THE FORTY ELEPHANTS

THE FORTY ELEPHANTS

ERIN BLEDSOE

BLACK STONE
PUBLISHING

Copyright © 2022 by Erin Bledsoe
Published in 2022 by Blackstone Publishing
Cover and book design by Alenka Vdovič Linaschke

Any historical figures and events referenced in this book are
depicted in a fictitious manner. All other characters and events
are products of the author's imagination, and any similarity
to real persons, living or dead, is coincidental.

Printed in the United States of America

First edition: 2022
ISBN 978-1-6650-1989-7
Fiction / Historical / General

Version 1

CIP data for this book is available
from the Library of Congress

Blackstone Publishing
31 Mistletoe Rd.
Ashland, OR 97520

www.BlackstonePublishing.com

*To Papaw, you read every revision and believed in me
when I didn't believe in myself. You left this world the same week
I found out all my dreams were coming true.
Thank you for waiting for me.*

PART I

CHAPTER ONE

LONDON 1920

Some steal out of desperation. Some steal because they like it.

I do it for both reasons.

"I'll have a scotch," says my chosen target.

I flash him a smile. "Anything else?"

His eyes travel the length of my body while I eye the gold watch fob dangling from the vest pocket of his double-breasted, peak-lapel suit. It teases me like the vendors at Piccadilly, waving fresh bread and fruits in front of a herd of starving children dying for a bite.

"What's your name, doll face? I've never seen you before," he asks, adjusting his trousers before reaching out to put his hand on my hip. "And I know all Kate's girls."

"Not all of them." I throw him a wink, and he leans closer with a lecherous grin. His hand slides down my thigh, groping at the form-fitting pants that are part of the scandalous uniform all the cocktail waitresses have to wear at the 43 Club.

"Tell me your name, love, and I'll give you a nice tip for fetching my drink."

I lean in. "Which tip?"

He roars with laughter. Men with money adore the power that comes with it. More specifically, the power it gives them over women. They'll do anything—say anything—to get us to break. Fortunately for me, that also makes them careless. He lowers his defenses with every inch I draw closer, leaving him mine for the taking.

I press my cheek to his and whisper sweetly, "I like being called beautiful," as I reach for the watch. As soon as I feel it inside my palm, a shiver creeps up my spine, leaving goose bumps behind as a reminder that this job, one I was born into, is my only calling.

"Beautiful it is. Can I see you after your shift? I can give you anything you want."

You already have.

"I'll be back with your drink." He tries to reach up for my face, but I promptly back away toward the bar, discreetly tucking the timepiece into a hidden pocket in my shirt.

"I need a scotch and two champagne cocktails!" I call to the barkeep, tapping the bar to get his attention, then glancing back to scan the customers while I wait. I can't help it. The crowd is like a three-ring circus performing one wild act after another.

It's a Monday night at the 43 Club, but it's as lively as if it were a Friday. The wealth of London is here, toasting drinks and laughing as they spill champagne on their Savile Row suits and couture dresses.

As a little girl, I used to daydream about being one of them—the chosen elite. I'd pretend my tiny room was a Mayfair town house and my cotton dresses were all fine silk. My mum said I could make myself believe anything with imagination, while my dad, a master thief himself, made sure I understood I'd never get anything that fine unless I took it.

Wartime convinced me of the rightness in my dad's view; dreaming wasn't going to get me anywhere.

"You're the new lass. Alice, right?" The barman slides me my drink orders on a stylish mirrored cocktail tray. "You've never done this kind of work before, have you?"

I take him in slowly, inch by inch. He's got a body a girl could have fun with, slim and muscular, a strong jaw, and gorgeous full lips. The only flaw I can find is a small scar near his left eye. I briefly imagine running my fingers through his hair before leaning in a little closer. "Is that a question or an accusation, Rob?"

His eyes widen, but instead of questioning how I've learned his name so quickly, he shrugs and responds, "Maybe both?"

I play along. "What gave me away?"

"It's the way you look at the crowd . . . I can't tell if it's fascination or disgust."

"Maybe both?" I tease.

A grin pulls at his lips. "When you work at joints like this, you get used to the clientele fast."

I sneer in response. "I just saw a bloke chunder into his top hat and then almost put it back on his head to finish the dance. I don't think anyone gets used to that."

His brows furrow together. "So this is your first time?"

I glare at the accusation, but I see only amusement in his growing smile.

"I never said that."

"Worked at all sorts of clubs in this city, yeah? What'd your references say—Murray's over on Beak Street? They say the crowds are worse over there."

He's on to me. In truth, I have no real experience, only the list of falsified character endorsements that Mum forged to get me this gig. My employment papers change depending on the job, and so does my name. I've been working since I was fourteen, and six years later, not a thing about my papers reads true. I am whoever I need to be. During the day I've been working as a maid for a wealthy theater owner, biding my time until the moment is right to rob him blind.

At night I serve cocktails at this club.

I grab the tray and dart off, plonking Mr. Handsy's drink down and making my way around the room in time with the jazz band's music, a toe-tapping rhythm bursting from their instruments and consuming everyone on the dance floor. I look away from the band just long enough to hand the two cocktails to a few socialites, who are pointing to the crowds with judgmental glares. Sometimes I wonder what it's like to be a Bright Young Thing, terrorizing London with gossip and games. They'll be here until dawn, dancing between drinks and secret slips of cocaine.

"This band is divine," one of them says.

The other nods in agreement. "Let's dance before they grow frightfully tiresome?"

I watch them slip away into the crowd, and the upbeat tempo makes my heart beat faster. Sweat trickles down the nape of my neck while I search for my next mark through plumes of cigar smoke and swaying bodies—and then I find her, a party girl in a fancy dress with a jeweled handbag. I weave through the room to get to her, past the crowded tables and hooting crowds, and all too suddenly, all I can hear is my shallow breathing.

And all I can see is her.

Women are difficult. I can only get close to them by staging accidental bumps or trips, which gives me just seconds to lift what I want: a silver hairpin, gold earrings, or a ruby ring. Women are a risk, but women are a treasure trove.

I get in close, and just as I'm about to slide the sparkling handbag from the girl's shoulder, she jerks around and snatches my wrist up with a low growl. "Don't even think about it, doll."

I instinctively prepare a hundred excuses and then decide what I'll do if she snitches to Kate and Kate calls the coppers. Panic fills me, but just as I open my mouth to say something—anything—I hear her say my name. "Alice?"

Gobsmacked, I stumble back. "Maggie?" Her name drops out of my mouth in a breathless whisper, and for a moment, the music in the club fades into the background. Even though I can still smell the sweat and stale air, I feel like it's just us. Me and my long-lost friend.

"You work here?" Her voice betrays equal surprise, but then she looks down at her bag and her mouth pulls into a devilish grin. "You're losing your touch."

I struggle to find the words. Is she really here? All these years later?

"Three years and eight months," I say out loud, still in a haze.

The Maggie in front of me looks nothing like the girl with worn clothes and bloody fists I grew up with. She was a scrapper like me, with a talent for thievery and getting by. But her right hook was always better than mine. When we first met, her brothers had her fighting a man in the Pit as the crowd shouted bets around them.

Back then the streets called her the Reaper.

The woman she is now is quite dazzling with her thick, ivory fur capelet and freshly cut bob, although no amount of makeup can soften her brazen expression.

I marvel at her. "Look at you, putting on the posh! You've come a long way since stealing chocolates in Lambeth."

She clears her throat. "That was ages ago."

I glance around her. "Where's your beau?"

"Don't have one."

I look over her again, a closer scan that renders me speechless. Under the wrap, she's wearing a black cocktail dress, intricately beaded and dripping with fringe. There's not a single rip in her stockings or scuff along her slick T-strapped pumps.

I force words out of my mouth. "Your brothers didn't tell me you were back in London."

"I've been back for a while," she confesses. "I just haven't gone to see them. They made it quite clear the last time we spoke that I wouldn't be welcome at home."

My mind flashes back to the night she left without a word, leaving me doubled up with worry, imagining every possible horrible scenario. Until one morning, after months of thinking about her, I woke up and decided she was dead.

And if she was dead, there was no use missing her.

That familiar pain of longing returns in waves, the anguish of remembering how much she once meant to me threatening to overwhelm me. I can't let that happen. Not here, and not now.

"It was brilliant seeing you, but I should get to work," I tell her, glancing back to see the barman searching for me in the throng, a fresh tray of drinks waiting on the bar in front of him. He's even prettier this far away, standing in front of bottles of booze lining the mirrored wall behind him. "That one already thinks I'm a bit dodgy."

I turn to leave, but she reaches out to stop me.

"I heard about your dad, Alice."

I shrug nonchalantly. "Twelve months with good behavior."

"How's The Mint faring without him?"

"That's none of your business now, is it? I should really get back."

"Can we talk after your shift, then?"

I eye her suspiciously. "What do you want, Mags? To crow over how good the years have been to you and how awful they've been for me? How I stayed with my family, and you left yours? I can't imagine what else we'd have to talk about."

"Have you heard of Mary Carr and her gang of thieves?" she asks without missing a beat, and a certain fear grips me.

Dad always taught me never to say the words aloud, certainly not in a busy place like this. He'd declare, *"If you want to stay in the shadows, keep your mouth shut and be invisible."* His advice never fails me.

A thief needs to be invisible.

I shake my head and glance around warily. "No, should I?"

"The Forty Elephants? They're making quite the name for themselves. Don't you ever read the paper? Mary Carr is our leader, and she's—"

"*Our?*" I arch my brows at the word. "You're involved in this gang?" All the words make sense separately, but not together. "You're in a gang?"

"This isn't like any gang you've heard of."

I scoff a bit, letting out a deep, weighted sigh. "I doubt that."

"Mary has a good thing going," she insists. "She's a real chancer."

"So what then, you nicked all of this? The dress . . . the bag?"

She laughs at the notion, then smooths out her dress. "We never wear what we steal. I bought this myself. Thanks to Mary Carr, I have a new life, choices I never thought I could have." Her face brightens. "You want to meet her?"

My jaw tightens in response. "You want me to join a gang?"

"Don't be sore, Alice." She pauses. "She's here, and I already told her we used to run together when we were girls. That you're a talent, like your father. She knows everything. She'd love to finally meet you."

I blink slowly, and my limbs go numb. The air in the club feels hot and stuffy, threatening to choke me. I'm flooded with memories of the girl I used to know and the one I'm staring at now. How could she ask me that? But more important, how could she have spent all this time bragging about our shared childhood memories to the very person she abandoned me for?

"I thought you were dead, Mags," I finally declare, my voice like ice. "We didn't hear a word from you after you left. No letters . . . nothing."

She hesitates long enough to catch her breath. "We always dreamed of getting out. Why would I look back?"

"I sat up at night watching those dark, gloomy streets, waiting for a cab to come along and drop you in front of Mum's shop. Meanwhile, you stayed gone, getting chummy with some gang leader, bragging about all the memories you had no trouble leaving behind?"

Her gaze travels around the room before returning to me. "It's not like that, Alice. I can be proud of the girl I was without wanting to be her again."

I stand firm. "Well, you seem to have forgotten that the Diamond family doesn't join gangs . . . so you can take your offer and piss off."

She tilts her head. "Still in Daddy's shadow, then?"

My body heat rises. "Out of your brothers' shadow, but in a new one, then?"

"Mary is nothing like them."

"Perhaps she's worse?" I use my finger to gesture at her dress, burying the envy and replacing it with a bitterness I can taste. "At least your brothers didn't ask you to wear this ridiculous costume."

The vibrant room around us suddenly feels small and unattractive, and silence stretches between us. Then a long, thoughtful moment passes where all we do is stare at each other. I don't know what she's thinking, but I know what I'm thinking.

She is a stranger to me, and it kills me.

Finally, with some hesitation, she says, "Good luck, Alice."

"I don't need luck."

Rob finally spots me and begins forcefully signaling me to come over; I welcome the excuse to leave. I make my way back to the bar quickly, but his playful nature has now all but vanished. "If people don't get their drinks, they stop buying them. We both lose money. I make the drinks, and you serve them. That's how this goes." He points at a collection of cocktails. "These are for the booth in the back."

Before I take up the tray, I awkwardly adjust my shirt and long trousers. I've been trying to get used to the feeling of the coarse fabric against my legs all week.

"Kit problems?" he observes.

"I've never worn pants before," I admit, not counting the rare childhood moments when I acted like my dad, marching around our house in his trousers, chasing down my brother, Tommy.

"Because women don't wear trousers. They don't own clubs either, yet here we are."

He jerks his head at the 43 Club's owner, Kate Meyrick, who is bouncing from group to group like the epitome of a social butterfly, laughing and chatting with each person. Nobody knows how she got to be the queen of the nightclub world, but she's here, nonetheless. When I interviewed for the job, she asked me one question: "What happens if a customer tries to put his hands on you?"

I immediately answered with the truth, replying, "I'd kick him where it hurts."

She hired me on the spot.

"Kate enjoys breaking the rules, so you better get used to the pants," he finishes, pointedly gesturing to his uniform—trousers with suspenders that loop over his bare chest and a matching necktie. "At least you're fully clothed. Kate gets a right laugh out of dressing her women like men and dressing her men like"—he searches for the right word—"this."

I smile and make a big deal about shamelessly looking him up and down. "But who can argue with this view?"

His face reddens, and he points to the booth again, then taps the tray of drinks. I see Maggie walk over and sit down with the girls there, and I realize the cocktails are for her group.

I fidget with my hands for a second, then push forward determinedly, balancing the sloshing delivery on my shoulder as I make my way over to the booth. Four women are sitting in the cushioned seats, dressed in thick furs and loaded down with jewels from head to toe. Pearl sautoirs hang from their necks, accompanied by ruby drop earrings and gold bangles that catch my eye even in the dim light. They look like the mannequins in the window displays at Selfridges.

"Finally," says one, impatiently snatching a glass off the tray before I can set it down. The twin next to her does the same.

Maggie sits on the other side, beaming a mite too victoriously for my taste, assuming I'm here by choice. She looks over at her companion, a woman in a blush-pink dyed chinchilla wrap and a feathered, silver headdress styled on top of locks of golden hair like a queen's crown.

On her fingers, I count seven diamond rings. Small stones but expertly cut. I briefly replay the memory of my dad on his knees beside me as a girl, teaching me how to tell the difference.

"A well-cut diamond is luminous, brilliant, and a poorly cut one is dull."

Then I would peer up at him with a curious smile to ask, "Which one am I?"

"Brilliant, my girl. Brilliant."

I shake the memory away and focus on her fingers. Unlike the other girls, who take no notice of my presence beyond guzzling their cocktails, she smiles directly at me. She's got to be at least a couple of decades older than the rest of them, but she's aged gracefully, with just a few wrinkles at the corners of her eyes. I should relax at her friendly attitude, but her Cheshire-cat grin leaves me tense and feeling like she knows a secret I don't.

Is this the famous Mary Carr?

"Sorry for the wait, ladies."

"Give us a whiskey instead?" Maggie asks with a smirk. "You know I'm not a gin girl."

"One might argue you're hardly a girl at all," teases one twin, and the other giggles.

"Keep opening your gob, Norma, and I'll put my fist inside it," she fires back.

The older woman snaps her fingers. "Maggie, play nice tonight."

"No promises, Mary," says Maggie with an eye roll.

Mary returns her gaze to me while Norma and her sister shove past to the dance floor.

I clear my throat. "Can I get you anything else?"

"You have fast hands," compliments the older woman—Mary Carr, I presume. "I've been watching you collect from the crowd. You're talented. How do you know our Mags here?"

Our Mags? I purse my lips and ignore the comment. "Collect?"

"Steal," she says, her voice dropping to a whisper. "But we prefer the term *collecting*. Less harsh, and well, *stealing* is such a dark word. Not something we'd want anyone to hear us gossip about."

"We?"

"We're like you." She points to Maggie and then over to the twins dancing the foxtrot. "Collectors. Only we stick with the shops down the West End, where the real rewards are."

My imagination runs wild. "You pinch from department stores?"

I've never had the guts to do anything that risky. Every time my father tried, a copper would drop him to the cobblestones and drag him off before he even had time to pocket a hatpin.

"All kinds of stores," she answers, complacently running her fingers down her pink fur. "Some women are born into it. The finer things in life." She stares out at the posh ladies in the club. "Some are not. Some women struggle every day for a taste of what other women take for granted."

I'm regrettably hypnotized by her words, watching her mouth move, anticipating what will come out next. "Me and my girls were not born into the finer things, but we have them. Do you want to know how?"

My throat goes dry while I twist to look back at the bar, where Rob's staring at me dead-on.

"Do you?" Mary's voice vibrates in my ear. I swing my eyes back over to her.

"How?"

"We have the balls to take them."

I pause for a minute to find my voice. "There's a fine line between guts and stupidity. I wager my balls are just as big as yours. I'm just more careful where I flash 'em."

She snorts in response, then gives me a broad smile. "Oh, I like you! I'd like to give you a chance to audition."

"Let me get you that whiskey." I clear my throat and quickly depart, aware that Mary's watching me as I walk away. My pockets are filled with things I've pinched, *collected*, and someone in here knows it—my mind races. I return to the bar and lean over the counter to call for Rob.

"Oy! Do you know those girls?"

"I wouldn't say I know them, but they come in every Monday night to celebrate."

"Celebrate what?"

I get the sense he doesn't like that I'm interested. "They're trouble." He pulls today's newspaper from beneath the bar and slaps it down in front of me, then points to the front page. "They're the Forty Elephants."

I glance down and read the first few lines. "A gang of female shoplifters?" Strangely, I've never heard Dad mention them. Usually, he's going on about all the gangsters that plague London's streets, especially the McDonald brothers, who are currently waging war with the Italians over bookmaking at the racecourses. We can't get him to shut his gob about them, but he's never said a word about a gang of girls.

Rob chuckles wryly. "A swarm of locusts robbing honest people more like. Their leader, Mary Carr, has been in and out of the courts five times this year alone."

"But not sentenced? How?"

"They can catch her all they want, but until they find the goods she stole, too, it's just speculation. They say she keeps it all at a warehouse somewhere and then fences it before the coppers can track it down. Got all kinds of connections to this city and the men that control it. I know she's aligned with the McDonalds, at least."

My fingers dig into my palms, leaving deep, curved indents. "You mean the Elephant and Castle gang?"

He nods.

"Does Kate Meyrick know who they are? Why would she let them in the club?"

"My guess is they pay her a fat amount to party here. Kate is all about favors for favors."

"How do you know all this?"

He pours some champagne. "I got good ears. I know all kinds of secrets. That's the burden of being the chap that makes the drinks." He doesn't sound angry, just exasperated. "But you know what they say . . . everyone has a secret in Soho."

I don't realize how worried I look until I see the casual expression on his face shift into concern that mirrors mine. "What's wrong?"

"Nothing," I say vaguely with a dismissive wave. "Don't be daft. I just hear terrible things about the gangs."

He knows I'm lying because he's quick to say, "I'll have another lass take over their drinks."

"No." The word comes out quick, rough. "I'll handle it."

"Listen, Alice, if you know what's best for you, keep your head down and stay away from those girls."

I take a deep breath and stand upright, fancying his concern. "I'm not a child. I can handle myself. With that baby face of yours, I might even be older than you."

His lip curls in a miffed-looking pout as he hands me Maggie's whiskey. "You sure you don't want another waitress to do it?"

"I said I'll handle it." I grab the glass.

He shouts at me on my way to the booth. "Don't call me baby face again! This is a man's face, you hear me? A man's face!"

I march to Maggie and Mary Carr and set the drink down with a frown. I figure it's best to just get things over with now and not let it go any further. "Thanks, but I'm not interested, and I'd appreciate it if you kept my collecting to yourself. I need to keep this job."

Maggie ignores me, taking the whiskey and tossing it back in one deft movement, but Mary Carr takes my hand, her long, elegant fingers gripping my wrist. "Why not?" She observes me evenly. "Maggie told me all about you and your family, and I've seen that you're already quite skilled."

I pull my hand away, recoiling with a low hiss. The envy I felt moments ago, staring at a friend who had risen far beyond her humble origins, has faded away now that I know there's an invisible collar around her neck. "Don't waste your breath trying to sweet-talk me. I don't join gangs. It's a Diamond family rule."

Her eyes widen. "Maybe that's where your family has gone wrong. A gang *is* a family. A gang is a home. Ours is a sisterhood. I take care of my girls."

The uncontrollable laugh that bursts from me paints a tiny frown on Maggie's face, but I don't pay her any mind. She knew better than to try to recruit me for something like this but did it anyway. "The answer's still no."

That silences Mary Carr. Instead, she stares deep into my eyes as if she hopes to see something there—a weak spot, perhaps? Something she can manipulate to sway me to her side. Maybe she's found such weaknesses in other girls.

She won't find it in me.

I am my father's daughter. There is no weak spot to find, nor softness to exploit. I cannot be manipulated or broken. I'm made of steel.

"Can I ask why?"

"Yes," I answer coldly. "But I can't promise I'll give you the truth."

She chuckles, but it sounds forced. "Maggie was right about you being stubborn and pigheaded."

"Pigheaded?" I force out the same laugh she did. "Coming from Maggie Hill?"

Maggie doesn't even look up from her empty glass.

Mary folds her arms across her chest. "You might change your mind."

"Let me know if you need any drinks, ladies."

As I walk away, I hear Maggie say, "I told you not to waste your time."

When my shift ends, I hustle out the back door to the well-lit Soho sidewalk, where stylish motorcars are parked and strolling couples kiss under lampposts. Musicians are still playing on some of the street corners, and though there's barely any traffic at Berwick Street Market this late, I can still imagine faint echoes of hawkers shouting from their stalls. I take a deep breath, letting the night air fill my nostrils, slowly preparing my already aching feet for the walk home.

"Oy," calls a voice from a private side entrance of the club that I assumed was reserved for Kate alone. He's a broad-shouldered chap, clearly soused. He winks my way. "You one of Kate's girls? Six shillings for a dance and two pounds for more, yeah? That's the price for a little fun?"

I glance to the side door again. Kate didn't mention a secret entrance for men wanting a little fun, and it certainly wasn't a part of the job description.

"I'm just a cocktail waitress," I tell him. "And since you don't seem to need any more drinks, piss off, yeah?"

He gets closer. "Three pounds, then? I like tall women."

It takes considerable willpower to check my temper as I let out a deep exhale. "If only I favored fat drunks."

The smirk that was spread across his face vanishes. "You've got a mouth on you, you cheeky bint. How about I tell Kate Meyrick and get her to give you the boot?" His hand leaves his pocket and greedily paws at my breasts. "Or can we come to another agreement?"

I don't have time to think before the red rage boils over. I yank his arm back and twist, hard, until he's whimpering in pain.

"I'm just a cocktail waitress," I say again, emphatically.

He thrashes and groans.

"Everything all right?" I hear Rob ask. I whip around. He's outside the main entrance, having a smoke but standing alert and eager like a hunting dog on a lead. I release the man with a hiss.

"Just grand."

Rob jerks his chin at the man. "Maybe you should catch a cab, sir. It's time for you to head home."

The man stares at both of us, but his eyes linger on Rob's lithe, muscular form before he stumbles away. I shake my head and force my clenched hands to ease.

Rob looks me over. "Did that git hurt you?"

"I hurt him," I say, resolute. "Could have broken his arm if I wanted."

"Too bad. What man doesn't want to save the girl and be a hero?"

"I'm not a girl, and I don't need saving." I know I'm being too short with him, but I'm still heated, and part of me wants to dash after that arse and make him wish he never laid eyes on me.

"I can see that." He twirls his smoke between his fingers before offering me a drag. I take a single puff and hand it back. The smoke fills my lungs and slows my racing heart.

"Who taught you that?" he asks.

"Who taught me what? To tell a man no? Or how to break his arm when he decides not to listen?"

He grins. "Both."

"My dad."

"Strange thing to teach a young girl."

"More fathers should teach their daughters to fight the same as their sons. The world is a violent place, as is London."

"Parts of London," he reasons. "Parts of this world. It doesn't have to be all or nothing. There are other options."

A cackle bursts out of me. "Are you implying I should have had a reasonable conversation with that tosser instead? A bleeder who had no intention of listening?"

"I'm not saying that. I'm just saying that sometimes there are ways of avoiding battle."

I straighten my shoulders, eyeing him more seriously now. "How many battles have you avoided?"

"Not enough." His voice grows distant, and he looks down at his feet. "All I'm saying is, you see things differently when you've been in a real war."

A heavy wave of regret fills me. Most of the men in this city can say they went to France to fight, and yet, I somehow thought him exempt with his carefree charm and quick wit. "I shouldn't have come at you cross. My brother, Tommy, was in the war, and he came back with more demons than he left with."

He nods. "Most of us have."

I long for life to come back to his features. To see that grin again. "Well, thank you . . . for that."

He chortles a bit. "You hated saying that, didn't you?"

"I loathed it." I roll my eyes dramatically.

And the grin returns. I smile back and point at the private entrance. "I didn't know the 43 was a brothel, too."

His eyes hold no judgment when he says, "Plenty of lonely men came home from war needing a little comfort. They offer the same thing at the Piccadilly Hotel. Five shillings for a song and dance."

"But here two pounds can get a lass into bed with you?" I can't contain the cross look pulling at my face.

"Kate didn't ask if you wanted to do both? Work in the club and be a comfort girl?"

"Comfort girl?"

"That's what she calls them."

"A whore," I correct him, shaking my head. "I thought Kate was different. That's why I wanted to work here. A woman owning a night-club! Avoiding police raids, challenging the law at every opportunity, and coming out on top." I can hear my voice growing louder. "Turns out, she's just like all the men, exploiting what women have between their legs."

"I wouldn't say exploiting," he says, gesturing at some of the comfort girls who have just come outside. They're dressed in glittering lamé with strings of pearls around their necks. Not as dazzling as Mary and her gang, but far better off than anyone I grew up with.

"You're telling me that if I want anything posh or nice, I either have to nick them like Mary or sell my body like those girls? You think we only have two choices in life?"

"I think bugger all," he blurts. "I don't judge a woman for what she'll do for a nice set of pearls. I'm no saint. I cast no stones."

I cross my arms over my chest. "You said earlier everyone has a secret in Soho. So what's yours?"

"I'll tell you," he says. "But you have to let me take you to breakfast."

I blink slowly. "I just nearly broke a man's arm in front of you, and you're asking me on a date?" I feel another blush coming on. "You take all the new girls out for breakfast or only the pretty ones?"

"Only the pretty ones," he says with a roguish look, offering me his cigarette again.

This time, I refuse it with a wave of my hand. "I can't."

"Can't or won't?"

I walk past him but not before saying, "Maybe both?"

CHAPTER TWO

There's nobody on the streets in Lambeth this late, and I long for the sound of hooves pounding against cobblestones and omnibuses rumbling by. The quiet reminds me I'm alone and has me continually looking into the shadows for movement. A quiet London is a dangerous London.

A horn blares as a motorcar suddenly races up behind me, and I nearly jump out of my skin. I've already reached for the knife in my garter when I see Maggie hop out of the Ford Model T that pulls up alongside me.

"You should fetch a cab. Not safe to walk around here at night."

I wave the butterfly knife in my hand, trying not to let my wobbliness show. "You know I always carry a blade with me, Mags."

I maintain eye contact and do my best not to goggle too obviously at her car. I can't imagine having a motorcar of my own, to say nothing of new silk stockings. A wave of jealousy hits me, but then I remind myself of how she achieved it all.

"You know better than to ask me to join a gang," I say flatly.

"Let me give you a ride home. We don't have to talk about any of that on the drive. It can just be a friend helping another friend. I'm certain your feet are aching."

They are throbbing from the night I've had dashing around the club, but I don't believe she just wants to do a good deed. The Maggie I knew wouldn't give up that easily. "I'm perfectly capable of walking."

"I want your company," she insists, moving around to open the passenger door for me. "It's just a ride."

And as if she can control the weather, a drizzle starts to fall. I shoot her a glare, and her lips pull into a wicked smile. "Not going to walk home in the rain, are you?"

I let out a heavy groan of exasperation before giving in and slipping into the seat. "You're driving to The Mint in this car and that outfit? Just know that I am not to blame if you find yourself in a half-dozen stickups."

She laughs but stays mum, keeping her word not to mention Mary or the gang on the way. It's a strange silence between us, two friends who have grown apart. I have so much I want to ask her but instead stare out the window, watching the well-kept residential homes and shops grow fewer by the minute.

Daylight in Lambeth is a dream. Beneath the sun's ruthless blaze, the streets have a life all their own. On the way to work, I pass green-grocer stands stuffed with baskets and crates under bright awnings, used bookshops with tellers shouting from the curbs, and men and women strolling with bright, cheery grins and finely tailored clothes.

But on the way home, the only pleasant scene we're offered along the sleeping streets is a shabby organ-grinder shuffling along with his hat out for coin. I've come to find peace in both. The chaotic nature of London's day and the eerie silence that follows a rising moon.

I take a deep breath and let my shoulders ease into a more relaxed state until the quiet serenity fades as my neighborhood comes to view—a district called The Mint, where the roads are blackened with London's grime.

Commissioner Horwood dubbed it the "criminals' district," a grim neighborhood where chimney soot settles on your clothes and skin and never entirely washes off. If a man is murdered here, the policemen don't even bother coming, knowing the body and evidence will be long gone before they arrive. It's a den for thieves, killers, and liars—folks who get by thanks to their dubious talents.

My mum's storefront is small, with a peeling sign advertising fortune-telling. It's not much to look at, but she gets plenty of customers desperate for answers, praying they leave with pleasant news. She doesn't disappoint.

Maggie parks across the street, looking out the window with distaste. Her family, the Hills, were my dad's right hand before they moved on to Chinatown.

"I don't know how you stay here," she finally says. "How do you come back after spending time in Soho, around people who are actually enjoying their lives?"

"Family," I remind her. I reach for the door and get out.

She's quick to follow, walking around to meet me face-to-face before I can dash away into the shop. "I said I'd keep my gob shut during the ride."

I shake my head. "You could have just left it at two friends saying hello, but you had to make it personal. You had to do something that makes me feel like you don't even know me at all. That you've changed in ways I can't forgive."

"That's awfully dramatic considering I'm certain you could use the money."

"We'll be fine. We always survive."

"So your plan is to survive forever when you could be thriving?"

I pinch the bridge of my nose. "Why are you pushing this so hard? You've been in London this entire time and never sought me out."

"Mary asked me to recruit you years ago, but I didn't. When she said she was going to try to find you herself, I threatened to leave if she did."

My eyebrows lift a little. "Where was that restraint tonight?"

She squares her shoulders in response. "Because when I saw you . . . I saw so much promise. While I appreciate what Mary has built, I know there's more expanding to do. Bigger scores. Challenges she turns her back on because she believes we're better off playing it safe. But I know I can do more, and the girls can do more. They just need to be shown. If you and I show them—show Mary—the possibilities, we'd be more than just entertainment for the papers. We'd be a proper threat to London. We'd have something all our own."

My mind reels at the thought, and the envy returns. When we were girls, there wasn't a thing we couldn't accomplish together. The possibilities now, as women, feel endless. But caution overwhelms me—not only at the idea of joining a gang but trusting Maggie again. I don't think I can.

I cross my arms over my chest, narrowing my eyes. "You want to recruit me because I don't mind rolling up my sleeves and getting my hands dirty? Or because you've always been on some quest to prove to your brothers you don't need them to be important?"

"This isn't about them."

"Don't lie to me! The least you can do is be straight with me."

"Don't you want more than this?" She waves her arm around, gesturing at the smoggy streets. "We talked about it all the time when we were girls—being more than The Mint. All you've ever done for as long as I've known you is sacrifice for your family and pick up after Tommy. When will you decide that enough is enough?"

I seethe. "We were girls dreaming of a world that does not exist." I let myself fully take in that swanky Model T since I'll never ride in it again. I burn it into my memory before saying, "Good luck, Mags."

Then I leave her and go inside.

The rusted old bell hanging above the door announces my entrance. Inside there's only a slight difference from the dim streets to the weak, tea-stained light illuminating the shop. Mum looks up from gathering tarot cards splayed across a table with a worn, fringed cloth on top. Deep red—her favorite color. When I was young, we lived in both stories of the building, but when Tommy left and Mum started her business, she turned the downstairs into a haunting, colorful scene lit by over a dozen candles. Framed paintings of animals dot the walls; bottles of dirt and herbs, purple crystals, and even a few animal skulls litter tables near the seating area at the door.

My personal favorite is her "book of the dead," a small notebook with scribbles and drawings that she uses during her séances. Her methods vary from client to client. Sometimes she reads cards or palms. Occasionally she even peers into a glass ball and mutters rubbish words she's made up to sound like she's speaking in tongues.

All of it lies, a brilliant charade she's perfected over the years. Her only real talent is reading people—a skill I like to think we share.

"Alice!" She flits across the creaky floorboards to take me by the chin and kiss my cheek. "How was your first night? Kate and her club everything you'd hoped they'd be?"

Not entirely, but there's no reason to tell her that. "Sure, I'm well chuffed. The place is packed with rich wankers, all pissed from too much champagne."

She smirks and opens her hands in anticipation. "Let's see what you got!"

I unload my pockets of all the night's bits and bobs, and she sorts through them, deciding what she might sell and what would be smarter to keep. The things we keep are those that could come in handy when Dad's away. Sometimes Tommy's mates come around gobbing off about unsettled debts, and something shiny holds them over. Or sometimes it's just someone in The Mint who needs new shoes or a hot meal.

"Excellent night," she compliments.

"You, too?" I ask, pointing at the deck of cards.

Her cheeks flush slightly. "A woman came looking for a way to kill her husband. I told her that wasn't the business I deal in."

I can tell she's lying; I'm the only person who can. Her nostrils flare, and she gets all twitchy. Movement of any kind means a lie. I groan and go over to the bookshelf that has a small compartment concealed in the bottom. Inside Dad keeps his trapper knives. There are six of them in total, but when I open the box, I count only five.

He despises guns and says they're only to be used as a last resort. That's why he owns only one, stuffed under Mum's mattress, but keeps over a hundred different knives underneath the floorboards in the kitchen.

"Are you daft? You sold her a knife?"

She places a hand on her hip and lets out a shaky breath. "It was hard to turn down what she offered. She came in here looking for answers, wanted me to read her palm and tell her he'd eventually meet his end. But that would not happen, Alice. He hurts her, and I gave her the option to hurt him back."

"We don't sell weapons; we don't sell drugs."

"Play it safe while your father is away." Mum finishes the oft-repeated mantra in annoyance.

"*Safe*," I emphasize with a snap. "I pick pockets, and you pick minds. Dad's orders."

"We're safe as houses," she reassures me. "It was just a one-off." She lowers her voice to a whisper. "Our little secret? Your father need not know."

I let out a groan and roll my eyes just as Louisa dashes down the stairs. Her long plaited hair brushes against my face as her thin arms wrap around my neck. She was born sickly. Our mother was certain she wouldn't make it. But she did.

We try to keep her from our less savory family activities. I want her to be young as long as she can, even though she's becoming much more curious about the illegal side of what we do.

"Mum sold a woman a knife," she gushes. "I heard the whole thing!"

"Hush, Louisa," Mum hisses at her.

"I told her she oughtn't do it. Dad will be furious. She let me play the palm reader tonight with several clients. I fooled them, too."

Our mother exhales and says, "I told you to go to bed. I don't want to hear any more of your cheek!"

Louisa turns to me with a roll of her eyes and ignores Mum. "Do you think he has it coming? Her husband?"

"Don't talk like that," I scold, urging her back up the stairs to our bedroom. "I'll be up soon. Go keep the bed warm for me."

She frowns and disappears. Once she's gone, my mother and I gather up my haul. It's strange: the longer I stare at all the beautiful things I collected, the more I think about Mary Carr with her lovely blush fur and gang of thieves. The feeling of riding in Maggie's car.

Images of her elaborate headdress dance in my head.

"You remember Dad talking about the Forty Elephants?"

"They've been all over the papers," Mum says disinterestedly, then sniggers. "Making quite the spectacle of themselves all about London."

"Maggie's joined them."

I watch her arch a skeptical brow. "Maggie Hill?"

I press my lips together, then nod. "I saw her tonight."

"Goodness, it's been years." She places a hand on her hip. "Has she gone to see her brothers yet?"

"No . . . and no plans to. She was at the 43 with her gang. Their leader saw me collecting and told me I was talented."

She snorts. "*Collecting?*"

I shrug. "That's what she called it. Mum, you should have seen what she was wearing. Gorg—"

"No, Alice," she cuts me off immediately, and her shoulders sag. "I don't care what rubbish she spit at you or what she was wearing. They're allied with the Elephant and Castle gang, which means they're enemies of the Italians. Gangsters fighting endless wars on the streets. That's not for us, and you know it."

I sneer. "You can sell some stranger a knife, but I can't talk about Mary Carr's gang without a lecture?"

"Maggie's made her bed. Let her lie in it."

I shake my head, starting up the stairs before I spot three plates on the kitchen table. I pause and twist around to look at her. "Did you have company tonight?"

She hesitates. "Now, Alice, stay calm. Don't get arse over tits about it!"

My throat constricts. "Tommy's home. Where is he?"

"He just came for supper."

"Where is he?"

"It's nothing."

"Where the fuck is he?" I yell too loudly like a wild thing that has no place in a home. I have my dad's temper, it's true, and sometimes it gets the better of me.

Louisa is looking over the railing in a blink, gawking at the scene with her mouth gaping open. "I wanted to tell you. Mum said I shouldn't."

"You had Louisa lie for you?" My anger grows.

"He's down at the pub," reveals Mum, her voice a shaky whisper. "Please, Alice, don't get your knickers in a twist. I never get to see my boy. Don't run him off."

I bolt out the door. "I told you not to let him back in after the last time."

She follows me out into the street with a plea. "You don't get to decide that!"

I toss a sharp laugh in her face. "I already have."

I jog to Ralph's pub. It's the only spot in The Mint where you can enjoy a decent bite and a drink without having to look continually over your shoulder. During the war Ralph clocked six enemy gunners with a single rifle, then took a flamethrower to the rest of their unit until they surrendered. When he came home, everyone chipped in and bought him the pub.

As soon as I get inside, the barmaid points to where Tommy is chatting up a pair of prostitutes. I don't need her to point; I could spot him anywhere. He's got the same bright ginger hair as our father and his trademark spectacles. If you didn't know him, you might think he was the kind of smart that comes from books. You'd be dead wrong.

"Now, Alice, don't go starting trouble in here," says Ralph when he spots me. "Take it outside."

At the sound of my name, Tommy pushes up and races away. I chase him out the back, grabbing him by the shirt to pull him down into a nearby rain puddle.

He hits the ground with a thud and groans. "It's always a pleasure, sister."

"What the bleeding hell did you do?"

He rolls over to his side, holding his arm now coated in mud. "I just came back to visit."

"Nooo," I grind out. "You came back because something's gone pear-shaped. That's the only reason you ever come back. You think these streets will protect you because of what our dad has done to protect them, but we're fed up with you, Tommy. The Mint won't do a damn thing for you. I won't either."

"Mum said I could stay." He wriggles upright and reaches for his hat.

"And I'm saying sod off." I snatch the cap and toss it a few feet away. "You think you're Dad now?"

"Someone has to take his place when he's gone, and God knows it's not you. What did you do, Tommy? Tell me!"

He leans against the pub's stone exterior and takes a flask from his coat pocket. He takes two long swigs and then shakes it with a frown. "Excuse me, I need a top-up."

I block the door with my body. "What did you do!"

His gaze turns downward. "I saved Dad. I paid a barrister a fat sum. He has connections to a judge who will lessen Dad's sentence on appeal, maybe set him free altogether."

"A barrister makes you a promise, and you believe him?"

"I have it on good authority that he's a man of his word."

"By whom?"

"The Hill boys."

I shake my head. "You've been in Chinatown? Gambling? Asking favors of Patrick and Eli?"

"I just went for a name and the amount he'd want."

My mouth goes dry. "How did you get the cash to bribe him?"

His bottom lip quivers, but he turns to the side so I can't see. "Never mind that right now. I just want to spend tonight with my family. Tomorrow, I'll run. I'll run as far as I can."

He's gotten himself into some pretty big messes before, but never so great that he's been as truly scared as he is now. "Who's after you? Did you start safe-breaking again?"

"I stole from the only people I could think of who would have that kind of cash, and they're going to kill me for it. Please, Alice, just let me have tonight."

I want to say yes. For as long as I can remember, my dad always has. No matter the trouble Tommy brought with him, he was forever welcome home. But as much as my heart urges me to acquiesce, my mind reasons otherwise. "The last time men came by, they threatened to take Louisa if you didn't pay up. We almost lost her to a sodding brothel. If everyone in the neighborhood hadn't pitched in to fight them off, she'd be gone."

"I did this for her," he insists in a low plea. "I did this for us. We need him. The Mint needs him."

"But I'm here," I bellow. "I always take care of us when he's gone."

"But you're not him! You'll never be him, Alice."

I sort of startle. "But you think you can be? Who did you do this for, Tommy? Him or yourself?"

"Does it matter? I saved him. Me. Not you, Alice. Me." He lifts his hands widely, gesturing to the smoggy air around him. "I have finally done something he can be proud of."

I shake my head and do my best to speak in a steady voice when I say, "When this plans of yours fails, who will save you, Tommy?"

He tries the flask again as if it might have suddenly refilled. "Why can't you see? I did this for all of us."

"You did this for you, and you're a bloody idiot for it."

What if he's right? What if he's finally got into a scrape he can't get out of? Or that I can't get him out of. I run my fingers through my hair and close my eyes. "I'm sorry, Tommy, but you can't come home. I'll get you a ticket to New York tomorrow. The first boat. I just need to have Mum fence some of my haul."

"Maybe they won't know it was me. I was careful. Maybe I don't need to run."

"You're never careful." I dismiss the notion. "Meet me at Victoria Station tomorrow morning. I'll have a ticket. If you don't get on the train willingly, I'll shove you."

I leave him in the alley to mull things over, and I go back up the block to where my mother waits in a panic just outside our front door. She's shivering with only a thin shawl around her shoulders. "What did you do?"

"I did what I had to."

I push past her to the stove so I can warm my hands. She follows a second later, ready to peck at me like an indignant mother hen. "You go tell him he has a bed here! You go tell him he's always safe here."

"That would be a lie, Mum," I say.

"He's my boy," she utters, not even bothering to hide the tears streaming down her cheeks. "You cannot turn away my son. Your father would never allow this!"

"Your darling boy can do no wrong, can he? Never mind that he nearly gets us all gutted monthly . . . you'd never know it from the way you blather over him. You expect everything of me and nothing from him. You're the reason he is the way he is."

"You want more affection, then? Is that what you're asking for, Alice?"

I huff bitterly. "You'd drop dead before acknowledging that I'm the actual head of this house when Dad is away, and not your favorite stupid, little boy."

For a moment, she's speechless, silently puffing up with anger until she bursts out, "You've never loved him!"

"I've never loved him?" I repeat the words far louder and more viciously to block out the deep disdain in her tone. "Do you imagine I clean up after him because it humors me?"

"Don't pretend you don't like to crow over him when he's low and swoop in to fix everything. You've always resented him because he is your father's son, and you are a—"

"A woman?" I don't deny it. "Resentment doesn't mean I don't love him."

She yanks her coat off its hook by the door. "I'll go to him now. I'll tell him he can come home."

"He'll be on the first boat to New York tomorrow."

Another gasp. "He wouldn't go without saying goodbye!"

"He's not coming back." Although I'm fuming inside at this all-too-familiar fight over Tommy, my stomach turns at having to be so cold to her. To refuse her the goodbye she wants from her only son. "He knows I mean it this time, Mum. It's unlikely whatever trouble he's in follows him to water. He'll be safe . . . isn't that what you want?"

She sinks to the ground, all the fight leaving her just as quickly as it started. I kneel next to her and lean my head on her shoulder, letting a single tear escape and run down my cheek. And suddenly, our home full of memories and laughter throughout the years as a family of five feels cold and bare. Her eyes glance to the table as her pained expression deepens. We have the same thoughts, I imagine. Her thinking this was her last meal with Tommy, and me knowing I've missed it.

"I'm going to bed," I say to her gently. "I have to be up early."

She nods, taking one shallow breath after another.

Upstairs I hear Louisa's feet dash across the floor, down the hall to our bedroom. She throws open the door and slips inside. I catch her just as she makes it to the bed and tucks in snugly. "What all did you hear?" I ask.

"Is it true? You told Tommy he couldn't come home?"

I reach for her hair and tuck some of it behind her ear. "I did."

Unlike our melodramatic mother, Louisa doesn't feel the loss as keenly. Her constricted chest eases with deep, audible relief through a breathy sigh. "Those men won't come for me again?"

"Never."

She's satisfied with my response and hums happily. "Then tell me about the club. Tell me what everyone was wearing and drinking." She jumps out of bed and closes her eyes, then begins to spin around so that her nightgown flutters against her legs. "Were they dancing?"

"They were doing it all," I say brightly, putting forth my best effort to sound breezy and cheerful. "It was all very glamorous." I regale her with stories of the 43's outlandish patrons as I undress and snuggle under the covers, patting the spot next to me. She gets in, sighing dreamily.

"How was school?"

She rolls her eyes and ignores the question, replying quickly with, "Is Kate Meyrick as extraordinary as the papers say? Did you see her?"

"I did."

"I wish I could meet her! A woman owning the most popular club in the city! I fancy she spends her afternoons having tea and posh little cakes, planning her next move." Her voice suggests she thinks of it often, dreams of it even. Just as I used to do when there was still a little girl inside me who spent her nights dreaming of a different life.

"I'd do anything to wear flashy satin gowns and catch a man's eye just by walking past him on the street."

"One day," I promise her. "One day, you'll wear tiaras and jewels and mink coats." I lift her chin a little. "But catching a man's eye can wait."

"You know I'm a woman now, Alice. Plenty of girls my age are getting married. My classmates say you're years behind, and if you don't get a move on, your womb will wither and dry. Before you know it, you'll be a lonely old hag."

I laugh. "Is that what the girls at school say about me?"

"They say other things, too."

"Like?"

"Our family is dangerous . . . that Diamond girls are dangerous."

I breathe in, trying to find the right words. "What's so wrong with being dangerous?"

"I don't want to be dangerous," she admits. "I want to be roaring happy. I want the sun!" She twiddles with her thumbs. "But they also say that Diamonds never leave The Mint, so I should stop mucking about. Do you think they're right?"

I consider it for a long, tense moment. "Yes."

Her eyes jerk up.

"I will probably die a lonely old biddy with a dry womb."

She giggles, and I pull her into me. Maybe we will never leave The Mint. Perhaps she'll never marry a nice, respectable man or wear satin gowns, but I'll never let her think there's no hope.

CHAPTER THREE

They arrive like a storm, loud and powerful, breaking in downstairs. The iron bars of our bed tremble while they wreak havoc in the shop, shouting taunts at my mother. "Come down, Lady Diamond. We're returning something to you."

I blink the shadows from my eyes and sit up with a gasp. Louisa pops up and screams, quickly covering her mouth a second later.

I hear Mum's feet patter across the floor, and she barges into our room breathlessly, her robe only half on.

"Don't go down there," I implore.

I hear the tinkling crash of shattered glass, and Louisa whimpers into her hand. "Who is it? What do they want?"

Mum's hair, usually wrapped up in a scarf, is in a plait down her back. She looks a right mess, but when she sees how terrified my sister is, she ties her dressing gown tight and pats Louisa's head. "Stay up here," she mouths to Louisa, retrieving a carving knife from the lintel above our door.

I hurriedly scoop up our bedding, tying one end of the sheet to the bedpost and throwing the other end out the window. "If they come up, jump out the window. Go to the pub and get Ralph. He'll keep you safe."

Louisa nods and curls up under the sill.

I grab the dagger I keep under the mattress and descend with my mother down the wooden steps into the danger that awaits us. Two burly men greet us with stern, unwavering stares, looming around my mother's table like prospective clients.

I study the room inch by inch. Two more men by the door: one is sitting in the armchair reading a book he's plucked from Mum's bookshelf while the other is pacing in front of the cracked door smoking a cigar. Four men against two women.

Not great odds, but we've handled worse.

"Ah, the illustrious Lady Diamond," says one of the men at the table. He holds a cane in his right hand and is dressed in an elaborate bespoke suit, bowler hat, and polished brogues. Next to him, his much taller companion wears a nearly identical ensemble. Both have the same coloring and features, which means they must be kin. Cousins? Brothers? I take a moment to burn their faces into my memory—if they dare hurt us, I'll remember what they look like when the time comes for revenge.

My mother, however, seems to know something I don't because she's pale as a ghost. "Wal and Wag McDonald." She approaches them hesitantly, the raw confidence in the way she holds the knife slacking.

The McDonald brothers? I stare harder. Their reputation precedes them—a fearsome pair always mentioned in the papers for unsolved murders and drive-by shootings. I've never met them before and had no desire to, which is one of the reasons I refused Mary Carr outright.

Why have they traveled all the way from Elephant and Castle in the middle of the night?

"My man isn't here, Wag. Tommy isn't either," says my mother, the slightest hint of a shake in her voice as she takes a slow, careful step back.

"We know about your husband and his fate. It's a shame. You have our sympathy," Wag says in a conciliatory tone. He pulls a chair from our table and takes a seat while Wal stands behind him, both hands behind his back. A few feet from them, the goon by the door lurks like a guard dog. I don't like that I can't see his face—that he hides in the shadows waiting for an order.

"Your husband has nothing to do with this, Lady Diamond, only your son." Wag waves his hand, and a different goon comes in, dragging Tommy by the hair. He's beaten to a pulp, and one of his eyes is swollen shut. Shiny, purple bruises stretch along his face. My entire body goes rigid, my mouth curling in, the anger filling me from toes to fingers. I did not think it possible to hate a stranger, and yet I've never wanted to hurt two so badly.

"Your boy's been cracking safes again and decided he'd do one of ours. The only reason he's not dead is because of the gunrunning job Thomas did for us last year."

"Gunrunning?" I ask aloud.

"Not now, Alice!" Mum flaps her hand in the air to quiet me. "How much did he take?

"Upward of a thousand pounds."

I choke when I hear it, and my mouth falls open with shock. A thousand pounds? We'll never be able to pay that back no matter what we do.

He casually flips over one of the tarot cards on the table. "Did you foresee this, Lady Diamond? Didn't you bother to gaze into your crystal ball this evening?"

His brother sniggers jeeringly. I snigger back at him with a hiss.

What a fucking tosser.

"I have an idea," he prompts. "Why don't you read my palm? Tell me what I should do. Tell me what I *will* do." He peers behind me at the staircase. "Is Louisa sleeping through all this noise? I'm sure she isn't. Curiosity can be a powerful thing for a child, but she's hardly a little girl anymore. Sixteen, almost a woman."

The fact that he knows so much about us, specifically about my sister, has my fingers curling tightly around the blade in my hand; I imagine plunging it into his chest. He's learned enough to threaten us, hurt us, and he wants us to know it. I glance upstairs, relieved not to see Louisa at the top listening.

A pounding starts in my ears, and I don't even recognize my fevered voice when I say, "Maybe he did you a favor? If Tommy can rob the likes of you, clearly the papers have you two wrong, or your security is shit."

Mum looks at me with daggers for eyes.

The goon sitting in the armchair jumps up and takes a dramatic step forward, but Wag lifts his hand to stop him. He opens his mouth, I imagine to talk more about all the things he can do to hurt me, but I get the jump on him by shoving past my mother to face him head-on.

"If you mean to intimidate my family and me, I promise you, you'll come to regret it."

He grins as if I've told him a joke instead of making a threat of my own. "You know, these streets talk about you, Alice Diamond. The fighting spirit of a man with your father's temper to match. I imagine you're thinking about all the ways you can make us pay for this. A battle, perhaps?"

"I wouldn't be afraid of it—you're just another criminal. You're no different from any of us in The Mint. You've just got better clothes."

"You won't get a fight from us," says Wal, finally joining the conversation. "What good would that do? Some of us would die, and the debt wouldn't get repaid. We're here to talk business. We don't want to kill Tommy. He's useful, a genuine talent when he's not drunk."

"Then what do you want?" My mother clears her throat, flashing the knife, but the motion betrays her trembling hands. "What's the deal?"

"He comes to work for us to pay it off. Safe-breaking for us. We've got plenty of use for a bloke with his kind of talent."

"No," I spit. "He's not going to work for you."

"Over my dead body," growls Mum.

"You're not in a position to negotiate," says Wag, looking pointedly at Tommy on the ground.

I nearly cry, thinking about how much pain he is in, but I control the urge. I won't show weakness in front of them. The Diamond name depends on each of us staying strong, even when we desperately want to break.

"How long will you give us? To pay it back?" I ask urgently.

Wag sighs. "We know you can't."

"How long?" I shout it louder. "Skip the small talk and get on with it so I can go back to bed."

Wag crosses his legs as he pulls a cigarette out of his coat pocket. One of the goons briefly steps out of the shadows to strike a match and light it for him. "Have a seat then. If we are to talk business, let's talk like gentlemen."

I ease cautiously onto the chair across the table, my gaze locked with his. I toy with the knife in my hands, flipping it with my fingers.

"Tell me something. I've spent years trying to persuade your father to bring his family to Elephant and Castle—to serve under our leadership. He could prosper with us. Your entire family could, given your arsenal of talents. But he always refuses. Why?"

I rub my forehead. "Why does it matter?"

"I don't enjoy being turned down."

"That must make you very popular with women."

His brother lets out a snort at that, and Wag raises an eyebrow in reproach.

"You'll be doing me a favor if you answer, and considering all this, I don't believe I'm asking much."

I glare at my mother and wet my lips, stalling because the explanation he's asking for is a story I don't fancy telling. I make a point of leaving the past in the past. It's the only way you survive in The Mint.

"Tell him," says my mother, moving behind me and placing her hand on my shoulder.

I lean in to give him my eyes, wanting his undivided attention for this. "Years back, when I was a child, the Italians came here to recruit my father. They knew they'd have a formidable alliance together. He told them no like I'm telling you no right now."

"I can't imagine that went well."

"They were insulted, so they went down to my uncle's place and slaughtered his entire family in their sleep. One man, one knife . . . six dead bodies."

I was with my dad when we discovered the bodies. I can still smell the metallic tang of sour blood if I think about it for too long.

Mum's voice cracks when she says, "A coward in the night . . . killing children. They were innocent."

"Joining a gang is not joining a family; it's the death of a family," I finish her thoughts.

"We are not the Italians," he responds with a small pinch of desperation. "We are their enemies. The enemy of my enemy is my friend."

"You are all the same to us. You've all killed innocent people, and for what? Controlling racecourses? When we kill someone, it's because we have no choice. When you kill, it's for power or who's got the bigger cock at the end of the day. A man hurts your pride, and he's dead. That's not our way."

The brothers exchange a quick, silent glance. Wag runs his hand down his face in consideration. "You want to make a deal, then?"

"A deal," I confirm. "We'll pay you back with interest. Just give me a few weeks."

His mouth quirks to the side, then he holds up his hand. Two fingers. "Two. One thousand pounds with interest."

"Thirty percent," interrupts Wal politely, as if he can somehow excuse the intrusion with manners.

Wag nods. "Thirty percent interest. If you don't pay it back in a fortnight, your brother comes to work for us."

He looks out the window, and a thoughtful moment passes where he is so deeply considering something that his brows pinch together. "The moment we arrived here, we were tailed by a dozen chaps looking to see what kind of trouble we brought. They weren't afraid of us. The only reason they didn't attack is because we had Tommy."

I smile with shameless triumph. "Like I said, in The Mint you're just another criminal like any of us here."

Wal joins him in looking out into the smog-filled darkness. "They wait even now, watching this shop for some kind of order from him."

"Not from him," Mum corrects darkly, looking down at me.

Wag fiddles with his hat in confusion. "The Mint follows your husband . . . does anything he asks. He has his own gang here, even if he doesn't want to admit it. Men and women who follow his code. His ways. Why would they not follow his son while he is away?"

"They won't follow Tommy," I restate stonily.

"They follow you," Wal says suddenly, his voice alight with curiosity. "You're the real head of the Diamond family when your father is away, then?"

I feel my nostrils flare. "Given what Tommy just bleeding did, it doesn't take a brilliant man to figure out which sibling is the one in charge."

A smile splits Wag's face. "I've never negotiated with a dame over something like this. We do business with Mary Carr, but her line of work is tame. We talk of percentages, goods, and services over late-night drinks. But you're in the same business as us, then, aren't you, Alice? Wicked things done with sinister folk. This is uncharted territory for me."

I lean in. "Striking a bargain with a woman doesn't change the territory. The only difference between us is what's between our legs."

Another grin. "We have a deal then."

"And if I pay it off? We are even?"

"We're even," he agrees. "We'll sod off and leave you to these piss-stained streets as we did your father."

I nod, not sure how I'll manage to scrape together that kind of cash, but my demeanor is confident and nonchalant when I respond, "Done."

We both stand. He straightens his coat and gazes around the room. "It's a pity that you were not born a man. Instead, Tommy is your father's heir, and you're the one who must clean up his mistakes. When will you decide enough is enough?"

My eyes stray to Tommy once more. "How far would you go for your family?"

"Too far," he says. "I have danced with the devil himself."

"I would do the same."

Wag finishes the cigarette and flicks it at my mother's feet. "Well, then. We'll be on our way, and I assume you'll be calling off the blokes outside? I don't want any difficulty leaving."

I walk outside, where the smoggy night air blurs the streets, and the only thing visible is the busted streetlamps. Even though I can't see them, I can feel them hiding in the darkness, lurking like animals stalking their prey. In truth, I don't want to call them off. I want to see them work their blades into McDonald flesh for the beating they just gave Tommy. But killing them isn't going to fix this. It would just spur a bigger war that we couldn't win.

I lift my hand to the fog, and they resurface. One by one. Some men, some women, a few adolescent boys. All talents. All gifted with something dark. Ralph is heading the troops and has two sets of long knives in each hand. They glisten like the diamonds I snatched off fingers and necks at the 43 only hours ago.

"Alice," he says, his voice low. "Ye need a hand?"

"Let them pass," I say.

Wal and Wag tip their hats and get into two motorcars waiting along the roadside. Before he closes the door, Wal says, "I'll be seeing you ladies around. Have a swell night."

Ralph retracts his blades and watches their cars disappear into the distance. "Was that who I think it was? What did Tommy do?"

"I'll handle it," I assure him tersely and go back into the house without another word.

Inside, my mother and I both rush to my brother and turn him over, blinking back tears. "Get me some rags and hot water!" I say.

She runs to fetch clean towels.

"You daft bastard." I reach for the wool blanket on the sofa to cover him. "You could have nicked anyone. Why them?"

"I'm sorry," he cries, curling into the blanket. "I just wanted to do something he'd be proud of . . . for once. I wanted to help. You were right, Alice. You're always right."

I rub my hands briskly up and down in his arms to warm him. "I will remind you to tell me that again in the morning."

He snorts a little, then rolls over in pain, clutching his stomach. "What are you going to do? How are you going to get that much money?"

"I'll think of something. I always do."

My mother returns with tea towels and hot water boiled on the hob. I dip one of the cloths and pat it around the gashes on his eye.

She combs her fingers through her hair. "What on earth did you steal that money for?"

Tommy and I say nothing, but our silence says everything.

"Alice? Tommy?"

Tommy coughs again, and I hesitate, but then tell her the truth with a reluctant sigh.

Her mouth goes agape, and she throws a few slaps at Tommy's head. He holds his head and grunts but does nothing in response.

"You stole that money because of an empty promise? You know how hard your father has worked to keep us out of the gang wars and you walk right us right into one?"

I blink slowly, recalling a single piece of the conversation with the brothers that is sticking with me. "What gunrunning job were they talking about?"

She pauses for a moment. "Your father owed them a handsome amount some time ago. A debt he couldn't repay. He used the loan they fronted him to plan a raid on a warehouse in Southwark, but it went awry. They said they'd forgive the debt if your father agreed to run some guns for them. He did it, and that was that."

The revelation makes my heart plummet. "Oh, how fucking brilliant! Dad told us the most important thing was never to get involved with gangs, but he did."

She stands abruptly. "We did what we had to do. That's all there is to say on the matter. You should go to sleep, Alice. I'll finish taking care of your brother. You have to be up in the morning for your job with Mr. King. It's important to gain his trust now more than ever. You get a lay of the land and loot the place, and we're able to pay off the brothers. Do you know the combination to his safe yet?"

Yes. I've known since the day started, but I lie. "No," I say, looking down so she can't see my eyes. "He locks his office every day when he leaves, and I'm not allowed to clean it. He's a bastard, but a smart one."

"Alice," she says my name with pure disbelief. "It never takes you this long. What's going on?"

"I'll find out the combination," I say, avoiding answering her directly. "But what if the contents aren't enough?"

"We will think of something else." Her eyes harden. "Whatever it takes to keep Tommy out of their clutches. He'd be a slave to them, you know that."

"I know."

"We have to save him."

"I know."

"I can't lose him, Alice. I can't." The words come out a quivering mess, her hands starting to shake.

I take her by the face firmly and force her to look me in the eye. "I know, Mum."

In the morning Louisa and I get dressed in silence. Downstairs my mother has breakfast on the table, and the circles beneath her eyes suggest she never went to sleep. Tommy stays on his makeshift pallet as we eat. I wait for Louisa to leave for school before catching a tram to the Kings' town house in Highgate.

I arrive a few minutes late, and by the time I reach their door, Alba, the housekeeper, has it open, waiting for me with a displeased frown. "I've accepted you're not good at much of anything, but the least you can do is to be on time."

"Forgive me," I say.

She examines me with pursed lips. "Did you race all the way over here? Your hair is a mess." As she reaches to smooth some of the stray tendrils, I admire her beauty. Her skin is a rich, gorgeous brown, and her eyes hint at a youth full of adventures she'll never disclose now that life has caught up to her.

I fancy she looks older than she is because of the stress of her job. "Mr. King wants Pearl dressed and ready for luncheon. She'll be making a formal apology to his friends for last night, so make sure she looks appropriately demure."

"What happened last night?"

"Just get to work. Less of your mouth moving and more of your feet."

I take her insults with my usual dismissive eye roll. Like Kate's club, the Kings' home is a modern beauty. Dark paneled walls surround black-and-white herringbone marble floors, and though the foyer is empty, I suspect that last night it was crowded with guests drinking and gossiping about Mr. King's latest show. I can already imagine the man, standing in front of his mahogany bar in his bespoke Shaftesbury Avenue suit, preening and faffing about like a false king.

Alba exhales. "Mrs. King's been in her cups, as usual. You'll have plenty to do to get her looking presentable. Think you can manage it?"

"How sloshed are we talking?"

"Does it matter? If it's too difficult a task, I'm certain we can find another sitter. A less mouthy one, too. Capable of following simple orders."

I was hired to be a second to Alba, bossed about and given the tasks she's likely earned a right to pass on. Instead, on my third day on the job, I stopped King's wife, Pearl, from tossing herself off the balcony during a drunken tantrum. Now I take orders from Pearl, and Alba resents me for it daily.

"I'll have her decent," I assure her, moving up the grand staircase to Pearl's rooms. Unlike the rest of the sleek, modern town house, her rooms are a Victorian, floral mess. Even her silk sheets have small dandelions on them. I've thought about pinching them more than once.

There's nothing like silk against your skin.

I peek into her gigantic dressing room and then venture into the bathroom, where I find her soaking in her claw-foot tub full of bubbles. She stares up at me and moans dramatically. "I'm so pleased to never get a moment to myself and always have you here with me every morning." Her voice is dry with sarcasm. "Have I ever properly told you how much I appreciate your presence?"

I grin in response, taking a seat on the edge of the tub and handing her a sponge. "Every day for weeks. You been moping around all morning?"

She groans in response.

"Why so down? Get into a row last night over something?"

"It was my beloved's birthday." She rolls her eyes with distaste, and I suddenly notice the delicate skin under her left eye is tinged purple. If I were to close my eyes right now, I'd see Tommy on the floor, bashed up with the same purple bruising. I clear my throat and pull my shoulders back. "What happened?"

"Everything was all done up to impress the prats from the theater, but I mucked it up."

"He hit you again?"

"I provoked him." She grins with delight, thinking back on it. "He was acting ridiculously, chatting up a chorus girl young enough to be his daughter and trying to get her into bed with him. He was making a fool of himself, so I toasted his ability to still get it up. He can, you know, despite all the snow. I don't ever see it, though; I close my eyes every time he's on top of me." She giggles richly. "I said it in front of everyone . . . it was glorious. It mortified him."

I'm not laughing because the bruise unnerves me. Mostly because I've become attached to her, but also because when men hit me, I hit back. Pearl King is different. A survivor, not a fighter. All the spirit she had was beaten out of her long before I came along.

"I'm broken, Alice. What do you expect?" It's as if she can read my mind or my face. "Broken means I've got nothing to lose."

I take a deep breath in response. Admittedly, I don't know what to do with broken, which is why every time I have a chance to rob her, I find a reason to wait another day. Week. Month.

I dip my finger into the bathwater. Cold. "Let's get you out and clean you up."

She stands up, dripping water, and I reach for a towel; then, once she's dried off, she slips into a silk negligee trimmed in lavender ribbon. Getting her groomed and dressed is time-consuming. She's a creature of infinite laziness, dragging herself around with little enthusiasm until there's a drink in her hand.

Pearl King used to be in all the papers, a budding starlet who started acting at a young age and blossomed in the spotlight. Mr. King's favorite actress. She was a sight to behold, so I've read. But after their marriage, she's now better known for her exploits—drugs, parties, excessive drinking. Sometimes I'm not even sure how she survives them.

By the time Pearl is clean and downstairs sipping a cup of tea, my mind focuses more and more on the events of last night. The debt is real. Yesterday happened, and I will have to do something to fix it.

If I don't pay it back, I damn us all.

"What's going on?" Pearl's eyebrows arch with curiosity as she folds the newspaper in front of her. "We always talk about me, but you're the mystery. I'm fine with it, but how about today, just once, we switch places?"

"It's nothing, Mrs. King," I say while pouring her some milk. "Family troubles."

"So, you're allowed to know every detail of my tragic life, but I can't even get a glimpse into yours?"

I half-smile at the comment, then take a seat at the table. "My brother did something foolish, something that puts my family at risk."

She leans in, curiosity piqued. "Risk? What kind?"

A part of me is tempted to tell her the truth—I feel confident she'd keep my secret with all the secrets I keep for her. But outsiders can't be trusted, especially ones with full bellies. She's lived in luxury so long she'd never be able to understand my family or our situation. "It's complicated."

"Do you need money?" She stiffens at the idea. "Not that I can give you any. Harold controls everything." She gives it a long thought. "But you can take anything from my closets—sell them. I've got some pieces I've never even worn. Take them all!"

I smirk and shake my head gently. Hocking her couture might make a sizable dent in the tab but won't pay it off in full.

"You're not going to hand in your notice, are you?" The wry tone I've grown accustomed to is replaced with one that is soft and vulnerable. "You can't quit. I could very well die without you. I almost did die without you."

There's no melodrama in her voice, only raw sincerity. I reach out for her hand, a hopefully comforting gesture to ease her mounting anxiety. "I will not quit. But do as he asks today. Don't give him any reason to punish you." I look over her bruised eye again. "Promise me you'll play the part? Say what he wants you to say?"

She pouts and rolls her eyes. "There's no fun in that."

Mr. King suddenly appears, rushing out of the library as he yells for Alba. His booming voice echoes through the halls like thunder. He turns to the dining room just as I pull my hand away. "Skiving off, are we? You're being given a wage to cook and clean, not eat my food and prattle incessantly with my vapid wife."

I jump up and nod curtly. He watches me with a steady glare. To his credit, he's an imposing man with a broad, heavyset physique and salt-and-pepper hair that would intimidate anyone in passing. Well, anyone but me.

He grows silent, radiating palpable waves of anger. Pearl's shoulders shake, but she raises her face to stare at him attentively.

"I'm going to one of the theaters for a few hours, but I'll meet you for lunch," he says, adjusting his vest. "I expect you to be gracious and apologetic with our guests. You'll behave as a wife should and not embarrass me one iota further."

"You want me to lie to their faces and say I didn't mean what I said last night?"

He storms over and grabs her by the chin. I instinctively move closer, two steps that feel more like leaps, and grab the chair to stop myself, my heart pounding against my chest. Pearl's face goes pale. He's squeezing hard enough to make her wince.

I search the room, and my eyes land on a fork. I imagine stabbing him with it. The sharp tines digging into his flesh until he's bleeding, scrambling around like a fish caught on a hook, screaming to Alba for help. Would I get away with it? I judge the distance from him to the door. I could run. But how far would I get?

"If you don't say what I told you to say, I'll have you committed," he says in a low growl, teeth bared. "Do you understand me, Pearl?"

She's quick to nod submissively, and he releases her with a throw. She cradles her jaw carefully and returns to her breakfast with an audible swallow.

"And you." He waves at me, searching his memory for my name. "Alice? Alba tells me you were late this morning. If you can't get here on time, find another job. Understood?"

My entire body urges me to lash out at him, but I force the impulse down and give him a demure response. "Yes, sir."

"Don't mess this up," he says again to his wife in parting. Before he leaves, he quickly strides across the foyer to lock the library door, then slips the key into the pocket of his suit.

I just need a moment without Pearl at my side to nick the key, unlock the door, and break into his safe. Maybe this is my wake-up call—if I don't rob them soon, I might do something stupid and kill this bastard with a fork.

But leaving means I'll have lied to her about not quitting, condemning her to face her fate. I lie all the time. At least once, every single day. Why do I feel guilty now? Why do I feel a pain in my chest at the idea of abandoning her?

I close my eyes and try to bury the emotion.

I cannot save her. I cannot save everyone.

Mr. King leaves with the key and relief fills my body.

Maybe tomorrow.

CHAPTER FOUR

I leave Mr. King's and take a tram to Chinatown, where the Hill boys have their operation. The clatter and rattle of the tram hurtling down the tracks makes it impossible for me to think beyond my anger. I clutch the wooden seat until my knuckles turn white, lightly tapping my foot against the lower deck.

When I finally step off, I lift my hand to block out the bright afternoon sun, then blink the scene into view. Chinatown is bursting with colors, narrow streets lined with shuttered homes and shops, a beautiful contrast to The Mint's muted shades of gray. I pass through the bustling market, where the cured meats and exotic spices fill my nostrils, but I don't stop to buy anything because there's a collection of faces watching me, stalking my steps through the market.

I am a stranger to their streets, and they want me to know it.

Despite their fevered stares, I feel no intimidation or wariness when I stop outside the Hills' small gambling house and give the man at the door my name. He nods and says nothing, walking inside for a minute before waving at me to follow him.

The smell of cigar smoke consumes me. There's a single open area full of round tables with men yelling and gambling in a dope-induced haze. There are no windows to give any sign of time passing, just a growing collection of empty liquor bottles. They could have been here for hours or days, and they wouldn't know unless they stepped outside.

Some chaps are poorly dressed, leaning over the tables, wallowing in their grim luck. Others are dressed in expensively tailored suits, suggesting that outside this den, they are men of status and power—personas they leave behind when they walk through the door.

"They're in the back." The bouncer points and returns to his post outside the door.

Behind a black curtain, Eli and Patrick are hovering around a desk with various documents on it. Men scatter about, more hired brutes to stop anyone from stepping out of line.

"Alice!" Patrick stands to embrace me. He has a kind face, with smooth, youthful skin and lush fair hair. He kisses my cheek and takes my hands. "It's been a long while. Shall I fetch you a drink?"

I step back, keeping my expression stern. "Which one of you saw Tommy last time he came to visit?"

"I did," says Eli, staring at me firmly. The opposite of his brother, Eli is hard around the edges. He has large eyes and a sharp chin, body covered in battle scars he wears with pride, going out of his way to keep his shirtsleeves rolled up and collar unbuttoned. His head is now shaved of the unkempt blond curls that I was always so fond of when we were children. It's almost painful trying to swing my anger his way.

"You gave Tommy information about who he needed to pay off to spring my father?"

"I told him that it had worked for a friend of mine." He stands up and starts toward me with a shake of his head. "But that there is a fifty-fifty chance anything comes of it."

I pull my fingers into a tight fist and shove past Patrick to throw a quick, forceful punch that snaps Eli's head back. He stumbles, then pulls up with a primal growl. He wants to hit me back—I can see it in his bared teeth—but he doesn't. Even as blood drips from his left nostril, he doesn't. He's never hit me, and he never will.

We were lovers once, not so long ago. I used to love the animal he'd become if pushed just right. The darkness inside him that he often kept reserved only for business. But now, I want to hurt that animal and send it running for its cage. "You fucked us! You've killed Tommy!"

One of his guards already has me in a viselike grip, trying to force me to the ground, but Eli lifts one hand, and he stops.

My fist throbs in pain. One of my knuckles busted open from the hit; I can feel the cold air on the wound.

Eli takes a handkerchief from the pocket in his vest and reaches for my bleeding hand. I resist, but he pulls roughly until he's able to wrap it around my knuckles in a tight knot. A muscle in his lower jaw tics. "What's happened?"

"Don't be thick! You knew he'd do something foolish with that information. You should have come to me. You should have told me."

"Tommy asked for a name. I gave it to him. He left here laughing at the idea of paying the barrister. I didn't think he was serious about it."

"He robbed the McDonald brothers."

Patrick stifles a choked gasp. "How much did he steal? Is he dead? Is Tommy dead?"

"No," I admit grudgingly, pulling my hand away with a hiss. "He's not dead, not yet. But the whole thing went tits up, as usual, and guess who came knocking down our doors for it?"

"What do they want?" Eli's brows arch with concern. "We can arrange a way out of London for him. Tonight, if need be."

"Him leaving doesn't change the debt he owes!"

Patrick blinks slowly. "How much does he owe? We can help."

"I don't want your bloody help." I pull my throbbing fist to my chest and close my eyes. "I am here to tell you both to stay away from my brother and my family. I don't want to hear your name come out of his mouth again." I start toward the door.

"Alice," prompts Eli, following me with several immense steps. "Just because we shared a bed doesn't mean I'm expected to tell you every-thing. Tommy is a grown man."

I stop and turn around. "Not because we shared a bed, Eli, but because of what my dad did for you." I wave my hand around the room. "You wouldn't have any of this rubbish if he hadn't taught you how to be your own man. If he hadn't pushed you to go bigger, venture outside The Mint. For that, at least, you *will* tell me the next time Tommy comes around asking for names." At the door, I stop to say haltingly, "By the way. Maggie is back in London. Running around with Mary Carr."

"The gang of little lady hoisters?" Patrick asks.

Eli lets out a terse laugh. "She's pulling your leg. You know Maggie wouldn't do that."

"Saw her myself at the 43 all decked out in jewels. Doing well and fine."

Patrick shakes his head. "She left because she didn't want to follow our rules, but then she joins Mary Carr?"

"I suppose that goes to show all the things she'll give up about herself before coming back to you boys." I eye Eli when I say it. Again a muscle in his jaw tics.

"Why are you telling us this, Alice?" His voice is low, ferocious.

"This is me showing you the respect you didn't think fit to show me."

I'm halfway through my shift at the 43 Club when I spot Maggie at the bar chatting up Rob. It's been years since we've seen each other, and now she's at the club where I work to have a casual drink two nights in a row.

I study Maggie and Rob discreetly from the other side of the bar. Rob expressed nothing but distaste for Mary and her girls last night, but now he's talking to Maggie like they're old friends. I open my mouth to call out an order to him but stop when I see Maggie slip him something.

"Don't you have better things to do?" says a disapproving voice behind me, and I spin around, grabbing the tray of drinks I set down to spy on Rob and Maggie.

Kate Meyrick is frowning at me, her sullen expression clashing with her colorful silk dress, cut in the latest style and complemented by an ostrich feather headband and a long necklace of sparkling, iridescent beads that immediately catch my eye.

Shiny always does.

"Sorry, Mrs. Meyrick, I just got distracted."

She adjusts the cream-colored gloves down her fingers, then grins.

"Rob has a way of doing that. He's a pretty one." She eyes my shirt and fixes it, straightening a fold in the fabric. "Save yourself the trouble though. As my mother always told me, honest men are the best men."

"Rob's not honest?" I ask, ashamed of the quick spark of anxiety that flickers in my chest.

"No man is honest. So the best man is no man." She says it like a playful song lyric, hardly taking it as seriously as it sounds.

"It's not just him distracting me," I tell her. "It's this place." I make an expansive gesture. "It's something else."

"She's a beauty." Her smile widens with pride. "My life's work."

"How'd you do it?" A question I'm sure she's been asked before, but I can't help it. A woman owning a club is one thing, but the hottest nightclub in London? I want her story, all of it, every single delicious detail. She defied the odds. She's on top of a world dominated by men. I need to know more.

"Aren't you the curious one? I adore curious women. Risk, that's the answer. Don't be afraid to take them. Taking risks is the only way women will ever get ahead of men in this city." She doesn't give me a chance to reply before she taps my tray. "Now, back to work."

I turn around, and Rob is right in front of me, somehow having slithered clear across the bar without me noticing.

Before I can speak, he hands me a note written on a cocktail napkin. "For you."

I set down my tray of drinks and unfold the napkin.

Meet me in the booth in the back. —M

"Thought you didn't like them—Mary's girls?" I say to him. "All that talk last night about reckless girls stealing from honest people. Never said you were pals with one of them."

"Pal is a stretch." He looks down at the napkin. "Take my advice: whatever she asks, say no."

I point to the space where he'd been with Maggie only minutes ago. "If you're not pals, then what are you?"

"Old acquaintances," he answers. "How do *you* know her?"

"Old acquaintances," I counter.

I take the napkin and curl it into my palm, but before I can escape the bar, I feel his hand on my arm. His fingers move down to Eli's handkerchief still wrapped around my knuckles. "What happened here?"

I pull my arm away. "You fancy me, don't you, Rob?"

"I do," he says without missing a beat.

I swallow, taken aback by his honesty. "You shouldn't."

He shrugs. "You're right. You're too tall for me. I don't mind a mouthy dame, but those stems are intimidating. I like my girls short."

I glance away and suppress a grin. "For the record, I don't like it when men touch me without asking."

He lifts his hands. "It won't happen again."

I lean in a little and lower my voice, reaching up to adjust his bow tie. "I said to *ask* next time, not that I don't want it to happen again."

I see a blush creep up his face as I walk away triumphantly, delighted I've won this round.

I slide into the booth with Maggie and throw my hands down with a heavy sigh. "To what do I owe the pleasure, Mags? I believe I made myself clear last night."

"I wanted to say you're right. I should have known better than to ask you to join a gang. I just wanted to give you the same chance I had."

"I already told you, you don't owe me anything." I shimmy back out, but she's quick to grab my bandaged hand. "Did this happen last night? I've been hearing gossip about the McDonald brothers coming to The Mint."

I tense, seeking something to say that will put her off the scent, but she doesn't give me a chance.

"It's Tommy, isn't it? He's always been a real shit. What does he owe them? What did he do? Tell me so I can help you."

I pull my hand away and slam the bruised knuckles against the mahogany table to make myself extra clear. "I don't want your help! I saw your brothers today. They didn't believe me when I told them you joined Mary, that you serve her like a dog."

She shoots up in a fury, her face the same fiery red as her hair. "I am no one's dog! Mary and I are part of a team. It's my brothers that treated me like a dog. They'd throw me in the Pit to make them money but force me to leave the room when it was time to talk business. Didn't matter that I'd be useful or that I had excellent ideas; I'm a woman and their sister, so I couldn't run with them—it wasn't my place." Her voice is booming, but after a quick peek past me, she calms herself and sits down. The spark of who she once was is gone, like a flame being blown out, leaving only the smoke behind.

"Mary likes you, Alice, says you have talent. She planned to give you an audition before your little scene last night."

"Audition?" I snort. "Was my performance for you last night not enough?"

"She'll test you with something riskier."

"Diamonds don't join gangs," I say again, but with less enthusiasm. I'm worn down from the events of last night, and it's challenging to keep the exhaustion from my voice.

"How much does Tommy owe, then?"

I run my hand over my face and sit back down with a plop. "A thousand pounds."

The amount doesn't shock her. "You can make that with us. It'd take two weeks, maybe three."

"I only have two."

Her eyes widen. "What was the deal, then? And if you don't make it? What then?"

I fold my hands across my chest. "If I don't make it in two weeks, they get Tommy."

"Blimey!" She blinks quickly, and her posture crumples. A moment passes while all the uncertainty and shock inside her seem to settle; then she lifts her shoulders back up with a firm movement. "If I give you my cut for the next two weeks, we can do it."

"No, I won't ask you to do that."

She gives me a half-hearted shrug. "You didn't ask me. I'm doing it anyway. Two weeks, we pay it back together. If you still want to leave, leave."

I hang my head. "It can't be that simple. You think she'll let me leave once she finds out I'm an earner?"

"It is that simple," she assures me. "The girls that follow Mary do so willingly. She knows the best way for her to succeed is having girls who want it just as badly as she does."

I throw my arms up and sigh dreamily. "I admit, seeing you like this makes me envious. You look like you belong in a Mayfair town house, and I look like a kitchen maid on a good day. But I don't want trunks of expensive dresses enough to sacrifice my freedom for them."

"We are not like the men."

"Oh, don't spit me that rubbish! A gang is a gang."

"This is different. You have to see it to believe it. Give it a chance."

I say nothing in return, and for a long moment, we sit together like we used to. Maggie always had a way of letting me figure out what I needed to without nagging at me to tell her about it. I long to tell her how much I've missed her, but my mind screams out in warning against it. She cannot know that I've been lonely without her.

Finally, she breaks the silence with, "Every morning, she has breakfast at Franny's near the Strand. Meet her there around half eight, convince her to give you an audition. Show her you are every bit as talented as I've said."

I shake my head. "What if it isn't enough? What if she refuses me? I insulted her by laughing at her offer."

"She won't refuse you." Her voice is absolute.

"I can't join a gang," I repeat, more to myself.

"This gang war between the men—it's just that, between the men. You love Tommy, your father. Little Louisa. But when will you love yourself? When will you know yourself outside of what your father has always expected of you? This is freedom, real freedom."

It sounds too good to be true. Freedom always has a price. I let out a slow breath. "What made you do it? What made you leave us?"

What made you leave me?

Her entire body tenses, her shoulders stiffening. A lengthy silence follows before she speaks. "Mary offered more. More everything."

"You were the Reaper," I remind her, and she shivers involuntarily. "You were the best fighter in The Mint, maybe all of London. You were somebody to our streets."

"All my life, my brothers had been telling me what to do, and my mum was right behind them, telling me to listen and obey. Mary came around, offering me a chance to decide. For once, someone asked me what I wanted. Women don't get that. At least not women like us. Your father never asked you if you wanted this life, did he?"

She's right, depressingly so, and I can't deny it. But still, I hesitate—deeply considering my uncle and his slaughtered family. The McDonald brothers beating my brother nearly to death. Rob's warning.

I cast him a quick look. He's mixing something up for a couple staring longingly at each other between drinks.

Maggie sniggers. "Let me guess, Rob told you to walk away?"

I avoid answering the question. "How do you two know each other?"

"He's what we call a defector."

"Defector?"

"The black sheep of the McDonald family. Changed his mind about being part of the family business after he got back from the war and went clean. Rumor is he did some awful things in service of his country."

"He's a McDonald?" I can't help the rise in my voice as the horror of such an idea leaves me shaking. "No, the third brother is named Bert, and my dad said he died in the war." He can't be a McDonald brother. He can't be a part of the same family that stormed our house in the night with my beaten-up brother, making demands. Not him. The idea guts me.

"Bert, Robert, Rob," answers Maggie casually. "That's him, and he looks alive to me. They used to call him the Demolitions Man—could make a bomb of anything in minutes. Now, instead of bombs, he makes drinks."

I struggle with the revelation for a long minute before Maggie jumps in again. "He wasn't in deep with any of their schemes, just helped with the logistics, you know?"

I stare at Rob, who is busy stocking bottles on shelves with Kate behind him, talking at the back of his head. Maggie slides over another napkin with an address scribbled on it. I'm guessing for Franny's.

I don't say anything else, and she gets up and leaves. I fold the napkin and tuck it into my pants along with the other one, then move to the bar. I wait for Kate to go back to her office before I snatch the rag out of Rob's hand and hurl it at him. "You're a proper shit!"

He catches the rag with a glare. "What's your problem?"

"You're my problem! You tell me to say no to Maggie knowing damn well I don't have a choice, thanks to your brothers!"

His mouth drops open, and he lets out a strangled laugh. "I don't even know what you're talking about!"

"That's a load of tosh! Don't lie to me!"

"I'm not lying! I don't talk to my brothers. I mind my business." He shakes his head, looking to me and the bar and the booth in the back where Maggie had been, trying to connect the dots. "What business do you have with my brothers, anyway?"

"You honestly don't know?"

"I honestly don't know what the hell you're talking about."

I shake my head with a spiteful hiss. "Well, lucky you. Just sit back here and tend bloody bar while the rest of us have to deal with your family's shit." I take my tray and throw one last glare at Rob. "I catch you looking at my legs again, baby face, and I'll break a glass over your bloody head."

The night slips by fast, and I'm too distracted by Maggie's words to pocket from the crowd. It's wild that I'm considering doing this, knowing my dad's furious wrath will come down on me when he finds out.

He wouldn't do this to save Tommy. He'd do terrible things, but he'd never join a gang.

But I'm not him, and maybe for Tommy's sake, that's a good thing this time.

I work mindlessly until closing, then head home to tell my mother about Mary Carr's offer. She brings her fist to her mouth and bites it. She paces until the shawl slips off her shoulders. "You should have told Maggie no. You should have told her to bugger off!"

"I told Maggie no. It didn't change much. It's only a meeting anyway. I have to audition for her. Perhaps I'll fail." I search the shop for Tommy. "Where did he run off to now?"

"I sent him to get fixed up. Ralph said he'd give him a few stitches and a bottle of something to take the edge off."

"I could use a bottle of something," I mutter.

"I don't want you to do this." Her posture grows stiff, her features pinched with doubt. "Mary might be sweet to you or give you a generous cut of the take, but that's because she knows none of that matters. You'd belong to her. She could change the rules and force you to do something you don't want to do. She'll have all the power, and you'll have nothing. That's not a position you want to be in."

"I don't belong to anyone. Yet again, you think so little of me."

"The second you defy her, she'll have the brothers break down our door again. How is this any different from Tommy working for them?"

"I'll bide my time, pay off the debt, and be done with her. It's a plan—the only plan we've got."

"Why would she even agree to take you in now? The McDonald brothers want you to fail, and they are allies. You can still clean out Mr. King."

I try not to let uncertainty creep into my voice as I say, "The situation with King is complicated."

"Complicated? How?"

"I don't know if I'm going to do that anymore."

A laugh bursts out of her. "You only got the job with King to loot him. That is always the plan when you take a job as a maid for the rich."

I move to the center table and sit down. "It's not that simple anymore. I haven't had a chance to get into the safe yet, and he hurts his wife."

"What does that have to do with anything?"

"I don't know if I can leave her. He could kill her if I do."

A moment of silence passes between us, and then another laugh, far more bitter, escapes her mouth. "You are a thief, Alice. You don't sympathize with a wealthy stage actress, thinking you might be able to save her! You imagine she'd think twice about saving you?"

"Is it so surprising that I might care for something outside of these goddamn streets?"

She folds her arms over her chest, her eyebrows pulling together to create an all-too-familiar crease in her forehead. I'm about to get a lecture, a strong one. "You don't want to hear this, but nothing you do will save a woman like that."

"I am not here for a session, Mum."

"She will stay with him, Alice, no matter the abuse, before she gives up those satin robes and lavender baths. I promise you that. I don't want to hear about this again. You will rob King, and that is the end of it!"

I jump up and rage at her, my chair falling to the ground with the brash movement. My words come out as more of a growl. "You don't tell me what to do! I decide what I'm going to do to pay off the debt. Not you!"

She takes several steps back, eyeing my fists uneasily, and I'm reminded of Pearl trembling at breakfast. A sharp pain pulls at my chest. I don't want to scare the people I love.

I reach out hesitantly and take my mother by the shoulders gently, adjusting her shawl apologetically. I tighten it around her body. "Forgive me, Mum."

She reaches up and tucks some hair behind my ear, giving a nod in response.

My lips thin, and I say nothing while flopping down on the run-down sofa, blowing out a breath of pure exhaustion. If I closed my eyes now, I'd be asleep in seconds. "What if there is nothing in that safe? We need to prepare for the worst. I could rob his house, but there's no telling how long it will take to fence the goods."

She groans with disappointment and takes a seat beside me. "If there's nothing in it, then we have no choice. Maybe if we're lucky, your father never finds out."

"And when he does?"

"God helps us both."

We share a cigarette in silence before I wander upstairs to check on Louisa, but the bed is empty.

The McDonalds.

Icy panic grips me as I swing wildly around, hoping she's somehow hidden in a corner and not kidnapped—then I hear the window creak open. A gush of cold night air slaps me in the face, and I see a figure crawl through.

Her slender legs come in first, lowering down as the rest of her follows. She adjusts her dress—my dress, actually—and turns around. I note a pattern of love bites on her neck, along with her disheveled hair and glazed eyes. Then the smell—the smell is like a knife to the gut. She reeks of the opium den next door.

"Alice," she squeaks, alarmed. "It's not what you think. I was just getting some air."

"Who is he?" I can't manage any other words.

"There's no he."

"Don't lie to me."

"You lie to me all the time," she counters, on the defensive. "Last night, I asked for the truth about our family. You couldn't even tell me the truth with gang members knocking out our windows. Go on, tell me, Alice. Tell me we are dangerous. Tell me I will never leave The Mint and that one day I will step into Mum's shoes. Or worse, yours."

"I'm not going to let that happen."

"Tell me, Alice! Tell me that my dreams of escape are silly. That I will only ever be a girl from The Mint."

"I told you I'd find a way to get you out!"

"You didn't get out." Her gaze drops, her lower lip starting to tremble. "You like to think I am a silly little girl that you can keep in this dark room forever, but I am not."

A fury fills me. "So this man is your plan, then? Your way out?"

"What if he is? Just because the answer to your problems can't possibly be a man doesn't mean the answer to mine can't be."

"You're just a bloody child." I gesture at her body, my dress, loose on her breasts and hips. "You're only sixteen."

"I'm woman enough for him."

"Who is he? You smell of the den next door. Tell me the name or I'll go over there and burn the place down just to make sure I get him."

"You wouldn't."

"Don't test me, Louisa. The bloke's name?"

When she says nothing, I grab the matchbook in the top drawer of the nightstand to make my point, then race down the stairs. She chases me with a cry.

"Don't do it! It's Jacob. It's Jacob Sloan!"

"Jacob Sloan?" My breath stalls in disbelief. Jacob is the son of a retired muscle for hire, Richard the Butcher, who owns a meat shop down the block. He's not a man Dad ever crossed. Not just because he's nearly three hundred pounds of pure force, but because he's been loyal over the years. Unshakingly loyal.

He's a man I shouldn't piss off, but every breath I take to regain control is another inhale of icy fury as images of Jacob touching my sister fill my head. My skin flushes until I'm sweating. There are indeed plenty of girls her age getting married in this city, bedding men older than them. Mum married Dad at fifteen. But Louisa won't be one of those girls, so bloody help me.

Mum starts up the stairs as I race down them. "What's happened? What have you cocked up this time, Louisa?"

I race to Dad's lockbox and select one of the serrated knives from his collection, one that my smaller hand can grip perfectly, then leave the shop. The opium den is guarded by a woman named Liza, who is always too high to do anything other than collect entrance fees from her desperate customers. She doesn't even notice me barge inside.

The layout is open, with old army cots and threadbare sheets, and the entire place smells like a wound that's going putrid, releasing a thick, sickly sweet smell that overwhelms everything else.

I gag and cover my mouth with the neck of my shirt as I make my way through, stepping over people and trying not to breathe too deeply. I observe the messy, candlelit interior as I move quietly inside. If Jacob hears me coming, he'll run.

I cautiously pull back curtain after curtain, peeking through and then closing them. When I finally reach a room in the back, I throw the door open to find Jacob sorting money into a cashbox. When he spots me, something about my expression makes him leap up and scurry behind the small table. Or perhaps it is the sight of the dagger. "Now, now, Alice, don't go doing anything you'll regret."

A tingle sweeps down my spine as I shake my head. "Who says I'll regret it?"

"Your father wouldn't allow this! We're a family in The Mint. We don't threaten each other."

"He'd feel differently if he saw the marks you're leaving along my sister's neck. His baby girl." My voice rises, and I'm growling through my words. "Maybe I'll tell him when he gets out and watch him storm this place instead. Squeeze your throat until your face turns purple while I laugh in the background."

I'm caught by surprise by the feeling of something slamming against my back. Louisa's arm wraps around my torso as she grabs my blade, her scrawny arms startlingly fast.

"Let go, let it go!" She huffs, her feet kicking at my legs. I elbow her in the ribs until she releases me with a squeak, and then I grab Jacob by the collar with disgust. I can smell his foul breath and see the sweat beading down his forehead. He's a squirmy little bloke—the first to hide during a skirmish out on the streets. Even now, he whimpers like a frightened child in my grasp.

He's the worst choice, and I won't have it.

I hold the knife up close, right against the stubble along his chin. "You touch her again, I'll find out, and I'll be back to cut you from nose to navel while every damn person in The Mint looks on."

I can feel the fear radiating off his skinny body. His eyes flick to Louisa sobbing behind me.

I jerk him by the collar. "Don't look at her! Look at me! She can't help you. Do we understand each other, Jacob?"

Bottom lip quivering, he nods jerkily. I place the knife down and let him go, but not before delivering a forceful punch to his head with my uninjured hand. The impact sends a sharp jolt of pain up my arm, and my whole hand explodes with agony. Both my hands are torn up, a mess of blood and purple bruising. I try to pull them into fists again, but the action is painful. They barely bend. It takes everything I have not to wince at the intensity of the sting. But I keep my face calm and finally clench my fists. If my dad could see me now, he'd slap his legs and howl with pride.

On the ground with blood pouring from a cut above his eye, Jacob lets out a high-pitched whimper but doesn't try to get up. He waits there, curled into a ball like a frightened dog.

I grab Louisa's hand and yank her out the door. Once we're outside, she shoves me back a few steps. "You're not my father! You have no right to tell me who I can see."

Mum emerges from our front door and immediately hones in on my hand, taking it in hers with a kiss. "Why didn't you use the brass knuckle-dusters if you intended to knock him about?"

Louisa is pure, cold fury. "You're allowing this?"

My mother's lips curl. "Did you sleep with him? Don't lie to me. I'll check between your legs if I need to."

Face red, eyes flooded with tears, Louisa shakes her head. "No."

"Good," she says. "You know what happens to girls that bed men for fun? They end up with a child, and then every choice they've ever had goes away. You'll marry him, live with him, be obedient to him because he is the only thing that will keep you and your child alive. Is that what you want?"

Her voice says it all, hinting at the consequences of such actions. Consequences she understands and has lived. I am certain there was love between my parents as I grew up, but maybe it wasn't always that way. "You want to spend your life under a man like that?"

Louisa shakes her head, clutching her chest, opening her mouth but unable to find words. Now that my back's not up, every part of me wants to comfort her as I always do. But she needs to feel the sting of our mother's words, so I resist.

"No." The word comes out of her mouth in a low whine.

"I can't hear you."

"No, that's not what I want. I was only having a little fun."

I move past my mother and face Louisa head-on, still resisting the urge to hold her, assure her I'm doing this for her own good.

But she's right about not being a child anymore, and I have to stop treating her like one. The lessons she learns will stick only if she learns them the hard way. "Fun's over. Now go to bed."

Chapter Five

In the morning I arrive at Franny's with a cautious determination and a drag to my step. I walk past well-dressed men and women enjoying leisurely breakfasts. A waiter rushes by me with a tray of fat cream cakes and golden, crusty pastries, and my eyes latch onto the mouthwatering sight until he melds into the scenery.

The restaurant is filled with the smell of fresh coffee, and I inhale its rich, earthy scent as my stomach rumbles with desire. If my dad were here, he'd be tsk-tsking beside me and saying, "Don't fill your head with daydreams, Alice—be practical. You'll never eat in a place like this, but if you hustle, you'll at least eat."

I think of that as I search for Mary Carr.

Finally, I spot her sitting in a secluded corner in the back, wearing the same thick fur and headdress she had on that night at the 43 Club, only in a different color. A shade of sky blue. She hasn't seen me yet, which means I can still reconsider. I can leave now, and she'll be none the wiser.

But I'm not confident that I can loot King's safe and leave Pearl behind, and I'm not sure what he has will even come close to the amount I need to fix Tommy's screw-up.

This is the only way. Two weeks and I'm out. I can do this.

I command my feet to move forward, ignoring the smell of the yeasty bread browning in the oven, leaving my stomach in knots. I'm not here to eat. I'm here to talk business.

Mary looks up impassively from her newspaper as I approach. She signals the waiter, who puts down a stack of crumb-smeared plates to rush to her. "Bring my guest the same thing I'm having, will you?"

"Right away, ma'am." He nods briskly and scurries off.

Her gaze travels up and down the length of my body. "Who told you where to find me?" she asks finally.

I sit down in the chair across from hers. "Maggie said you have breakfast here every morning."

Her brows arch. "How humorous. One moment, I have no idea who you are. Just some name that Maggie mentioned, a childhood friend. Then this morning, I hear that the McDonald brothers have business with the Diamond family. That this Diamond family controls The Mint, a den of criminals. At the head of it is you. A woman." She lets out a bubbly giggle that hinges on hysterical. "I had no idea we were so similar."

I cut the small talk. "You've heard about my brother's debt, then?"

"I don't know all the details." She shrugs before taking a long sip of coffee. "We're allied with the brothers, but distantly. They would never share information about their unrelated business with me. I deal with goods and profit, and they deal in war. I do not want to know who they slaughter for power. That's not what I want."

"What do you want, then?"

She gives me a wide enigmatic grin. "I want to give every woman a chance to wear silk and ride in cars they own. To understand that being a woman doesn't mean we can't make our destiny."

I shake my head scornfully. "It's easy to talk about destiny when you're eating here, sipping coffee in your expensive outfit."

The mention of coffee seems to conjure the waiter, who magically appears by my side to set down a coffee cup and a plate of eggs, beans, and toast. The smell of the fresh brew is spectacular, reminding me of the first job I ever helped Dad on. We emptied the register of a gourmet chocolate shop near the Strand. He rewarded me with a coffee-bean truffle, and I swore I'd tasted heaven.

"Is that why you're here, Alice? To talk down to me for having all the things you wish you had?" Her voice is calm, not at all bothered by my remark.

I wonder if perhaps this is just routine for her. Talking up a poor girl in need of a break. Here, where she's surrounded by cinnamon and yeasty dough, staring at a woman dressed in fur and diamonds. Foolishly, she'd fall for this brilliant charade without a second thought. How many women have you trapped, Mary?

"Eat something," she suggests warmly with the most engaging smile. "You're looking peckish."

Despite my stomach imploring me to devour everything in one bite, I only take a dainty sip of coffee and place the cup back on its saucer with a gentle clink. "No," I finally say. "I came because I'd like to take you up on your offer if you'll still have me. Maggie says it should be easy to pay off my family's debt in a couple weeks if I'm running with you."

She exhales dramatically. "I told you that you had a talent at the 43, and I meant it. I also think desperation can be a powerful motivator. But I don't think you'd be a suitable fit, after all."

My heart races. "That wasn't the case the night we met. You're a thief, just like me. The only difference between us is that you don't have rips in your stockings."

She retrieves something from a silver beaded handbag on the table—a tube of lipstick. "I don't recruit women like you. Women like me."

"Can you stop talking in riddles?"

"In The Mint, you snap your fingers, and there are men at your door willing to do your bidding because of your father's reputation. You are accustomed to being in control. You do not follow orders. You make them. I cannot have that. I cannot have you challenging my orders."

I don't argue with her because everything she's saying is right. I let out a lighthearted chuckle, forcing the tension from my posture, even though under the table my leg is jiggling madly. "Perhaps it's for the best," I say in a calm tone. "Dad would toss me out on the street for disrespecting everything he's built."

"What has he built? A nest of low-level criminals safe from the gang war? It's all rubbish. Though he might pretend that his intentions are noble, he knows he has power over those people. And he's too smart ever to give it up."

For the moment I forget that I need her. That I should beg for a chance and stop mouthing off. "My father doesn't control The Mint. He brings order to it. Those people are his family and friends. He doesn't own them. He is nothing like you or your precious McDonald brothers. He'd laugh at me for even considering this."

I realize quickly that I am proving her point.

"Let your father laugh," she continues strongly. "He'll stop soon enough when he realizes what you've become. After all, a woman cannot fight or be outspoken. A woman like you cannot think or vote. How could she possibly do what a man does but even better? Let all the men laugh. The world will come to know us. It's a shame that I cannot trust you to listen to me. We could do glorious things together."

I'm astonished by my speechlessness. It's hard to believe—a female gang of thieves, under no man's law, running by their own rules. I have power in The Mint, but only because my dad gave it to me. And that power doesn't come with rewards like dresses and cars. It only comes with pain, anger, a numbness I've had since I was born as I've been forced to endure my dad's many lessons about what comes along with our family name.

I shift my position in the chair and lean forward. "Let me at least have the audition. Let me show you can I follow orders."

She takes a sip in consideration. "Do you have a day off from working for Harold King?"

I lean back. "How do you know I work for King?"

"I have connections all over this city, Alice."

She pulls something from her coat, a small notebook that she opens and skims. "You've done this over a dozen times this year. You get in as a maid at some toff's house, spend a week getting a lay of the land, then wipe them out. A new alias every time so they can't track you down. Only you've been at Harold King's for over a month. Why are you still there?"

My stomach fills with bitter dread at the ever-present reminder that I cannot seem to shake wanting to help Pearl. "It's complicated."

"Is it?"

I hesitate for a moment. "He beats his wife. I—I've grown fond of her, and I don't feel right leaving yet. He's got a safe, and I know the combination. But as soon I take what's in it, I've got to leave. I can't go back. I can't help her. Maybe next week, I read a column in the paper about how she mysteriously fell down the stairs."

"Has this ever happened before?"

"No," I say sharply. "I don't get attached. I never get attached."

"You sound upset with yourself."

"I am," I admit.

She gives me a strange look. "Imagine that . . . softness in a girl from The Mint."

"It's not softness."

"It's compassion, loyalty outside of your family. I value these things in my girls. They are excellent qualities."

"You mean weak," I snap irritably. "I'm not weak. I plan to do it. I just don't know when."

She takes a moment to reply. "Tell me what the deal is between you and the brothers?"

"My brother, Tommy, nicked a thousand pounds from them because he's a fool, and they found out. If I don't pay it back, they put him to work safe-breaking for them."

"That doesn't sound awful. It's clear your brother needs someone to keep him in check."

I clear my throat. "It's not going to happen. My brother will not work for them."

She nods with understanding. "Then, that means it will make them angry if I recruit you to be one of my girls. They don't want you to have an opportunity to pay them off. They want to win. They are betting on you losing."

"I don't lose."

Mary grins widely. "Me either. Do you have a day off?"

"Tomorrow," I reveal with some hesitation.

She gathers her things. "Maggie will pick you up and get you set up for the audition. Should you pass, I'll welcome you into my little world. You can decide on your own if it's worth it or not."

I shake my head with confusion. "You're going to go against them on purpose?"

She rises from her seat. "Every so often, it's good to anger your allies. It teaches them you still have the power to do so. They expect me to refuse you. They'll know to ask me next time, instead of simply assuming I'll put their interests above my own."

A sense of relief overwhelms me, but I don't forget to say, "To be clear, when I've paid off the debt, I want out."

"The freedom to stay is yours, and so is the freedom to leave. But you will not want to leave."

I let out a bitter laugh. "You don't know me like you think you do."

She adjusts her navy gloves, pulling them down each wrist with a tight jerk. "Oh, I know you, Alice. I was you, in some sense—a girl born poor, a baker's daughter. I was told my entire life I'd never be anything more than that. Then I decided my fate was my own, and here I am. There is more to life than the burden of your father's and brother's choices. I'm not a baker's daughter anymore, and you don't have to be the queen of the poor."

She stands with that same mysterious smile that leaves me more unnerved than comforted. "I'll pay the bill," she says.

I watch her waltz out of the small café. She passes men and women on her way to the exit, and they marvel at her graceful walk. Her composure. The way she carries herself. I'd assume she's a woman of means if I didn't know better, born into money and status and good breeding. I'd never put her down as a pickpocket.

She's conned all of London—and that could be me.

I leave Franny's and arrive at the King town house early. Pearl is still sleeping, and Alba is busy cleaning up the remains of breakfast. King's overcoat is hanging by the door where he left it when he came home last night. I manage to rummage through it and sneak the key under my apron while Alba has me scrubbing floors.

When she leaves through the swinging kitchen doors with plates in her hands, I tiptoe over to the first-floor library and unlock the door. On one side of the room, wall-to-wall bookshelves, and on the other, framed posters of all his most popular stage shows signed *King* at the bottom. Across from the marble fireplace, a towering safe rests on a mirrored console table.

I've known the combination since my first week here yet found excuses to come in every day since then. But with Mary's words fresh in my mind, I push myself forward. She thinks my compassion for Pearl isn't a weakness, but how can it not be? If I didn't care about her well-being, I'd be long gone by now.

If I'm lucky, the contents of his safe might be enough to pay off the McDonald brothers in full, and I'll be free of this altogether. No Mary, no gang, no debt.

But what would happen to Pearl?

I take another step closer to the safe, drumming my fingers against the white cloth apron around my waist. Before I can decide what to do, I hear the light taps of feet coming up behind me.

Pearl stands at the door with both arms crossed over her chest as she gives me the once-over. She's dressed nicely this morning in a low-waisted Georgette dress with her hair done up in plaits. "Thinking about robbing us?" Her voice is playful, but I struggle to respond in kind.

"Of course not," I say quickly. Too quickly.

She grins. "Well, there's nothing fun in that safe." She adjusts her necklaces. "Just deeds to his theaters and his will."

I try not to show my disappointment.

"If there were cash in there, I'd have stolen it a long time ago and fled this oh-so-happy home. Sometimes I imagine where I'd go . . . I hear America is booming."

She takes a step inside the library and gazes around. "Did Alba send you in here to dust or something? Well, never mind that. Come with me! I'm taking you to eat."

"Oh, I've already eaten."

"I haven't," she retorts. "You wouldn't deny me the company, would you?"

I manage a smile. "Never."

When we arrive at Claridge's for my second fancy breakfast of the morning, Pearl takes a seat at a reserved table. Even wearing her borrowed burgundy morning dress, I feel out of place looking at the sparkling chandelier and the bone china I'm tempted to pocket. I can hardly see Pearl past the large flower centerpiece in the middle of our table.

Men and women goggle at us from afar, whispering to each other while lemon cakes, pastries, and dainty sandwiches are served, and I can hear piano music coming from the ballroom we passed on our way here.

First this morning with Mary and now here? This doesn't feel like my life anymore.

I stare back boldly to challenge their attention when I realize no one is looking at me. Pearl King is still very much a household name, it would seem, and one that has this entire restaurant in awe.

Pearl sits erect and tilts her head haughtily. She doesn't make eye contact with any of the other patrons, acting as if we are the only two in the room.

"Tea," she says to the waiter, who stands attentively at her side.

"Earl Grey today, Mrs. King?" His voice is light, hopeful. As if he believes that remembering her order will give him a place in her thoughts.

"Yes," she says kindly, bestowing a smile.

He stares at me with less enthusiasm. "And you, miss?"

"Tea is fine," I say. As the waiter hurries off, I mutter to Pearl, "Everyone is staring."

She pulls a folded newspaper from her bag and peels back the page. "They always stare. I'm used to it."

"I'm not," I admit. "It's unnerving."

The waiter brings our pot of tea, and I put a small dash of cream into my cup before pouring.

"Were you that great of an actress?"

Her brow quirks. "You've never heard of me? My performances?"

This is the first time we've ever talked about her once-promising career. "I don't go to the theater much."

"You don't need to go to the theater to get a newspaper."

"Theater drama isn't exactly my priority, and I read slow."

"They're not staring because of my time on the stage. I've been a mess lately—the papers like this version of me much better. Offstage drama sells more copies. I'm curious, what shows have you seen, if not mine?"

I shrug nonchalantly. "What does it matter?"

"I want to get to know you better, Alice."

I don't want to tell her the truth: I've never been to the theater. I scramble to come up with a lie while taking a slow sip of my tea. "There's one headlining now, at a theater near the West End. I went with my mother last week."

"*Pretty Peggy* is at Shaftesbury right now. It's marvelous, isn't it?"

"Marvelous," I agree, smiling through the lie.

Her eyes thin, and she stares in a way that makes me nervous, like every word out of her mouth is some kind of bait I'm taking. "I know you have secrets, Alice. You don't trust me with them."

My gaze drops. "I don't trust anybody, Pearl. Don't take offense."

I let the silence linger between us. She eats, and I drink, but her next words catch me off guard, too loud for comfort. "I think I might kill him."

I choke on my tea and force myself to set the cup down on the saucer. "What?"

"My husband."

"I can't have this conversation with you."

"Oh, don't play innocent, Alice. You've told me very little about your family, and I assume it's because you have some skeletons in your closet."

I straighten my back at the comment and feel my mouth go dry. I don't have time to lie before she says, "It's why I trust you."

"You're not thinking."

"Do you have a better idea?"

"Divorce him!"

She laughs lightly. "And then what? Find a job in the working world?"

"Women do it all the time. You can find work!"

"I'm a disgraced stage actress, Alice." There's regret in her voice. "I won't have a shilling to my name if I leave him, and he'll ensure no theater in town considers me for a role."

I lean back in my chair and groan. "He grows worse by the day, doesn't he?"

"I can get him roaring drunk and have him stumble over the balcony. Then it's an accident. Hell, I almost did it myself."

I shake my head. "It's not so simple. You're a woman in this city, and he's a man, which means they'll blame you, especially with your history. There has to be another way."

Her eyes water, and the gravity of her misery shakes my core. "What do you propose?"

I think for a long moment, then say the first thing I can think of. "Men like him have secrets. If we find them out, we can blackmail him."

"And if he's good at burying his secrets? We've been married five years, and I've yet to discover something I can use to my advantage."

"Then you leave this life behind," I say firmly.

"I've been a poor girl," she says with a wave of dismissal. "If I'm poor, I'm already dead."

"You won't have nothing," I assure her, then hesitate over my next words, sure I'm crossing a line I shouldn't. "You'll have me. I'll help you."

I realize how attached I've grown to her, and I don't know how to feel about it just yet.

"Oh, you'll get me maid work?" She chuckles at the notion. "Imagine me trying to scrub a floor or wash a dish. How positively dreadful that poor family would have it."

I don't laugh. I can't. Nothing about this is humorous to me, but she always seems to find a way to giggle about her misery.

"There's life beyond this," I insist. "Even if you can't see it."

Her eyes fix on me. "Why are you so nice to me? I imagine you've worked for plenty of privileged women like me. I'd hate working for me if I were you."

I answer honestly, offering my best smile. "Maybe I have a weakness for women like you."

"Women like me?"

"Women that don't know how to survive without a man."

She shifts in her seat and looks down. "It's not that."

"It's not?"

"I just don't know how to survive without money. So long as he has all the money, he has all the power."

"That's not true. Money isn't power. Power is power." I take another sip of tea. "We are doomed from birth. The second we come into the world, a man is frowning at us, bitter that we don't have cocks."

"You're right," she says, elbow on the table and chin in her palm. "I am doomed."

A horrible feeling slides over me at the sight of her daydreamy face. My words are settling too deep inside her head. I don't want her to think she can't have a new life, one where she's free of her husband's abuse, but I know that kind of fresh start will only come with a lot of turmoil and pain. Maybe I don't see how it's possible now, running away without losing everything, but I don't want her to lose hope.

A hopeless woman is a dead woman.

"Some women, special women, defy the odds. Take fate into their own hands and get to start over. That's going to be you. We'll figure it out together."

Women like Mary Carr.

Her lips curl up into a grin, cheeks brightening. "Together?"

"Together."

Chapter Six

In the morning I wake up to my mother looming over me. "Maggie's outside the shop."

She watches her from the window while I get dressed and pin up my hair. By the time I'm ready to walk out the door, Louisa has already left for school, and my mother is downstairs waiting to follow me outside.

"Louisa is gone already?" I ask with a frown. "She hasn't talked to me since what happened with—"

"She'll get past it."

"And if she doesn't?" I fiddle with my coat. "She's as stubborn as me, which means I shouldn't expect much for a good year or so."

She places a hand on top of mine with the most comforting smile she can manage yet it does not quite reach her eyes. "Right now, one thing at a time. Focus on today. I will handle Louisa when she gets home tonight. Tommy is doing better, so I say it's time for a much-needed family dinner."

The idea does bring me some relief.

She opens the door to walk me out, greeting Maggie with a frown. "Welcome back, Maggie. Although how welcome can a girl feel when she won't even go to see her kin? Shame on you."

A scowl darkens Maggie's face as Mum barrels on. "You be sure to tell your lady boss that this is only temporary. My husband will be out soon, and he will remedy this. He will fix all of this."

Maggie gives her a sardonic smile. "As always, a pleasure to see you, Lady Diamond."

Mum's gaze moves over to the posh motorcar parked on the street—different from the one Maggie was driving at the 43. This one is a sleek Rolls-Royce with maroon leather seats. "You really are like one of those toffs now, all flash with no street smarts. Someone around here's bound to see a car like that as an opportunity. They won't hesitate to take it from you."

"Well, then we better get going." She winks at my mother sassily, then starts the car, sending a luxurious-sounding rumble reverberating down the street.

I slip into the passenger seat, and at first the drive is quiet. Finally, somewhere between drumming her fingers against her leg and chewing at her bottom lip, she says, "You told my brothers I was back?"

"I did," I confirm.

"What did Eli say?"

"Not much. You know Eli. Patrick looked like he wanted to cry."

She swallows loud enough for me to hear. "I miss them sometimes."

"But you don't regret leaving?" I ask her again, hoping for a new answer.

"No." Her voice is sharp and firm, but her expression doesn't quite match. "You'll come to find this life is well worth what we might have to give up. Women like us don't get chances like this often."

"Women like us?"

"You know what I mean."

I can't deny the truth in her words, but our circumstances are different. "The difference is you have a choice. If I don't join Mary to pay off this debt, my family suffers. This isn't a choice. This isn't freedom."

"Maybe it seems like that now," she reasons. "But when you've got that debt paid off, and you see the profit you make under Mary's guidance, you won't want to give it up."

"I'm paying back my family's debt, and then I'm done."

"We'll see."

We drive to the West End, where the daylight somehow mutes the parade of shops we pass along the road. During the night the district shines like the beacon it is, drawing men and women from all over to its theaters and department stores, which are far grander than anything in Soho. Not a night goes by when there isn't some glamorous event. The papers talk all about the balls, garden parties, and charity events hosted by up-and-coming actresses. A spectacle of crowds, talent, and most important, the rich. But now, there's just the flat morning light shining on windowpanes, leaving me feeling more somber than I'd like. I frown a bit, wondering when I'll finally see the magic of it all.

We pull up to a dress shop, and Maggie parks the car, gesturing to the side of the building where an alley takes us to the back door of the shop. "I'm taking you in to meet our draper, Agatha. She'll fit you into something posh."

"I'm telling you right now that I can't afford anything made on Oxford Street."

"Don't fuss about prices," she insists. "Just let Agatha work her magic."

I nod, and we move inside where there are mannequins everywhere, each wearing outfits in various stages of completion. All the shelves are stacked with colorful fabric, and at the center of it all, an older woman with silver-streaked hair hunches over a black beaded dress with a needle and thread. The dress is sheer with jewels embroidered in the bodice.

"You're late," she says sharply without looking up. "If you can't be on time, you don't deserve my services."

"Oh, come on, Agatha, it's your favorite customer." Maggie grins ear to ear and holds her arms out wide.

Agatha peers up at her with a narrow, unamused expression, then looks over to me. She lifts a pair of spectacles hanging from her neck. "This the new one?" She stands to get a better view of me. "I must make something fresh to fit her length. The usual three?" She brings out a measuring tape and wraps it around my waist, then measures my shoulders and bust, memorizing all the numbers, writing nothing down. "I'll have them ready in a few days."

"You got anything we can borrow now?" Maggie points to my outfit. "Something stylish."

Agatha waves at a small rack of dresses. "Pick something, but quick. I've got a customer out front."

"Anything?" I peek at the rack she motioned to and marvel at the material, the array of deep, sultry reds and blues. I'm almost afraid to touch them. Agatha must notice because her mouth transforms from a frown into a knowing grin.

"I love the way the new girls marvel at my dresses."

I push through sleeveless and cap-sleeved scoop-neck dresses with low waistlines in chiffon, velvet, and taffeta. And then, at the back, thick fur coats that feel like heaven against my fingers.

Agatha laughs a little. "What is she for the score? Face or hands?"

"Both," answers Maggie, which is news to me. "Maybe none. Just her audition today."

Agatha reaches for a yellow chiffon dress with a deep V-neck. "This one then. It contrasts with your black hair well, and your skin will glow. When you walk into the store, they will stare and wonder what man is spoiling you rotten."

I take the dress and feel the fabric between my fingers, imagining myself in it. "Does it have to be a man spoiling me? Maybe I came into the money all on my own."

Agatha's brows rise. "She'll fit right in with you girls. Get dressed now, I have work to do, and I don't want any of my customers seeing me consorting with the likes of you. I expect the dress returned tonight. Intact."

Maggie beams as Agatha disappears to the front of the shop. "Intact."

I slip into a curtained area to try on the dress, unsure of how it will look on me. I step out and peer into a long mirror in the room's corner that is partially hidden by several haphazardly stacked mannequins. She's right. The contrast is beautiful, and I almost don't recognize myself.

I can hear my mother's voice in my head. *Girls from The Mint don't wear dresses like this.*

Maggie must sense my self-doubt because she's quick to join me by the mirror and place her hand on my shoulder. "Confidence is key. If you doubt yourself, they'll doubt you. You were smooth at the club, fearless. That's who you need to be now. Can you do it?"

I laugh under my breath. "It's too late to say no, right?"

"We're in this now." Maggie's wicked smile should leave me unnerved, but it doesn't. I feel a tingle all over, the anticipation nearly leaving me breathless. I want to get started. Right this minute. Maybe I don't know what I'm getting into, but I do know what I'm good at. If Mary wants a gifted collector, she's found one in me.

Mary slips into the room and startles us both. "Sorry I'm late. You look lovely." She takes a step closer to get a better view of me, studying the angles of my face. "Let's get you made up? Maggie, meet us the salon?"

Maggie nods, exiting through the same door we entered. And though I'm a grown woman capable of handling myself in every challenging scenario presented to me thus far, being alone with Mary leaves my throat dry. "What's wrong with my hair?" I ask.

She gives me a sideways look. "If you are to dress the part, you are to look the part."

We jump into Mary's breathtaking Vauxhall and stop by a salon advertising "fresh new bobs," where a woman cuts off my long locks with little delicacy. Every snip of the scissors is a strange reminder of the life I'm leaving behind for the new one in front of me. I struggle to keep tears from my eyes as the hair piles beneath my feet. It's foolish, truly. It's only hair, and most of the time, I find it a nuisance. Brushing it, pulling it up, having my mother tighten it into a plait identical to hers. Hair doesn't define me, so why can't I hold myself together?

The woman then styles my chin-length hair with expert precision and powders my face and lips with more color than I've ever had on my skin. The result is someone new.

I stare at her a moment too long in the mirror. My ashen skin is lit with color, and though my eyes are still a dull brown, there's a sense of mystery about them now. I still have my dad's narrow nose, but with the blush on my cheeks and the bob framing my face, I look nothing like my family.

Nothing like the leader of The Mint when her dad is gone.

The sadness from the loss of my hair seems to disappear in a snap as I stare at a confident woman who doesn't have a care in the world apart from what clothes she will wear tomorrow. This woman isn't carrying burdens placed on her by her father or brother. This woman is an unfamiliar person.

I don't know her, but I want to.

Mary extends her hand with a smile, urging me out of the chair, which is still covered in my chopped hair. "Let's finish up the look."

We walk outside, and to complete the image, Mary grabs a fur from the back of the car, a plushy cream one, and pulls it around my shoulders. The feel of fur against my skin sends chills down my spine. A kind of excitement I thought only a man could give me.

At first, I feel out of place, ashamed even. This isn't the woman my dad raised, so taken with her looks and comfortable in her skin. He'd rage at the idea of wearing a fur coat instead of fencing it and using the money for something practical: family or The Mint.

But then, as each minute goes by, I embrace the power of a beautiful dress and a thick fur, painted lips and freshly cut hair. My breathing grows ragged, and I sigh with contentment.

"You look the part. Now a name," says Mary. "Should someone ask, you must be ready."

I continue to stare at my reflection in the car window and consider her words. "Dad used to call me Annie when he was angry with me."

"Why Annie?" Mary asks.

"He had a sister named Annie."

"I remember him talking about her," adds Maggie, emerging from her motorcar, parked tightly behind Mary. She eyes me up and down in one quick swoop with nothing but glistening admiration. "She was always causing trouble, throwing rocks at store windows to protest for the vote. She ran away with a communist, didn't she?"

I nod slowly. "They both got killed during a union strike against the railway. Dad was devastated."

"Oh, I love a rebel! Ready for your audition, Annie?"

I take another moment, just one, to embrace Annie. This dynamic woman will draw in fools with her beauty and then rob them blind. Never before have I felt that I could use my beauty as a weapon.

Alice is not beautiful. She's made of steel, with no loyalties outside of her family and The Mint. She cannot afford to wear furs and stockings without rips.

But Annie can.

Finally, I let out a breathless, "Ready."

Mary tucks her arm into the crook of mine and walks with me. Maggie follows behind, casually smoking a cigarette.

"Every woman in the gang has a purpose," Mary begins with a nod. "When we plan a score, there's always a threesome. A face, a pair of eyes, and skilled hands. Without each, we doom a score to fail." She points to a gathering of beautiful girls near a street performer, each uniquely dazzling. "Girls like that, they're the face. The distraction. They come in, and the shopkeeper stays busy taking care of them while invisible girls steal from the stores. These women don't need beauty. Simple is always overlooked."

I nod, taking in her words, imagining the scene in my head. A shopkeeper speaking to a lovely woman who looks like she has money to blow while a plain woman wearing modest clothing steals behind him. "Women like Maggie are the eyes?"

"Yes," she says enthusiastically. "Maggie watches the shopkeeper, she watches the face work her magic, and she watches the hands. Should she suspect a score is going bad or see any coppers nearby, she's trained to get the girls out safely. It helps that she knows how to throw a punch.

"Rough around the edges works for these women," she continues to explain. "But I think you're different. A proper catch."

"Me?"

She halts and stares at me dead-on. "Maybe you're a rare breed, a woman who can play each of these parts. I've had girls like that, little chameleons. They're special." I can't tell if she means it or if she's just trying to get me to be as enthusiastic as she is. Whatever her intention, it's working. My heart is racing, beating against my chest in a frenzy.

Like my father, I am too easily flattered.

"Just tell me what to do." I bounce on the balls of my feet, a fluttery feeling in my stomach. "Let's get on with it."

"We'll start here," she says, motioning at the street full of men, women, and children. They're distracted and trusting, so they won't see it coming. They're easy targets, but I want more. Better.

"You dressed me like this to have me pickpocket off people walking down the sidewalk?" I don't hide the insult in my voice.

"We all have to start somewhere."

Behind Mary stands Selfridges in all its glory. The large Greek-inspired columns seem to go on for days, and I remember how in awe the city was when the structure was first built. It's rumored nearly ninety thousand people turned out to see it on the opening day.

"What about Selfridges?" I ask, partially because I know what a gold mine it is, but also because I've never been inside. The papers have some flattering descriptions of the glamorous department store, but I've always wanted to have a look myself.

Maggie sniggers from behind us, tossing her smoke to the ground. "I told you she's got some balls on her."

Mary looks at the department store, then shakes her head. "Selfridges? No, out of the question."

"Why?"

"It's not a good idea for anyone except experienced hoisters."

"How else do you expect me to gain experience?"

Her mouth turns up. "Harry Selfridge was the first to put his merchandise out on the showroom floor instead of taking shoppers into private rooms. His displays are always big and brash. He wants shoppers to touch and feel things before buying them. This makes it all the easier for us to snatch and run. However, he caught on and hired a store detective, who acts as a direct line to the coppers, should he catch anyone stealing. The girls that go into Selfridges not only have to have the skills, but they also need to evade a trained detective on the lookout."

"Store detective?" I've never heard of such a thing.

"Mr. Selfridge takes his business very seriously. He's not afraid of us, and he shows it."

I feel the hair on the nape of my neck lift. If I get caught on my first day, that's it. I'll end up just like my dad, and my brother will go to work for the McDonalds. But what happens if I succeed? What happens if I prove myself worthy of the highest of scores on my first day?

"Let me have a gander at it," I say. "I'll take the risk."

Maggie scoffs. "She said it was out of the question. Just start slow, Alice."

"I can't afford to start slow," I bark, the words coming out more feral than I meant them to. "If I'm in this, I want to go all the way." I look Mary in the eyes. "I'm asking you to trust me. And if I succeed, we skip this stage."

"This stage?"

"The stage where I am an amateur who gets the lowest jobs. I want big scores. I want to run with the best girls. I want to pay off my debt to the McDonalds as quickly as possible."

Her eyes grow wide with excitement. Her entire face lights up and flushes pink. "You are brave."

"I never had a choice to be anything else," I say. "Let me do this."

Maggie moves in. "This is an awful idea, completely absurd."

"Not if you have me," Mary insists. "I'll be your eyes. If we do this right, there's no reason we shouldn't succeed." Her gaze snaps to me. "But if we don't, if I have to save one of you girls, it'll be Maggie."

Her words settle at the bottom of my gut, but I don't let them deter me. "Fine."

We walk together through the revolving doors letting men and women in and out in a constant flow. Inside, Selfridges greets us with brilliant displays beneath crystal chandeliers. Groups of customers stroll along and jump at the newest deals displayed on countertops stacked with scented soaps, powder puffs, and embroidered handkerchiefs. I don't know if the flowery smell filling my nostrils is from the fresh roses scattered about the sales floor in sleek vases or the perfumes being sprayed in the air as customers pass by.

I wander slowly to admire all the details, but a woman in the store's signature green uniform stops me as I pass the information booth. "Welcome to Selfridges. Can I help you with anything today?"

"It's my first time." The words slip out of my mouth, and I realize I can't move. I'm standing stock-still in a trance. The attendant walks around the bronze-trimmed, mahogany counter to greet me properly.

"First time? A marvel, isn't it?" Her face glows with pride. "Here for a new dress? Or a fresh pair of shoes?"

I shake my head. "I'm just browsing."

"Our lifts can take you to any department you please. Clothing, housewares, and a shoe department. The Palm Court restaurant if you find yourself parched. But that's not all." She looks me over. "A hair-dressing salon should you want to touch up your beautiful bob!"

"We'll find our way," interrupts Mary. "Thank you."

"We don't talk to anyone when we come into stores," says Maggie. "We don't want to leave any lasting impressions on the shop attendants."

I nod, still transfixed. In front of me are the makeup and perfume departments, a bewitching setup meant to lure women in with enticing fragrances that have me dwelling on Pearl's lavender bath. The girls behind the counter wave me over, bouncing on the balls of their feet when I make eye contact, lifting cut-glass perfume bottles, and misting their scents into the air. For a fleeting moment, I forget that I am the predator here and gladly let them pull me into their sirens' trap. They want to douse me with a spray or two along my neck, and I'm not only willing but eager. I'm enchanted.

Maggie stops me with a quick arm pull, jerking me back to reality. "Remember why we're here."

Mary adjusts her fur overcoat, beaming with confidence as we walk, a stroll that gives off the impression that we belong here, and nobody would dare say otherwise.

We stop near a jewelry display where a young woman waits behind a counter of diamond necklaces, all hanging from long-necked mannequins. Even on such a dull prop, the gems catch my gaze and keep it.

Mary lowers her voice. "You wanted a chance to prove yourself."

She tilts her head toward an emerald necklace on display. It's shaped into a massive oval instead of cut down into small pieces to run along a woman's neck. A necklace that wasn't designed to go with every dress but to stand out. The first thing they see when you enter the party and the last thing they think about when they sleep at night.

It's a showpiece.

A man and woman are already looking down at it, asking the salesgirl questions. "You want me to steal that?" The words fall out of my mouth almost too loudly.

"Not you, us," says Maggie, and the words bring a great sense of relief.

Mary nods and retreats to the door. "I'll be your eyes, and Maggie is your hands. You play the distraction." Before going too far, she eyes something to the far left of the jewelry display—a short man with a waxed mustache. "That's our detective. If you see his eyes linger on you for more than a minute, we're caught. Don't take a chance. Don't risk it. Just leave."

I peek at him, taking in his tailored suit, the pocket watch in his hand, and the whistle hanging from his neck. He is alert, scanning the crowds intently. It's almost amusing how openly he plays his role.

We need to blend in to steal, so he needs to blend in to catch us.

Or so I tell myself.

With Mary gone to the store's periphery to keep guard, I gaze long and hard at the emerald. All around me families are shopping with their children in tow. Their smiles and laughter remind me of Louisa and the risk I'm taking. If I get caught, I may never see her again.

My hesitation must show because Maggie pulls me into the ladies' powder room with enough force to knock me off my feet.

"What's going on? You're frozen out there, drawing attention to yourself."

"I just got nervous, that's all." I glance into the mirror above the round porcelain sink to see her again—this new me.

"The Alice I know doesn't hesitate," she reasons. "You know what you are capable of and who you are. You saw the opportunity at the 43, and you took it. It's no different now. You wanted this. Show Mary that you're everything I believe you are."

"I was just thinking about Louisa," I explain with a breathy sigh. "I don't get caught at the club because I am careful, and the crowd is drunk. Too legless to notice a stray hand in the dark. When I pretend to be the help to rob the rich, I use a different name. Once I've stolen from them, there's no chance of me getting caught because they never know who to look for."

"How is this any different?"

I wave at the luxurious bathroom to match the grand store. "Here, in broad daylight with a store detective watching, I'm about to take my biggest risk. And if I get caught, and I'm not there to protect my family anymore, what will happen to them with Dad gone? Who will keep The Mint safe?"

I feel dizzy, my legs and knees weak. I've never known fear during the hunt, not like this. I'm good at this. I know I am. I am my father's daughter. Why can't I find myself? Why can't I bury the fear?

"Keep thinking about them," Maggie insists, her voice low and forceful. "About Louisa, and Tommy, and The Mint." Maggie takes hold of my shoulders. "Think about everything that necklace could do for them. Not just to pay off Tommy's debt, but the life you could have with it. The life you could give your family that your father never could."

She breathes, and disappointment crosses her face. She's staked so much on me, and now I'm failing both of us. "Nobody will give us a break. We don't get that unless we're lying on our backs. We have to take what we want. We have to do things that frighten other women. I know you understand me, Alice. I know you are just as frightened as I am."

"I understand," I utter. "I understand more than anyone. You know that."

"I know—that's why this is your moment, and I don't want to see it slip past you. I don't want you to walk away from this because I know what you can do with this opportunity. All you have to do is take it."

I look into her eyes for a long moment before nodding.

Annie—this new me—has to take the risk.

We leave the toilets together and venture back to the display. I move in, opening my mouth to speak to the salesgirl, but the emerald catches my eye again. The way it's cut, the way it shines. Almost fictionally so. My father has stolen plenty of jewels, and none of them have ever had such a flawless luster, particularly emeralds, which are nearly always a little cloudy. Even the highest quality jewels and diamonds have flaws. I think about it, putting something so pricey on display for the world to see and touch. It can't be real. I avert my eyes past the salesgirl, the departments, and then to the lift. I wonder if perhaps the genuine emerald is somewhere else, only given to the buyer after the transaction is complete. Maybe the safest way for Mr. Selfridge to protect his merchandise is to hide it.

I turn to Maggie, then glance past her to Mary, who is hovering near the front entrance and growing impatient.

"It's a fake," I whisper to Maggie as we meet near a display of silk scarves. "The real one is somewhere else. If that's not real, it's fair to assume none of the displays are real."

She pauses carefully, and something about her expression tells me this isn't news to her. "It being real isn't the point of the audition."

I feel my mouth drop open. "You'd have me risk everything on a fake emerald?"

She presses her lips together firmly, but before she can say a word, I glance out into the crowd. "No," I cut her off before she can explain. "If I'm taking this chance, we're leaving here with something real."

I focus on the crowd. Before, I only noticed the families, but now I concentrate on the single men with expensive watches and the individual women sporting diamonds along their necks and ears. The fur coats, the exquisite silk, the array of bags filled with already purchased goods as they browse for more. "We rob the crowd. We get real goods. If that isn't enough for her, then maybe this opportunity isn't what I thought it was."

Maggie chews her bottom lip. "The crowd is even more of a risk. Someone could call out if they catch you."

I adjust my cream fur overcoat, reaching into my dress to explore the deep pockets so cleverly sewn into the seam. "Are you in or not?"

The moment of uncertainty in her eyes vanishes as she pulls her shoulders back. "Pick your targets carefully. Do nothing foolish."

"I won't steal from families," I tell her.

Maggie chuckles. "A thief with morals?"

I breathe in, then study the crowd to find my targets. A quirk in the way a man smiles that tells me he's not always gentle. A childish party girl with yesterday's makeup still on her face. An elderly woman who holds a small dog and snaps at shop attendants as they stumble around trying to meet her demands.

I focus on finding it, the darkness in the surrounding people, and my body takes over when I do. My hand stealthily slips into bags and pockets as I slither through the crowds while only occasionally catching the attention of an admiring man.

I stop at a glass display case where a shop assistant offers me a ruby red lipstick sample. She applies it to my lips, marvels at the color, and while she searches for other samples for me to try, I snag the gilded tube and disappear back into the madness.

A silk scarf, a beautiful set of pearls, all tucked into my dress pockets, which I load endlessly without being noticed. There's no bulk, not with the coat around my shoulders.

The detective in the corner is within eyesight, and I recall Mary's words. If he's staring at me, I'm already caught.

I search the crowd for Maggie. She's near the door with Mary, urging me out. She looks pointedly at me and then the store detective. Mary's eyes say it all: it's time to go.

But I don't heed their warning just yet.

There's a giant pink diamond on the finger of the elderly woman. I noticed it just moments before when I'd lifted a pair of gorgeous velvet gloves from her bag. She's not focused on her shopping bags; she's holding on to her little fox terrier as it snacks on treats she keeps feeding it from her coat pocket. The chap behind her carrying all her items is struggling to keep himself steady as she adds more purchases to the pile.

He's my opening.

Him and that little dog.

I try to focus on Maggie's urgent glares and Mary's anxious fidgeting, but the diamond lures me closer. *I can get it.*

Appearing next to me as if by magic, Maggie bumps into the bag man, who nearly drops a hatbox trying to let her pass. For a moment, her presence stuns me, and I'm frozen in place. How did she know what I was planning?

I quickly blink back to the moment and use the bag man's vulnerability to my advantage and rush over to Maggie. The three of us bump into one another, creating a chaotic, fumbling mess.

The man tumbles into the older woman, and her little dog flies out of her hands, landing feetfirst onto the floor. I scramble over and snatch him up while she struggles to find her balance and avoid flying shopping sacks.

"Pardon me," says Maggie to the bag man. "I'm far too clumsy for my own good."

The terrier wiggles in my grip, eager to get back to her owner and her coat full of treats.

A nearby clerk offers the elderly woman his arm to help steady her, and her eyes shoot daggers at me. I hand the dog over, and as it seems to dawn on her that my intentions were helpful, her expression relaxes. "Oh, thank you. Thank you for catching my sweet girl!"

Our hands cup, mine in hers, as I pass the tiny terrier over. I slide the ring off her finger with ease, and she nuzzles her precious dog before scrutinizing the surrounding confusion, intent on finding someone to blame. I tuck the diamond into my coat, and while the detective scrambles to clean up my mess, I flee the scene.

Outside, Mary is livid, storming down the steps onto Oxford Street in a fury.

I rush to catch up, still far too proud of myself to let her anger wound me.

"What in God's name were you thinking?"

Maggie materializes in front of me. "It was a good score, Mary. Don't you want to see what we got?"

"Both of you disregarded my orders."

I shake my head, sidestepping Maggie to address her. "You sent me on a fool's errand. You knew that emerald wasn't real. I wasn't going to risk everything for a glass bauble."

"You failed to follow a simple order. If I cannot trust you to obey me, you cannot join me. That scene at the end? That was reckless. Why go back to the woman you'd already stolen from?"

I retrieve the ring from my coat. "Because of this."

She is physically moved at the sight of the diamond, staggering back a step, but she doesn't gasp or make a sound. Her mouth moves soundlessly like a fish as she gawks. She reaches for the diamond to study it. Beautiful, pink, cut to perfection.

Real.

"They say diamonds are the way to a woman's heart," I tease with a grin.

"You got that off her finger?" Mary cannot fathom it. "Brilliant! How did you manage it?"

A long tense silence passes between us as we realize something momentous has just occurred, as we suddenly all understand what we can do together and how far it might take us. Mary pulls the ring onto her finger, and her eyes roll with pleasure. "You're a wild one, Miss Annie. Perhaps an excellent investment, after all."

Maggie's lips pull up into a grin. "Diamond Annie. That's what we'll call you. You'll be a legend with the girls when they find out about this."

I try not to show the excitement filling my gut, rendering me flushed. "What do you say, Mary Carr? Did I pass the audition?"

"We will go far together, Diamond Annie." Her way of saying yes, I hope. "But let me be clear, if you disobey me again and drag Maggie along with you, I will toss you out without a second thought. I don't give second chances, but I'm giving you one. Don't make me regret it."

I don't like to be threatened. Nobody threatens me in The Mint—but Mary has all the power right now, so for the moment, I resist the urge to deliver a sharp retort. I swallow the insult and say, "I understand."

"Keep the fur," says Mary with a grin. "A welcoming present."

I breathe deeply, clutching the cream fur tightly. "I'm in?"

"Welcome to the Forty Elephants."

Chapter Seven

We drive to South London, to Elephant and Castle, where the bustling of traffic consumes the air and the rasp of trams leaves my ears ringing. The streets are so congested that Mary's smooth glide through them leaves my eyes wide. How she's somehow able to maneuver through it so effortlessly is beyond me. When she clears the traffic, the noisy trams are replaced with equally loud and crowded streets. We pass a dozen street stalls and the glitzy department store William Tarn & Co., where I closely watch men and women exiting with large shopping packages.

Mary finally stops at an enormous warehouse and parks out front.

We take a small path along the side of the building, winding down to the back entrance. A man waits by the door, standing watch. I think I hear Maggie call him Lou as we approach. He's casual and friendly with Maggie, but as soon as he notices Mary, his expression sobers, and he reaches for the door.

We enter a treasure trove of stolen goods. Jewelry of all kinds is spread over a long trestle table, awaiting inspection by a fencer. There are racks of dresses and furs as far as the eye can see. Row upon row of shelved goods, an organized mess of everything imaginable, all being carefully sorted and recorded by several women with tall ledgers. In the back, I even notice a few motorcars being cleaned by a woman with a rag.

They look our way and then chatter among themselves as Mary points us to her office in the back. The carpet is thick and soft, silencing my steps.

Inside is a large well-appointed room decorated with paintings and extravagant art. A sizable rosewood, leather, and ivory sofa sits in the corner with various coats littered on top of it. Two ebony side tables stand on either side with Tiffany lamps and various boxes of rings and trinkets. As if Mary spends her nights inspecting the stolen goods herself, or perhaps, relishing in her daily victories.

On her red lacquered desk are more ledgers filled with names and numbers. I peer at the slender columns of notes, all scribbled in her cramped handwriting.

She has us unload our pockets onto the desk before instructing Maggie and me to wait outside while she counts and inspects the takings herself.

As we wait, the twins from the 43 show up with four handbags dangling from their arms. One has two evening bags made of expensive leather and beaded silk. The other twin carries a metal mesh bag plated with gold and a Dresden pearlized mesh bag with a smooth enamel finish. They place them down for inspection then walk our way in unison, hips swaying step-by-step to the same beat.

The one who carried in the mesh bags speaks first. I notice her hair is a shade darker than her sister's. "First day? How was it? It can't be too good if you're waiting outside Mary's office with a frown. I'm Norma. This is my sister, Grace."

Maggie scoffs. "Been at it all day and only came back with four handbags, eh?"

"Mary told us to take it easy, you know, being we're her top contributors this week."

"My name's Alice." I manage a convincing smile. "And don't get too comfortable at the top. We had a marvelous day today."

Norma's bottom lip twitches. "Listen, new girl, keep talking to me like that, and you won't be in this gang long."

I laugh a little. "Here I thought this was supposed to be a sisterhood?"

Grace takes a step closer and squares her shoulders. "We always get rid of the lippy girls. You don't want to make enemies of us."

"You don't know who I am," I tell her. "So for that, I'll forgive your mouth. But I can assure you that I am the one you don't want to make an enemy of."

"Back off, Grace," growls Maggie. "You know what happened last time you got in my face. This time I'll slap you hard enough that not even your makeup can cover the bruise." She lifts her fists, and the action sends Grace back a step.

"Leave them alone, girls," calls a woman from the back. She's almost too gorgeous to be real, with wide cornflower-blue eyes and curly, blond hair. "You see the loot they brought in today? It was impressive. Mary had a desk full of things to log."

She looks like she belongs wrapped in a box, a pretty porcelain doll that a little girl squeals over opening on Christmas morning. She's a face. She has to be a face. Send her into a shop, and she'll distract anyone with eyes.

Grace flashes her a glare. "Stay out of this, Charlotte! You're halfway out of the gang anyway, so you don't have a say anymore. Alice will be your replacement."

Charlotte ignores her and walks over. "Nice to meet you, Alice. I'm Charlotte. Maggie always talked about her childhood friend that taught her how to collect. She's not fond of many people, so you must be special."

"I wouldn't say special," mutters Maggie, rolling her eyes.

I open my mouth to ask about Grace's comment, *"halfway out of the gang,"* but Mary joins us before I can. She strolls out of the office with a bounce in her step.

"News, ladies. We have two new top contributors this week." The twins seethe in front of us. "Mags the Hellion and our newest recruit, Ali—" She pauses and glances my way, stopping with a grin. "Diamond Annie."

"Diamond?" Charlotte sounds intrigued.

Mary pulls out the pink diamond, and the girls gasp.

"Diamond," she answers, unable to hide her glee. Everyone in the warehouse claps while the twins glare daggers at us, not bothering to conceal their fuming.

"Mags the Hellion?" I ask with a grin.

She returns my grin. "Charlotte is Sweet Lotte. The twins, well, they're the twins."

They both give the same scowl.

Maggie sneers back. "Our nicknames don't define us, but they gave us a fresh start in this world. A way to leave our real names behind and embrace who we've become."

Mary's smile widens. "They're a talented team, Mags and Annie, but they'll need a third."

"I can do it." Charlotte lifts her hand. "At least until my beau and I tie the knot." So that's the explanation. Once she's married, she's out of the Forty Elephants.

"Wonderful. Congratulations, girls. I'll have the goods fenced within the next few days, but we celebrate now. I've arranged for us to have a good night at the 43. Go party, have some drinks on me. In the morning, we'll discuss moving you to Elephant and Castle. Has your family always lived in The Mint?"

I nod. "As long as I can remember."

"Well, let's change that. You're moving up in the world. You should live like it."

I laugh at the idea. "I can't leave The Mint, and I wouldn't want to give anyone the wrong idea. This is temporary."

"You still think you will pay the debt and leave? After what you did today?"

"I stole. I steal all the time. Today was just like any other day."

"No," she counters, taking a deliberate step closer. "Today, for the first time, you were exactly who you were always meant to be. Today, you were Diamond Annie."

She's right. Today felt good, extraordinary. I saw the world in front of me for what it truly is—mine for the taking. *Ours* for the taking.

But I don't let any of that show when I say, "Today, I played a part. That's all."

We all head to the 43 Club to celebrate, with many of the girls following us from the warehouse. They surround me, talking and giggling as we enter the club, praising me endlessly. I hold on to Mary's gift, the soft cream fur, while a glowing feeling tingles on my skin, and it's not something I'll soon forget. Friends haven't come easy to me over the years, especially after Maggie left. I mentally scold myself, instructing my mind not to let this camaraderie go to my head or influence my decision-making in any way.

I'm only in this until the debt is paid. There are no friendships to be made. These girls only care about what I can do for them, and Mary's the same way.

We sit at the bar, and Maggie toasts our success. "I knew you could do it. I'm glad you auditioned."

"You said you wanted bigger scores. I can't think of a bigger one than Selfridges."

"Thank you for trusting me."

"I've always trusted you, Mags. You might be the only one I ever have."

"Are you ever going to forgive me for leaving? Or will you remind me of it daily?"

"I still haven't decided."

She glances at Mary and the girls as if she needs to make sure they're too far to overhear before saying, "I think you and I can go a long way together if we can leave the past in the past."

I try to pull words from my throat, reassurance that I can leave our history where it belongs. But the betrayal is still fresh for me, a wound that has healed but left a scab that I pick at every time it feels like we're getting close again—a reminder that she left me, and she could leave again.

But for the sake of succeeding, I bury the doubt for the time being and lift my half-empty glass in agreement. "To new beginnings."

She clinks hers against mine before downing its contents. I raise the glass to my lips to drink it but place it down on the bar top instead.

As she signals for another, I notice Rob sneaking me a glance.

Maggie sees me staring and shouts at him. "Rob! Come over here and let us tell you about our day! That's your job, isn't it? Make our drinks and listen to us yammer?"

He lets out a snort and moves over. "Always the charmer, Maggie," he says before his eyes meet mine. "Still planning on throwing a glass over my head?"

I shrug. "Who can say? The night's young."

"Honest to God, I didn't know about my brothers' business with you or your family. I didn't even know your last name until yesterday. Your papers say 'Alice Black.'"

"Well, I'm not going to use my real name on my papers, am I?" My voice drops to a careful whisper. "I'd appreciate it if you wouldn't tell Kate."

"Your secret is safe with me."

"Is it?"

"If I had known, I would have told you."

I shake my head. "It doesn't matter anyway. I've had enough of your family this week to last a lifetime, so let's end the conversation for good."

One girl calls Maggie over, and when she's gone, he leans close to me and whispers, "You're punishing me for my brothers' choices?"

"They're seeking retribution for my brother's actions."

"You seem to enjoy your punishment though," he adds, a hint of frustration in his tone. "Not entirely fair. I'm not at all enjoying mine."

I give him a dirty look. "That's none of your business."

He nods. "You're right. It's not. That's the way you'd have it, anyway. I'm an open book, Alice. If you have something you want to ask me, I'll tell you the truth. I've only ever been truthful with you."

I want to hate him. I hate his brothers. I barely know them, but what I do know is enough. I should feel the same toward him, but try as I might, I can't muster up any anger, any reason to doubt that he's honest. "Who are you, then? Rob the bartender, Rob the Demolitions Man, or Rob the defector?"

"I'm all of them," he replies with some disappointment. "I love doing this, making drinks. It's not anything special, but it's easy. The man I used to be when I worked with my brothers was someone shameful, dark. I loathe him, but he's still a part of me. I don't know if I can ever leave him behind entirely. But I'm done fighting wars that aren't mine."

"You're a pacifist now, then?"

He pours a drink and toasts himself. "To peace."

His words settle. "You're telling me the truth?"

"I'm telling you the truth."

"Why? You don't owe me anything. We're strangers."

A relaxed smile crosses his face. "I'd like to change that."

My mouth goes dry, and a flush of warmth fills my body. I can't remember the last time I felt this way about a man. Maybe Eli, though we were so young that it feels like a lifetime ago. I don't want to be strangers either, but now I feel like we don't have a choice. "Maybe I felt the same before I found out who you are. I don't trust your family. I don't know how to trust you."

"Let's start over," he asks. "Let's try again."

The girls circle me once more, and Rob clears his throat as he moves down the bar to help some customers.

"Annie," says one of them, approaching me warmly. Her hair is a mess of curls cut into a tight bob with a splash of freckles alongside her nose and eyes. She reaches out for a handshake. "I'm Rita. The haul you and Maggie pulled in was damn impressive. I wanted to shake the hand that slipped off that gorgeous rock."

"Thank you. Nice to meet you, Rita."

I mean that, too. Compared to the twins, she's heaven.

We chatter on pleasantly until Mary makes her way over, and the girls part like the sea. "Kate Meyrick would like a word with you."

Kate moves from behind Mary to greet me. "My, my, how far my new cocktail waitress has come."

I shake my head. "I guess you could say that."

Kate perches on the empty stool next to me while everyone continues partying loudly around us. "Well, I can share a certainty with you. It's one I give all you ladies. I will protect my business fiercely. Should you think about stealing from my customers, there will be consequences."

I'm relieved that she's unaware of the collecting I've already done in this place. I remain calm. "You're not going to fire me, then?"

"No," she says. "Mary says that your time in the gang is limited."

"It is."

"Then there's no problem."

I nod. "How long have you and Mary been friends?"

She laughs. "I'm not friends with Mary Carr. I'm not even friends with Commissioner Horwood, who comes in here regularly. We all have our parts to play. I have to smile and provide services to people I think are absurd or even repulsive, for my club's sake. My club and my daughters are all that matter to me. You can stay on here as long as you keep your hands off my customers and your business away from mine."

"Understood," I say tersely. Her tone is stern with judgment. I should let it roll off my back, but I don't. "I imagine you did some awful, repulsive things to get this club to where it is. How else would you have gotten to the top? A woman owning the hottest club in a city run by men?"

She holds my gaze. "Your point?"

"My point is, say what you will about women like me and women like you. But we're not so different. You didn't get to be the Queen of Nightclubs without a little rule-breaking."

She says nothing, just smirks my way for a few long minutes. "Do we understand each other, Diamond Annie?"

I lift my drink to hers. "We understand each other."

"Very good." Her smile returns as if it never disappeared. She returns to the madness, and Maggie takes her place.

"She give you the old 'don't steal from my club' threat?"

I nod and take another swig of my drink. "She did."

"Take it as a compliment. She only does it to the ones Mary favors." Maggie lifts her glass again, this time filled with whiskey. "Now, let's celebrate."

CHAPTER EIGHT

I can already feel the hangover thumping at my temple when Maggie and I catch a cab back to The Mint. I lost track of how many drinks we had, and now, with the threat of morning coming in a few short hours, all I want to do is cuddle with Louisa and sleep.

When we arrive home, my mother helps me walk a teetering Maggie inside. We place her on the sofa, and I throw a blanket over her.

Mum scoffs. "Some things never change, do they? She was always sleeping over here when you two were girls."

I start to reply when I see an unfamiliar face sitting with Louisa at the center table. "A session this late?"

My mother's expression tenses. She moves away from the sofa and over by the guest, placing a gentle hand on her shoulder. Her face is puffy and the color of cream, littered with freckles, and her eyes hold me with an intense stare. Everything about her feels somber. "This is Christina Noon. She's Tommy's girl."

Ah, that explains her face. I chuckle a little, searching the shop for Tommy before saying, "Do yourself a favor, Christina, find a new man." I take off my fur coat and hang it on a hook by the door.

Christina manages a smile that tells me she won't heed my warning. "Tommy told me about you, Alice. It's nice to meet you finally." Her voice shakes a bit, and I notice her cheeks are flushed. Tommy made her cry, poor girl. "He hurt you?"

Her face scrunches up with displeasure.

"Where is he?"

My mother throws her head to the door. "Been at the pub all day and night."

"Shocking," I spit.

"Tommy told me we'd run away together. I was waiting at Victoria Station for him, but he never showed. I thought he might be dead." Another tremor ripples through her voice. "We love each other."

I step toward her, trying not to let my exhaustion turn my voice too bitter. "Get out while you can. Loving Tommy is a curse. We can all speak on that."

"Alice," interrupts my mother. "Christina is, well—"

"I'm having his child."

My heart skips a beat, and I let out a shallow breath. It's hard to explain the feeling residing in my gut—a strange mixture of dread and happiness. A baby could change Tommy for the better or for the worse. "Does he know?"

"I planned to tell him at the station."

I pinch the bridge of my nose and reach for my coat again, slipping my arms inside as I walk out the door. My mother follows, giving me a delayed head-to-toe gaze, then delicately taps the fur to feel it between her fingers. "What is all this? You look, well—you look beautiful."

"This is the job," I say, briefly touching my dress. "This is paying the debt."

"I take it you passed her audition. Shall we fence the dress?"

"Did you think I wouldn't pass?" I shake my head slowly. "No, we're to be careful with this dress. Upsetting the woman who made it is the last thing I want to do."

She takes my hand. "Go easy on Tommy."

I pull my hand away. "You didn't seem to mind me being hard on Louisa when it was deserved, but you ask me to be delicate with Tommy?"

"I'm asking you to be kind, Alice. That is all. He made a mistake. We all make mistakes."

"None of us quite as often as Tommy though."

I pull away from her and head down to the pub. The customers glance up from their tables to nod respectfully before Ralph points grimly to the end of the bar, where my brother is slumped over with his head in his hands.

"Ralph, can I have the room for a few minutes?"

He nods and bangs his fist twice against the bar top, the signal for closing shop. "Clear out."

Men take last drinks, collect their coats, then stand to leave. When the room clears, Ralph follows the others, shutting the pub doors behind him. I take a seat next to Tommy and down the last of his drink. "You can't drink yourself to death."

He squints at me with puffy, red eyes. "Give me a few more days. I'm just getting started."

"I'll tell Ralph to cut you off."

"If I go work for the brothers, I'm as good as dead already."

"You're not dead yet. I'm still working on it."

He stifles a hopeless cry. "I made a mistake. I didn't think it through. I've killed us. I've killed all the people here in The Mint. Everything Dad has built. What will happen to us, to them?"

"It's not over yet," I say, more confident than ever after my successful day with Mary. "But there's a girl at the shop named Christina."

He lifts his head again, more alert. "She's here?"

"Says she's your girl."

His smile flickers away. "Tell her to leave. Tell her I'm no good for her."

"I've already given her fair warning."

He manages a chuckle, then rubs his forehead. "Then tell her I don't love her. That always works."

"That would be a lie, wouldn't it?"

"Does it matter? Sometimes we lie to save the people we love."

"She's having your child."

He doesn't look at me, and a long silence follows. He presses his lips tightly together and reaches for the glass, having forgotten I emptied it. "She said that?"

I take his hand firmly, and he turns to face me.

"You'll go to her, and you'll make an honest woman of her. Father had his flaws, he still has them, but he'd make you do the same thing."

He doesn't respond, so I soften my grip on his hand. "You're scared, and you should be. It will not be easy."

"She and that babe are better off without me. You know that, Alice. We both know it."

I shrug in disagreement. "I don't know that, and you don't know it either."

His bottom lip trembles, and his finger circles the rim of his glass. I pull him toward me and press my forehead to his, the only way our father ever knew how to express love. "You can't change what you did, but you can change this. Make this right. Take her somewhere nice. Tell her how you feel." I pull out a few shillings and hand them to him.

He bites his lip before nodding, and he doesn't pull away when he says, "I'll make it right. I promise."

We exit the pub and go our separate ways: him toward the house and me over to where Ralph is waiting, guarding the outside. His gaze flicks up and down. "You clean up good, girl," he says, handing me the lit cigarette between his fingers.

I smile and take a quick drag. "Any news for me?"

"Hannagan got pulled doing a robbery in Lambeth; the family isn't doing so well."

"Two girls, right?"

"Yeah," he says ruefully. "Trying to keep them from the cathouse."

I nod, discreetly running my fingertips over the silky fur of my coat before shrugging it off my shoulders. "You got someone you can sell this to tonight?"

He takes the coat with a certain unease. "I can ask around if that's what you want."

"Give them what you make off it. I'll get more next month."

He takes off his frayed wool coat to give to me.

I lift my hand. "Keep it. I got another one at home."

Not as beautiful or soft, but it keeps me warm.

"Anything else?" I ask.

"Jacob Sloan is raging over what you did to him."

"I'm sure he is."

"You need me to take care of him?"

"No. We can't punish a man for being pissed off. Not fair, is it?"

He grins a little. "What happened with the McDonald brothers? The streets are talking."

"What do the streets say?"

"They say that Tommy needs to go."

"Tommy does need to go," I confirm. "With everything he's done to bring trouble to the neighborhood, I don't blame them for demanding it. But let me be the one to walk him out. I've got some business to finish, and then I'll see it done."

I awaken before morning to a gun in my face and Louisa screaming next to me. My instincts pull me up from the threadbare sheets, and I force myself to remember how to stand.

My mother darts out of her room, dashing past the gun to grab Louisa and pull her away from the weapon.

I blink until I can see Jacob in the dim light. He shakes the gun and shouts, "Get up. Get out of bed."

I briefly wonder how he got past the front doors and Maggie slumbering on the sofa. Then I see our open bedroom window, and my memory flashes to Louisa sneaking in and out of it. He did the same.

I stare at him dead-on. If he were drunk, I'd see it in his eyes and be able to forgive him. But he's not drunk at all, just angry. He knew exactly what he was doing when he broke into our house and started making threats, which means I cannot forgive him for it.

Father says a man must take responsibility for his actions even if he's wrong, mad, or vengeful. He must own his mistakes.

"Jacob, think about what you're doing."

"Shut your mouth!" He takes a quick, aggressive step forward. "You have any idea what it's like walking around here with the reputation you gave me? Beaten by a woman? You have to pay for what you did."

I note the pistol shaking in his hands. "My father will find out about this."

"They say it could be months before he's freed. I plan to be long gone by then." He looks at Louisa. "I love her. We had plans, plans I intend to keep. Plans you will not stop."

Now I glance to Louisa, and he and I both wait for some sign that she returns his feelings. When there isn't one, and he understands that there won't be, his fury grows. He turns his gun in her direction.

I rush forward, but he's quick to yank her from my mother to his side. My mother pulls and fights with him while Louisa screams, slapping at his shoulders. "Jacob, don't do this!"

A vein in my neck begins to pulse, and white-hot fire burns through me. "I will only ask you once . . . put down the gun and let her go." My voice is ice.

He starts to respond, but in what feels like an instant, Maggie lunges into the room and swipes a knife across his thigh. Bright red bloodstains bloom on his pants, and he stumbles toward the window with a shout that verges on a whimper.

Maggie leaps at him like a wild animal. She shakes him by the shoulders and pushes him back into the wall with a loud slam.

His gun slides over to my feet.

Maggie keeps him to the wall and presses her knife against his thigh. "Move, and I'll cut your balls off."

"Stop," pleads Louisa. "Please stop. You don't have to do this. Just let him go. He won't come back. He won't."

Maggie looks at me, waiting for my word. My silent "yes." This is the girl I knew, the scrapper from The Mint, who wasn't afraid of anything. And if Louisa weren't watching, I'd gladly give the signal. I'd watch her kill him without blinking and feel nothing at the loss of him.

But my father wouldn't. There's a reason people go to him for guidance and order. He'd do this by the law of The Mint. A fair battle and a public challenge. "Let him go, Mags. If we do this, we do this right."

Maggie hisses and walks back.

I pick up the gun. "We don't use guns in The Mint, Jacob."

Louisa runs to stop me, reaching for my hand. "You don't have to do this. You can let him go, and the streets will be none the wiser."

My mother pulls at her violently. "You will not challenge her in this. You will watch."

"Outside," I tell Jacob, ignoring Louisa's pleas. If I look at her, I might waver. "Go now."

I shove him until he walks down the stairs and out the front door, and I sneak the gun to Maggie to hold. "Knives or fists?"

A few people peer out from their homes, watching the show.

Louisa cries behind me. "Please, Alice, don't."

I've always wanted to send her away one day so she can have a different life, free of this violence and pain, but now I know, with Jacob standing as a reminder, that sheltering her keeps her weak. It would hurt her more than help her. She needs to understand our world and how we handle men that threaten us.

"I wanted to keep you from this," I tell her as warmly as I can manage in front of all the folks starting to gather. "I wish I still could."

Maggie marches up beside me, and just like that, it is as if there are no forgotten years between us. "I can do it for you."

"No, you can't."

Jacob watches our exchange in fear, then shouts, "Knives."

Ralph walks over somberly and hands us each two blades. He steps back, and Jacob takes a step forward, gripping his knives for dear life. A moment of silence passes heavy with tension as we wait. A time intended for our families to gather, ready to say goodbye because one of us must lose. Men and women emerge from the shadows and their dark homes to watch. Ralph points at a lad and says, "Go get Richard!"

I chew my bottom lip while the anticipation twists at my insides. I don't want to wait. He doesn't deserve the consideration.

"When you're gone," he utters, the fear in his voice replaced with newfound strength, "I'll challenge Tommy next, and then your father."

Is he trying to get into my head? He can't possibly have that kind of ambition. And if he does, where did it come from and how long has it been brewing?

"When they're gone . . . the Diamond family reign ends."

"I'd keep my mouth shut if I were you, boy," cuts in Ralph. "Your father should be along shortly."

But he doesn't stop. "Then Louisa is mine."

"She'll never be yours."

"You won't have a say if you're dead."

"Alice, please. We can end this now," cries Louisa from behind me. "Don't do this. We can still talk about this."

But all I can hear in my mind is *"Louisa is mine."*

I block out Louisa's cries and throw my knife with expert precision. My thoughts momentarily drift back to Dad teaching me to sling blades at targets, him standing in my path to test my resolve.

The knife slices through the night air in a perfect arc, plunging into Jacob's chest. He stumbles soundlessly onto his knees, clasping the handle. I thrust another at his gut. He falls on his side with a thump, bleeding out.

I close my eyes and imagine myself by the river Thames with Eli, back when we were young and in love. We would lie on a wool blanket and listen to the water for hours, eating stolen strawberries and cheeses. I had never felt so at peace. Not before or since. When I open my eyes, men are already lifting Jacob's limp body by the hands and feet.

Ralph takes me by the shoulders. "Alice . . . this isn't how things are done here. How will we explain this to Richard?"

"I saw his hand twitch," I lie coldly. "He stormed my house in the night with a gun. He had no intention of playing fair. I threw mine before he could throw his."

Ralph's eyes narrow cannily, seeing through the lie with ease. "There will be consequences for this."

"Take his body to his family. If they need help with anything, come to me."

With a sigh of reluctance, he nods.

I turn to Louisa but find her gaze unmoved, staring at Jacob with an emotion I can't place. "Louisa, it just happened."

Still nothing. Not a blink, or a twitch, or even a tear. I can't read her mind, but I already feel the regret seeping through me. My mother takes Louisa inside to soothe her, while Maggie gazes at the smear of blood on the street where Jacob's body was. "It's been a long time since I've seen a man die."

I place my hand on her shoulder. "Thank you for tonight. I'll be inside shortly. I need to talk with Ralph."

She nods, and I walk far away from the shop before rounding a dark corner. I hide in a small, gloomy alleyway where a stray black cat watches me with caution, pawing at trash along the cobblestones. I sink to the ground and cry into my hands as Louisa's horrified expression fills my mind, the image burned there forever.

A moment passes, and I let out a calm breath, clean off my face with the back of my hand, and get up, but my knees give out, and I wobble back down. But before I can quite hit the ground, Maggie's in front of me, her firm hands taking hold of my shoulders, not allowing me another attempt at standing. Through the dim, narrow light casting into the alleyway, her expression is illuminated. A compassionate, overcome frown. She sinks beside me, resting her head on my shoulder like she used to do when we were girls.

And for a moment, just one, we are those little girls again.

"I forgot how good you are with knives," she admits.

I sniff. "Is that a compliment?"

She pulls out a cigarette, half-smoked, and lights it for me. "You remember what your father used to tell us?" She puffs out her chest and lowers her voice an octave. "Girls from The Mint aren't allowed to cry." She thinks on it for a long moment, then chuckles to herself while I take a drag of the cigarette. "Then we saw him crying like a baby when Tommy got home from the war. And that one time the group of orphans came around here caroling. He tried to hide that single tear running down his face."

I stifle a laugh. "He always tried to hide it."

"Is that why you're hiding it?"

My mouth goes dry. "I wanted something different for her. I didn't want her to see this side of me . . . this side of these streets. I thought I could keep her locked in a room, where I made her promises of something better and would eventually just move her out of here."

"It didn't work for us, Alice. Why did you imagine it would be any different for her? Look, let her be angry with you . . . but she will understand one day. Not today, maybe not tomorrow, but one day."

We finish the cigarette together, and when I'm finally ready to move again, Maggie follows. At home, I walk up to our room to find an empty bed, then drift down the hall to my mother's room and find Louisa there with her.

I sit on the edge of the bed and reach out for her hand. The moment my fingers graze over hers, her eyes jerk open. She says nothing, but the distant look in her eyes makes me feel as if I've lost her for good.

She pulls her hand away and tucks it into the blanket.

On top of the dark events I carry with me all night, on the way to the Kings' town house the following morning, Maggie reveals I tried to drunkenly seduce Rob at the 43 Club and the girls had quite a laugh over it. I can't contain the horror in my voice when I say, "I kissed him?"

"You tried to kiss him," she counters from next to me in the cab, touching up her hair and face using a tiny compact mirror. "It was glorious, truly." She tosses the compact into a handbag and pulls a fresh cigarette from a gold case while I sit frozen, trying to recollect what happened, but everything before the fight with Jacob is just a blur.

"You're telling me this now?"

"You honestly don't remember? I drank far more than you, and I remember everything."

A self-conscious chuckle escapes my mouth. "It's easier to lie."

"We're independent women," she reasons brashly. "We shouldn't be shy about wanting a man and showing it. You just shouldn't be blackout drunk when you make your move."

"I don't want him."

"You don't have to lie to me. I saw the way you looked at him."

"He's a McDonald, even if he says he isn't."

She rolls her eyes. "If you want to fuck him, just do it already. You said you wanted to plenty last night. Get it over with so he's not a distraction."

I quickly change the topic, trying to shake the image of his drunken, loose lips from my mind. "You girls celebrate that way every week? You should have warned me."

"We celebrate hard. I should have warned you. I'll pick you up when you're done playing maid," she teases. "We'll hit a few shops along the Strand. You know, I don't even have to drop you at that rich old bloke's place. You don't have to do that anymore. The gang could be your full-time gig."

"We'll talk about me quitting after we get paid. And we're stopping by the 43 before we hit anything," I say, unable to shake the scene she painted of me throwing myself at Rob. The cab stops, but before I get out, she says, "Don't tell Mary about what happened last night. Don't tell her what I did."

I scoff. "Don't tell her you defended my family and me? That the real Maggie Hill came back from the dead?"

She rolls her eyes. "Would it be so bad if she were dead? Why do I have to keep her alive for you?"

"You don't."

"You remind me daily that I cannot leave her behind, as much I want to. Mary spent time on me. She showed me I don't have to be violent to get what I want. She'd be disappointed, knowing what I did."

I narrow my eyes. "This woman you are now, this part you're playing, it won't last."

"Why can't it?" she shouts, her fingers balled into a fist until her knuckles turn white. "Why can't you let that girl you knew go? Last night was a mistake. I lost my temper. It won't happen again."

"No, it will happen again," I retort. "You didn't lose your temper. You knew what you were doing. You felt more comfortable swinging that blade around than wearing anything Mary puts on your body. The

Maggie I know is still here. Nobody said you have to be one kind of woman. There's no rule that you can't be beautiful and clever but also fearsome and wild. You can be all these things."

Her eyes stay forward when she replies with, "No, I can't be. Not with Mary. She doesn't understand the woman I was. She wouldn't understand it now. She gets her way with tricks and ploys. She will tolerate nothing she deems uncouth. Please don't tell her."

"You know the only difference between this life with her and the one you had with your brothers is your posh dresses and your fancy new motorcar."

I get out quickly, and as I walk up to the town house, I hear her say, "That's a damn big difference!" She blows out a puff of smoke, and before I can get another word in, she's gone.

I'm almost at the service entrance when I hear a panic-filled scream coming from inside. Usually, I'd knock at the kitchen door and wait for Alba to open it with that distinct stare of disappointment she reserves just for me. But today I push inside and rush through the kitchen to the foyer where Pearl is on the floor, helplessly clutching a split lip that is dripping blood.

Mr. King towers above her, holding her wrist in a viselike grip to keep her from squirming away.

Alba is just behind them with a broken teacup at her feet.

He brings his hand back again, hitting Pearl's face in the same spot. The sound his palm makes as it slaps her skin leaves me unnerved. This time she doesn't scream. "You will not go to that party! I am your husband, and I demand it!"

He reaches down, trying to grab something out of her lap—a red envelope with green trim. Pearl lets go of her face to clutch it as if for dear life.

Alba looks away and sinks to the floor to clean up the porcelain shards as if the scene in front of us isn't happening.

But it is.

I close my eyes and try to remember who I'm pretending to be. Here, I am Alice Black, a docile maid, dependent on Mr. King's employment.

With Mary, I am Diamond Annie, a sly and fashionable thief who can use her beauty to her advantage. Last night I was not playing a part. Last night I was Alice Diamond, daughter of The Mint. I killed a man in the middle of the street while all The Mint watched.

I cannot ignore that woman inside me now.

I cannot turn away.

I grab a heavy crystal vase sitting on a credenza and smash it to the ground. Mr. King is distracted by the noise and stops what he is doing to gaze at me bemusedly.

I pick up the biggest, most jagged shard of glass and move toward him, gripping it tightly.

"Don't touch her again!" The words come out loud and sincere—a voice I'd wager he's never heard from a woman before. I become rigid all over, every muscle in my body alive with pure, untampered hatred. My ragged breath is loud in my ears, the only sound in the room besides the grandfather clock ticking away near the staircase. I find my voice again, but what comes out is more animal than human. "You touch her again, and I'll show you all the creative things I can do with this piece of glass."

His posture stiffens, his face red, and though I see a glimpse of reserve in his feet as they take a single step back, amusement fills his expression. "You wouldn't. You'll never get another job in this city if you do."

I hold my ground, and his eyes shift to the blood dripping down my palm. The cut from the shard stings like hell, but I don't lessen my hold. A little blood proves to him I'm serious and wild—not the girl he thought I was. I tilt my head. "You can't run your mouth if you're dead."

His eyes widen, and his upper lip curls back. He takes another step away from Pearl, but not far enough for my taste.

"You think I'm afraid of you? You think—" His words dry up midsentence.

"All your life, women have been afraid of you. You need that fear. You feed off it. Without it, you wouldn't know who you are. Without it, you'd be nothing." I slacken my grip on the crystal to slice forward into his forearm. He releases Pearl with a gasp, staring unbelievingly at his wound as the blood seeps through his flawless shirtsleeve to mingle on the floor with mine.

He holds his arm, and Pearl drags herself away, crawling to the staircase.

"You cut me!" Harold yells breathlessly, shaking his head back and forth in denial.

"I'll do worse," I warn him, then turn my attention to Pearl. "Pearl, fetch your valise."

Harold growls through the pain. "She won't leave. She'll never leave me."

Maybe he's right, and there's no sense in pretending otherwise. I glance past him at Pearl trembling on the staircase, tears streaming down her blotchy face. She is soft; there's no denying that.

"It's your choice, Pearl. You have one, even if he wants you to believe you don't."

She waits a moment, long enough to nearly convince me that Mr. King's terrible words are the truth and I won't be able to persuade her to be someone she's not. Even my own mother warned that a woman like Pearl would endure anything to keep her privileges. But then, she calmly wipes the blood off her face and dashes up the stairs to pack.

Holding the piece of glass to guard Harold, I wait patiently, startled by the strange similarities of last night and today. Ralph's words are heavy in my mind—*"there will be consequences."* What will they be? How bad will they be?

Pearl returns in a rush, silencing my thoughts. On our way out the door, I hear Harold demand Alba to call the police.

We take a cab so far outside the city I start to wonder if Pearl's given the driver the right address. But we eventually arrive at a small flat: a little heated space with no color on the walls. There's a bed, a stove, and a beautiful blanket thrown across a battered, old chaise longue. And though the flat seems abandoned, I can tell she's been here before because the moment she unlocks the door, she lets out a loud, comfortable breath.

She then takes off her coat, heads for a loose floorboard in the corner, and shimmies it upward. There's a box inside, filled with stacks of bills and fancy jewelry. "I bought this place secretly," she says. "During my time at the theater, I had the director slip me cash here and there. Nothing big enough to catch Harold's attention. I'd squirrel it away. This flat wasn't expensive, but I didn't have much left over once I bought it, just what's in here. It won't last me long."

She takes the box and sits on the edge of the bed. "Six months, maybe a year."

For a moment, I'm breathless and don't have words. She did this all by herself, which means she's always had the intention of leaving. I want to ask her why she waited so long, but I resist. "We'll figure it out," I say, somewhat unconvincingly. I hadn't thought past getting her away from him. Had she not suggested coming here, I don't know where we would've gone. "Stay here for now. Don't talk to anyone. He finds out where you are, and he'll drag you back."

"He'll kill me," she corrects me with little emotion. She seems numb.

"He won't touch you again." My words don't change her expression, but she nods in response. I point to the envelope in her hand. "Out of all the things you could have taken when you left, you bring a letter?"

"This?" She lifts it and laughs. "This isn't a letter. It's an invitation, and it's why we got into a fight. Have you ever been to Selfridges?"

I try to sound nonchalant when I say, "Hasn't all of London?"

She sighs dreamily. "Every year on Christmas Eve, Mr. Selfridge throws a party. The most exclusive event of the year for the crème de la crème of London. I've been getting the invitation every year since Mr. Selfridge saw me in *The Girl from France* at the Vaudeville Theatre. Harold has never gotten one."

I raise my brows. "The invitation doesn't have a plus-one?"

"It does," she says simply. "But why would I bring him? It's addressed to me and me alone. It drives him insane. This year, he demanded I not attend. Said that me going without my husband sends a nasty message." She lays the card down. "I refused."

"All of that because his pride was hurt?"

"It's always his pride."

A tense silence lingers between us, and I think about Maggie on her way to pick me up at Mr. King's town house. "I have to go, but I'll be back tomorrow to check on you. We'll work out some kind of plan then."

She places a hand on my arm to stop me before I can leave. "Why are you doing this?"

"I don't know," I admit.

"Because you're a good person?"

"I don't think that's it." A good person doesn't do what I did to Jacob last night. "You needed a push. I pushed you."

"You needed that job, didn't you?"

"Not that bad."

"There's got to be more to it then. Giving up a good job for a stranger."

I let out an exasperated sigh. "I don't like when men hurt women. That's all there is to it."

"Do you think you could teach me?"

"Teach you what?"

"How to fight back as you did."

"That wasn't fighting back."

"Can you teach me?"

"Depends."

"On what?"

"If what he said is true. That no matter what, you'll go back to him. That all of this is for nothing."

Her face is anything but reassuring. "Thank you for this."

It's not the answer I was hoping to hear, and she knows it. She sinks back onto the bed and rummages through the box, spreading out the contents. I'm not done fighting for her to believe in a life beyond Harold King's control, but for now, there's nothing I can say to prove otherwise.

"I'll be back tomorrow," I assure her.

CHAPTER NINE

To my relief, Maggie's car is outside the warehouse, where she and a few girls are chatting over smokes. When she catches sight of me, she jogs over with a confused gaze. "What happened? I'm supposed to pick you up later."

I tell her what happened with Pearl King. She shakes her head. "You know it's not your responsibility to save all the lost girls in this city."

I click my tongue in response.

The girls have never seen me in my maid's uniform, with its sizable lacy collar, lace-trimmed apron, and ribbon headband, and most laugh good-naturedly as I approach, but the twins sneer. "Servitude looks good on you, Diamond Annie."

I let the comment slide as Maggie pulls me into the warehouse. "You arrived just in time. Mary has some cash for us."

The thought gives me butterflies.

Inside, Mary is busy inspecting a new automobile that must have come in sometime last night. "One moment, ladies." She examines it closely while jotting things down in a notebook in her hands.

"So I suppose this means you're done with the second job?" Maggie's brow perks up at the question.

I shrug. "I don't see Mr. King welcoming me back anytime soon."

Mary walks past us into her office, leaving the door open behind her. We move inside and I watch her gather money from her office safe, then shut it with a loud clank. She pays us one hundred pounds each, then hands me a large brass key. "Did Maggie tell you how all this works? I get fifty percent of your take."

The words startle me into speechless disbelief for a moment. "Fifty percent?"

She laughs. "All the girls look like that when I first tell them." She leads us outside the warehouse and gestures down the street to a set of flats. "Walk with me? I'll show you your new place."

I force my feet forward. "My new place?"

"I pay for the parties, the drinks, the food, but most importantly, the security. The McDonald brothers are my business partners, and when we need help from them, they supply it. If one girl gets caught, they use their connections with various top men in the city to secure a quick release. We need them."

"We need them?" I repeat the words to ensure I heard them right. "Half of what I make trying to pay them back goes to you and then to them?"

Her words don't settle well with me. As we approach a block a few streets down, the anger builds to the point of exploding, but before I can let it out, Mary gestures at the building. "This is where the girls stay."

We enter the lobby, and I shake my head. "I told you, I don't need you to provide new housing. I don't want this to be another debt I owe."

"You don't have to live here, but so long as you're a part of this gang . . . you have a home here."

I feel a tiny grin creep across my face, and my body feels weightless—as if her words alone could make me fly. I scan the building in awe. "I don't think—"

Inside, we step into the lift and take it up to the third floor, where I'm greeted by a long hallway and four doors.

"Two bedrooms. It's yours so long as you keep supplying like you did yesterday." Mary reaches over to shake my hand but stops. "No men in the building overnight. It's a rule."

I think about Charlotte. "Charlotte is engaged, right? Once she's married, what happens to her then?"

"Out of the gang," she confirms glumly. "I have nothing against a woman falling in love. Love is fun, inspiring. It makes us feel alive.

Marriage is another thing. Men don't enjoy having a woman committed to anything but them."

I consider my firsthand experience with Pearl and Harold, then
nod in agreement.

"What about you?" She tilts her head, making a study of me. "Got
a man in your life?"

I shake my head. "No man, and no plans for one."

"No matter, no man stays the night. You want to sleep with him,
do it at his place. Understood?"

"Understood."

"Welcome home, Diamond Annie."

I swallow and consider it. I think of the things I could do, the places
I could take Louisa. I could get her out of The Mint, but I also know
how my father will feel. Not only have I joined a gang, but I'll be allying myself with the McDonalds. The same men who beat Tommy to a
pulp and stormed our shop at night with their demands. All of it runs
through my head until my stomach is in knots. "This isn't my home."

She grins. "We'll see. I've got another shop I want you and Maggie
to hit tomorrow. Enjoy yourself."

I wait for her to get back into the lift before I unlock the door. It's
not like Harold King's town house by any means, but it's perfect for me. I
take my shoes off, walk over to the Aubusson rug by the fireplace, and run
my fingers across the set of gleaming silver candlesticks on the mantel.

"What do you think?" Maggie asks from the door with Charlotte
and Rita giggling behind her. "We wanted it to be nice so you aren't
moving into an empty space."

"It's the nicest place I've ever lived," I reply honestly. I turn to the
three of them and don't hide the emotion in my voice when I say, "Thank
you for what you did for me."

Charlotte and Rita rush over to hug me, but Maggie stands apart,
beaming.

"We have to go on a quick errand," she says. "Take a look around.
I'll be right back."

I wander down a wide hall to find the bedrooms—one smaller with bluebird wallpaper that would be perfect for Louisa. I close my eyes and imagine her trying on new dresses and hairstyles, getting ready for a day in town.

I leave her room and go into mine, one I'd share with my mother if I could pry her out of The Mint. The space is airy with an emerald-green velvet settee, but what makes me stop in my tracks is the bed covered in new peach-colored silk sheets.

I don't think twice about it.

I take off my clothes, all of them, and throw myself on top of the bed. Against my skin the fabric feels like I always imagined it would. But also, somehow better.

I want to wear these sheets outside, everywhere I go.

I hear the front door open and make a dash for the robe someone left hanging for me in the closet, then peer from my room into the hallway. Maggie strolls inside with a bottle of something dark clutched in each fist. Charlotte and Rita follow, carrying a bulky gramophone. "We're not done celebrating, Diamond Annie!"

I let out a moan. "I'm not yet recovered from last night. I can still smell the gin in my hair."

Maggie lifts one bottle. "Then another round won't hurt, will it?"

Charlotte waves me down. "Come now, my beau and I tie the knot in a few weeks. I'm approaching every night as a potential celebration."

"Too seriously," adds Rita with a chuckle. "Drunken Charlotte has a taste for far more men than just her fiancé."

Charlotte hits Rita on the shoulder. "Shhh. We are a sisterhood of secrets."

Maggie throws her arm around Charlotte and hollers at me. "Don't make me come get you."

I pull the robe around myself and stare down the hall, taking in the scene in front of me—all these women welcoming me with open arms into a strange new family. I don't have many friends; I never have. My life has been finding ways to survive and protect my family, leaving no room for simple joys or connections.

A girl from The Mint can't be this lucky. A gang is not a family.

My father's lessons haunt my mind, feeding me doubt.

When will it all go away? Will I ever stop hearing his voice in my head?

I remind myself again that I'm only in this until the debt is paid. That all of this means nothing. That they mean nothing.

"I'm coming," I say, joining them for drinks.

I leave midcelebration to stop by the 43 and confront Rob. It's still before hours, which means the club is dead aside from the cooks, a few bartenders, and Kate looking over her books at a booth in the back. She glances up from her work and says, "We're not open yet, not even to you, Diamond Annie. Come back for your shift."

"I just need to talk to Rob."

"Rob rarely has so many visitors. Someone else came by to chat with him. They're out back," she says with a wave of her hand. "Make it quick."

I take a long hallway to the door that exits into the small back alley where we leave the trash and empty crates. I push open the door an inch, but the sounds of rough conversation stop me in my tracks.

A voice I recognize sends a chill down my spine. "You need to come home."

Wag McDonald.

"The Italians are out for blood, and you're an easy target. We need to end this. The distance doesn't work anymore. I can't protect you at a distance."

Rob sighs in response. "I'm not going anywhere. I like it here, and if they're coming for me, they're coming. I'm not hiding in Elephant and Castle."

And though I can't see Wag's reaction, I imagine his face pinched with irritation. "Fine, if you're sticking this out, I want you to carry a gun, a knife, something."

"I don't need a gun."

He grunts again. "You're dead if you don't fight back, Rob. Sabini slaughters entire families to make his point."

I roll my eyes. "Using my family history to your advantage, Wag?"

He continues quickly, "What's to stop him from shooting up the club just to get a little McDonald blood?"

Rob clears his throat. "If I'm going to die, I'm going to die. A gun or a knife will not keep it from coming. I'm not spilling any more blood. I'm not walking into the grave with any more dead men beside me."

"Rob, just listen to me—"

"Thank you, brother. But if that's all, I need to get back to work."

"You're stubborn as hell."

I slip away and run back down the hallway, throwing myself so quickly onto a barstool that I nearly topple over. Kate gives me a little smirk and goes back to scribbling in her ledgers.

I breathe out and smooth my mussed hair. Rob emerges a moment later, spotting me and smiling as if someone hadn't just warned him of his likely impending death.

"Back so soon? Most first-timers need a day or more to recover. Someone should have warned you that those girls party long and hard."

"And day and night," I add. "I've just come from another party of theirs."

He shakes his head. "When they're not robbing London blind, they're drinking from sunup to sundown."

"So I tried to kiss you?" I cringe internally at my abruptness.

"Tried, yes." Rob bows his head to hide a smug grin.

"It won't be attempted again, I assure you."

"You assure me?" His brow quirks playfully.

"You're so pleased with yourself, aren't you?"

"Fairly pleased."

"It won't happen again," I say, louder now, getting off the stool to leave. His hand darts out and grabs mine to keep me from bolting out the door like a skittish colt. "I think you and I both know that it will happen again . . . but next time you'll remember it."

For a moment, we stay frozen with our eyes locked and his hand cupping my wrist. Then he slowly releases it to move down to my fingers. The sensation makes me shiver, and I unwillingly think that maybe drunk me had the right idea. Or perhaps it's been too long since I've been with a man.

He lets go. "Sorry. I remember. No touching."

"Let me save you the trouble. We'd make an awful pair." I decide to be blunt to get this over and done with. Maggie said he was a distraction, and she's right. Anytime he's in the room, I ignore what's in front of me to stare at him.

He begins cleaning large glass tumblers with the 43's interlocking numbers engraved on them. "It doesn't matter if we would or wouldn't. I trust Mary Carr hasn't given you the full list of rules yet? No men. At least nothing serious. Apparently, men complicate things."

I flash him the same cheeky grin he gave me earlier. "And anyway, I don't do serious."

He gives me a piercing stare that makes my smile fade. "I'll throw you over my shoulder and take you upstairs right now for a little fun if that's what you want. But when we're done and you leave this place, you will still feel like something is missing . . . and so will I."

His words leave me unnerved and excited all at once. I'm not used to men talking to me like this. If any boys from The Mint felt affectionately toward me growing up, I never knew it.

Eli was my only beau before we decided love was for children.

Rob doesn't know the real me, so he's not afraid, and I like him for it. The rush of emotions is a new sensation, and I have difficulty finding the right response. "You assume you're what's missing in my life? Is this what you use to get other girls to go to bed with you? How many times has it worked?"

He manages a terse chuckle, but the amusement doesn't reach his eyes. "You're the first to call me on it."

I shake my head. "You don't want any of part of this." I use my hand to wave at my body from head to toe. "Body, mind, soul . . . none of it. I promise you."

"Can I tell you a story?"

"Does it matter if I say no?"

He looks past me at Kate. "When I was a boy, my father was always trying to teach my brothers and me the business. He thought we were too soft. One day he took us to The Mint, where I first met Thomas Diamond."

I shake my head to tell him to stop but can't get a word in edgewise before he continues. "My father told him that a man from his streets was responsible for a dozen missing children. This man ran a trafficking business on the side, snatching kids from the slums and selling them off. But that directly violated an unspoken rule. One that every circle of crime knows."

My heart beats so loudly that I wonder if he hears it. "You don't deal with the business of children."

He nods. "When Thomas got the proof, he rounded all the families up that had lost children. He gave them each a shiv and let them take turns. One stab for every missing child. My brothers and I turned our heads. We couldn't watch it. I looked at Thomas instead and saw he was making his children watch too. The boy, like us, couldn't stomach it. But the girl—she never blinked. She watched each person stab the man until it was done. She didn't turn away."

I grow tense as the memory floods my mind. "It was a lesson."

"Was it?"

"Even the people we trust can betray us."

His eyes grow soft. "I told myself I would never forget her face, and when I found out your name was Alice Diamond, it all came together."

"I don't remember you," I tell him.

"Well, I'll never forget you."

He takes a crate of empty liquor bottles and starts moving to the basement stairs at the back of the club. I glance at Kate still buried in her books and decide to follow him. "I overhead you outside with Wag."

"You're following me now?"

"Even with his warning, you won't protect yourself?"

"If Charles Sabini comes for me, he's coming with friends, and one weapon will not change much."

"You'd just die, then?"

"I'm not afraid of death."

"Everyone is afraid of death."

I halt at the bottom of the stairs and lean my back against the wall, trying to appear casual. He places the crate down on the ground and pushes his body against the opposite wall with the same air of composure, making the space between us feel endless.

On purpose, I suspect.

"Why don't we just be honest with each other, Alice. What are you afraid of?"

"What makes you think I'm afraid?"

"If I were to kiss you now, right here, you'd melt in my arms. I know you fancy me as much as I do you."

He's not wrong.

"But you're afraid of wanting me. Why are you afraid?"

I take a deep breath, looking him up and down. "You first, Rob. Give me your fears, and I'll give you mine."

"I was engaged before I went to war," he reveals slowly. "When I returned, I found her with another man. I almost killed him." He points to the scar near his eye. "This isn't from a battle, despite what I tell people. It's from her—Annalise—throwing a teapot at my head to stop me from choking her lover to death. I was going to kill him, then I looked down at my hands, and I realized that I didn't even know myself anymore. I was just someone else's monster year after year and the violence . . . the anger . . . I didn't know how to control it. I was done with that man right then."

"And you came here? Kate hired you?"

"She put up a tussle at first, but my brothers tipped her off about some raids when she first opened, and she doesn't fancy being in anyone's debt."

I roll my eyes. "How charitable of them."

"Your turn."

I think about it, gathering all the reasons I've avoided men most of my life. My pulse races. "What if the truth scares you away?"

"I promise not to run."

"Men make promises all the time that they can't keep."

"Try me."

I let out a shallow breath, and the rush of nerves leaves my stomach in a flutter. "The first man I slept with was older than me, too much older. He was a business partner of my father's named Declan Toole. I asked him to stop, but he didn't. Later my father found out and strangled him to death. He brought me over after and made me look at the body, so I'd know he wasn't going to be coming after me again, and then he taught me how to stop a man who can't listen. He made me punch a wall until my knuckles bled."

It should feel horrifying, revealing something so raw and personal. I've never even told Louisa. But instead of terror, I feel relief, followed by a sliver of guilt. Maybe if I told my sister, she wouldn't have been so willing to go off with Jacob. To her, my reason for hurting him was just to protect her. And it was, mostly.

But I'd be lying to myself if I denied that my memories were part of what made me so eager to lash out with my fists. That when I hit him, I remembered Dad's satisfaction when he showed me the odd angle of Declan's corpse slumped up against the wall, the enormous purple bruises around his neck.

"I think maybe he thought I stood a chance before Declan."

"What do you mean?"

"To be innocent, just his little girl. I shield my sister Louisa as much as I can. I think he'd hoped to do that sort of thing for me. I always knew he had to do dreadful things sometimes, but the brutality . . . he did his best to keep me away from it before that."

"But he changed his mind?"

"He realized that not teaching me was hurting me. That this world is not kind to little girls who don't understand it. This world is cruel. He taught me to match that ferocity so I could survive."

"But not your sister?"

"She is learning a little now. I wish I could keep it from her."

"Even if not knowing could hurt her as it did you?"

"I don't want her to be like me."

Rob looks me up and down, but I don't see judgment in his eyes, only a sympathy that has his fingers curling into a tight ball—a glimpse at the volatile nature he wishes he didn't have. I glance down and laugh at myself. "You'd think I'd stay away from violent men after that, but I ran right into the arms of another one. He asked me to marry him, and I almost said yes."

He takes a step forward. "But you said no?"

I take a step closer to him. "I said no."

He takes one more. "One of my toes is longer than all the others."

I can't control the snicker that escapes my mouth.

"You laugh, but it's very off-putting. I have to keep my socks on at all times."

He wants to kiss me; I can see his eyes drift down from my eyes to my mouth.

"I've liked you since that night in The Mint all those years ago. I was just a boy then, but there was something about you. This girl standing among all these men, watching when we couldn't. You were terrifying and strange to me, but so beautiful."

"I am not afraid of wanting you," I reveal slowly. "I don't believe good men exist, but if I ever were to find one, I'd get away from him as fast as I could. To save him."

He goes very still and looks deep into my eyes. "From what?"

"From me." I take one last step, closing the distance between us. "I have seen things, hurt people, killed many men. I have blood on my hands. You said you did not want to fight any more wars. You say you want peace, but I am war."

"When you're around, I don't hear them."

"Them?" I shake my head.

"The men in my head, the lives lost to the Demolitions Man. When you're around . . . I don't hear them. You are peace to me, Alice Diamond."

He's close enough that I can feel his breath on my face. "If you tell me to stop," he begins slowly, lifting his hand to touch the side of my face and then curve around the base of my neck, "I'll stop."

"Why aren't you scared?" I ask quietly.

"Why aren't you running?"

I bring my lips against his. He tastes like gin and smells like that mix of sweat and stale cigar smoke that eternally lingers in the club. I'm not soft about it, not delicate. I take in the shape of his mouth, his full lips, and the way our breathing mingles between each staggered sigh. The way he tastes . . . I won't be able to forget it.

Somewhere far away, I hear a door open and heels click against the ground. We part quickly, moving to each side of the stairs just as Kate descends. She snaps her fingers. "Alice, get out of here, and Rob, you've got a bar to stock."

"When will I see you again?" His voice is light, hopeful.

Kate snaps her fingers again.

I grin but don't look back as I climb the stairs and exit out the back door. Once I'm on the street, I feel each gust of wind wrap around my body like an embrace, and my steps almost turn into skips. I let myself enjoy the moment, touching my lips where his were, before I get on the Tube to Elephant and Castle.

Chapter Ten

The next few weeks pass like a fever dream. I spend most of my days collecting with the girls and my nights working in the club, only visiting The Mint to check on the family. I paid Tommy's debt with ease, and now in my absence, he's taken over; though as usual, he manages to get by doing the bare minimum with Ralph and Mum picking up the slack. But the more I'm there, the less I'm collecting with Mary, so sometimes I wait days before going back.

This is the longest it's been. Four full days without a check-in.

I blame the girls, who never seem to stop, jumping from one score to the next with Mary rooting them on. More often than not, I fall straight into bed at my new flat after a late party, the hum of the ongoing trams outside acting as a strange lullaby that puts me to sleep at night and an alarm that awakens me in the morning.

Today is the first of December, and winter is upon us. A light snow is falling outside the church where Charlotte is getting married, and she's dressed to match in a lacy white gown and ivory fur capelet. Though I don't share the other girls' sadness over her leaving, I will miss collecting with her. She's the perfect face with all the right tools to distract shopkeepers long enough for me to pocket their wares and make my escape, and I loathe replacing her.

Her soon-to-be husband is a young, ambitious man who works as a bank clerk. He's clean-shaven and wide-eyed, handsome enough but soft around the edges. I imagine he has no idea about Charlotte's past, and I'm sure she intends to keep it that way.

Most of the girls are present at the wedding. Maybe once there were forty girls, but now they've dwindled to about a dozen of Mary's finest. A select bunch that passes from store to store like a violent storm, leaving invisible chaos in their wake.

In the same way that we only go into a store in small groups, we avoid congregating in the parish hall too. We move in clusters, chatting to one another. I've been accepted into one composed of five other girls: Maggie, Rita, Evelyn, Vera, and our departing Charlotte.

After the ceremony and reception, we celebrate at a small dance hall in Soho, where Mary supplies the drinks and—behind the scenes— drugs. Between songs, girls slip away to Mary for a pinch of cocaine, an addiction she seems to feed with delight. It keeps them lively and willing to jump at her every request. She often offers some to me, but I refuse.

We all sentimentally toast Charlotte's nuptials, then rage on to the loud, toe-tapping jazz that has even my ungraceful body moving to the beat.

"I hate to see a girl like that go," says Mary tipsily, joining Maggie and me at a table in the back. "Especially when it's to a man. It means he won."

Maggie chuckles. "You'd rather lose her to a woman?"

"I'd rather have lost her to anything but a man."

I stare down at my champagne flute, toying with its delicate stem— the liquid splashes in a circle inside the glass. The girls love bubbly, but I have little taste for it. It's much too sweet. I look up at Mary, still lost in thought, and make a snap decision to take advantage of her mournfulness to bring up something that's been itching at Mags and me for weeks.

I glance at Maggie, who instantly reads my mind, nodding her head with a swift jerk.

"Have you heard about the Christmas Eve party thrown by Harry Selfridge? When I was working for Harold King, I saw the invitation on his wife's vanity." A lie. But I don't want Mary to know that I've got Pearl hidden away or that I'm slipping her funds.

She wouldn't understand.

She'd believe it shows a chink in my loyalty to the Forty Elephants.

As far as she knows, her gang is my sole focus, and that's how I'd like to keep it.

Mary nods casually. "It's a massive party for the elite of London and all the world."

"Have you ever thought of taking it on?" I inquire.

She snorts condescendingly. "I've certainly dreamed of it, Annie. But it's an impossible feat. Not only would we have to get in without an invitation, but security would be tight. And if we do something like that, it will change the nature of what we are."

Maggie's brows arch. "The nature of what we are?"

Mary pinches her nose as if the conversation exhausts her. Or maybe it's that she's said all this before to some of the other girls, and she doesn't favor repeating herself. "Do you want to know why we've remained successful?"

"Because we are talented," I say.

"No. Anyone can collect. We are not special. We are successful because we stay in the shadows. We don't venture out into the limelight enough to catch too much attention."

I shake my head. "The papers aren't too much attention?"

"The papers don't take us seriously, and so long as they don't, the police don't. A girl gang is quite a fun Sunday topic for Commissioner Horwood to laugh about over breakfast with his wife."

Maggie glances down, the conflict evident in her stressed expression. "You said the men who laugh at us would be sorry one day. Why can't they be now? This score could be the biggest thing we've done. It would make history!"

"It would be foolish." She looks at me when she says it, not Maggie. "We step into the spotlight and prove we're a threat, and we become the target. The police have caught me over a dozen times, and I'm released within a month because being a woman criminal makes little sense to them."

I press my lips together. "I imagine the McDonald brothers and all their extensive connections help too, don't they?"

"Of course. Their protection is invaluable."

I watch her fuss and fidget, growing more uncomfortable by the second. Why is she so against this?

"I only mean that so long as the coppers are too preoccupied with the men and their gang wars over the racecourses and bootlegged goods, we can use that to our advantage. Be successful in the shadow of their threat. We need to stay clever. If they're laughing at us, we have all the power."

I can't stop the snicker that erupts from me.

"Something humorous about what I said?" Mary says testily.

"I have never lived in a man's shadow."

She laughs deeply, her eyes cold and flinty. "Oh, yes, you have—your father's shadow. You only had power in The Mint because he gave it to you. It's no different here."

Once again her knowledge about me and The Mint leaves me unnerved. I suspect Maggie told her plenty about her childhood friend before I came along, but it feels like Mary knows more. More than I want her to.

Mary takes a long sip of her drink before eyeing Charlotte and her all-too-pleased husband. "Our success has come because the men above us are reckless and sloppy. They kill and draw attention to themselves, and we use that to stay safe. We collect from that party, and we become the new target. Mr. Selfridge will gripe until Commissioner Horwood hunts every one of us down. He is as protective of his magnificent creation as I am of mine."

She's not wrong. We would not be in the shadows anymore. But why is she afraid of that?

When I don't reply quickly enough to her liking, she leans in and asks, "Do you understand?"

Maggie nods, but I don't. I hold Mary's gaze stubbornly.

Vera comes up to the table and taps Maggie on the shoulder, breaking the tension. "Someone's here for you out back."

Maggie stands up with a confused look on her face but follows Vera with a shrug.

I watch them walk away as Mary moves around the table to sit next to me. "Did Maggie put this idea into your head, or did you put it into hers?"

I shake my head, quick to backtrack. "It was all me . . . and it was just a suggestion. We were drinking one night, and I brought it up." Not entirely true. Maggie has been pressing me about it, envisioning the profit daily. We could make the Forty Elephants a force to be reckoned with. But also, with the brothers paid two weeks in, I don't need the gang anymore. So if she wants to toss me, I can go back to my old life without any regrets, but I don't quite want to yet.

I like this. I like the girls, and though I'll never admit it aloud, I feel like I belong in this gang. And yet, it's difficult for me to believe every day. How can I feel like I belong here when my home is The Mint? My people are there, my family is there.

"Do not put suggestions like that in Maggie's head," she says, pulling me from my confliction with a dark voice. "You are a profit, a talent, and it would hurt us to lose you now. You have been a top contributor since your first week with us. Aren't you happy here?"

I sleep on silk sheets and wear beautiful furs and diamonds. I give back to my family, providing amounts my father never dreamed of. I have my own flat—even though it'd be nicer with at least my sister staying with me.

I am happy, so for the moment, I bury the words rising up from Alice Diamond of The Mint, who'd never accept being dismissed by anyone. "I am very content."

"Then no more plotting risky scores with Maggie, and do not mention Harry Selfridge's Christmas party to any of the other girls."

"I won't."

She smiles sweetly as if she hadn't made a threat to get rid of me a moment before.

Mags returns to the table and sits back down with a disgruntled thump. "It's Eli. He's out back."

I perk up. "Eli is here?"

"Yes, but not for me. He's here to see you."

I get up with a groan and push through the crowd of dancing girls, getting bumped and jarred until I reach the back exit of the hall. Maggie follows but stops at the door. "Do you want me to go with you?"

"No," I say. "I'll handle this."

"You're certain?"

"Yes."

I wait for her to return to the celebration before I open the door. It's still flurrying—I look up at the snowflakes whirling in the air and imagine my mother and Louisa wrapped in thick wool blankets and sitting around the stove drinking tea. A pang of guilt rocks me as I clutch the new fur around my shoulders and arms, keeping me as warm as a fire.

Eli is standing against the wall fiddling with a lit cigarette. He looks me over once.

"Posh, really posh."

I roll my eyes. "Why are you here? How did you find me?"

"I'm good at finding people. You know that."

I nearly roll my eyes again. "Can we skip the braggadocio?"

"Did you kill Jacob Sloan in a duel?"

The words slap me in the face with the memory of Louisa's horrified expression. I've only recently stopped having nightmares about it. "Hardly a duel. My first knife killed him, and the second was insurance."

His mouth goes slack. "Well, his father, Richard the Butcher, has turned some of The Mint to his side in his quest for vengeance. He claims the Diamonds have abandoned The Mint and no longer work toward everyone's best interests. He says you killed his son solely because he dared to touch Louisa, and worse . . . you didn't follow the rules. You didn't wait for Jacob's family to stand witness."

He's right, I didn't, and there's no denying it. "I killed him because he threatened me in the middle of the night with a gun, then tried to take Louisa against her will. He broke the rules long before I did. I handled it like my father would have."

"Did you? Would your father really have crossed Richard?" He shrugs the thought away before I can answer. "It doesn't matter, Alice. It's happening." He looks at the dance hall critically. "How long has it been since you've been home?"

"I'm only doing this to pay off Tommy's debt. I'm home as much as I can be."

"How close are you, then? To paying it off?"

I hesitate a moment too long. "They're paid."

He opens his mouth but only air comes out, and I read his mind. He did not expect that answer. When he finally finds his voice, he says, "Then what are you still doing here?"

"Since when does more hurt? The more I bring home to the family, to the streets, the better off we all are."

He gives a little laugh in response, calling me on my shit, and I seethe, wishing he didn't know me so well. "You're here because you like it. You like being in this gang."

"Maybe."

A muscle in his jaw tics. "You left unrest in The Mint. The people don't know that Jacob threatened you, only that he dared to touch your sister, which is not a reason to kill a man."

"Bite your fucking tongue, Eli," I snap. "My father never shied away from killing a man who touched a girl before she was ready to be touched."

Everything about his tense state softens, a spark of recognition in his eyes as if he'd forgotten about Declan entirely. He reaches up to scratch the back of his head. "I'm not saying I don't agree with what you did . . . I'm just asking you to make The Mint believe you. The only reason this hasn't escalated further is that most of The Mint are still loyal to you. You need to remedy this before it gets out of control."

My heart races violently. The Diamonds have never been threatened in The Mint, not like this. I stepped away, and now if I don't return, my family will be at risk. I pull my fingers into a tight fist, feeling my nails dig into my skin. "Where is Tommy in all this? Did he marry that girl Christina? Every time I come home, he's not around. Mum says he's settling down."

Eli takes a slow breath, rolling his eyes. "When he's not at my gambling den, likely throwing away all that cash you say you're leaving your mother, he's at some whorehouse. Did you honestly believe you could trust Tommy when you left?"

"I didn't leave."

"You left," he growls. "You think I don't know when you're lying?" He points the tip of his cigarette at me and then the dance hall. "This shit with them is beneath you."

"Is it, Eli?" I arch my brows, sneering at him. "Or do you think I'm not good enough for it? That I should be cold and lonely in The Mint where you left me. You're not allowed to have an opinion about what's best for me anymore."

He seethes, flicks his gaze upward, then tosses the cigarette to the ground. "The Alice I know doesn't take orders from anyone. Not even for a fancy new coat. Go home and make this right. Richard tells his supporters that if they take The Mint, why not take Chinatown next? Get your house in order before your consequences come knocking on my door and the only Diamonds left in The Mint are dead ones."

I close my eyes, heat flushing through my body until my fur coat feels stifling. I flex my fingers and throw open the door and leave him without a word. Maggie is anxiously waiting close by, wanting more information. She follows as I grab my bag and rush outside the dance hall to fetch a cab.

Maggie studies me carefully. "What did he want?"

I don't speak because I'm not even sure what I should say. I'm livid, upset with The Mint for falling apart while I'm gone, but also with myself. How could I even consider leaving The Mint behind for furs and pearls? But most importantly, how could four days change everything? Has the unrest been brewing this entire time and I've been too distracted to notice?

"Alice, talk to me!"

"You don't want to see what I'm about to do."

Her nostrils flare in response. "Tell me what he said!"

"No!" I shout, turning on my heel to face my childhood friend. "You left Maggie Hill behind a long time ago, and you were ashamed when she came out to help me. Trust me when I tell you, the less you know, the better."

Finally, a cab sees me and moves closer. Maggie grabs my arm as I step toward it. "We are friends. Do you not trust me yet? Have I not earned it? Or do you still resent me for leaving?"

"No," I say honestly, looking back at the dance hall. "This is a job. You do your job, and I do mine. Friendship was us surviving The Mint together. Friendship was you threatening Jacob with a knife. Friendship was two little girls stealing from chocolate shops, promising each other they'd always have one another's backs. What we have here, it's not friendship. We work together, that's it."

Her posture goes rigid, and her face shifts into a deep scowl. "Is that it?"

"You are Mary's dog. You recruited me wanting bigger scores, more out of this gang, and more for yourself, but the second she says no to something, all that ambition drains away. You lower your head. The Maggie I knew bowed to no one." I don't realize I'm shouting until my throat goes dry from the frigid air filling my lungs.

"I didn't see you put up much of a fight either," she counters.

I shrug. "It doesn't mean anything to me. Not like it means to you. I wasn't going to get you tossed over some fantasy score. What do you have outside this gang?"

The question leaves her speechless.

But I don't have time to dive into her inner revelations or try to convince her she's more than this. "I need to go home, Mags. There are things I left behind coming back to haunt me, and right now, they are more important than the gang. I'll be in touch."

"What are you saying? Is this you quitting?"

"I'm saying that Diamond Annie is freedom. Fresh air. I feel alive when I am with you and the girls. I love it. But Alice Diamond is not going anywhere—the more I try to run from her, the closer she sticks to me. Mary says I cannot be both, but she is wrong."

The cab halts in front of us, and the driver gets out to fetch my door. Maggie grabs my hand tightly before I can take a step closer. "Stay. Fuck it all and just stay. No obligation, no family burden. Just stay."

I push her hand away with a firm, decisive shake of my head. "Take care of yourself. I'll come back when I can."

My return to The Mint is without fanfare. No one greets me as the cab pulls in along the street to drop me at the shop. I only see Ralph waiting in a chair by the door, the dark circles under his eyes betraying his sleeplessness. He stands when I get out and clears his throat. He is smiling, but his lips are thin, stretched.

"Ralph, how long have you been out here? Who is watching the pub?"

"I closed it down," he says. "A few days at least. Richard came in trying to recruit—you put enough drinks in a man, and a stupid idea seems wise."

I sigh heavily. "How many men have gone over to him?"

"A handful, maybe."

I look down the block and say, "He's around now, I assume?"

He nods. "Always watching, but he won't come out knowing you still have men loyal to you. He'll wait until it's dark and you're alone. He knows he can't match you in the daylight."

"Then we root him out," I declare. "He has another son, doesn't he?"

"Alister," he answers. "Works in Chinatown with the Hill boys."

"We'll get him and use him as bait."

"Then what?"

"Then we do this fairly. Him and me in the streets with all The Mint watching and a fight that will decide who takes over from there. That's what my father would do."

The notion scares Ralph. "He will want to fight with fists, Alice. He knows he cannot win against you with knives."

"Then we fight with fists." I share his fear but ignore the flighty feeling in my legs. Richard is a brute like my father. He could kill me fast and easy for all The Mint to see, and walk away with everything.

I swallow to soothe my dry throat. "Where is Tommy? He's never around when I'm home, and I'm tired of my mother never having answers for it."

"Last night he was at the whorehouse." He points down the block. "Sleeps there often with Jacqueline."

Jacqueline. His childhood sweetheart.

"What of his wife, Christina Noon?"

He shrugs. "I'm not sure."

I breathe out. Eli is right. There is no reason for me to put any hope in Tommy to make things right. Four days. All he had to do was keep this place together for four days. I place my hand on Ralph's shoulder. "I will find Tommy, but when I get back, you'll go get some sleep. I'll take my mother and Louisa out of The Mint until I return with Alister."

He sighs audibly with relief but says, "I don't mind watching them."

"I know, Ralph, but you need to take care of yourself. I'll need you at your best tomorrow."

Inside the shop my mother is wearing a deep green taffeta dress. Her hair is cut into a bob like mine. My father would hardly know her, and he'd scold her for chopping off one of his favorite things about her.

"Alice!" She places a glass bowl down and walks up to embrace me. "Are you home for the night? I can cook something for dinner."

"Why didn't you tell me about Richard Sloan?" The words come out rougher than I intend.

She shrugs far too casually. "There's nothing to tell. He's a nobody. Ralph is worried, but I'm not. He's not the first man to challenge the Diamond family."

"Eli came today and said Richard's recruited a handful of men and has plans to move to Chinatown once he takes over The Mint."

Again she shakes her head as if this is all a minor inconvenience. "Diamonds have led The Mint since long before you were born. Your grandfather took control of this place, and that power isn't going anywhere. Certainly not to Richard Sloan."

I rub one temple with my thumb. "I will bury this before it grows any worse. But first, I will fucking find Tommy, and after I'm done giving him a beating, he will remedy this with me."

I hear the stairs creak and look up, expecting Louisa but seeing Christina instead. Her voice is a low plea when she asks, "You know where Tommy is?"

I can see it in her eyes, the misery that comes from trusting in my brother and watching him fail. "I do," I tell her, then look past her. "Where is Louisa?"

My mother hesitates. "She's not in school anymore. She asked for a job, so I forged her papers."

"She's not in school? When did this happen? She was here last week!"

"After you left, she asked if I could help her get a job."

"Where?"

"The Savoy," she says proudly. "She landed a spot there as a maid and is quite taken with it. She'll be staying in her quarters there with the other maids, but she promises she'll visit." Before I can rage, Mum steps forward and places a hand on my shoulder, just as I did to Ralph a moment ago. "She's happy there. You wanted her to be free of The Mint, so let her be free. When she's ready to come home, she will."

I long for her now. I wish I said more the night before I left. I wish that every time I dropped off money I came inside to promise to her I'd be different. That she'd never see what she saw again. But that would be a lie.

She knows who I am, my place in The Mint, and there's no fooling her anymore. No sheltering her.

She's better off far away, but I feel a dull ache in my chest at the thought of not being able to embrace her. I can feel my eyes water, but I don't let tears escape them as I look back up at Christina. "After I collect Tommy, we're all going to stay at my place in the Elephant until we resolve this. Both of you pack your bags."

"I don't want to leave," protests Mum. "There must always be a Diamond in The Mint."

"We are not leaving," I assure her. "It's one night."

Christina turns around to go pack her bags, but I stop her. "Never mind, come with me. My mother will fetch your things."

She takes the steps down cautiously, and I wave her out the shop door. The boardinghouse-turned-brothel is just a few blocks down from the pub—a brisk walk. I take off my fur overcoat and wrap it around Christina's shoulders, exchanging it for a thick wool one. She shivers into it and grips it around her body, fingering the sleek bristles. "I've never worn anything like this."

She sounds like me, weeks ago, when Mary put the first fur on my shoulders.

"Is it true what everyone says about you? That you killed a man? My father always said that a man who thinks he has the right to kill another would never be welcome in heaven."

I sigh. "Well, then how fortunate that I'm a woman." I turn the conversation to more comfortable topics. "Where did you meet Tommy?"

"I met him at church," she admits.

I let out a booming laugh. "You're lying. You must be."

"Was he always like this? Before the war?"

"Irresponsible? Reckless?"

"Yes."

"That's Tommy."

"He was hurting, and I comforted him. We talked, and he told me everything. His family here in The Mint, his dreams of being able to travel the world. Even his talent for safe-breaking. I wanted adventure, and I thought he'd be the one to give it to me."

"You will get your fair share of adventure with Tommy, but he will bring you as much pain as happiness."

"I know," she says, choking up. "But there is no going back to my father. He will not let me come home."

"You *have* a home, Christina." We stop walking, and I turn to face her. "You are in this family now, and the women in this family must be made of steel. You will know pain, loss, and suffering, and you will have to fight every day to prove yourself to The Mint. But once you do, it will respect you. I have looked after Tommy and cleaned up his messes for years, but it's your turn now. If you don't stand up for yourself, he will never be a man for you."

She nods, stifling a cry.

We continue to the brothel, and the madam, a long-time friend of the family, welcomes us in. "Tommy is in the third room down the hall," she says right away, and I pull Christina along to the room, where I'm overwhelmed with the smell of sweat and musky sheets. Inside, Tommy is lying fast asleep, and Jacqueline is sitting at the edge of the bed, slipping on her knickers.

She jumps a bit, rushing across the room for her robe. "Alice? Who's your dame?"

"This is Christina Noon. She's Tommy's wife. Carrying his babe."

Jacqueline's eyes grow wide. "It was nothing personal, doll. He paid well."

Christina doesn't reply, at least not aloud. But her eyes say it all—the strange familiar horror that comes when a woman finds out Tommy isn't the man he promised he was.

"He paid with my money," I cut in, picking up a pillow and throwing it at Tommy's face. He flops out of the bed and rolls onto the floor, jumping up.

"A hundred pounds," I bargain. "You never let him in your bed again."

Her breathing goes ragged.

"Jacqueline," says Tommy. "She's bluffing."

"I'm not bluffing." I reach into my coat on Christina's shoulders and pull out a small envelope, then hand her five twenty-pound notes.

"Do we have a deal, Jacqueline? Never again."

She gives Tommy a small look of longing, a pout, but quickly takes the cash. "We have a deal." Jacqueline slips away before Tommy can get a word in.

Tommy's face heats red. "What the hell are you doing back here! This is my business, not yours! You left!"

"Now I've come back," I say. "To right a wrong, and this time, you will help me." I take a demanding step forward. "You will help me fix my mistake . . . just as I have helped you fix all of yours."

The corner of his lip turns up. "*The* Alice Diamond made a mistake?"

Finally, with a cherry face and a trembling lip, Christina bolts to him and slaps him. Once, twice, and then she's pounding her fists on his chest until she is sobbing. "You bastard!"

He holds his stinging cheek.

Christina continues to hit him. "Why! Why are you like this!"

"I—I don't know," he stammers gravely, taking her by the shoulders. "I'm broken, I'm just all wrong! Something in here is wrong." He hits his head with the flat of his hand several times, and my mind drifts back to when we were children, and he'd grow so frustrated with himself that he'd slam his head into walls when Dad reminded him of his mistakes. All the things he couldn't do right.

My body grows heavy as I realize that all my life, I've loathed him because I've had to remedy his mistakes, never realizing that the burden of being a failure weighs on him too. I slowly let out a deep, pained breath.

"I'm bad, Christina. I'm bad for you." His eyes grow wet with tears. "Everything about me is bad. I can't do anything right."

I see myself in him right now; I hear the words I said to Rob clearly in my mind. Tommy doesn't believe he deserves anything good, and I don't either. How did we both end up so broken?

Christina snatches the hand he's using to bang on his head. She pulls it down past the fur to her growing belly. "You did something right," she says sincerely, her gaze unwavering. "We did something right."

"Forgive me," he says, muttering it repeatedly until her crying lessens, sinking down to press his forehead to her belly.

"I hate you," she whispers.

"I know," he says. "I hate me too."

Chapter Eleven

I take Tommy, Christina, and my mother to my flat to get them settled in, but word must have gotten to Mary quickly because she meets us near the lift. "What's going on?" Her eyes lock on Tommy specifically. "I meant it when I said no men."

I close my eyes, needing to find my voice before I say, "They're not safe in The Mint right now. It'll only be a few nights."

Mary squares her shoulders in response. "Doesn't your family run The Mint?"

"In my absence, things have gotten complicated."

To my surprise, any suspicion resting in her features vanishes. Then, she places a comforting hand on my shoulder and offers me a smile. "Stay as long as you need. Your family is always welcome here."

I watch her carefully, baffled by her charisma, trying to determine whether she's being genuine or not.

"It won't be long," I insist.

"Don't rush, Alice. Maybe this is the sign you need to leave that life behind?"

Ah, that's it. I'm welcome here because the farther away I am from The Mint, the easier it will be to keep me in the gang.

I play along for the moment. "Maybe you're right. Thank you, Mary."

Once I see them settled safely inside, I stop in at the 43 for a drink. It's my night off, but with everything that just happened, I want to see him, even if I'm just watching him tend bar and chat with customers.

I walk inside to find another bartender in Rob's place—a stranger. I ask around until one of the servers reveals he's off tonight and that he conveniently lives above the club in a small bedroom he rents from Kate.

Several knocks later, he opens his door with a half-grin. "Diamond Annie, Alice Diamond, or Alice Black? What do you prefer?"

I salute him with a mocking sneer.

"You're the last person I expected to see here. You've been avoiding me."

"I do that after I kiss a man. I warned you."

He nods. "You did."

I peer into his dark flat. "Can I come in for a drink?"

"All I've got is scotch."

"That'll do."

He waves me inside. I glance around the room, eyeing all the little things that make up his everyday life: a small soot-stained stove, a faded woven rug, and a wrought-iron bed. On the windowsill is a can filled with cigarette butts, and around his bed are stacks of books, worn and dog-eared.

I settle near the door with my back against the wall. He pours me a drink and hands it to me. "I'm happy to see you, don't get me wrong, but why now? You don't say a word to me during your shifts. Just drink orders."

One massive swallow later, I give him a long stare. "Today I returned to The Mint to find out that my family's power is being challenged."

"Challenged?"

"I killed a man, and his father is seeking vengeance." I wait for his expression to grow long with horror, but it does not, so I go on. "To do things fairly, as my father would, we'll fight in the street for all The Mint to watch, and the winner takes control." I lift my glass his way. "So I figured if my hours are numbered, I'd come by and see you."

He runs his hand over his mouth and shakes his head, letting out a loud, frustrated huff. "You don't have to do this. You could walk away from it. It was never yours to begin with."

I roll my eyes. "You sound like Maggie. I didn't come here tonight for advice."

He takes a step toward me, and I feel like we're back in that basement. "Then why did you come? What do you want from me, Alice?" His voice is low, sultry. I adore the way he says my name. He stops a few inches in front of me, and I drown in his smell. "Honestly."

"I don't know." I breathe out the words.

He reaches up for my face, then uses his thumb to push down on my lower lip and open my mouth. I can see the memories flicker in his eyes, recollections of the last time our lips touched. "I think you do."

"Mary says no relationships with men. Just lovers."

"Just lovers then?"

His voice is tempting and deep. He reaches for my legs and slides his hand under the hem of my dress, pushing it up my thighs inch by inch. He does all this without breaking eye contact, and my exposed legs shake from the chill.

"Tell me what you want from me."

I take his hand and move it between my legs. "Here."

His fingers wander while his mouth devours mine. But the more I kiss him, the more I like him. I've thought about his mouth too much the past few weeks, and the idea that I can't forget him unnerves me. I excel at forgetting men.

He should be no exception.

I break the kiss and take him by the shoulder, putting pressure on it until he sinks to his knees, face between my legs. "Here."

He pulls one of my legs over his shoulder, and I feel his mouth gliding up my inner thigh.

For the moment, I allow myself to get lost.

Throughout the night he doesn't sleep soundly. He must be dreaming he's still at war, thrashing around, yelling things that make little sense to me. I eventually get up and sit at the edge of the bed to watch him. With the moonlight coming in through the window, I can see the scars along his body. All the marks that measure his time spent fighting.

I want to stay until the morning.

In a different world, I do stay.

But that feeling of doubt settles in deep as I watch him, and I imagine all the beautiful things we could do together and then all the ways I could hurt him. So, I get dressed and slip out into the crisp predawn air as quietly as possible, then catch a cab back to my place.

Tommy is sharing the spare room with Christina, and my mother is tucked into my bed. I slip under the sheets with her, resolving to let myself lie like this, curled next to my mother like a little girl, for just a few moments before heading to Chinatown.

Just as one of her hands sleepily reaches out to stroke my hair, I hear a pounding outside. I let out a groggy moan, and I drag my feet to the front door. I turn the latch and find Mary standing tensely in the hall. She shoves her way inside without so much as a word.

"It's early," I note, rubbing my eyes, so desperate to close them.

"Are you sleeping with Rob McDonald?"

The question startles me awake. "Are you following me?"

"I know everything about my girls. It's a part of the job."

"That's a yes then." I think about the only person who knew I was headed up to his place. Kate Meyrick. I shake my head.

"You are not allowed to sleep with him."

I take a step closer. "Allowed?"

"That's right."

I desperately try to gather my thoughts and arrange them into words. Just yesterday, she assured me that my family was welcome here, but now she's throwing out demands and new rules. "We're allied with the brothers."

"Which is why this can't happen. We don't mix business and pleasure, and this isn't up for negotiation. You will not sleep with him again. You will not see him again outside of when I am present at the 43. I want you to quit your job there too. No point in keeping it when you've got bigger things to worry about."

Not only is she pushing to get me far away from The Mint, but now she wants me to quit my second job? Admittedly, I don't need it anymore, and it's tiring to keep up with. But it's the only time I get to see Rob, and the only break I get from both my lives.

"I feel like I have to repeat myself because you're not hearing me." I raise my voice significantly. "You can't tell me who I'm allowed to fuck, Mary."

"You will end it!" She bellows so loudly that I choke on my protest. "I have worked too long and too hard to be seen as a business partner to them and not a woman. I've worked too long to be treated as an equal."

I gasp at the words. "Equal? They don't see us as equals. You said it yourself; we only survive in their shadow. We are only successful if we can use the city's fear of them to our advantage. When we are in the papers, it's a tabloid story. It's a drama. When they are in the papers, men and women write to their MPs to encourage reform. We are a joke to the commissioner, and we are a joke to them!"

Her face is splotchy and red. "You don't get to say things like that to me! You clearly don't understand your place, so allow me to illuminate you. The moment you said yes to joining my troupe, my word became law. Everything you have, I can take away. I can snap my fingers and send you crawling back to that gutter I found you in." A haughty laugh escapes her lips. "Where you're clearly not welcome anymore. So you belong to me."

She takes a step closer. "If I tell you to jump, you jump. If I tell you to collect from a store and then set it on fire, you will do so with a smile on your face. If I say no Rob McDonald, you'll end things with him. Do we understand each other?"

"No, we don't," I growl out, almost feral. "Tonight, I will fight a man with my bare fists for threatening my family. I stabbed a man dead in the streets before I joined you. I snap my fingers in The Mint, and men will kill for me."

Her eyebrows lift a little. "From what I hear, not for long. You still need to win your fight against the Butcher, don't you?"

I part my lips to ask how she could possibly know that but swallow the words down, not wanting to show her she's got the upper hand. "Nobody owns me, Mary Carr. Nobody controls me. You made a grave mistake thinking I would be like Maggie. Thinking you'd train me like a dog."

She folds her arms across her chest with a Cheshire grin, and a tingle sweeps down my spine. "You were nothing without me, and you'll be nothing again—just street trash. But if you want to play dirty, let's play dirty. I was aware the moment Louisa left The Mint. I have spies all over London. They told me when she got a position at the Savoy with fake employment papers. What a shame it would be for her employer to find out. Falsifying your employment papers is a serious offense in this city."

I let out a breathless gasp. "You're threatening my family now?"

"I need not hurt you with some big physical display, Alice. Perhaps you think being clever is not being brave, but I don't give a damn about bravery. There is no honor here. This is not the war. There is no code. There is only my way or no way. So from this point on, you will do as I command without protest if you want to keep your darling sister safe."

I look down, letting out slow, hissing breaths from between my clenched teeth. I shuffle through the memories of how all this started— all the words she said to convince me she was everything I needed. I not only fell for it, but I walked confidently into her trap without a second thought.

I don't blink when I say, "I could kill you right here and now if I wanted to. Solve all my problems."

"Maybe. But if you don't believe a woman like me has certain measures in place against that eventuality, then you still don't under- stand the difference between us."

I ball my fist together and lift my arm, on the verge of springing at her, but my body freezes midmovement. Hurting her will not help here. Nothing my father taught me will help at this moment.

The tenseness eases from her shoulders, and her mouth upturns from a frown to a gleaming smile as if she senses submission in me. "I didn't recruit you because I believed you'd be like Maggie. I knew I could manipulate Maggie from the start. She craves praise from a maternal figure, a chance to leave behind brothers who only used her. I turned her from an aggressive little girl to a creature of elegance and trickery.

She was a follower in need of a leader. She was easy. But you—I had no illusions that I would be able to tame you. I recruited you because although you are street trash, you are talented street trash. And if I have your little sister, that means I have you, don't I?"

I close my eyes and replay everything—meeting her, agreeing to the audition. Her praise, her generosity. Every step she took to ensure I was hers from the beginning. She played me like a fiddle, and though every instinct warned me away, I let myself be entrapped. All the muscles in my body tighten at once, and the flat—usually so comfortable—feels too warm and overbearing. These walls were never mine, not really.

"Louisa is innocent in all of this." I stutter out the words, feeling cold all over.

"So are Tommy and his new bride," she says with a careless shrug. "It'd be a shame if something were to happen to them too, wouldn't it? I love a happy ending."

My heart skips a beat. Mary had a plan for me from the very beginning, and there's nothing I can do to change it. All I can do is take my life back.

But first I need to take back The Mint, then I need a plan for Mary.

She lets out a heavy breath and stretches her arms with catlike laziness, all too satisfied with herself. "You will break, Alice, and when you do, this will all be easier." She steps past me into my flat. "Oh, and something you should know about Rob. He's an informant for the commissioner. So, whatever lies he fed you about why he is no longer involved with his brothers were just excuses to get you in bed. He is *very* involved."

I don't want to believe her. I want to believe him. "You're lying."

"He works both sides so that his brothers always stay one step ahead of the coppers. Clever, no? But I don't trust clever men, certainly not clever men with a direct link to the law. You and him are done."

An informant? Rob, the man who preached honesty, is living that big of a lie? I shake my head and focus on Mary, on what's in front of me. "You know, Mary, you have a flaw."

"Oh?"

"You talk too much."

She grins, then a sound catches her ears. She looks down the hall at my mother, gazing out from the bedroom door. With a smirk Mary turns to leave. When she opens the front door, I see Mags standing outside with wide eyes, obviously eavesdropping.

Mary passes her with a snap of her fingers. "Sorry to keep you waiting, Mags. Let's get going."

Maggie looks at me for a brief, dreadful moment before following Mary.

My mother storms down the hall as soon as the door shuts behind them. "This is the reality of this gang, is it?"

I cover my mouth, then rub my lips in thought. "Are you hoping I'll tell you that Dad was always right, and I've fucked us?"

"No. I do not plan to lecture, only to ask what you'll do next."

I don't have to think about it long. "I'm going to ruin her, but first, I'm going to handle Richard Sloan. Keep Christina here, but go wake Tommy and tell him I'll be back in a few hours to pick him up."

I knock on Rob's door for a full minute before he answers. He looks like he was just starting to get dressed. I glance behind my shoulder at the streets below, searching for Mary or anyone watching, then slip inside and shut the door.

He takes a seat on the bed, where the sheets are still in disarray from our evening together. "Back so soon?" he teases, grabbing our glasses from last night to refill them.

"I don't want a drink," I say. "Are you a police informant?"

He drops one glass, and it shatters next to his bare feet, but he doesn't move to clean it up. "What? I don't know . . . Who told you that?"

"Is it true?"

His breathing goes ragged, and a visible shudder takes over his entire body. "Who told you, Alice? Tell me who told you!"

"Mary," I declare with a grimace. Though I knew it to be true coming from Mary's mouth, hearing it from him leaves a hardness in my gut. A part of me, an insignificant part, hoped she was lying. Rob was supposed to be an exemplary man, too good for me. Honest. Fucking honest.

"That's impossible," he insists, finally sinking to pick up some of the glass. "Nobody knows but my brothers, and they'd never tell her."

"She says she has spies all over the city. She knew things about me too."

"I don't understand. I'm careful. Commissioner Horwood recruited me after the war. My brothers thought it was a smart move, having someone on the inside. I balance the line, but I balance it well, and it keeps me from the worst of the violence."

I pace the room, my feet restless. All this information is flooding my head in relentless, incoming waves. I can't pause to process it—I don't have the time. "He trusts you then? He believes that you are done with the family business?"

"He doesn't doubt me," he confirms. "And if he ever does, I give him something good, some intelligence that will reaffirm my loyalties." His expression softens, and he reaches out for me. "Alice, I wanted to tell you. I thought about saying something last night. I wanted to."

I lift my hand to stop him. "Did you know why Wal and Wag came to The Mint when I first confronted you about it?"

"I swear, I didn't. We keep a distance to make things look as real as possible."

He continues picking up the glass carefully. When all the large shards are collected, he fetches another glass from a cabinet but changes his mind midpour and drinks from the bottle.

"I wanted to trust you, Alice. I feel like I can."

"You can't," I tell him firmly. I take the bottle from his hand and down a long swallow until my throat burns, then thrust it back at him. "And it's smarter that you don't."

He shakes his head. "Then what is this between us? If there can be no love or trust?"

"I don't know," I admit weakly, chewing at the inside of my cheek. "I know that when you're around, I feel like I don't have to pretend to be someone I'm not." I press my hand to my head, trying to find the words. "When you touch me, when you kiss me, I feel like I'm finally safe with someone—a man. There are cruel men all around me, and then there's you, Rob."

His cheeks redden. "I feel the same with you, Alice." Again, he reaches for me, and again, I thrust his arm away with a push, denying myself what I want.

"But I don't have the luxury of feeling safe. Don't you understand that? So if there can be no love or trust, there can be kindness between us. Friendship."

"I can't be your friend, Alice."

"You can try, can't you?"

He recoils at the thought, running his fingers through his hair in frustration. "If you're asking me to try, I will."

I lower my head and gather my thoughts. "Mary is a clever woman, and one day, there will be something she wants from your brothers, and she'll leverage your secret to get it. We can both agree that her knowledge is dangerous?"

"Agreed." The word comes out pained and deep.

"I want you to give the commissioner the location of Mary's warehouse. He will raid it, find plenty of stolen goods from various high-end stores, and haul her in." I take a seat on the bed, desperately trying not to think about last night, tangled up with him, skin to skin. "You said it yourself, if he can't find the goods she's stolen, he'll never be able to hold her."

He sits down next to me slowly, staring contemplatively at his hands. "You want me to double-cross her? It would hurt you. It would hurt the girls and destroy the gang."

"If the Forty Elephants cannot survive without her, then it needs a rebirth." I think about our family history with The Mint and how Richard Sloan could turn men to his side because our hold on the neighborhood weakened when I left.

"Does this mean you're done with the gang?"

"I don't know," I admit with a shrug. "But I'm done with Mary." I lean in to kiss his full lips one more time, then stand up to go. "If something happens to me, don't let your brothers hurt my family."

He stands urgently. "What are you saying? What's going on? God's sakes, Alice, tell me something, please."

"Promise me." I reach for his hands and squeeze them without mercy.

He pulls me into him, his hands reaching for my face to hold me still. "The fight? If you are going through with it, I'm going with you!"

"No, you're not," I tell him with a shove. "This is my fight."

"It doesn't have to be."

Another kiss, so quick and unsteady—my lips shaking against his. "Remember your promise."

Before picking up Tommy, I visit Pearl with some lunch. Finger sandwiches, strawberry cakes, and lemon tarts from some of her favorite spots. She's reading in a corner chair when I come in but jumps up with delight when she spots me. "I'll put on some tea," she says, scurrying over to the small kitchen nook. I thought she'd be crazed by now, unable to handle the boredom, desperate for a night out with drinks or a shopping spree along the Strand. But something about this place soothes her.

Maybe because it's so far away from her husband.

I notice a few empty liquor bottles spread about and tidy them up for her, also surreptitiously slipping a few bills inside her handbag.

We sit and have tea together on the small balcony. The afternoon sun is pleasant for early December, and with only a few birds chirping outside, I understand why she enjoys this place.

For the first time since Charlotte's wedding, I'm able to quiet my thoughts.

She breaks the silence. "Are you going to tell me how you came into that money you tuck away for me each time you visit? I know you have your secrets you'd like to keep, but when are you going to trust me with some of them?"

I want to tell her everything. I want someone to talk to about it. But when I open my mouth, nothing comes out. I glance at the newspaper in her chair, tucked snuggly beside her leg. I motion at it and reach for it, flipping through the pages until I find something, a small article about the Forty Elephants, and point to it. Somehow that feels better than saying it aloud.

She glances down at the headline, and her eyes widen. "You're in this gang?" Her voice is laced with excitement. "I read about them weekly. They're such splendid fun!"

Fun. Maybe it was fun at the beginning at least.

"Tell me more! You must!"

I shake my head. "I shouldn't."

She exhales slowly and crosses her arms over her chest, her lips pushed out into a petulant frown. "You tell me something like that and then refuse to elaborate? This is a better story than anything in a book. You're a gangster?" She shakes her head in disbelief. "Why on earth were you working for us?"

I manage a half-smile. "He's rich."

"You were going to rob us?" Her eyes glitter with intrigue. "No wonder I caught you in the library!" Her brilliant smile fades a bit. "But I don't understand why you'd help me then. What do you have to gain? If you intended to rob me, you'd have done it by now. I'm expected to believe you're a thief with a heart?"

I hadn't considered the notion until now. "I wanted to help you. I just didn't know how."

"You need to take your envelopes of cash back," she says with a quick shake of her head. "What if this doesn't last? You have a family. I'm not your family. I'm not your responsibility, Alice. I need not be your burden."

"You're not a burden," I snap. "I will work out a way for you to get enough cash so you can have a fresh start. I don't know how yet, but I will."

I initially thought I'd be able to save up enough running under Mary, but now that won't be an option. I reach for my teacup, already cold from the light wind. I take a long sip anyway. "I hope that I will see you next week like always, but certain things are at play. Things I don't have control over. If I don't come back, take what money you have and leave."

"If you don't come back?"

"If I don't come back," I repeat the words to make myself clear. "If I don't come back, I need you to swear to me you will buy a ticket and leave London. I need you to swear to me you will not grow desperate and go back to that man."

Her eyes water. "What kind of trouble are you in?"

"Because if you go back, he will kill you. Not today, not tomorrow, maybe not in a year. But one day, he will hurt you bad enough that you won't heal. Do you understand me?"

She takes a deep breath and sits upright. "Alice, I won't swear that until you swear that you'll be all right. You are all I have right now. Tell me how to help you!"

Finally, the fear that I might not beat Richard surfaces, and my bottom lip trembles violently. I fight the tremor in my fingers and take her hand to squeeze it. "Don't go back to him."

"OK."

She's just saying it because I've asked her to, and now I know if I don't make it, she won't either.

Chapter Twelve

When I return to pick up Tommy from my flat, Maggie follows us out of the building to the cab. I'm able to ignore her entirely until she steps in front of us and blocks our path. "Where are you going?"

Mum and Christina are helping me shove my things into the back. "I have to take care of something in The Mint, and then I have to come back here and take care of something else."

"I want to help."

Tommy looks Maggie over with a grin. "You look real fine, Mags."

"I can still beat your ass, Tommy," she growls.

He lifts his hands in mock surrender.

Maggie returns her attention to me with urgency. "Tell me how I can help."

"Why does it matter to you?" I flare. "You heard every damn word she said to me, and it made no difference to you. She owns you. You're not my friend, and you're not Maggie Hill anymore." I try to shove past her, but she blocks me again. "If you don't move, I'll move you myself," I grind out.

"I am Maggie Hill," she says firmly. "And I'm with you. Whatever you're about to do in The Mint, I'm with you. Whatever you will do to Mary"—she pauses and hesitates—"I'm with you."

I don't believe her. How can I? I shake my head. "I don't have time for games, Mags."

"I'm with you," she says again, more robustly.

"We'll see about that," I counter. "My first stop is Chinatown."

Her eyes drop. "For what?"

"If you're with me, Mags, you're with me. All the way. If you're not, that's fine. Just don't get in my way."

She takes a moment to consider, then nods. "Let's go see my darling brothers." She motions Christina and Mum to follow her. "But we're taking my car so I can show it off."

"Drop us off at home first," insists Mum with a dramatic eye roll. "I have no interest in witnessing your reunion with your brothers."

Maggie nods. "Fair enough."

When Tommy, Maggie, and I arrive at their headquarters, we're not granted entrance this time and are instead instructed to wait outside for Eli and Patrick. When they finally come out, we don't say anything for a few long minutes, and the silence begins to unnerve me. Eli and Maggie stare at one another, each radiating aggression until I clear my throat. "I'm here for Alister Sloan."

"And a drink," cuts in Tommy with a finger up. "Can I just go inside and help myself?"

"No," snaps Eli.

Patrick's eyes me sharply. "Our bookie, Alister? It's hard to find an honest man who's good with numbers. He's a treasure to us."

"I will not hurt him. Just use him as bait to lure Richard tonight."

Patrick arches a brow. "What do you plan to do?"

"How do we solve anything in The Mint? Challenge him to a fight and end this nonsense."

Tommy chokes on his own breath. "What? That's your plan?"

Eli moves from his tense stance against the side door and stares at me critically. "If you challenge him, you know he'll call for fists."

"I appreciate the concern, Eli. Now can I borrow your bookie or not? I'll make sure nothing happens to him."

Eli scoffs. "You know you cannot guarantee a promise like that."

Patrick looks at Maggie. "What is your place in all this?"

"I'm helping Alice," she says. "Being a mate. That's all."

"You can be a friend to her but not a sister to us?" Eli growls. "You've been in London all this time and never came home. Not once. You know Mum passed away last year, praying she'd hear from you before she died."

"I heard about it," she says solemnly. "I was at the funeral, actually, in the back."

"Why the back?" Patrick inquires, sounding far more wounded than Eli, his eyes watering as he looks at her. As if, all this time, he also prayed to hear from her.

She clears her throat. "Mary said I couldn't come home, so I didn't."

"What a life you chose with Mary Carr," utters Eli with contempt. "Is it worth it?"

I snap my fingers between them. "We didn't come here to explain motives, Eli. You told me to get my house in order, and that's what I'm doing."

Eli gives his brother a curt nod, and Patrick goes back inside and returns a moment later with Alister. He looks just like Jacob, only thinner. He regards me calmly and says, "I mourned the loss of my brother when I heard of his unfortunate end, but it's been years since I've seen him or my father. I know nothing of what he's been plotting in your territory."

Maybe I believe him, maybe I don't.

I'm a proficient liar. He could be the same.

Only one way to find out.

I cross my arms over my chest. "I can forgive the handful of men your father's smooth words swayed to his side. I allowed him to sway them when I disappeared too long. But he is a simple man with a simple mind, can we agree on that?"

He sniggers. "My father and brother both had simple minds. I was fortunate to take after my mother's side in that respect and left them both behind without a second thought when Eli and Patrick gave me a chance."

"You feel you belong here then? A bookie in a gambling and drug operation instead of the rightful owner of a butcher's shop?"

"I belong here. My loyalties are here."

Eli rolls his eyes impatiently. "Where are you going with this, Alice?"

"It is not strange to me that a man with a simple mind seeks vengeance, but it *is* strange to me that a man with a simple mind seeks to not only take control of The Mint but also expand his influence to unfamiliar Chinatown. He does not know how business is run nor have the muscle it would take to pull it from the Hills. But you know who does?"

Alister's cheeks flush a bit, and his eyes harden. "If you want to do business like a man, then state your accusations rather than playing around with this mess of words."

I half-grin, but my throat constricts. I could be wrong about this, very wrong, but I persist. Maybe it's Mary rubbing off on me? Perhaps I can be clever too. "I'm not accusing you of anything, but I find this situation odd. There are too many things that don't add up."

Patrick and Eli exchange a look.

I continue, "If your loyalties are here, like you claim, rooting your father out of The Mint is in your best interest and mine."

"She's right," adds Eli, his voice skeptical. He places a hand on Alister's shoulder. "We trust that you have nothing to hide. I'll go along to make sure nothing happens to you."

Alister's mouth turns down. "If you think that's best, I'll do what I can to help."

Alister and Patrick return inside, but Eli remains to observe me with a serious expression. "Don't come around here making claims like that without bringing them up with me first. We trust Alister. He doesn't have a hand in this."

I give his words some thought, then repeat the same thing he said to me with cold precision. "Do you think I owe you a conversation beforehand because we *shared a bed* once?"

His lips curl into a scowl. "This isn't the same thing!"

"It's the same damn thing," I grind out. "I don't ask permission from anyone, certainly not to voice a thought that should have come to your mind long before it came to mine."

He opens his mouth to speak again, but I point to Maggie's car parked on the side of the road. "We'll be waiting out front for you when you're ready."

Maggie, my brother, and I stride away, and once we're far enough, Maggie asks cautiously, "When I left, you and Eli were mad for each other. What happened?"

I roll my eyes. "Not the time or the place, Mags."

At the car Tommy lets loose into a panic. "You can't fight Richard, Alice. He will kill you. Maybe he doesn't have any brains inside that big head, but it is big. His arms too. You cannot fight him. You will die!"

I take him by the shoulders and give him a shake. "I'm handling it, Tommy."

He recoils from me. "NO! There is another way! There's always another way, and if there isn't, I'm fighting in your place."

"You've got a child coming. You're not fighting him."

"Try and stop me."

I grab him by the collar. "Stop, Tommy. Just bloody stop!"

He swallows hard. I release his collar and adjust his shirt, smoothing away invisible wrinkles. "You're not fighting anyone. I need you to live, for our family and for your new one. So, I just want you to watch and listen and maybe learn something. Do you think you can do that?"

I anticipate an ugly altercation. Tommy always has something to say, even if it's just pointless vitriol. But to my surprise, he swallows down any argument rising in his throat and gives me a slow, understanding nod. I back away from him.

Maggie, somehow reading my mind, pulls out a smoke. She lights it and hands it to me. I take the slowest drag possible without drawing breath.

"He's right, you know. There is another way," Maggie says.

I groan audibly. "You too?"

"You can walk away from this. Start life afresh with your family somewhere else. No Mint, no responsibility, no gang."

"Running is always the answer for you, isn't it?"

"I was happy with Mary, happier with her than with my brothers."

"Then why are you here?"

She takes the cigarette from me to take a drag herself. "My brothers didn't believe in me. They deserved me leaving as I did. But you didn't. We always said we'd stick together, no matter what. We promised each other we'd get out of The Mint together. I owe you for doing what I did."

Talking about the past doesn't change the present; all it does is bring up old hurts better forgotten. My gaze drops, and my ribs tighten. "Past is the past."

She inhales deeply. "I'm here now, for what it's worth."

I refrain from snidely reminding her that I'm still wounded, just like Patrick. That at times, I, too, resist crying, remembering how lost I felt without my best friend. She's heard enough of it. She knows she hurt me, and further punishing her isn't going to change anything. I take her hand in mine and squeeze it once.

"It is worth something," I say, and she smiles.

Patrick and Eli exit the front door with Alister behind them. We drive to The Mint, where Ralph is again watching our home in a chair by the door. I get out to scold him but instead shake my head and smile. "You are a creature of habit."

He stands up and grips my shoulders fondly. "I don't want anything happening to this place."

"Get back to the pub," I say. "Let the men know that I have Alister. Word will travel fast. If Richard comes to you for answers, you tell him I'm the only person he needs to ask."

He hums his acquiescence, giving Eli and Patrick a not-so-welcoming glare before heading down the block.

"We used to be mates," says Eli.

"The best of friends," adds Patrick.

"The past isn't the present," I say, unlocking the door. "You're not mates now, so behave." I open the door and wave them inside. "We'll wait here. It won't be long."

Hours pass rather slowly with the eight of us in such a small space and nothing to occupy our time but a few bottles of gin Patrick brought along to ease the tension. I don't go upstairs, fearful I'll dwell too long on Louisa's face the last time I saw her and distract myself from the moment at hand. But I give the boys the option to sleep if they want, all except Tommy. I send him out with a list of connections my father stashed away for emergencies—men and women who owe him a favor— so that if we need the backup, we'll have it.

Mum and Christina sit on the sofa, sorting through old baby clothes, whispering back and forth while Mum occasionally smiles and reaches over to caress Christina's round belly. I try to imagine myself in Christina's place, had things been different. In that life, I would have agreed to marry Eli, and we'd have children now. Little feet scurrying along the floors, making my mum smile that same way. I wouldn't be here, fighting this fight.

But just as a strange sense of longing fills my gut, I shake away any sense of regret. If I'm not fighting this fight, if I'm not the woman who decided this path long ago, I wouldn't be me.

I look away from them and glance around the room. Alister waits with a book in his hand near the stove.

Patrick warms to Maggie, and they drift to the kitchen, where I can see them quietly exchange stories together, reminiscing over lost time. Eli doesn't join them or even attempt to eavesdrop.

He waits with me by the door, watching the misty street outside the windows. "I don't want anything to happen to you."

The words catch me off guard. It's been a long time since Eli and I have been kind to one another. I pull a note out from my overcoat pocket and hand it to him. "Keep this. It's an address. There's a woman there that I helped get away from her abusive husband. She will go back to him if I don't return. Make sure she doesn't."

He stares at the address with a strange look before folding the note and slipping it into his vest pocket. "What would you have me do?"

"Ger her out of here. Anywhere. She'll die if she goes back to him."

He peers at Maggie over his shoulder. "Why not give this to Maggie?"

"I want to trust her," I tell him honestly. "I want to forget everything and move on, but I can't. She says she's here to be a friend to me, but when has anyone ever been a friend to me without wanting something in return?"

A question for myself more than him.

"This woman, who is she to you?"

"Just someone I met."

"A stranger? You want me to save a stranger?"

"Just do it, Eli. Please."

He lets out a deep, weighted sigh and nods, then stares at me too long for comfort. "Tell me something, Alice. This thing with Richard, why are you doing it?"

A brittle laugh escapes my mouth. "You came to me demanding I get my house in order, or have you already forgotten that pleasant conversation?"

"But you could have said no and left these streets behind for good. Stayed uptown with Mary and the girls. Why did you come back? Why even face Richard at all? Is it for your father? Is it for your family? Who is it for?"

"Me." I pick up the half-empty glass of gin I left on the windowsill and take a long drink. "It's for me, Eli." I point to the street. "You think Richard Sloan would have challenged my father like this? Do you think these streets would have questioned him for what I did to Jacob? Never. They wouldn't have done a damn thing because he is a man. But I am a daughter and not a son." I scoff bitterly, thinking about it. "My father, despite raising me in his giant shadow, put Tommy in charge of The Mint before he left for his last score and didn't come home. Tommy sleeps through a storm while I walk outside to face it. At this very moment, little girls are watching through their windows while their fathers prepare for the fight."

"You're doing this for them then? For the little girls of The Mint?"

I don't give him my eyes when I say, "Someone has to show them that men can't just take things from us whenever they please. But no, I'm doing this for myself. The Mint is mine, and tonight I will earn it." I look past him at Maggie. "I have a favor to ask."

"Another one?"

"Bring Maggie back into the family."

"No."

"Tomorrow morning, there will be no Mary Carr and no gang."

He arches a brow. "What did you do?"

I shrug. "She threatened me, and I did not kill her. I consider that growth."

He laughs richly, catching the attention of Patrick and Maggie before they return to their conversation. "She won't come back, and you know that."

"Convince her it's in her best interest and yours."

"How is that?"

"What Mary built isn't new. She's just smarter about it. Arranging fencers and buyers, training girls to stay in certain spots in the city where the coppers are thin. They do all the work, and she gets half their take in exchange for protection and a place to live." I shake my head, considering it more seriously. "Maggie can lead them, and they can take on bigger scores with you and Patrick acting as security and providing the fencers and buyers. I've seen Mary's books. She pulls upward of five thousand pounds in two weeks. Wouldn't you like a taste of that?"

His features shift into awestruck disbelief. "Even if I said yes, they won't work with men. Mary recruits girls on the idea that every man in their life is looking for a way to break them and that she is their freedom from that."

"She's not wrong," I say. "But a partnership is different."

"Isn't she partnered with the McDonald brothers?"

"Supposedly, but I don't know what part they play in all this yet. So far, we have done nothing risky enough to need security." I give it more thought. "Just consider it. Propose it to her."

He exhales. "What about Louisa? She will wonder what happened to you. She will mourn you."

I choke back the emotion daring to break out from the captivity of my throat. "She will mourn, but only because she did not say goodbye. You didn't see her face, Eli. That night I killed Jacob, I lost her. She saw me for what I am."

"And what is that?"

"A monster."

"We are both monsters," he agrees glumly. "We work with the devil in these streets."

"The world made us monsters. My father made me one."

"Your father made me one too."

"Do you hate him for it?"

He shakes his head. "I love him for it. If I didn't become a monster, other monsters would have eaten me up."

I keep watching the street, trying to imagine myself as someone else. Rob asked me, and I couldn't even give him a proper answer. Who am I outside the monster?

Eli grabs a bottle of gin to pour some more. "You know if you die, I die."

"I know."

Ralph emerges from down the street a few minutes later and knocks on the door. Eli opens it with a certain unease.

"He's coming," says Ralph.

CHAPTER THIRTEEN

The streets are cold, but I leave my mink coat hanging over the banister and take a moment to change my clothes, donning the scratchy cotton I've worn most of my life. But my makeup and hair are reminders that Diamond Annie still resides in me, and for a moment I wonder if I can be both.

Maggie places a hand on my shoulder and lets out a staggered breath. "You sure you can do this?"

"No."

"Your father would be proud of you."

I roll my eyes a bit. "What's his admiration if I'm dead?"

She shrugs. "True."

Mum stands up to join me with Christina following behind her, but having them so close to the battle would only leave me unnerved, constantly checking back to assure myself of their safety. "Stay in here, will you?"

Mum's eyes harden. "I'm not missing this, Alice."

"Watch through the window then? You both are something they can use against me . . . especially Christina." I move past Mum and place a hand on Christina's cheek. "You're carrying the future of these streets inside you. No matter what happens . . . stay inside. If everything goes wrong—"

"Run?" Mum finishes my sentence with a smirk. "It will not go wrong." She presses her forehead to mine briefly, then retreats to her spot on the sofa with Christina.

Eli and I walk outside, followed by Alister and Patrick; Tommy jogs up the street in the nick of time. I lean into him. "Any luck?"

He tilts his head a bit. "Not much."

I open my mouth to reply, but the streets catch my attention. I hear no wind, only the soft shuffle of feet rustling along shadowy alleys. Eventually, my challengers move as one into the light of the moon with Richard at their head. I recognize some of the men, but most are new to The Mint. Behind me Ralph brings forward men with weapons bulging from the lining of their coats—older men who wouldn't dare challenge the Diamond rule.

I haven't seen Richard in years, but as he walks forward with no sense of fear—a tall, robust man with scarred biceps the size of my head—I suck in a sharp breath. I can hear my father's voice in my ears, his warning that there are some men we do not cross.

Richard could throw me clear across the street without breaking a sweat. Break my hand with a flick of his wrist. Crush my windpipe if he catches me by the neck. If he gets his hands on me long enough, I'm dead.

My skin grows clammy, and my stance is rigid. I press my lips firmly together to keep them from trembling. What happens if I lose?

What happens to Pearl, to Maggie, to my mother, Louisa, and Tommy?

What happens to the girls that followed Mary? Where will they go if Eli doesn't reach out to them? Will they even follow Maggie?

What will Richard do to The Mint? What will my father do to him when he finds out what happened here?

And in that final silent moment, before words are exchanged and a duel is set in motion, my mind lights up with thoughts of Rob's face. His grin, his scar. The way he laughs.

Maggie jogs up next to Tommy, and they both stand beside me. "I told you," she whispers. "I'm with you."

I close my eyes and try to remember the way my father looked when he faced impossible odds. Was he this terrified? I'd have never known. I remember my mother's voice saying, "You are made of steel," and I think about those little girls watching from their windows right now. I am not fearless, but for them, I must look like it.

"Richard Sloan," I say warmly like we're old pals.

"Alice Diamond."

Alister joins the conversation, briskly moving between us. "Father."

Richard places a hand on his shoulder, his brows pulled together. His voice drops to a low whisper when he asks, "Son, have they hurt you?"

"He's safe with us," cuts in Patrick. "We'd never hurt him. He's good for business. But this—" He waves his hand around. "This isn't good for business. We can still avoid war if we handle this now. A conversation among gentlemen."

The shadows break where men, women, and soot-stained children emerge around us to watch the challenge. Entire families. The pressure tugs at my stomach. How will they fare under new rule?

"The time for conversation has passed," says Richard. "And there are no gentlemen here, Patrick. The Diamond family has abandoned The Mint." He looks at me. "You killed my son because he dared to want your sister. And you broke our laws. You didn't wait for his family to stand witness."

I carefully spin around to make sure I have everyone's eyes on me when I respond in a loud, calm voice. "I killed Jacob because he broke into my home in the middle of the night and put a gun to my head. Not only to hurt me but also to kidnap my sister. I was well within my rights to fight and kill him as I did."

"I witnessed all this," announces Maggie. "I saw the entire thing."

Richard's men look around, exchanging glances, but he doesn't give them time to think about this new information. "Means nothing," he spits out bitterly.

"I'd say it means everything," says Ralph. "She did what anyone would do, and the duel was fair. I saw Jacob start to pull his knife, Alice just had quicker hands." Not entirely true, but Ralph's loyalty is unbreakable, and I make a note to never take advantage of it.

Richard shakes his head furiously. "I don't care if it was fair! Being under the thumb of one family isn't fair. And it stops now. We don't need to bend and scrape to your father or listen to his every word. He thinks staying away from the mobs is the way to live, but we both know full well the profit that comes from being their associates. That's why ya left, isn't it?"

I flinch as his words echo my own to Mary at Charlotte's wedding. Expansion, letting the girls be bold, planning bigger scores. Maggie and I had asked her for more, and she denied us.

Is that what The Mint deserves too? Is that what it wants?

"Alice," cuts in Tommy, rolling up his sleeves. "Let me do this! You know I can take a hit."

"No, Tommy."

"Let me make up for everything. You wouldn't have joined a gang and left the area had it not been for me. This is my fault."

"No," I say, putting my hand on his shoulder. "I need to do this. It needs to be me." I press my forehead to his and gently tug on a lock of his hair.

"I will fight to take us into the new world," continues Richard, shoulders out, head high with unshakable bravado. "No knives, only fists. The winner takes control of The Mint and may expand into whatever neighborhoods we wish. That includes Chinatown."

"You can have Chinatown over my dead body," growls Maggie.

Richard laughs deeply. "How about this? I fight you both. I'm not afraid of two girls. But when I win, I get The Mint and Chinatown. No fights. You take your men and leave." He gives Eli and Patrick a firm glare. "You go quietly."

I expect Eli to step in indignantly at such a brash and insolent assumption about rearranging our territories. Instead, he laughs so profoundly and exuberantly the echoes bounce up and down the street. "You stupid shit," he spits, looking at Maggie with evident pride.

My tense shoulders ease. The Butcher doesn't know what he's done.

Eli strides in front of us both. "We got a deal."

"Sir," interrupts Alister with a cough. "Risking your entire operation on a sister you haven't seen in years is a poor gamble. The numbers don't add up."

Eli cocks his head. "A long time ago, I didn't put enough faith in my sister. I won't make that mistake again. And I'm not gambling on her. I'm gambling on the Reaper."

The men around us start to whisper.

"The Reaper?" Alister looks around confused.

Tommy chuckles behind us, taking out a smoke casually as if he's ready for a show.

"Can I tell you a story, Richard?" Patrick asks lightly as Maggie and I exchange a grin. "You're new enough to these streets that you couldn't possibly know about a fighter they called the Reaper," he continues in a singsong voice, and if I were to close my eyes, I'd see him walking around the Pit taking bets.

I squeeze Maggie's hand once before we separate, and we take slow steps around Richard, caging him. I pull off my coat and hand it to Tommy while the crowd encircles us, their feet light against the ground. Old gas lamps shine from the windows and storefronts, but a mist of darkness clouds the air, making it difficult to see how many are watching the fight. Are there ten or a hundred faces looming around us?

I take over Patrick's story, so Richard's gaze is on me. "My father took me to the underground fights in Lambeth when I was a girl. The fights took place in this den called the Pit. One night I went and saw a man in the Pit who looked just like you, Richard. I said to myself, no one can beat him. He's too big, too strong. He takes one step, and he's got you. But the crowd kept whispering about the Reaper, a fighter that had never lost."

"That's the first night we met," says Eli fondly. "Patrick and I were just boys then, trying to make our way in the world. The Pit was easy money. It was the first time we met your father too, and he showed us how to turn our talents into real money. He changed our lives like he did many here in The Mint." He looks past Richard at his followers, hoping to remind them and make them feel guilty.

Maggie and I continue to circle Richard, and I keep my voice dark and low while uttering, "The Reaper came into the ring, shorter and smaller than the opponent, thin like a stray cat that has to fight for scraps in back alleys. The Reaper dodged every kick and blow—just too fast to be caught. Finally, the brute grew tired of the chase and overstepped. That's when the Reaper came in. Blow after blow, knuckles bruised against his sides and face. The Reaper clawed up his mighty body and twisted around his neck, squeezed his head with her legs until he couldn't breathe."

"Her?" inquires Richard, newly agitated.

"Her," I confirm with a broad smile. "Killed him with her bare thighs. I had never seen a woman kill a man until that night. It was beautiful."

Richard watches Maggie more intently now, positioning himself with his arms out to block an incoming attack. But I detect some disbelief in his pinched expression. How could it be true? This posh-looking woman he's never met—able to kill a man so quickly? If I hadn't seen it, I wouldn't believe it either.

My eyes briefly veer to Maggie. "In Chinatown she is the long-lost sister of the Hill boys. To Mary and the Forty Elephants, she is Mags the Hellion, an expert collector. But here, in the place that truly knows her, she is the Reaper."

Maggie heels off her shoes and tosses them to the side. Richard's expression shifts with unease as if all the pieces are finally clicking into place. He moves away from Maggie and positions himself to come at me first, the weaker one. Smart.

He swings his fist, but I crouch down and charge, using my shoulder to ram his middle until he lets out a breathless gasp. I pummel his abdomen and sides, jabbing until my arms burn. He grabs me by the hair and tosses me onto the sidewalk—a cheap shot.

I stumble a bit and reach for the tender spot at the back of my skull.

With me off the board, he turns to Maggie, who's still walking around him like a circling lioness. He rushes at her full force, and she moves swiftly to avoid his enormous hands. Under him, beside him, all around him, dancing on the tips of her toes. She gets a hit on him, a quick blow to the throat, and he stumbles, choking.

"Follow my lead," she says, and I nod.

We both do the same dance, dodging and moving, a quiet prance that leaves him swiping the air like an angry bear. Furious. He is growling with each swing. He catches me, tosses me to the ground with a painful thud that knocks the wind out of me. Tommy steps in to help me up, but I lift my hand to gesture him back.

My body is aching from the fall, and I feel a sharp sting from a cut above my eye, but I force myself up.

He never catches Maggie.

When she finally has the Butcher exhausted and tripping over himself, she throws a single punch to the chest that knocks the breath out of him. I throw myself into the fray, and together we continue to land hit after hit, the sound of our fists against his flesh reminding me of the sound of the meat tenderizer my mother would use to pound a side of beef in the kitchen.

The pain in my hand is so intense that my knuckles go numb, but I still pound him, and I don't stop, not until he's down on the ground, struggling to breathe.

Even then, we wait for him to move. His men shout at him to get up, to keep fighting. He pushes up a little, then falls back down. Eyes closed, unconscious.

Ralph doesn't cheer or signal our followers to clap. There is no noise from either side, just a quiet understanding of what has happened and what it means for us all.

I look up and manage a half-smile at Maggie, my unspoken thank-you, and she nods back at me, somewhat breathless.

I walk back to Tommy, barely registering the fact that Alister is missing before I feel the cold weight of the barrel of a gun against my temple. "Nobody move!"

"What are you doing!" Eli roars thunderously, and I look him dead in the eyes.

Alister lifts his head at Richard's men, a silent signal, and they each pull out a gun, outnumbering our weapons with bullets.

"So much for a fair battle," I mutter, looking at Tommy, now on his toes in preparation to leap. I shake my head at him, my eyes like daggers.

Alister jeers. "Your father would see this place stay hidden forever, but this is a brave new world, Alice. The men here, the talents of The

Mint . . . imagine what we could do in this city. That is why mobsters come here, begging for our help in their vendettas. The Mint is power."

Maggie makes a face and adds, "So much for not being ambitious."

Alister looks around at the army of eyes surrounding us. All The Mint. "I will lead you all into the sun if you'll let me."

Nobody tells The Mint what to do or who to follow. Perhaps he's right. Maybe we can be more. Maybe my father never asked what The Mint wanted, and that was his mistake.

"Do you want to be more?" I ask aloud, looking around at the men watching and listening. "If it's what you want, I will lead you. We can walk in the sun, bring our talents to the heart of London. But you need to know what comes with it. The commissioner ignores these streets. He believes we are a place beyond help, but if we put ourselves center stage, he will no longer ignore us."

I hear Mary's words in my head and repeat them. "We will be a target."

"Stop talking," demands Alister, pushing the barrel harder against my head.

"I will do what you ask of me," I shout. "I am my father's daughter, and I will serve you as he did. But Alister Sloan will not. He is not loyal to you. He does not care about you, and he does not understand you."

"I will kill you," he utters stridently. "It will be a shame because I can admit that you are unlike any woman I've ever known, but you are still a woman. You cannot go to war in a city run by men. You will fail."

"She won't," interrupts Tommy. "She won't fail."

"Stay out of this," spits Alister. "You are a waste. You're nothing. You slept while your own sister prepared to fight."

His mouth pulls up into a wolfish grin. "Who said I was sleeping? NOW!"

The sound of a deafening explosion leaves my ears ringing. Richard's men are thrown forward, guns flying from their hands while our men scramble to get away from the blast. I try to twist around and snatch the weapon from Alister but stumble forward instead, tripping over my feet and falling to my knees.

I look up, but my vision is just a blur of smoke and bodies.

I reach to claw at my ears, but the ringing grows louder and louder. I need it to stop. I can't think or see anything—my stomach twists in fear. If I can't see the enemy coming, I'm as good as dead.

"Alice!" Two hands reach out for me, then grip me by the shoulders to pull me up. I feel my body swept up in a single fluid motion, and the only thing keeping me from the ground is two firm hands and a voice I'd recognize even in the loudest of rooms.

"Rob?"

"Hell of a fight you put up there. Thought he had you." He sets me down away from the chaos and reaches out to touch my cheek. In a snap, the ringing in my ears quiets. I reach up to hold his hand against my skin, grateful I'm able to touch him again. "Where did you come from?"

He smiles that smile I love.

I shake my head. "Did you and Tommy plan this?"

"Tommy came to me earlier. Kindness between us, remember?"

I search the area for Tommy, who is standing next to Eli and Patrick. All three have Alister in a lock, and I shake my head in absolute amazement.

He wasn't sleeping through the storm. He was watching and listening, just as I asked.

Guilt rocks me. "You said you wanted peace, Rob . . . no more violence. This isn't peace."

"I told you, I'm at peace with you. If I lose you, maybe I go back to war."

With Alister beaten to a pulp, unmoving on the ground, Tommy strides over. "I hope you don't mind that I had a few names of my own. Your list was good though."

I get up to embrace him. "How did you even know about Rob?"

"You think I just let you leave The Mint with no idea where you went or what you were doing? I checked up on you, Alice. You're my sister. I couldn't just let you disappear on me."

I tug him back into me again. "You could have killed us all with that stunt, you know."

He chuckles deeply. "But I didn't, did I?"

Ralph and a few men drag Alister off, then Eli briskly joins us, sweeping a suspicious glare over Rob. "Rob McDonald? Here I thought the Demolitions Man was done playing with fire. Your brothers know you're here?"

"They don't," he declares. "I'd appreciate it if they didn't."

Eli opens his mouth to speak, but Patrick cuts in. "If that is the least we can do for you, then you have our word."

Patrick tugs Eli away, and past them I spot Maggie sauntering toward the pub. Before I can chase after her, Rob bends over and whispers in my ear, "I took care of Mary. He'll raid the warehouse tonight."

I nod, and his warm breath along my neck sends a chill down my spine. If I close my eyes, I can imagine him naked with nothing but the moonlight from his window to illumine his beautiful body. I want him now more than ever but resist the urge.

"Get out of here," I tell him softly. "I don't want anyone else recognizing you. I'll come by soon to thank you properly."

"No," he says with a shake of his head. "You owe me breakfast or dinner. A date, a proper one."

I press my lips together to suppress the grin pulling at my mouth. "A date."

He winks my way before disappearing down the street. When he's gone, I turn and smile again at Tommy, my heart swelling with pride. "I'm proud of you, Tommy. Dad would be proud of you. Maybe you can do more for these streets than I thought."

A hint of emotion flickers in his eyes, but when he clears his throat, his voice is steady. "I thought I might leave The Mint."

"What do you mean?"

"I got a baby coming, a family. I'd like to live long enough to see him—or her—and I think a straight job might be the way to do it."

I shake my head. "You don't do straight jobs."

"Mum can make up some references for me." He looks down at his feet. "I've made a lot of mistakes, but I got time to do right by my new family. I can take Christina and the baby out of here, away from The Mint, and we can start fresh."

Despite everything that's happened, I can't imagine life without him, though I also understand the choice and admire the man he wants to become. But my mind is a mess with worry.

Ralph jogs over to join us, and Tommy quickly changes the subject. "Do you think what Alister said is true? Does The Mint want more?"

"Hard to say," he admits. "The men of these streets do little talking, but I'll do my best to find out for you."

I think for a moment before saying, "Thank you, Ralph."

He points down the street. "Maggie is over at the pub. You should check on her."

I nod and wait for the two of them to head off before leaving the street brawl's settling chaos and hurrying over to the pub. Inside, Maggie is slumped over the bar, and the barmaid is pouring a glass of whiskey for her. I take a seat beside her and thank the barmaid with a nod.

"Richard would have killed me," I say to her softly, "had it not been for you. Thank you for doing it . . . I know you didn't want to."

Her brittle laugh penetrates the still air, and when she looks at me, I expect frustration. Anger. Signs she resented being put in that position. But her eyes are bright, expansive, and strangely inspired. As if through bloodying her fists, she's found herself again. "I love being Mags the Hellion, but I missed the Reaper. God, I missed her. Maybe if you can be both, I can be both."

"Is that what you really want?"

"I think so." She straightens her back and finishes her drink.

Eli and Patrick walk in, and Patrick quickly rushes to Maggie with a wet towel and gauze. He examines her bruised fists, then pulls her away to clean them up. Eli waves the rest of The Mint inside, insists that drinks are on him, and shuffles behind the bar to start pouring in Ralph's absence. Mine is the first drink he makes.

"Gin?"

"Always," I say, clutching the glass with a grin but only taking a small sip. I'm a bloody mess. My body aches from the beating it took, and I just want to lock myself in a room somewhere and sleep until the sun comes up.

"It won't happen again," he says.

"What won't happen?"

He doesn't blink. "I won't keep anything from you again." He lowers his head as he pours, continuing to talk under his breath but just loud enough for me to hear. "You're not with him, are you? Rob? I thought I saw something between you two."

I sort of startle. "You thought you saw something?"

"It can't be true . . . you being with a man from the very family that caused all this."

I want to defend him, explain that Rob isn't what Eli thinks, but I'd be lying. Rob is still working with his brothers. The same brothers that beat Tommy to a pulp. So instead of the truth, I lie to him. "It's not what it looks like."

I still don't know what Rob is to me, so how the hell am I going to explain it to Eli?

Maggie sits back down on the heavy wooden stool beside me and taps the bar to get my attention. "Now what is your plan for Mary? Don't tell me you don't have one because I know you do."

I nod, glad for the excuse to look away from Eli's unnerving stare. "Maybe I don't have one."

"Let me in," she insists. "Have I not proven myself to you?"

I glance down, unable to suppress the wicked smile pulling up the sides of my mouth. I take her by the hand. "Come with me, and I'll show you."

We drive over to the Elephant and park at a safe distance, about a block down. I motion for her to follow me out of the car to watch. In the charcoal light of the early morning, we wait until the coppers show up to raid the warehouse. They pull out goods and boxes, ransacking the place and breaking windows with their large truncheons.

I see Mary coming out, yelling obscenities and struggling as she thrashes and kicks to get away from the officer behind her. Even in the face of apparent defeat, she stands firm, showing no fear while they pull off her velvet coat with mink trim and strip her of her diamond rings. I think about the first time I saw those rings glistening in the club light.

How important I thought she was, making promises of all the things I could have if only I trusted her.

Finally, when she's down to nothing but her slip, they handcuff her.

"What did you do?" Maggie whispers in awe, stock-still. "Without Mary, without the warehouse, the girls won't have anything. The gang is done."

"No," I tell her with certainty. "Mary is done. You and me, we're just getting started."

The nervous set of her shoulders relaxes slightly, and she says, "Where do we go from here?"

"We collect from the grandest party of the year. We go down in history for doing the impossible."

She watches the raid continue. "How?"

"We must recruit someone else. Someone in society. Someone who is the ideal face. The best distraction." I think of Pearl, of the way everyone at Claridge's froze when she waltzed into the hotel. My mind drifts, but my eyes don't sway from the scene at the warehouse. I don't want to miss a second.

"But for now, let's just enjoy the show."

As the coppers drag Mary to their wagon, I catch her eyes and give her a small salute.

Your move.

PART II

Chapter Fourteen

At Pearl's little hideout, I sit on the edge of her bed, mulling over the decision I made and what it means for us. All of us. The gang. The girls. My family. Pearl, who I still must get to New York.

She acted unsurprised when I showed up at her door with Maggie and has remained quiet ever since pouring tea for the three of us, but I can see the heels of her feet bouncing with anticipation from her seat at the table.

I finally break the silence, saying to Mags, "Will the McDonald brothers use their connections to get her out, do you think?"

Maggie shakes her head in response. "I don't know if their influence will work this time. The location of the warehouse has always been a secret. It was meant to be protected by them, but they were nowhere to be found during the raid, which means . . ."

"What does it mean?"

"Maybe it's out of their hands. Mary always said if the coppers ever raided the warehouse, we were done for. That we'd have to rebuild from the ground up. That's why, besides Wal and Wag, only us girls on the inside know its location."

"Or maybe her connection to the brothers isn't what we thought it was. If they were not there to offer protection, maybe that's not what she's paying them for."

"Then what have we been giving her such big percentages for?"

I shake my head. "I don't know, but we'll find out. First things first."

I walk over to Pearl's reticule and fish out the slightly creased, crimson card from Mr. Selfridge and hand it to Maggie. "This is priority number one. We have a collection date."

I look down at Pearl seriously. "If we do this, we will have enough funds to send you to New York and set you up with a new life. The rest we'll use for us. The girls. The Mint. A new gang, a new family." I look at Maggie now. "One that we lead together. No rules, no threats, all ours."

"Ours?" Pearl questions.

"Ours. We'll need your help with this, Pearl."

"Me?" She laughs at the idea. "You can't need my help."

"The guest list alone will be a huge score." I hand the invitation to Pearl. "You're our way in. We do not even have to teach you the trade. You are the distraction. We slip in, collect, and then we all get to start over."

She shakes her head at the idea. "You're going to rob Harry Selfridge? That can't be done. Last year at the same party, he boasted that his store security was so tip-top not even Houdini could escape with a pocketed lipstick."

"I've already worked the store once," I say, and her mouth goes agape. "You what?"

"I don't see why we can't do it again."

Maggie claps enthusiastically, but Pearl grows more frantic. "I can't."

"You're an actress, aren't you?"

"Well . . . yes."

"Then consider this just another show."

Maggie clears her throat. "We will have to be cautious of Mary. If she gets out, she will seek revenge."

I roll my eyes. "I'm not afraid of Mary, and after what you did to Richard Sloan, you shouldn't be either."

"Our differences are why we should fear her," counters Maggie brashly. "We fight our wars in the streets. Our fathers used knives to make their point. Her revenge will be in the darkness when we least expect it. She is smart and calculating, and she will make us pay."

"We can't worry about a revenge plot that may never come. We only have two weeks until that party, so we either decide here and now that we are going to do it, or we walk away and plan something else."

Pearl holds the invitation nervously, considering the idea. "You're saying this is my ticket to New York?"

I take her hands. "Yes, that is what I'm saying."

"Then I'm in." Her voice doesn't shake when she says it.

Maggie studies Pearl, clearly taking her measure and seeing something wanting. "You'd willingly join us knowing what happens if you get caught? You'll lose everything."

She snorts and looks sarcastically around her small flat. "I've already lost everything. If we do this, I take my cut, and I leave England for good. I leave my husband's influence for good. That's all I want."

Maggie paces anxiously. "There are more factors to consider. We don't know Selfridges. We don't understand the building or the staff. We have no idea how even to escape once we have our loot. And there's a new Selfridges detective—a woman, Detective Betts. There was a column about her being the first female store detective in London."

I mull over what she's just told me. There's no way around it— we'd need someone working on the inside to pull this off. A legitimate employee to help us understand what we're up against—someone who'd be the perfect salesgirl—or at least look like one on paper. "I'll get a job there with references doctored by my mother. I'm new enough to the Forty Elephants that I haven't had a photograph passed across Commissioner Horwood's desk yet."

"Selfridges isn't like any job you've ever had, Alice. His standards are difficult, and you will be watched, monitored, and expected to be a perfect employee."

I chuckle a little. "I think I can manage it."

Maggie shakes her head firmly, still unconvinced. "We don't have fencers, and we'll need more trustworthy girls willing to be part of what we're doing. They're not all going to just drop Mary for us, you know."

"We'll go to your brothers, and they will arrange the fencers and buyers."

"No," she says sharply. "What Eli said before the fight was all well and good, but going back to them would make everything I've done pointless."

"We need them."

"Mary's people, we can find them."

"Sure," I agree with little enthusiasm. "But they're not going to give us a fair price. They know we're new to the game and will gouge us. Not just that, they'd always be *her* connections, not ours, and if she finds out what we're planning, she's sure to ruin it before we even get things off the ground. Your brothers will not cheat us. They will take what's fair."

"I don't care about fair," she utters. "I'm not going back to them."

"You care about your pride more than our success?"

"Don't you?"

I try to remain calm when I say, "We pull this off, and there's not a fencer or buyer in London that won't want to work with us. We make the terms. We decide who we want to work with and who we don't. We do this, and we won't ever need to turn to a man again for help. Instead, they will flock to assist us. But we have to prove ourselves first, just like we did in The Mint."

Her fingers curl into tight fists, and several minutes pass while she says nothing. I know what I'm asking of her is difficult, but I don't relent. If we're going to make this happen, we've got to make sacrifices. And as if she can read my mind, her brows arch seriously. "If you get the job at Selfridges, it needs to be our focus. No distractions. If I'm giving up my pride, you're giving him up."

"Who's him?" Pearl cuts in.

I look at her and shake my head. It should be easy to give Maggie the answer she wants. Rob and I haven't known each other long, and aside from our "friendship" and one passionate night together, he's a stranger to me. A McDonald brother with ties to the commissioner.

I have every reason to keep away from him, the least of which is to ensure our score's success. So why can't I give her the answer she wants without hesitation?

Have I let him in? Am I fonder of him than I care to admit?

"He's not a distraction," I lie.

She makes a face. "He's a distraction, and he's a McDonald. Until we understand the extent of Mary's friendship with them, we can't risk anything."

She's making a fair point, but even still, I have to force the word out. "Fine."

We all three exchange a look.

"Does this mean we're in business?" Pearl's eyes shine in a way I've never seen before. They're hopeful, bright, and inspired.

I look at Maggie. "Are we?"

The unease is still there when she says, "This better be worth it."

"It will be."

The staircase to Rob's place creaks and groans beneath my feet with each step. I don't want to say goodbye, but what I want doesn't matter anymore. I asked Maggie to return to her brothers, to damn her pride; the least I can do is stop seeing Rob.

I give the door a single knock. He greets me shirtless with a book in his hand, and I'm taken back to The Mint. The chaos of that bomb going off with his arms firmly around me, sweeping me to safety. The first night we met and every moment after when I swore to myself that I wouldn't let him in, sure I'd ruin him. Why did I let it get this far?

"So they took Mary away?"

I don't answer the question directly and jump right to the point. "I'm planning something with Maggie, and she thinks you're a distraction."

His brows arch, and his mouth turns down. "She's right."

"She is." I continue to gaze at him, down his neck and shoulders, imagining running my fingers along his chest.

"What do you want?"

"It doesn't matter what I want."

"Will it ever matter?"

A tingling ache floods my body, and I shudder thinking about his hands, our lips, the way his skin warms to my touch. I close my eyes to focus, then change the subject quickly. "Do you think your brothers suspect it was you?"

"Maybe," he says honestly, then reaches out and firmly pulls me through the doorway into his body. "But I don't care if they do."

I don't try to resist, at least not physically. We collide together, every nerve in my body coming alive, and for the moment, I can't feel my aching muscles and throbbing hands. Our savory kisses turn possessive, and his lips nip at my collarbone and neck, a desperation in his hands as they pull at my clothes, ripping off my brassiere with ease. I fall on the bed, and he hovers above me, where I catch his eyes for a moment. Just one. His lips part slowly, and he asks, "Is this you saying goodbye, Alice?"

I don't know how to answer him. I don't want things to end between us, but if I pick him, I may lose Maggie and the score. Our plans. I can't have both.

I don't know what to say, so I say nothing. I run my hands down his chest and pull at his pants. He kisses me from my breasts to my stomach, and my body writhes. I let him take me on the bed and then the floor.

As he slips out for his shift downstairs, I wait in the sheets with my head on his pillow. I can hear the traffic outside, the hustle of men and women lining up to get in the club. The music drifts through his window, but my mind is at peace. If I close my eyes, I could sleep until he gets back, but the longer I gaze at my swollen knuckles, the more I think about Maggie and our glorious fight.

How good it felt to have her back, and her visceral disappointment when she agreed to work with her brothers again. She asked one thing of me, and I haven't given it to her yet.

I get up and dress slowly, picking at Rob's clothes and books before letting the music get the best of me. I drift out of his place, down the rickety stairs, and slip in through the "private" entrance, finally getting a good look at Kate's side gig of loose women.

I pass each room slowly, not quite peeking inside but observing enough to know none of these girls are sleeping on threadbare sheets. Just as they're dressed in pearls and satin, passing me with a faint scent of rosy perfume on their necks, their rooms are lushly furnished too. Kate catches me just as I open the door to the club.

Her eyebrows lift a little. "You escaped the warehouse raid? Wonderful. I'm glad you're here. I need to let you go, Alice. I'm putting distance between me and all of Mary's girls . . . including you. It's unfortunate Mary could not protect her house, but I intend to protect mine. If there's nothing else that I can help you with, please leave my club."

"You can help me by keeping your mouth shut," I reply brashly. "I know you told Mary about Rob and me. You stop running your gob about me, and I keep the commissioner from finding out about your little side hustle here." I motion back at the plethora of rooms and men parading in and out; then I spot one who leaves me shuddering.

Harold King.

I take a deep breath and resist the urge to call him out for the scum he is.

Kate stares through hardened eyes. "What makes you think he'd believe you?"

I lean in. "I already gave him one woman he wants. Why not another?"

She pulls her shoulders back, and for a moment, she struggles to find the words. Her mouth just opens, then closes. Her lips thin. "Are you saying that you—"

"I'm just stopping in for a drink," I assure her with a smile. "On the house?"

I slip past her, bouncing on my feet with confidence I can't hide, shutting the door to the brothel behind me and embracing the nightclub air. I lean over the bar and call for Rob, and he happily slips away from shouting customers to flash me his grin. "You shouldn't be here . . . should have heard Kate going on about banning the Elephant girls from the club until the heat dies down."

I reach across the bar, opening my hand. "I want to dance."

He looks at me like I've gone mad, dropping ice into a small whiskey glass. A waitress shuffles past me without a word to grab it. "I can't leave the bar right now. Kate will fire me."

I shake my head. "Look, I don't dance. You take this offer now because you'll never get it again."

His entire face warms red. He gives the other bartender a nod, then walks around to take my hand. I lead him through the crowd of dancing couples, where the air feels warm and stuffy but somehow inviting. We dance the foxtrot, and he never misses a chance to lean in for a quick kiss to my neck.

If this must be goodbye, this is the memory I want to keep burned into my mind.

The next morning, I drive to Chinatown to talk over terms with Eli. We sit stiffly at a table like people barely acquainted, and the tension unnerves me. I explain my plan to him and what I'll need, but he rolls his eyes.

"I'm confused," he finally says. "Is this your plan or is Maggie in it with you? Because she's nowhere to be found." He makes a theatrical show of scanning the room, standing up and walking around with his arms spread wide. "Where is my sister?"

"She doesn't know I came here without her. I want to talk this over with you and get the numbers locked in without childish bickering."

"You don't even have the job yet."

"I'll get the job."

He rubs his palm over his eyes, then down his face, growing flustered with the conversation. "Are you fucking him, Alice?"

I roll my eyes, mocking him with an exaggerated groan. "Fucking men! I talk business, and all you can think about is your cock! Who I sleep with hasn't been your concern since you left The Mint."

He rubs his temple. "I asked you to come with me!"

"To be your wife!" I say furiously, standing up. "Not your partner or your equal, your wife. You asked me to be something you know I can never be. Who I sleep with now has nothing to do with our business arrangement."

He glances around at the few men scattered about the private room who might be listening. Patrick is at the bar nearby mixing himself a drink when he spots Eli's foreboding eyes. He clears his throat. "Let's give them the room, gents."

When it's just us, Eli continues his tirade. "If you're fucking him, you're fucking the McDonald brothers. You're in bed with them. You want fencers and buyers. Why not go to them?"

I stop him by hitting my fist against the table. "Because I ended it," I yell, breathless and exhausted with the topic. "Maggie asked me to."

For a moment there is a quiet tension between us when I think he sees through me. I did not end it with Rob officially. I did not tell him goodbye, and Eli has always been good about catching any unease in my voice. I know when my mother lies; he knows when I do.

But to my relief, he shakes his head and sits back down, letting out a heavy sigh. "Maggie knows what's good for business then. She's just looking out for the score."

I sit down with him. "She's smart, more than you give her credit for. We'll pull this off. We'll make something of this, something bigger than Mary had. But I need your help to do it."

He finishes off the gin in his glass before nodding. "I can make the arrangements to have the goods fenced and line up buyers, but I want thirty percent."

"Twenty."

"Twenty-five."

"Twenty."

He grins, then spits in his hand and reaches out for mine. "Consider it done."

I spit in my own, and we shake on it. "To new beginnings."

For a moment too long, he holds my hand, then pulls away. "And old stories."

Chapter Fifteen

"Posture," commands Pearl, circling me like a hungry bird, ready to feast on the remains of the woman I am to feed the woman I must become. She stands tall, beaming with confidence, checking my shoulders anytime I slump a bit to loosen my muscles. "You need to walk and talk like a lady."

I'm standing in the middle of her flat while Maggie is lounging on the bed, chuckling and sipping tea—thoroughly enjoying the show—and I loathe that I resorted to asking Pearl for help. But with my interview a day away and my dress fitting scheduled with Agatha tomorrow, I need a refresher. Being proper was the least of my concerns running with Mary the last few weeks. In fact, I'd all but thought pretending to be a humble, modest, working-class woman was behind me altogether.

"I am a lady," I tell her. "You should see these curves in a slip." I glance back at Maggie, and she grins. Before I can even snort to myself, Pearl claps her hands in front of my face.

"No!"

I blink, startled. "No what?"

"A lady never laughs at her own jokes . . . in fact, a lady doesn't tell jokes at all. It is always better to say too little than too much. You'll talk yourself right out of this job!"

I groan and reach up to pinch the bridge of my nose, but she pulls my hand down with another resounding, "No!"

"Stop that!" I growl, louder than intended.

She shakes her head with disappointment. "Do not get angry. Your tones must be soft, endearing perhaps, but never brash."

"I have a temper," I admit loosely. "I've never been any good at keeping my mouth shut."

"True," mutters Maggie.

I shift around to glare at her. "Don't you have anything better to do?"

"No," she answers honestly. "This is better than anything I had planned for today."

"You need to change." Pearl finally faces me and crosses her arms over her chest rather seriously. "Alice Diamond isn't going to get hired at Selfridges. Diamond Annie isn't going to get hired at Selfridges. You must become someone else. Someone you might not like . . . a woman you might not want to be."

I consider her words, and my stomach fills with unwelcome anxiety. I try to keep the unease from my voice when I ask, "You want me to be like everyone else?"

Pearl paces a moment before taking a seat beside Maggie on the bed. "You don't have to lose the drive inside you, Alice—the fire that is going to make the impossible, possible. But whatever tricks you used to get hired by my husband—or any of the esteemed toffs before him— are not going to work at Selfridges. Blend in, don't stand out, but show reverence. Appear driven enough to voice thoughts and ideas. I don't think . . ." She pauses for a few moments, and her gaze drops. "I don't think you can do this."

A tingle of fear sweeps down my spine, and I hate that her words, words that shouldn't make me shudder or doubt myself, somehow have. I pull myself together with the deepest breath I can manage, allowing the air to fill my lungs with sweet relief. "I can do this," I say, hoping I sound more certain than I feel.

Pearl frowns. "And if you can't? What if all this is for nothing? And we have no way out . . . I have no way out." All too suddenly, her voice is thick with fear, and I understand that her doubt is deeply fueled by fear of tomorrow. She's given me her life, her hope, and if I let her down, she has no idea what will happen to her.

"We can't think like that," cuts in Maggie, aiming firm glares at the both of us. "We've got one shot at this and no room for failure." She sets down her cup of tea and pushes off the bed to stand between us. She points at Pearl. "You keep teaching her everything you can. You pretended for years to love your husband—if you can do that, you can teach Alice how to pretend to be a lady for a few weeks."

And then she points to me. "You're Alice Diamond. You can do anything."

It's not a pep talk, but it does ease the tension building in my chest.

Maggie places both her hands on her hips and nods as if proud of herself for her short contribution. "Let's get back to work!"

"As long as it takes," I say, standing firm. "Tell me what to do, Pearl, and I'll do it."

With my forged employment papers in hand the following morning, I arrive at Agatha's dress shop with the best smile I can manage given my sleepless night. She needs to believe I'm taking a job to earn an honest income while Mary's away, not that I'm planning something on my own. Maggie claims Agatha has no loyalties, but it's better to be safe than sorry.

She moves hastily and dresses me in a plain but good-quality, two-toned gray dress and hat, flat shoes, and a tragically dull bag to match. I look in the mirror and hardly recognize myself.

Good. I need to be someone else to get this job. I keep Pearl's words in my mind, ever present—it is better to blend in than stand out.

On a cluttered desk, I spot a tube of lipstick—blood red. I don't resist the urge and start to apply it on my lips for a hint of color, but Agatha stops me with a *tsk*. She snatches the lipstick from me and places it back on the desk. "No lipstick. He might sell it in his store but having it on his employees is very different. You need to look to proper."

"Too bad proper means dreary," I say to myself, too loudly, but Agatha overhears my complaint and laughs. I clear my throat. "But if this is what it takes, no lipstick."

"Appearances are everything at Selfridges," she says matter-of-factly. "You need to look classy, but more important, be efficient. My daughter Beth worked there a few seasons back, and she said it was the toughest job she'd ever had. She said Mr. Selfridge came by once a week, and if he saw a speck of dust anywhere, he'd write his initials on the surface with his finger. If it wasn't clean by his next walk-through, people lost their jobs."

I sigh heavily. "How fun. Did Beth get sacked?"

"No." She rolls her eyes at the thought. "She married a Yankee and left for Chicago last year. I couldn't keep that girl still, no matter how hard I tried." She steps back to assess my overall appearance in the full-length mirror in front of us. No emotion is visible in her features that might betray a hint of how she feels about her handiwork. "You'll get the job if you can manage to keep your mouth shut. No guarantee you'll keep it though."

"Agatha?" I ask, and her eyebrows lift in silent reply. "How long has Mary had you on her payroll?"

"Long enough," she answers dispassionately.

"By choice?"

Her eyes shoot up to meet mine, almost defensively. "What do you mean? What are you asking me?"

I step down from the stool in front of the mirror. "This is a nice shop in a respectable area. You seem to have a plethora of honest customers. Mary must pay you a sizable amount to risk doing all this work for the Forty Elephants. Accessory to our endeavors? Should we get caught and the coppers get their hands on Mary's books, they'd see your name and know you've been creating dress patterns with custom pockets for collecting. Is it worth it? What she pays you?"

Her eyes narrow. I'm not careful enough with my words, but I want to know more about her relationship with Mary so that if it isn't what it seems, I can turn her to our side later.

"Haven't you ever heard the saying 'curiosity killed the cat'?"

"Cats have nine lives, don't they?"

"Keep your head down, Alice. Girls that ask too many questions find themselves back on the street in a snap. I've seen it happen before. Curiosity is dangerous." She pauses for a moment before continuing, "How are you faring since Mary's departure? I rarely see one of her girls seeking honest work."

"I was working as a maid before she recruited me. I'm used to going back to straight jobs. It doesn't pay as well, and it's certainly more grueling, but I know how to survive."

She laughs. "I don't doubt it."

I scan the walls near her main worktable. There's a photograph of a youthful woman who has Agatha's eyes and broad forehead. "Is that Beth?"

She doesn't look up when she responds proudly, "No, my other daughter, Dorothy."

"Where is she now?"

"Far away from London. I paid a heavy price to get her into an excellent school in the country. I'll see her for the holidays."

"Heavy price?"

"Curiosity again," she tsk-tsks. "Mary paid for it. The full tuition. All I do now is to work off the debt. When it's finally paid off, I'll be free of your kind."

"My kind?"

"Wicked," she declares before she snips off the last thread from my hem and stands up. "Now you look like a lady . . . but just remember"—she points to her mouth—"keep it shut and play the part."

I give her a fake smile back and catch a cab to Oxford Street with a newfound determination. I must get this job.

I don't have a choice.

I'm Alice Diamond. I can do anything.

Entering the store gives me a delightful flash of déjà vu, and I'm tempted to play the crowd again to see what kind of stash I can collect. But there's no room for mistakes until after the party, and I need to think of the good of the gang, which means keeping my head down until the right moment.

I walk to the lift, where a plump attendant with the rosiest cheeks I've ever seen sweetly asks, "Where to?"

"I'm not quite sure," I tell her. "I'm here for an interview, looking for seasonal employment."

"Floor four, directors offices," she says, shutting the lift. "Pays good, but if you don't mind me saying, you don't look the part. It's pretty girls for the sales floor. Girls like us end up doing things like this."

I blink slowly. "Girls like us?"

"Oh, I didn't mean to insult." She laughs a little nervously. "You're pretty enough to do it. You've just got some dirt under your nails."

I look down at my nails, now aware there is in fact dirt beneath them. A small thing Agatha and I missed during my transformation. "Girls who haven't had it easy in life, you mean, then," I say slowly. "I look like that kind of girl to you?"

She shakes her head vigorously. "I didn't mean it like that. Please, forgive me. I talk too much."

"You don't need to apologize," I insist. "I just didn't think the hardship showed."

"Here we are!" She opens the lift and turns to face me. "Third room on your left. Word of advice, if Miss Waller is doing your interview, ask questions. She doesn't like the quiet ones. They make her nervous and all."

I nod, noting the advice contradicts Agatha's comments about keeping my mouth shut.

"Oh, and miss? Don't tell anyone I told you anything. We're not supposed to disclose things like that. I just feel a little guilty, blurting out what I did before."

I smile to reassure her. "Your secret is safe with me, no insult taken. My hardships have made me who I am. I wouldn't take them back. Dirty fingernails and all." I flash her my nails, and she smiles softly.

"That's a fine way of looking at it."

I walk down the hallway and turn to the room, where the door is wedged open. A group of women stands around in their best dresses. I've always felt confident when putting on a persona for a con, but when I enter the room, I'm struck so suddenly with a fit of nerves that I sink into the nearest chair and search for my breath, somewhere deep in my chest, hiding there like a scared little girl on the first day of school.

There were stakes on every job I've taken before, but none as heavy as the ones I face now.

I force myself to sit calmly just as another woman sits next to me with her shoulders pulled back tight. The competition in the air is thick, building in silence as we discreetly take the measure of each other. All of us want the same thing, and only a handful of us will get it.

I wait—we all wait—for a little over an hour. The clock on the wall marks the maddeningly slow passage of time with loud ticks, and the longer I wait, the more impatient I become. Nobody comes to see us or even peeks in the room to check. Some women leave, short on time, while others sit around huffing with frustration.

Finally, wanting answers, I stand and head for the door. Not to leave. I'm not leaving without a job, but instead to storm up and down the hall until someone, anyone, tells us what on earth is going on.

I grab the doorknob right as someone else twists it open, and I collide with a woman. My papers flutter to the ground, and she is quick to grab them before I can. "Off in a hurry, Miss . . . ?" She pauses and scans my paperwork. "Black? Alice Black?"

I want to snap at her, demand some kind of explanation for keeping us all waiting for hours on end. But Agatha's advice pops into my head again, followed by the memory of the lift attendant immediately marking me as different from the other girls interviewing.

And then Pearl's warning—this position will not be an easy one to land.

"Just off to the powder room to freshen up," I say politely, lifting my voice. "We've been waiting for some time, but I didn't want to miss anything."

The woman before me has a stern face, a thin nose, and short hair. Her lips pinch together, but the expression isn't a frown. More of a disapproving twitch, maybe. "I made you wait because this, my dear, is

Selfridges. Here, the customer is always right, even if the customer needs your undivided attention for hours on end. That's the dedication required for this position." Her voice projects past me to the other women in the room. "This is a test of patience. I'm Miss Waller."

Well, consider my patience tested.

"The fourth-floor powder room is across the way, Miss Black." She scans my papers again, only this time more attentively. After she's done, she looks me up and down skeptically. "Impressive references, but it takes more than that to make the cut at Selfridges. We'll see what you're made of. You'll start today's interviews. Meet me down the hall in my office when you're done."

Chapter Sixteen

I slip inside the powder room to splash water on my face and stare into the mirror until I feel more collected. You can do this. You have to do this. With a loud exhale, I briskly make my way down the hallway, past several doors to Miss Waller's office.

"Miss Black." Miss Waller beckons me to take a seat, and I quickly refocus on the task at hand, spreading a pleasant smile on my face and walking over to the chairs in front of her desk. To my surprise, there's a woman perched on a high stool in the corner, furiously scribbling onto a pocket-sized notepad. She has an athletic frame and a tiny button nose. She's wearing a painfully dull, dark frock, and her plaited hair is pinned up at the nape of her neck; clearly, this woman doesn't care a fig about her looks, aside from her relatively new-looking ankle-strap Mary Janes.

Even Miss Waller is sporting stylish finger waves and a fashionable dress with a Peter Pan collar. But there's something about this other woman—her complete lack of concern over her unfeminine appearance coupled with the unblinking way she stares—that puts me on edge.

"Let's begin," says Miss Waller with a polite cough. "Pearl King is your last reference. The stage actress?" Her mouth makes that reproving little twitch. "You were a lady's maid for the Kings?"

"Yes, I was."

"Why do you want to work here then? This job requires a unique skill set."

I think of Pearl's hour-long bubble baths and how I had to slowly coax her into dressing for the day. "Well, I enjoy ladies' fashion and helping women look their best. It's what I excelled at as Mrs. King's lady's maid. And I've always loved the store. When I found out Mr. Selfridge was hiring extra seasonal help, I didn't want to miss the opportunity."

Something about my words has the woman in the corner peering down at me intently.

Miss Waller nods. "Is there anything I should know that's not here? It's important to be as honest and straightforward as you can."

I swallow down the lump building in my throat. "I handed in my notice to Mr. King before coming here. His wife will speak fondly of me, but I do not believe he will. He is cruel to his wife, and I couldn't stomach it any longer."

The woman in the corner writes something down.

Miss Waller's forehead creases as she examines me with an inscrutable expression. The silence between us stretches to the point that I'm filled with doubt. Maybe honesty was the wrong move. Perhaps I should have just made something up to align with whispered rumors about Pearl's constant drinking and alleged drug use.

"I doubt Mr. King would admit to such a thing, and I didn't want you to speak to him and hear something unfavorable," I continue briskly, trying not to fumble over my words.

Like I threatened to cut this throat with a shard of glass.

"But Mrs. King favored you?"

"She did."

I open my mouth to continue, but she lifts her hand to stop me. "There's no need to explain further. We won't be speaking with Mr. King, and I thank you for your honesty."

I place my hands in my lap and look down demurely, but I'm unable to resist peeking up out of the corner of my eye at the woman, who is still watching me with a strange intensity, scribbling observations in her notepad. Who is she?

The lift attendant said Miss Waller likes questions.

"I beg your pardon, but may I ask why there is a lady in the corner? Will I be interviewing with her as well?"

Miss Waller glances at the woman unenthusiastically and lets out a wry chuckle. "This is Detective Betts. She's our store detective for the season. You'll see her patrolling around the store, observing customers and staff, making sure everything is fine and good."

My heart skips a beat. This must be the new store detective Maggie mentioned.

"Fine and good?"

"She's in charge of preventing theft, which is why she insists on sitting in on all hiring interviews." Her bottom lip twitches. "No matter how much I protest the idea."

I play the fool. "Is theft something we need to be worried about?" I direct the question to Detective Betts, but Miss Waller answers for her.

"It's more of a concern during the holidays. You may have read about a group of female shoplifters, the Forty Elephants, in the papers as of late. They target shops, steal from them, then fence the goods before the police can find them." She waves her hand dismissively, clearly unperturbed. "But I believe theft will be at an ultimate low this year, especially now that their leader is behind bars."

"Yes, I've heard of them," I say, glancing down. "And I saw the article yesterday about the warehouse raid ordered by Commissioner Horwood."

"I can hardly take a gang of moderately successful female hoisters seriously when we have gangsters running rampant. Safeguarding against these women is a waste of resources if you ask me, but Mr. Selfridge wants to take all the precautions he can to prevent anyone from stealing merchandise." Miss Waller glances back at Detective Betts again. "I apologize if her presence has made you uncomfortable."

"Oh, no," I say, keeping my voice even. "If Mr. Selfridge is worried, he has every right to take all the precautions he can."

Detective Betts's eyes move from me to her notepad again. She scribbles something else down. Her silence is the worst. It's hard to read a silent woman.

Miss Waller glances at the clock on the wall behind her. "Clock is ticking! You'll do fine. Hiring isn't the hard part; training is. You must satisfactorily undergo a week of training with a more experienced sales-girl before we let you on the floor by yourself. You'll start tomorrow morning."

I nearly bounced out of my seat. "I'll pass," I say assuredly, forcing my eyes to stay on Miss Waller.

She nods. "Keep up the confidence. You'll need it."

She shakes my hand with finality, and I don't press my luck. I jump up and leave her office immediately, beaming with delight as I scurry back to the lift. When the doors open, I say, "Ground floor, please!"

The attendant gives me an overly excited look. "So how did it go? Good? Miss Waller's a real pain, isn't she?"

"It went brilliantly," I say, chipper. "Back for training tomorrow morning. She was a little tough, but I think Detective Betts is much more intimidating. But I'm told you lift attendants aren't supposed to disclose your opinions on things like that."

She giggles, enjoying the small talk. "Well, we lift operators know everything. All the business that ain't our business. That's why we're supposed to keep quiet with the customers and anyone who comes in looking to be hired. But you're in the family now! Don't worry about our resident store detective. Miss Waller doesn't care for her either. Too quiet."

"Does she talk to anyone? She didn't say a single word during my interview."

"She talks to Commissioner Horwood. Mr. Selfridge hired her through a private company, but he doesn't give her any orders. I'm not entirely certain how it works, but she takes her job very seriously."

I nod pensively. "Sure seems like it."

Back on the first floor, she waves me out. "Enjoy your day. I'll see you tomorrow!" Her voice bridges on hope.

"Sure. I'm Alice Black, by the way."

"Lucille Roth," she says sweetly.

I exit the building and breathe deep, letting the fresh air fill my lungs until I'm delighted and calm. I've got the job. Maybe it'll be absolute hell trying to keep it, but I've got it for now, and that counts for something.

"Alice!" I hear Maggie round the corner in a rush, shuffling past men and women strolling Oxford Street.

"How long have you been waiting?"

"Not long," she tells me. "We have a problem."

"I just got the job," I say with a frustrated snort. "Can it wait until tomorrow? I'd love to enjoy this one moment."

"It's the girls," she says glumly. "I went back to the Elephant to see if I could sway them to join us for the score. The McDonald brothers were there. They said they control the gang now."

"They what?" My voice comes out shrill.

She gives a curt nod. "We have to do this without them."

"No." I shake my head and run my hand through my hair, working out what I can do and what I shouldn't. I shouldn't storm the girls with demands—I don't need to make an enemy out of them. I need to focus on keeping this job, getting all the insight I can into the store, then collecting from it with Maggie and Pearl.

I need to ignore this information, but how can I? The girls are innocent in all this. But more importantly, I ruined their entire world by turning in Mary.

All the muscles tighten in my body, and I swallow away my sense and say, "We're going to see them. Right now!"

At the Elephant and Castle pub, we're greeted by a group of men guarding the front doors. We give them our names and wait for a good few minutes before being escorted inside, where I scan the men drinking around sturdy wooden tables under low lighting. The chatter stops when they see us, and the only sound left in the air is the faint clink of glasses against the tabletops.

I inhale the stale air, tasting the cigar smoke as it fills my nostrils.

"This way," says one man, leading us to a sizable drawing room behind a curtain where Wal and Wag sit opposite each other at a round table, laughing and talking. Wag even looks up and smiles at my entrance. The man who walked us in switches off the gramophone in the corner.

"Alice Diamond," says Wag, shuffling a deck of cards that he quickly puts down. "A pleasure to have you visit. We're so sorry to hear about Mary's unfortunate predicament."

I roll my shoulders back and look around at the place, feeling like everything I've been told is a lie. How the hell did my brother get in here without getting knocked on his arse? "How did Tommy get past all this security and into your private safe? This place is locked down."

"Dressed as a dame," says Wal, not bothering to hide the embarrassment in his flushed cheeks. "The girls said they spotted an unfamiliar face coming back here to clean up but didn't think much of it."

I laugh to myself. "Clever sod. Only Tommy."

"Only Tommy," agrees Wag. "We heard a fascinating story about your nighttime adventure in The Mint. Congratulations are in order. It's rarely, if ever, that we hear about fights involving a female victor—much less two. What can we help you with?"

I get straight to the point. "Maggie here tells me you're under the impression that you run Mary's gang now?"

Wal clears his throat, lifting a brow. "We own the gang now."

"No, you don't."

Wag chuckles under his breath. "You don't understand how this works, do you?"

I throw my arms up. "I'm here to understand. So maybe we talk like men and not like society matrons gossiping at a tea party? Tell me what I don't know because I'm sick of your fucking monologues."

My words strike a chord. A muscle in Wag's neck pulses. "Mary owes us a debt."

"A debt?" Maggie cuts in.

Wal eyes her thoughtfully. "A large one."

"Does everyone in London owe you two money?" I utter harshly. "How much?"

"Ten thousand pounds, with interest."

I try not to choke on my words when I say, "For what exactly?"

"A sum to get her enterprise up and running and various other gambling debts. You see, we need the girls collecting so the debt continues to get paid off. You never wondered why Mary took fifty percent?"

"She said it was for protection, the flats, the food . . . to keep us comfortable."

"It went to us."

My hands tremble. "Half of what the girls earn, on their own, goes toward Mary's debt?" I shake my head. "It goes to you?"

"Yes," confirms Wag. "Now, with Mary gone, we'll take over. The girls get to stay in their homes as they continue to collect, and we still get our cut."

My mouth dries, and my gut tightens as I force out a breath. "No."

Wag stands up. "I don't want any ill will between us, so I'll make you a bargain, Alice. You and your friend here don't owe us anything. Does that work for you?"

"It doesn't. I'm planning a score, and I want the girls involved."

"You're planning a score?" Wal repeats the words slowly, letting me know how seriously he is taking this.

"Maggie Hill and me," I confirm. "It should be very lucrative."

Contrary to Wal's somber visage, Wag looks amused. "How do you intend to fence and sell the goods from this mystery score without Mary?"

"We've acquired help from Maggie's brothers, the Hill boys. They'll provide the fencers and the buyers."

"The Hills?" Wal interjects again, looking to Wag. They exchange a look. "We've been trying to arrange a meeting with them for months."

"For what?" Maggie asks.

"Business." Wag dismisses her question with a wave of his hand.

Maggie gives a curt nod. "You're seeking an alliance with them because your war with the Italians is getting out of control. The more you fight, the more reinforcements Charles Sabini brings to London. You hold power now, but that won't last, will it?"

"You need man power. That's why you came to The Mint," I add, finishing her thoughts, now giving me a new perspective on the motives of Wal and Wag the second they stepped into The Mint and tossed my world upside down.

Wal finally stands alongside Wag. "Those are big thoughts for two little women."

"I am here to talk business," I growl out the words. "Not to decide what I should and shouldn't say because of what's between my legs. So for the sake of saving time, let's be open about what we want. I want the girls. What will it cost me? I can pay Mary's debt in two weeks."

"What score will pay off upward of ten thousand pounds?" asks Wag.

"That's my business, isn't it?"

Again, they exchange a look as if they can read each other's thoughts. "Same terms as before? We get The Mint if you cannot pay the full amount in the agreed-upon time?"

"No, I won't bargain with The Mint, but if I fail, we can talk about allying instead. A profitable friendship."

They both huff at the idea. "Alliance? The reality here is that the arrangement with Mary allowed her interest to be repaid from the goods she fenced while still adding to her ever-increasing debt, and that benefits us. We make more money having them pay it off over time. It's just good business to keep the contract we have and take control of the operation while Mary's away."

"And the girls who are unwillingly part of this bargain? Are they just supposed to trust that you'll take care of them? That you'll be fair?" I ask.

Maggie nods in agreement. "I wouldn't blame them for being wary, especially when they hear about what Mary's been doing to us all this time. But now that you're taking charge, if any of us should dare to ask questions, we'll just be beaten into submission, yeah?"

"We don't do business like that. We are not that kind of men."

I laugh richly. "Says the men who are taking something that isn't theirs and planning to exploit it solely for their own gain. Adding to a debt being paid by girls who had nothing to do with it? How is that not beating them into submission?"

Wag clears his throat. "This isn't up for negotiation. We are keeping the girls."

My entire body overheats, and I feel sweat trickling down the back of my neck as if it's early summer and not the start of winter, but I try not to let my anger get the best of me. I still have time to figure out how to get things lined up after the party. All that matters right now is getting the girls their freedom. I did this to them, the least I can do is try to fix it. And I only have one thing left to use as leverage.

One thing that could hurt them, force them to reason with me, but it's beneath me—something in Mary's playbook. Not mine. I find no honor in blackmail, but we have no future if I don't prevail here. The words taste bitter coming out of my mouth. "I know about Rob and his secret job."

Identical looks of horror spread across their faces. They both shoot up, wildly looking around the room and past the thick curtain to take stock of who heard.

"Everyone out!" they roar as one. "Out! Lock up the pub—we're closing early today. Now!" The men move chaotically, exiting with a swift unease until we are finally alone. No guards. No friends. Just us four.

Wag says in a menacing tone, "I suggest you tread lightly, Alice. Think about your next words."

"I know he appears to be an informant for Commissioner Horwood, but it's a double cross. He would never turn his back on you. It would be a shame for the commissioner to learn the truth about this. It would be even worse for the word to get out that he's a snitch—your allies would question you. Perhaps your entire operation would fall apart."

"You're threatening us?" The words come out of Wag's mouth weighted and slow.

"I didn't want it to come to this, but getting the girls out from under you is all I care about. Let them go, and you'll still have Mary's obligation paid in full, with interest, and then we'll all be free to move beyond this."

"You should know," Wal lets out tensely, "we watch him, our brother, protect him, and we know about the fling you two have been having."

"You care for him," agrees Wag. "I don't believe you'd intentionally endanger him."

He's right. I wouldn't. But he doesn't get to decide whether I'm bluffing or not. I stand tall and fill my words with ice, just like my father told me to do any time a man challenged me.

"Don't think I'm a bleeding heart because of my sex. Richard Sloan and his sons underestimated me. Mary Carr underestimated me. You know what has happened to them as a result."

Wag blinks with disbelief. "Are you implying you had something to do with the warehouse raid?"

I don't let the steel leave my eyes. "Two weeks. Do we have a deal?"

Once more, they look at each other. Several minutes pass with nothing but silence between us until Wag says, "We have a deal."

I shake each of their hands curtly and turn to leave, but Wal has one last thing to say before I go. "Know that this kind of shady business dealing makes us enemies after it's completed."

I let his words roll around in my brain and carefully choose my next move. I turn seamlessly on my heel to face them again. "Mary Carr knew about Rob. She's the one who first used this knowledge as blackmail to get me to take her orders. She had every intention of leveraging it against you in the future. I imagine she had far more vicious intentions. I am not Mary. I don't want anyone to get hurt."

They don't reply.

"But, gentlemen, should you still think me your enemy when this over, feel free to do what you think necessary. The Mint will be ready. And I promise you, the men fighting for me are much stronger than your dandified, gun-wielding guards in fashionable suits. My men are cold, hungry, and driven. A fight with me, with them, will be bloody, and you will lose."

Chapter Seventeen

I send Maggie to inform the girls about what happened and select a few she trusts to meet us back at Pearl's hideaway. Only Rita, Vera, and Evelyn arrive with her, with news that the twins raged at the idea of following any score led by me. We sit scattered about with only the lamplight glow bouncing off the walls to illuminate all our equally troubled features.

"What did you say to the McDonald brothers?" Rita breaks the silence while Pearl passes out glasses of gin. "They said we worked for them now."

"You don't," I reveal. "The McDonald brothers were going to take over our operation and have the girls continue to collect under their leadership, but I arranged for your freedom. For the moment."

"For the moment?" Vera's lips thin.

Rita's questioning eyes look past me to Maggie. "But Mary's been caught before, and they've never done that. They're spooked because of the warehouse raid, aren't they? They think the coppers are going to take us all away next."

Evelyn lets a small cry escape from her mouth but quickly claps a hand over her lips.

"There's more." I clear my throat, mentally preparing myself to deliver the grim news.

Vera gasps. "How can there be more?"

I try to find my voice but can't, so Maggie takes over. "Mary's in pretty deep with the McDonalds. She owes upward of ten thousand pounds, plus interest. The fifty percent cut she took from us? That was being used to pay them off in installments."

"Ten thousand pounds?" Rita repeats the amount over and over again until fury laces her words. "We've been paying off that bitch's debt?"

Vera shakes her head. "We give her fifty percent for protection and connections. You're saying most of that—if not all—goes toward paying them off? And they were going to ensure the gang kept performing as usual so they could keep raking in the money?"

Evelyn drops her gin and scrambles to the ground to clean it up. Maggie is quick to help her, grabbing the glass in one hand and taking Evelyn by the shoulder to calm her with the other. "Breathe. We'll do everything we can to protect you and your daughter. I promise. We're in this together."

Daughter? Evelyn has a daughter? What else don't I know about the girls? A pinch of guilt rocks me. We haven't known each other long, but at the very least, I could have tried better. I could have asked about them.

Mags gives me a pointed look, wanting me to share everything with them. The idea for our score. The plans. Yet still, I resist, all too aware of the repercussions we'll face if Mary were to find out from one of them. She still has resources and connections. She could see this entire thing fail if we're not careful.

"I knew about the debt," admits Evelyn gravely, surprising everyone but Vera. Her features suggest she knew, as well. "I questioned our percentages when I first joined the gang. Vera is good at knowing our merchandise's street value, and I'm good with numbers. The math never worked out right."

"Not once in all the years I've run with her," adds Vera. "Most of the girls don't know any better."

Evelyn nods, a tear sliding down her face. "When I questioned her about her take, she gave Cora's father our location when he got out of prison. We barely escaped with our lives. I've been running from him since Cora was born. Mary told me if I questioned her again, I wouldn't be so lucky."

The news shakes me. I knew Mary was a clever woman and heartless where I was concerned, but how could she put a child at risk?

Vera takes a long drink before clearing her throat and saying, "I've got a sick mother, living outside the city. When I started asking questions, Mary threatened to kill her. She knew where she lived, what illness she had. She knew everything."

"Not to mention the McDonald brothers." Evelyn waves her hand furiously. "Anytime we fall out of line, she uses them to scare us. She made it seem like they were the closest of friends."

"It's not friendship. It's business," I declare.

Rita leans over to Maggie, and the two of them have a brief mumbled exchange. "Maggie told us you two were planning something," she says to me finally.

My shoulders tense, and I glare at Maggie. "She did now?"

I wanted to be sure of where they stood before revealing the details of the score. Vera pulls out a large bag and takes a ledger from it. "This is just one, but I went to the warehouse after the coppers left. Mary keeps her books securely hidden so her networks are still in place when she's let out, and they can't be used against her." She runs her fingers along the edges of the record's pages. "They have everything. Her vendors. Her accomplices. The receipts of every deal she's made and information on all the coppers, delivery drivers, bankers she bribes to look the other way." She shifts from her seat and takes a stand. "We want to join you. We took these ledgers for you."

I shake my head, sure that I'm not hearing her right. "You mean you want in on the job?" I ask. "Not that you want to join *me*." I take the book from her and flip through its pages, reveling because I hold the innermost workings of Mary's operation in the palms of my hands.

"Both. What you're starting, we want in. All three of us. And maybe some of the other girls too, once they hear about it. More girls means a bigger score. There's nothing to lose here."

"There's everything to lose," I correct her, letting out a deep sigh before resting my elbows on my knees. "When someone confronts Mary, the first thing she does is go after that person's loved ones. She threatened my sister when I did not obey. Evelyn, she threatened your life and your daughter's life. Vera, she did the same with your mother. So if you get wrapped up in this with Mags and me, she could make them suffer when she gets out. It's a risk. A colossal risk."

I know I can protect my family regardless of my weak spots—The Mint will make up the difference. Maggie and her brothers can take care of themselves too. But these girls aren't like us.

I think back to when Mary first met with me and told me about the kind of girls she didn't recruit and the kind of girls she did. I go on hastily. "And it won't change the debt she owes. It must be paid. If it isn't, Wal and Wag will come after us. They'll get their cut no matter what."

"Unless . . ." Vera interjects, agitatedly pacing in front of the fireplace. "We pay Mary's debt in full straightaway. If we pay it, we're free of them and her. Nothing owed. We'd finally be able to step out from under their thumbs."

"We'd finally be free," I remark in agreement. "That's the deal I brokered with the brothers. The entire amount paid in two weeks. This score will be big but—"

"Not that big," cuts in Maggie. "We can't completely pay off her debt with it and come out with something for ourselves. Not if all we plan to do is collect from the guests at the party."

"What party?" Vera finally asks with narrowed eyes. "What is this big score you're planning? Maggie didn't tell us much."

I give Maggie the nod she's been waiting for, and she spills it without taking a moment to breathe.

"The party of the year?" Vera repeats the words, each heavier than the next.

"The score of all scores," Rita mutters.

Evelyn's eyes don't leave Maggie's face. "Why not collect from the store then too? If we collect from both . . . we're golden."

"More difficult," I add. "Collecting from the guests will be easy. I got a position as a salesgirl there today. We need to be intimately familiar with the store's layout and the party plans, not to mention the new store detective's habits. It's the only way we have any chance at succeeding."

"You got work at Selfridges?" Pearl finally joins the conversation with an infectious smile. "I shouldn't have doubted you!" She vigorously embraces me as if relieved, startling the other girls.

Rita clears her throat. "I'm sorry, but who is this?" She points to Pearl, and her look of raw confusion spreads to the other girls in the room.

"This is Pearl King," says Maggie.

"The actress?" Vera asks herself, tapping her chin. "I think I saw you in something!"

"Former actress," adds Pearl.

"What part does she play in this?" Rita looks down at the glass of gin but doesn't drink it. "Not to sound cross, but I don't trust rich folks."

"Pearl will help us," says Maggie strongly. "Her part in this is nonnegotiable."

Evelyn shakes her head, cutting off Rita from replying, and says, "All the jewelry on display are fakes, but there is a place that Selfridge keeps the real jewels. Perhaps his office or the office of his accountant?"

My mouth dries up in response. "I *only* want to steal from the crowd because the store detective won't be focusing on the guests' valuables. But she will be on high alert for potential thieves trying to use the party as an opportunity to filch something. I can't even imagine how well guarded the offices will be—if that's even where the real jewels are."

"We could start with a distraction," agrees Maggie, looking me in the eyes. "A bomb, maybe? Like the one set off in The Mint?"

I huff out a laugh. "You're suggesting we set off a bomb? You asked me to break things off with the Demolitions Man, remember?"

Maggie nods in approval. "My brothers can do it. Perhaps not as eloquent, but they'll get the job done. They'll draw everyone outside, which gives us plenty of time to get to the offices and find the safe where the real jewels are kept."

"I suppose you think it will just be wide open for us?"

"We need someone good at opening locked things," says Rita glumly. Another pointed look from Mags. "Anyone come to mind?"

"Ha!" I let out a knee-jerk laugh. "Now you're suggesting we bring Tommy into the fold? After everything he got us into with his safe-cracking and when he's just announced he's going straight?"

"Think about it," she reasons, placing both hands on her hips firmly as if everything is coming together for her and she's irritated that I don't see it. "He's one of the best safe-breakers in London."

I run my hand down my face. If I shed all my worries about the innumerable things that could go wrong, my imagination lays out a scenario that has me practically bouncing on the balls of my feet like a child. But I also know that the odds, even if we can organize everything perfectly, are against us.

Too many people are involved now, and there are too many wild cards to factor in—one of the most important being my brother. "I can't ask Tommy to do that."

"Convince him," urges Maggie. "I agreed to go back to my brothers, didn't I? You can, at the very least, get Tommy on board."

I feel a muscle in my jaw spasm. She has no idea I just threw Rob to the wolves for this. I stand up to face her head-on. "You're not going back to your brothers. I made a deal with Patrick and Eli myself."

"When did you do that?"

"Does it matter when? It's done. I've got the job, your brothers will arrange the fencers, and Pearl here is our ticket in." I motion at her with a careless wave.

Pearl lifts her drink into the air before taking a sip.

Rita's eyes narrow, lips pinched together. "I'm not convinced. Outsiders are dangerous. If the actress gets scared or makes a stupid mistake, she could bring all of us down."

I fold my arms across my chest, unyielding. "She wants this as much as we do. If we pull it off, she'll get a fresh start. She's just as determined as any of us," I say in defense of my friend. "Pearl can be trusted, and she is not to be mistreated. She's had enough of that to last a lifetime."

"Alice," interrupts Pearl sharply. "I can speak for myself."

"Then put down the drink and speak, woman," urges Maggie, reaching out to pull the drink from her hand.

Pearl clears her throat primly. "I can assure you ladies that I want this just as much as you. Alice here saved my life, more than I'd like to admit." Her body goes very still, and her eyes drop. "I owe her this, and I will not fail her."

I feel my mouth turn upward, but before I can get up to properly thank her, she cleans a stray tear off her face and snatches the glass back from Maggie to down the gin.

The girls mull over my words silently until Vera suddenly breaks out into a smile. "We can do this. Together. Then we'll finally be free of everyone trying to control us. Free of Mary and her lies."

"For the first time, we'd get the reward we deserve for our hard work," Evelyn concurs.

I study them cautiously. This is all fun and inspiring to talk about. But doing it means leaving Mary for good, the woman who, despite her faults, gave us all this life. Planning a daring, one-off heist with Maggie and me is one thing, but now these girls want me to be their leader and take Mary's place. I know how to lead The Mint. I know the men and women who live there. I know what they want from me and what they expect me to do.

These girls are not them, but maybe they can be.

Maybe my old family and my new family can be one and the same.

"We want in," Rita repeats, her voice loud, clear, and without a flicker of doubt, as if she can read my thoughts. "This freedom Mary sold us on—it's not freedom at all. We'll work with you and Maggie. A partnership between us all. A new gang."

"It won't be like before," I warn. "Without allying with men like the McDonalds, every thief in the city will think they can step all over us. Break into our homes, steal from our warehouse, do whatever they want to us because we're just women. So long as we don't have the guts to match the violence of men, we will always be at their mercy and disposal."

"We need to change," says Maggie firmly. "I can teach you how to fistfight, and Alice can teach you how to wield a dagger. We can match their violence if we must. We can become their equals. If they challenge us, we'll challenge them right back."

I give her a weary grin. "It sounds so promising when you say it like that, Mags, but the kind of women we would all have to become . . ."

"We'll do it," says Rita.

"Things need to change," agrees Evelyn. "We can change them." She holds up her drink. "A toast to us!"

"To the Forty Elephants!" shouts Rita.

"To Alice Diamond and the Forty Elephants." Maggie's cheer feels barbed, and a cloud passes over my face. I know what she's implying. I took it upon myself to handle the situation with her brothers alone when we had agreed to be equal partners.

Admittedly, I don't know how to share anything with anybody.

If the girls are going to change, I should too.

"To a new world," I finish, and we lightly clink our glasses together. I make eye contact with Maggie before taking a sip. "Together?"

It's my way of apologizing and promising I'll try harder to include her. To trust her.

She rolls her eyes once and then gives me a nod and a wink. "Together."

Later that night, while the other girls sleep sprawled out on blankets on the floor, Pearl and I sit outside on the balcony, sharing a drink and listening to the windy night air thump against the building. We wrap ourselves in blankets to keep warm, and I long for Louisa. On frosty nights we'd watch the snow from our bedroom window. Last year I promised her we'd go this winter to see the city lit up for Christmas and hear Big Ben chime in the new year.

I try to imagine her happy, working at the Savoy, far away from me.

"You've been handling all this well," I say to Pearl, eager to distract myself.

"It's nice to feel wanted . . . to be a part of something. Even if that something is illegal." She wiggles her brows and grins. "You seemed to resist the idea of including your brother."

"It's complicated," I admit wearily. She hands me the half-empty glass, and I take a long swallow.

"Are you worried he won't be able to do it?"

I huff and shake my head. "There's not a safe he can't open. But he's got a wife now and a baby coming. He told me he wanted out of this life."

"But he will do it if you ask him?"

"He will."

She sits back in her chair and tucks her feet beneath her. "You are lucky to have a family that loves you." She looks off into the distance. "My mother loved me. That's why she wanted me to marry Harold. She knew I'd have a better chance of making a life for myself on the stage if I was with him. I didn't find out he was wicked for a long time. When he offered me the chance to trade in my dreary, anonymous life on the farm for the dazzling lights of London, I took it. I left my mother behind to pluck chickens and haul a fruit cart back and forth to the markets every day."

"You were a child. Too young to know any better."

"Too young to know that I was abandoning her?" She shakes her head in dismissal. "I knew what I was doing. Maybe I'd have nothing with her, but at the very least, I'd have love."

"You have friends here," I say immediately. "And I don't use the word lightly. Frankly, I have no clue how to be a friend, much less keep one. My entire life has been about survival, and anyone outside of blood has just been a casualty of that war. But we're in this together now, so I'd like to try."

She takes the glass back with a chuckle and tips it toward me, saying, "To trying."

"To trying."

"America," she daydreams happily. "Perhaps I'll go back to the stage, make a name for myself again in New York."

The image of her somewhere far away from Harold King, blossoming and happy, makes me smile.

"What about you? If we pull this off—and that's a big if—you'll have crowned yourself."

"Crowned?"

"Dethroned Mary. The girls will look to you, and others will flock to join your gang, in awe of this great, impossible score you pulled off."

I press my lips together and give it some thought. "What becomes of me?" I ask softly, more to myself than to her.

But she leans in, intent on answering. "What becomes of you? I knew you were different when you talked me down from that balcony. I've never met a woman so formidable. You will pull this off, Alice."

I stare at her unblinkingly. "You're certain of that?"

She drains the glass. "I'm certain."

Chapter Eighteen

The next morning, Miss Waller has all the recruits line up for examination. I stumble in with a minute to spare and join the rest, all dressed in the same shade as the store's signature green. Miss Waller has a yardstick she's using to correct the girls' posture, commenting on elements of each woman she finds "unflattering" as she goes.

When she stops at me, she gives a long sigh of disappointment. "Dress good, posture good, but hair and makeup? Did you fall out of bed this morning?"

"I can do better," I say, trying not to let her see how much her insult stings. I spent too long chatting with Pearl last night and not nearly long enough resting, but I couldn't stop my mind from racing. I kept thinking of the girls, what I've done to Rob. What happens if I fail?

Miss Waller purses her lips with a nod. "We'll see, won't we?" She claps her hands several times. "Let's start your training. You've got a week or so until Christmas and less than that until the Christmas Eve event. Mr. Selfridge expects the very best for that party. Am I making myself clear?"

Her eyes seem to linger on me.

Together we all say, "Yes, Miss Waller."

The day is anything but slow, yet it still drags. Around every corner is another rule. Each new employee is expected to work a specific department, stationed there for hours until they are familiar with its products, only to get shuffled off to a new station once they finally start to comprehend the previous one.

I know the merchandise, but selling isn't my strong suit, and the more Miss Waller pushes me to dazzle, the deeper my irritation grows.

I keep smiling though, even as my feet ache and my stomach growls. I endure everything thrown my way because I need to find out all I can to give us the best advantage possible.

In the late afternoon, Miss Waller announces a short break for teatime. We can enjoy a quick respite but are due back to our departments in less than fifteen minutes.

After downing a cup of tea and a biscuit, I walk over to the lifts, where Lucille greets me warmly. "Welcome back!"

I smile through the pain of having my feet scrunched into unforgiving pumps. "Joy to be back." I let out a loud, painful groan. "I'm worried I won't be able to feel my feet for days after what Miss Waller's putting them through." I give in and peel off my shoes to spread out my toes.

Lucille clucks sympathetically at how swollen they are. "You know what you need? A smoke." She motions me into the lift.

"A smoke or a drink," I mutter, walking into the lift. "Where are we going?"

"This is the bargain basement," she says brightly. The lift opens to an entirely new world of merchandise—one that's a little more chaotic and designed for the working woman. "I come down here after every paycheck. I can't help myself. But there's a door in the back that leads to a tunnel." The excitement is evident in her voice. "It'll take you right to the Bond Street Tube station. Just a half a mile away past some fencing and lumber piles."

The information is so unbelievable that it takes me a second to process it. "A tunnel? Underground? I've never heard of it." It sounds made up, and I make my skepticism evident in my tone. But in the short time I've known Lucille, her blabbering seems to be honest. She's not the lying type.

She shrugs, lowering her shoulders along with her voice. "It's a private tunnel, still under construction. Mr. Selfridge's secret project. I sneak down to have a quick smoke sometimes when the store madness gets the best of me." She steps out of the lift and motions me to follow her.

The bargain basement isn't open yet, but everything is organized into festive holiday displays. I make my way through the sectioned merchandise, scanning the walls for any sign of a hidden door, confident it won't be precisely as Lucille is describing.

"Here we are," she says, reaching a narrow exit that appears to be locked, but when she reaches for the handle, it swings open with one powerful pull. "Lock's just for show, a warning to keep people out."

Inside, the drafty tunnel air hits me with a cold rush, and my feet sink into the damp earth. I observe the construction, study the interior, and a buoyant sensation fills my body—the inspiration pulling at all the doubt I've been carrying for the last few days. This is it. Our way out with all the goods we can manage, and no one will be the wiser.

My mouth goes agape.

"It's nothing fancy," says Lucille.

No, it is not. It is a forgotten, musky place that Mr. Selfridge isn't ready to stamp his name upon. Fortunately for me, I don't mind getting a little dirty.

"But it's a pleasant place to escape," she continues, handing me a cigarette and lighting her own. "Mr. Selfridge was supposed to finish it last year, but there have been some delays. You got a man?"

The abrupt change in topic has me a bit baffled and caught off guard. I don't know how to answer her question. I don't know what Rob is to me, or if we're even anything at all after what I did to him. "Complicated."

"Ah, those are the best ones." She bats her eyelashes with a playful grin.

"You got one?"

"Complicated. My dad died in the war, left me, my mum, and my two younger brothers. I got a man that wants to marry me, but it means leaving the city and my family. I don't know if I can do it."

Just that information alone makes us alike. I sympathize with her plight, and a feeling of guilt tugs at me because of it. She's a kind woman, for all I know, who doesn't deserve to be lied to.

I clear my throat and quickly change the subject. "How many employees know about this tunnel?"

Lucille shrugs. "I'm not sure. I just stumbled upon it, really." A minute passes, and she hurriedly tosses her cigarette to the ground and grinds it out with her toe. "We better get back. I shouldn't leave my station, and I'm sure Miss Waller will be hunting for you."

I nod in agreement, exiting the tunnel and then the basement, a million thoughts still whirling in my head as I try to plot out how to best use this information for the score.

Once we reach the lift, I pause and push my shoes back on my swollen feet. Lucille enters, but before I can follow her inside, I hear a door open from a small passageway to our left.

I peer down the long hallway.

"What are you doing down here?" The woman's voice is no-nonsense and slightly accusatory. I can barely see her from this distance, but she pulls the door open wider and starts to stride forward. I eye her indignantly, and then my entire body freezes. Detective Betts. I discreetly flap my hand behind me to signal for Lucille to close the lift and leave me to face the consequences alone.

I breathe in and out, relaxing my muscles. Talking about her and observing her is one thing. This is different. I'm interacting with her now.

I don't want to be noticed. I have to blend in.

"Miss Black, is it?"

Shit. She knows my name. My heart kicks up a beat.

I distract her with a question of my own. "You remember my name? How flattering."

"I know all the seasonal hires. What are you doing down here?" she asks again impatiently.

"Miss Waller told us to take a break and explore the store." In my defense, those were her exact words. "Many of the female employees were gushing about the bargain basement. I just wanted to see it for myself."

The lie must be convincing enough because she quickly looks me up and down and adjusts her enormous round glasses. She wasn't wearing them when I first met her. "It's good you're down here. I have a few questions about your references."

"Questions?" I ask without moving.

She walks back to the room, retrieves something, then strolls back to me without missing a beat. She shuffles through some papers in her hand before saying, "Your history is vague, very vague."

"I didn't think to include everything."

"What don't you want us to know about you?" Her voice stays steady and impenetrable, with no sign of emotion for me to read.

I struggle not to betray the clamminess spreading in my feet and riding up my legs. "Nothing, just personal things I didn't think were necessary to mention."

"Hmm." She studies the papers again. "Most of the new employees raved about their personality, their families, all the things that make them the perfect candidate for the sales floor. You leaving yours blank is very curious."

No. Not curious. Curious is bad.

"It's as if you don't want us to know you or remember you. I admit, your story about Mr. King was certainly a hook. Who doesn't love a woman standing up against a man?" She doesn't sound impressed. Instead, she appears to be mocking me. Making a joke of the things I said because she somehow knows I'm not the woman my papers make me out to be.

"I grew up in a dark part of town," I finally say, somewhat breathless, lowering my gaze. "I didn't want where I was born affecting whether or not I got the job."

Still, her features don't change. "I don't believe you."

My shoulders stiffen. "I beg your pardon?"

"There's something about you . . ." she says, her voice trailing off. "I can't put my finger on it, but it demands my attention. My curiosity. My eyes." She tucks my employment papers back into a folder in her hand. "I'll be watching, Miss Black." She motions me off. "I don't want to catch you wandering down here again. Understood?"

"Understood." I barely manage to get the word out before I sidle past her and nearly run to find the stairs. The air feels musty down here, making the sweat trailing down my back unpleasantly chilly. When I finally find the door with a small window overlooking the stairs, I dash through, my feet on fire with each step.

When I get back onto the main sales floor, Miss Waller spots me with a grave expression, snapping her fingers to send me running toward the huddle of women she's directing to new assignments. We are tasked with asking customers what they need and then trying to convince them to purchase things they don't.

The girls who accomplish this will pass their training.

I look around, still feeling like I'm on the edge of nausea. Close to giving in and diving for the nearest powder room, I hear Miss Waller's order, but I'm panicked, looking around for Detective Betts's prying eyes, sure I'm already found out. Every moment now is just bringing her another step closer to discovering my lies, and the anxiety is butchering my confidence.

If she digs too deep and lets her curiosity push her too far, she'll investigate my history too carefully. I've got to end this now before it's too late.

Miss Waller urges us to target a guest looking for something in particular and make the sale. But while I'm on the hunt, I spot Charlotte in the crowd, slipping her fingers into a lipstick display to retrieve a few while the attendant is turned around to look for something she requested.

I glance around, trying to spot the other two supposed to be accompanying her, but find she's alone. I don't know why she's here. She's married, supposedly done with collecting. However, the small amount of kinship I have with her is outweighed by my fear of what will happen if Detective Betts finds out the truth about me.

No score. No new beginning for Pearl or the girls. I fail in every way. I can't let any of them down.

My cheeks burn hot, and a dreadful thought comes to me as I quickly weigh the odds, glancing between Charlotte and Detective Betts. Charlotte snags a pair of silk scarves with ease.

If we're going to pull off our heist, I've got to get Betts's attention off me now. To do that, I've got to give her something—a reason not to suspect me. A reason that shifts the attention to someone else.

I have to betray Charlotte to protect the score.

I brace myself and then swiftly march over to Miss Waller and Detective Betts. "There's a girl over there, a woman. I saw her drop some scarves into her coat."

I see a flicker of doubt in Miss Waller's eyes, but Detective Betts is suddenly on high alert, eyeing the crowd through sharp, narrowed eyes.

"A woman?" Miss Waller asks suspiciously. "You're certain?"

"I'm certain." I turn and point to her as casually as I can. Charlotte hasn't noticed, still focused on dazzling the clerk and keeping him busy with false inquiries. "A few silk scarves and lipsticks."

Miss Waller glances at Detective Betts. "Isn't it your job to look into this?"

Detective Betts takes a moment, a quick one, to look me in the eyes. I show no sense of challenge. "I saw her. I'm certain."

She doesn't blink but nods in response, motioning at two security guards casually pacing back and forth in front of the main entry. She approaches carefully with a dazzling smile to match Charlotte's plastered on her face. A quick exchange of words passes between them, and then after giving a subtle nod, the two guards take hold of Charlotte's arms.

She screams and thrashes, making a scene for the whole store to see. Detective Betts dips into her coat to retrieve the scarf, then orders the men to take Charlotte to her office.

I don't know what will happen now, but Detective Betts gives me one last glance, and I might be mistaken, but it appears humble. A wordless thank-you with her eyes.

I stare at Charlotte's terrified face as the lift doors close, and the shame burns me until my knees grow weak. The crowded store feels like the bomb going off in The Mint—a loud ringing I can't drown out. I tell myself it had to be her or it was going to be me. I had no choice. I had to do it. But the reassurance doesn't help.

I reach out for the nearest counter to steady myself.

Miss Waller apologizes to the nearby shoppers and continues training, somewhat thrown by the moment but still focused on the task at hand. I follow her directions, praying the sweet relief will eventually overpower the guilt.

It never does.

When the day is over, I rush outside, wanting to feel the winter chill on my face. It's early December, but I can already smell the snow in the air.

"Alice?" I hear Detective Betts's voice behind me and jerk around, almost frowning, thinking she'll find a way to pull me back inside for something else.

I need to get away from this place for the night.

"There's a little café down the block, some of the best pastries in London. Do you have time for a cuppa? I'll pay."

I want to say no. Any conversation between us could further her suspicions.

Keeping my distance is best.

But her expression, still firm as she waits for an answer, tells me that saying no might be worse. "Certainly."

The detective orders tea, no milk or sugar, and a chocolate biscuit. I stick to tea, not wanting to give her the idea I'm staying for dinner.

"I fought for this position," she explains in a steady voice. "Edith Smith opened the door for women in the police force, but we're still few and far between and considered a joke by our male colleagues. According to Commissioner Horwood, being stationed in this position is more favorable considering the rise in female theft. The reality is, try as I might to find real police work under his leadership, he'll never be happy with a woman working cases in his city. But if I put away enough thieves during the holiday season . . . maybe he'll change his mind. Maybe I won't have to work for private agencies anymore."

I listen intently, nodding every so often.

"I have files about these women. Notes collected by other detectives, but none of them are incredibly detailed. I've been preoccupied with my reputation and trying to prove myself. Not only to London but to women like Miss Waller, who laughs when a woman is in a man's position because she thinks it means we're oddities, like seeing a duck in a pub. She has this idea that a woman's place in this world should be under a man and that there's nothing wrong with that."

Now I find myself leaning in, eager to listen instead of sip at my tea. How can my enemy be so unexpectedly fascinating?

"She does nothing without Mr. Selfridge's approval. I, on the other hand, sometimes think the less the men in charge know, the better."

Her words change everything. This woman, standing on the opposite side of the law, is not so different from me. She seeks validation, to be taken seriously, to earn her spot among the men who mock her ambition. She's driven, and that makes her dangerous. Very dangerous. But could I turn that danger to my side? I tilt my head a bit, deeply considering whether Betts can be swayed.

Can I use her ambition against her?

"The woman we caught had numerous items in her coat from stores all along the West End. Mr. Selfridge praised my efforts, and he understands now that the threat is still very present."

Your efforts?

"None of that would have happened if it weren't for you."

Much better.

"It was honestly nothing," I insist, trying to keep my voice even and my eyes unwavering. "I was just trying to protect the store. Maybe this arrest will prevent theft. The women seeking to rob the store this holiday season will be too frightened to do it."

She laughs a little, but it doesn't sound genuine. "From what I've seen and read, these women aren't scared of much. I admire their strength and daring, if I'm honest. But I plan to prove to my superiors I'm a force to be taken seriously."

Her eyes are filled with passionate fire. Intimidating and raw.

"You see, with Mary Carr away, the entire city believes the Forty Elephants will just disappear. But I think, with the throne left vacant, there will be a few out to prove themselves."

My stomach weaves together in a tight, unrelenting knot. It's as if she sees right through me. Then suddenly, she shakes her head. "Forgive me for getting carried away. I wanted to thank you, and I hope you'll come to me first if you see anything else. You're very observant. That's a rare quality, and it should be rewarded."

"It was nothing to praise. Honesty shouldn't need a reward." I struggle to keep my voice from wavering. I know why I did what I did. I needed to get Betts off my tail and focused on other things. Other women. But I don't feel good about it, and I wish I could have come up with a better solution. One that didn't involve Charlotte. I don't let any of this show when I smile and say, "If I see anything, you'll be the first to know."

She nods and takes a long sip of her tea. "I also owe you an apology for my accusation earlier. I did find your papers a bit suspicious, given your lack of personal information. But then I considered what I'd write about myself if I wanted employment." She rolls her eyes. "I'd do the same thing you did. Let my experience speak for itself. I'm not the type to linger on fancy words or dress myself up to impress anyone. I didn't come from the poshest of places either. I know all too well the shame that follows someone with a lower-class family or upbringing."

I thank her demurely. I still don't know how to fool her during the Christmas party, but I have a week to figure it out. She has a weakness: she's ambitious, driven. She'll do anything to be taken seriously.

That alone could be useful.

We spend the next hour talking about the store, Miss Waller's brash way of training, and how different London is from the detective's home in Winchester. I even manage to get a laugh out of her when I mention my aching feet—a pain she sympathizes with. When we part ways, she wishes me a marvelous evening, and I do the same.

But when I start down the sidewalk, a heaviness overtakes me. Just last night the girls begged to help me and follow me. I gave them hope. But what I've just done, they won't forgive.

I don't even know if I can forgive myself.

I hurl around the nearest corner, past a milliner's, and feel my entire body shake. My breathing is rapid, out of control. Charlotte's face flashes again and again on a maddening repeat. Not even the city's noises, the hurling omnibus whizzing by or the chatter of street vendors, can distract me.

I'm lost in her eyes—her weak, frightened eyes.

I spend the next few minutes breathing through my nose and out of my mouth, counting to myself. One to ten. One to ten. I feel just as distraught as I did the night I lost Louisa, only I don't have Maggie here to talk me off a ledge. So, I have to talk myself off it.

I had to do it to protect the rest of the girls, to protect the score. I had to distract Detective Betts, gain her trust. There was only one way to do that.

There was only one way.

One way.

Back at The Mint, I look for Tommy but find my mother alone in the house, cleaning up after a session. I let out a massive exasperated sigh. "Tommy gone?"

"Took Christina to dinner. Should be back tonight." She looks me up and down. "Something wrong?"

I avoid her eyes. "Everything is right. I got the job at Selfridges . . . I earned the trust of the store detective on duty. Everything is right, but I feel so wrong." The thickness in my throat grows unbearable.

My mother reaches up for me, taking me by the shoulders. "Sit down. Tell me about it."

"How about you read my palm?" I grin through the shame, taking a seat at her table. I close my eyes and see her face again. Charlotte's. Then Louisa's. All the innocent women who have suffered because of me. How many more faces will I add to their number?

"We haven't talked since before your fight with Richard Sloan," she says gently. "You did well, Alice. I know you think I've always favored Tommy, but I'm proud of you too."

"You *have* always favored him," I counter automatically. "But we've all got a soft spot for Tommy, despite his many, many flaws. After the fight with Richard, he said he wants to get out of this life for the sake of Christina and the baby." I feel a pang in my chest. "But I came here to ask him to do one last job."

"It's the least he can do," she reasons, still clutching my hands. "So why the long face? What's going on in that head of yours? People come here to talk, and I listen. Tell me."

I rest my head on her shoulder and let her have it. What I did to Mary, how I gave up Rob, Selfridges, the McDonalds, the score, and finally, Charlotte. When I'm done, I realize how distant she's been from all this. In a way, I'm grateful she's safe from it, but another part of me longs for her guidance.

I choke up a bit but clear my throat quickly. "But it's like you said, Mum—I am made of steel. I must do things other women don't and live with it. And I had to do it. Didn't I?"

She says nothing for a long time until the silence grows unnerving. "Mum, are you going to say something?"

"Yes," she answers. "That'll be two shillings."

I manage a laugh, and she smiles back, taking me by the cheeks. "The Mint was forced on you. The weight of these girls was not. You didn't have to help them, and you don't have to lead them."

"I want to," I say aloud, and it feels good to own it. "If I can lead The Mint, I can lead them. But I had to earn it in The Mint, now I need to earn it with the girls."

She releases my hands. "Well, then it sounds like you had to do what you did. Charlotte will haunt you, but there are casualties in any war."

I consider it more, then ask, "Have you heard from Louisa?"

"Not in a while," she admits. "You should go see her before this grand score. I have faith in you. After Richard Sloan, I am certain you can survive anything. But you'd have regrets if something happened and you didn't see her."

"I think she's already gone when it comes to me," I admit weakly.

Before she can reply, Tommy walks through the door, arm in arm with his wife. "Alice?" His voice is light, happy, until he studies my face a bit longer. "Eh, everything all right?"

I blink hard to keep the tears at bay, promptly scrubbing my face and standing. "Yes, but I have a favor to ask you."

"Anything," he says, removing his gloves.

"Can we talk in private?"

We head upstairs and sit by the windowsill to share a smoke. I tell him of my plans for the Selfridges heist and follow it up with, "The girls believe it's an imported Mosler safe. Mr. Selfridge is known to be partial to them. I don't know where it is yet. We assume his office."

His eyes widen significantly. "The safe that can't be opened. The whole world knows that."

"There isn't a safe you can't open, Tommy Diamond. And think about it—the funds alone from this score will set you and Christina up well. You can leave London, start anew in a nice big house in the country and raise chickens."

He laughs at the idea, but his expression is somber. "It's risky, Alice. If something happens, Christina will be left alone. That's the whole reason why I want out."

"I promise nothing will happen. I got a job there, so I'll know the place inside and out when the time comes. We won't have a problem getting out. You're just opening another safe, loading the contents into a bag, and leaving as a rich man."

"No fucking way. You got a job at Selfridges?"

I smile proudly.

Still, he hesitates. Tommy has never been shy when it comes to pursuing big scores, and the fact that he's unsure now lets me know how serious he is about turning over a new leaf and becoming a better man for his family. The guilt continues to gnaw at me, and I start to wonder if we can pull the heist off without him. A light rain starts outside, small drops of water slipping down the windowpanes. Just as I'm about to open my mouth and recant everything I've said, he slaps his knees.

"I'm in," he says confidently. "There's no lock I can't break . . . dare I say it, not even one belonging to Mr. Selfridge himself."

I take a deep breath and pull him in to press my forehead against his. "Thank you, Tommy."

"Don't thank me, Alice. I owe you this. I owe more than this, but it's a start."

The sound of someone pounding at the front door cuts our conversation short. We both rush down the stairs to a frantic Maggie. "Pearl's gone."

"What do you mean, gone?"

She throws her hands in the air. "Gone! I went out to see if I could convince more of the girls to join us, and when I got back, I saw her fighting with a man in the street. Before I could get close enough, he threw her into his car and drove off."

Chapter Nineteen

Maggie waits in the car outside the King town house while I slip out and walk up to the door. I knock once, twice, and then finally, a gloomy-looking Alba answers.

"I just came to see Pearl," I tell her.

Alba glances behind her shoulder nervously. "You best be getting out of here."

She tries to shut the door, but I swiftly stick out my foot. I note a drop of blood on the cuff of her sleeve, and a sense of panic overwhelms me. "You tell me where she is now, or I slam this door into your face on my way in."

She hesitates, clearing her throat quietly. "A hospital near Camden Town. She had an accident." Her voice shakes some, giving more away than I believe she intended. "But it wasn't an accident . . . He brought her back home. She kept trying to leave and he got angry." Another tremor in her voice. "She's in awful shape."

My heart sinks. I open my mouth, but nothing comes out.

"You stupid girl." She spits out the words with a growl. "You thought you could win against a man like that? You need to go, Alice. I told you where she is."

I push on the door with my foot, my bottom lip trembling with a bitter fury. "Is he in there right now?"

"No, he's by her side to ensure she goes home with him. I don't know why you're surprised." She gives me a look that suggests I'm daft. "It's no secret that the day you started working here, she suddenly fought with him more. You made her believe she has the power to make her own choices, to decide when she's had enough." A low huff escapes her mouth. "If there's anyone to blame for her current state, it's you."

I laugh cruelly. "You'd rather I'd been like you? Watch him beat her black and blue and then pretend nothing ever happened?"

"I have a family," she says without remorse. "I need this job. Forgive me for choosing them over a spoiled little rich bitch with no sense of the real world. She knew exactly what to say to make him lose his temper, and she did it every time. She never learned. Maybe now, she will."

I can't get another word in before she slams the door, and I hear the lock click.

A swell of anger rises in my throat, threatening to choke me as I return to the street. Maggie gets out of the car to meet me. "What happened?"

I knew there was always the possibility that Harold would find her, but I allowed myself to think otherwise. Maggie reaches out for my shoulders, and her firm grip helps me keep my balance. "Alice?"

"We need to make one more stop." My voice is breathless, uneven, nearly hysterical. "Camden Town. The hospital."

We arrive at the hospital in record time. Maggie parks and follows me inside through the large doors. The air smells of freshly laundered towels and death. I ask the nearest nurse for Pearl's room, and she points me to the private ward, down a long corridor with mahogany-paneled walls scraped from trolleys bumping into them.

Even as we enter the ward, rich with the smell of perfume and fresh flowers, I find no comfort in the money spent to treat patients of higher status. The sum Harold paid for her comfortable stay is just blood money, feeding the doctors and nurses the idea he genuinely loves his wife and would never harm a bone in her body.

I push myself to walk to Pearl's bed and take her hand. Her eyes are bruised and swollen, and there is a wide gash on her chin, likely from the signet ring on his finger cutting into her jaw. Her nose is broken, disfigured in a way that makes me feel terrible for not remembering how it looked before.

This image of her, beaten and broken, will remain with me forever.

Maggie arrives through the door shortly after me, her face long with surprise. She rushes toward Pearl to take her other hand, trembling with fury. "He did this. Her husband?"

"He did this," I confirm without a doubt.

Maggie's brows knit together, and then her gaze is drawn past me. I hear heavy feet slowly stride in behind me. I don't need to hear his voice to know it's him. Harold King.

He stands with a fresh bouquet in hand, and he's decked out in a tailored three-piece suit. Not a drop of blood on him. "Well, if it isn't our long-lost maid." He lifts his arm to tap the tender spot beneath his clothing where I cut him. "I still remember your parting gift."

"I know you did this, you bastard!" Fire consumes me, and I lunge at him. Maggie stops me with a forceful push. I feel her hands against my chest, knocking the wind out of me.

"Don't," she warns in a voice too low for Harold to hear.

Harold sighs heavily in response, but the remorse doesn't reach his eyes. "It's a shame what happened. A motorcar just hit her last night, sent her clear across the street before speeding off. I've alerted the authorities, and they're on the hunt for the man—or woman—who did it. Not to worry, justice will be served." I don't realize I'm crying until I feel a tear slide down my cheek, betraying me in front of him. I'm quick to clean it off with the back of my hand.

"Justice will be served," I agree, my voice heavy and loud. "You can be damn sure."

A scowl creases his face. "I admire your passion, little maid. But I think you'll be a happier woman when you realize you're nothing in this world without a man. We have all the power. What we give, we can take."

"You think you have power? You know nothing of power," I say, so coldly that the sound of my voice startles me. Does it even belong to me? Or does it belong to the beast inside me? I didn't want to hurt Richard Sloan. I had to.

I want to hurt Harold King. I want him dead. I want his blood on my hands. "You will regret this."

"My wife learned her lesson the hard way. I'd hate for you to have to endure the same method of tutelage."

I fight Maggie's hold on me, desperate to hurt him.

"Let's go," says Maggie, refusing to let go of my arm. "Let's go now, Alice."

She drags me into the hall and back outside. When we reach the car, I yell, "You shouldn't have stopped me. I wanted him to hurt. I wanted him to bleed."

I pause, somewhat taken aback by how strongly the words flew out of my mouth without hesitation.

"Get in the car," she orders, and I stubbornly take my time slipping into the passenger seat.

She doesn't look at me when she says, "You don't beat a man like Harold King by attacking him in a hospital. He's a gentleman with a lot of influence. He'd call you mad, and they'd lock you up before you had time to blink. No score. No girls. No nothing." She shakes her head, a flush of emotion turning her cheeks red. "You take a man like that down with a gun, a knife, just like you would a rabid animal. You hunt him when he's alone. You make sure nobody sees. We will take care of Harold King together. But now is not the time. We need to focus on the score. Not just for us, but for Pearl too. She was our way in, and now we're without an invitation."

I know only one other person who might have gotten invited to the party of the year. "Maybe we ask Kate Meyrick? She must be invited. She's made quite the name for herself. Although, our last conversation wasn't the most pleasant."

"What did you do?"

I shake my head. "It's not important."

"We can ask," agrees Maggie. "But she'll have a price."

"Everyone does," I mutter.

"We're also down a girl without Pearl. She was going to be our face. I was going to teach her how to collect this next week, show her the ropes," adds Maggie. "We need as many girls as we can get. Perhaps I'll ask Charlotte! She never wanted to leave the gang. Mary forced her to after her marriage. She'd gladly join us, and we already know we work well with her."

I knew it would come up. Eventually. I was just hoping it would be after the score. We already have so much going against us, and I don't want any turmoil with Maggie.

But I don't have a choice anymore. A moment passes as I struggle to find the words. The right thing to say. Is there even a right thing?

"Something happened," I say, swallowing over the lump in my throat. "Detective Betts suspected me from day one. I don't know if it was my interview or my references, but she made it clear she was going to be watching me."

Her eyebrows lift a little. "Where are you going with this?"

"Charlotte was at Selfridges. I saw her stealing and told Detective Betts. She had her arrested."

Her mouth falls open.

"I had to do it, Maggie. I had to take the suspicion off me so we would stand a better chance."

"You turned her in?" She gets out of the car quickly as if she can't stand the sight of me.

I get out with her, and my instincts turn flighty. I'm riddled with guilt and fear. How am I ever going to convince her to forgive me? "What would you have done?"

"Anything else," she grinds out. "Maybe she meant nothing to you, but I've known her for years. She was kind to you, and most important, she was my friend."

I nod, taking all the insults she hurls at me because I know she needs to let it out. "Look, I didn't do it lightly, and the guilt has been eating away at me ever since. But I didn't see another way. This woman, Detective Betts, she's serious. She's smart. She'd have found me out if I didn't give her reason to trust me instead."

She shakes her head in response with a look of pure disgust. "And you know why she trusts you now? Because she can't fathom that you'd turn in one of your own. Nobody is that callous."

I splutter indignantly, but she carries on. "Would you do the same to me? If betraying me was for your benefit? You say we are in this together, but every step you take is on your own. You only know how to be alone!"

"You are right." I emphasize the three words as strongly as I can. "I've been at it alone a long time, Mags, and I feel like I can only count on myself. I don't like what I did, but I did it for you and Pearl and the girls, who are all depending on us to pull this off. I did it for us. I don't want to be the person to decide these things, but someone has to be." I repeat my mother's words. "Charlotte was a casualty of war."

"What war?" She lifts her arms in a fury. "If I am to go into battle with you, at least tell me who I'm fighting!"

"Everyone!" I yell back, matching her fury. "Men like Harold King who break women for sport. Women like Mary who manipulate poor and desperate girls to their advantage. The McDonald brothers seeking to control us. Richard and Alister. Your brothers, who never saw you as anything more than a circus sideshow that brought in some cash. This whole bloody world! It is us against everyone."

Maggie takes a deep breath and holds her head, tears trickling down her face. My heart pounds as I take a step forward, nearly choking on my words as I continue, "I have done terrible things to protect my family, and if you think I will not do the same for you, for what we're trying to do together, then you haven't been paying attention."

Her fingers ball into fists as she debates my words. Even if they make all the sense in the world to her, it doesn't change what happened. It doesn't change that Charlotte meant something to her and that she was kind to me. She didn't deserve what happened to her, and nothing I say will change that.

"I need some time alone," she says, but it sounds more like *time away from you*. "I'll meet you back at Pearl's place later. Evelyn and Rita want to go over the plan again and get Tommy up to speed on his part in all of it. Now that we've sacrificed things—people—the sacrifices must be worth it."

I nod slowly. "I agree."

She starts toward the car door but stops. "No more secrets, Alice."

I have more secrets. I am made of secrets. But for the sake of peace, I say, "No more."

"I mean it. I'll be done for good otherwise."

"No more secrets."

In the morning Maggie is still distant, but she agrees to come with me to talk to Kate tonight and see if we can strike a deal with her.

For now, I report to Selfridges, where Miss Waller has all the recent hires gather in the library for a discussion about the upcoming Christmas Eve party. Everyone chatters excitedly while I look at them in dumbfounded awe. I just barely survived our training period, but they all seem to be flourishing. Aside from Lucille, I've made no other friendships. I've been too preoccupied to even consider it, which isn't wise.

Being the outcast means I bring more attention to myself. The isolated one is always the suspicious one. That's why we run in packs when we collect. I've got Detective Betts off my back for now, but nothing will stop her from suspecting me again later.

I need to socialize.

I walk across the library toward a group of girls chatting. I join the conversation just as one of them says, "You hear there will be celebrities at the party? The biggest social event of the year."

The one speaking notes my appearance. "Oh, hello, Alison, is it?"

"Alice," I correct her.

"I'm Patricia," she says. "This is Kathy and Renee."

I look at them both. "Sorry, we weren't introduced sooner."

"Miss Waller's been hard on you," observes Kathy. "We all had a bet you'd throw in the towel by now. I would have."

I smile. "I've worked for worse than Miss Waller." I try not to consider Harold for too long. "The pay is good, and as you said, this is the biggest event of the year. Who wouldn't be honored to be a part of it?"

"I'm only in it for the food," reveals Renee with a blush. "My cousin worked here last year. She said every year before the party, Mr. Selfridge treats his employees to a huge Christmas dinner. That's also when he gives out the bonuses. I know you're a new hire, but all employees are invited."

I nod slowly. "That seems delightful." But I can't go, even if it would add to the part I'm playing. There's too much to do to prepare for the score, and I'd feel guilty having just a moment of fun. "What a generous man. Have any of you ever met him?"

"No," says Kathy. "We'll see him at the party though. Likely with a new youthful beauty from the stage. He's always got a starlet on his arm."

"It's quite scandalous," confirms Patricia with a grin. "But I can't say I'd refuse the attention if he looked my way."

Renee slaps her shoulder playfully. "You have no shame!"

Miss Waller walks into the room minutes later and clears her throat. "As most of you know, in less than a week, Mr. Selfridge is hosting his famous Christmas Eve party here. The guests are handpicked and will get a first look at some of the latest designer fashions and the newest gadgets from inventors all over the world. Some of you will work on the sales floor while others will handle refreshments. This includes drinks and food, and assuring the guests are comfortable at the event."

I let out a deep breath. Essentially the same thing I did at the 43 Club but in a less scandalous outfit. A small sense of relief fills me as I consider it. It will be easier to direct the girls if I'm wandering the crowd instead of stationed at a fixed department.

Miss Waller goes on, emphasizing the importance of the party and that we all understand our jobs and don't let our attention waver, even with all the distractions that will surround us. Finally, she reads off the list of those who will be stationed at each department and those who will be acting as servers. I wait with my toes curled into my shoes for her to say my name. But she never does, finishing the list and tucking the paper away.

"Let's get back to work, ladies," she says promptly.

"Excuse me, Miss Waller. I didn't hear my name."

"That's because I didn't call it, Miss Black."

I blink, then shake my head. "Are you tossing me? I'm doing my best."

"Stop, Miss Black," she says with irritation, lifting her hand in front of me. "I'm not firing you. It seems you left quite the impression on Detective Betts, and she has requested you have a special role at Mr. Selfridge's event. Now before you ask, I don't have the faintest clue what it is. She went over my head to do it."

"I was hired for the shop floor," I say, confused.

Miss Waller shrugs. "Detective Betts's job is to be on the lookout for shoplifters, a serious job and far more important than the sales floor. Betts has never taken on an apprentice before."

I have to keep my mouth from going agape. "Apprentice?"

"That's my assumption. I wouldn't know, though, because she thinks she's above the order of things around here." She rolls her eyes and runs her hands down her sides. "Just tolerate her throughout the party. Do as she asks. When it's over, I'll find you a regular position on the shop floor so you can stay on with us. You've worked hard for it. Don't think I'm not acknowledging that."

I open my mouth to reply, a polite thank-you for what feels like a compliment, but she's quick to snap out her next words. "Now, go. Detective Betts is on the roof last I heard, strolling the pleasure gardens. See what she wants. Don't forget your coat."

The lift doors open to the serene garden air. During the summer, the rooftop is supposedly busy with a tea service and exclusive garden parties for special guests. I've heard rumors of extravagant fashion shows that draw all of society. It's hard to imagine it in the dead of winter though. Snow rests upon most of the benches, and the garden is just sad-looking patches of barren stalks. No wonder the roof is closed this time of year. Winter hardly does it justice.

She's strolling down the long cobblestone path and staring out at the gray sky, looking curiously at peace as if this gloomy, quiet place is her sanctuary. I pull my coat around my body tightly and scurry to meet her. "Miss Waller says you have a job for me," I say, wanting to get to the point so I can get back inside.

Without looking at me, she leans against a nearby pillar. "When I was a girl, I saw a woman rob a watchmaker. The police asked for a sketch of her face, and I gave it to them. They told me I'd be a great detective one day. They weren't serious." She laughs to herself. "They were just sweet to me, but I took it to heart. I fought for years for the chance. Catching thieves is what I settled for, and up until the other day, I thought I was pretty damn good at it."

My upper lip twitches in response. *Collectors*. We prefer the term *collectors*. "And you want me to do it with you?"

She turns to face me, burying her hands into her coat pockets. "You saw something I didn't, and I've got so much pressure on me to prove myself to those who don't think I'm capable. An extra set of eyes can't hurt. I'm not too prideful to ask for help when I need it."

She just keeps getting more admirable with each conversation. How are we so alike and so different at the same time?

I play like I don't know what she's talking about. "What gives you the idea I'll be any good at spotting them? It was just luck with that woman before. I was hired for the shop floor."

"Yet you don't look like you particularly enjoy the shop floor. This could be a bit more exciting and give you a chance to stay with the company after the season ends."

I want to refuse her because I don't want to be closer to her than I already am. She's good at noticing details and picking up on the tiniest cues. But the more I consider it, the more attracted to the idea I am. I can steer her clear of Maggie and the girls—keep her distracted with someone else. If I'm able to earn her trust, truly, there will be nothing standing in our way.

"It would be a little more exciting," I admit. "But I don't want to disappoint."

"I don't need you to be an expert overnight. I just need extra eyes."

Denying her would be suspicious. I'm playing the part of a woman in the working world who should be delighted with the offer of more. I force my mouth to curve into a convincing smile. "When do we get started?"

She responds with a grin. "How about now?"

CHAPTER TWENTY

The detective takes me to the main floor to observe the bustling crowds of last-minute shoppers buying gifts and gawking at the elaborate displays. All the salesgirls are busy speaking with customers, cheerily making recommendations, and answering dull questions. It's all a song and dance, and I'm thrilled to be away from it for the time being. There's only so much "playing nice" I can do before the cracks show.

"Now from what I've gathered, the Elephants run in packs of three," she says, leaving me suddenly unnerved. "One stays near the door to keep watch, while the other two enter the shop. The girl near the counter is always pretty, a face that grabs everyone's attention while the other girl, the talented one, wanders the store and pockets what she can."

I laugh nervously. "You are good."

She rolls her eyes dismissively. "Observation is not a talent. I see what anyone else would if they looked close enough. Now look closely."

I nod slowly, gazing at the crowd, looking for any collectors I might know. "I don't see anything suspicious. Or rather, anyone." No one is standing near the door, silently communicating with a girl at the counter—nobody in the crowd warrants suspicion. Though I'll admit, I'm not trying particularly hard, and I'm confident after word of Charlotte's capture spreads, none of the girls would be foolish enough to collect from here.

"It looks like a safe shopping day," I say aloud.

The detective studies the crowds and places her hands behind her back. "For now. The Forty Elephants never work alone. That's where their strength lies, in working together. Mary Carr instilled these beliefs in them for a reason. They may not always be close to one another, but their eyes always seek each other out. The first rule isn't about getting the goods. It's about taking care of each other. They create these bonds, you know. Unbreakable." She says it with no emotion as if she's talking about packs of lions hunting on the savanna.

I gather my voice. "How do you know all this?"

She's supposed to be new to London and therefore less likely to understand us.

"Commissioner Horwood gave me his notes on them, spare as they were. I studied them fiercely. We have caught Mary Carr on numerous occasions, but the courts never sentence her. I believe that she has connections to powerful men, and those men make sure she is freed each time. Commissioner Horwood denies this. He'll deny it until he's in his grave because if it's true that would mean his entire city is corrupt. That nobody can be trusted and that criminals like Mary Carr, or the McDonald brothers, actually own London instead of its lawgivers."

I hang on to her every word, listening so intently that the hubbub of the store fades into the background. "But you believe it to be true?"

"I believe that a woman like Mary Carr has a vast network of accomplices, but until we have the proof in our hands, a list of names, she will always find a way to escape proper punishment. I know she'll be out by the new year."

"That soon?"

"That soon," she repeats the words with a sigh of disappointment.

I nod slowly, and our training continues. She doesn't teach me much outside of necessary observation and study. We catch a little boy tucking a small toy train into his pocket but nothing more.

"Come with me, I want to show you something." She walks to the lift, and I follow along while Renee and Kathy cast me suspicious looks. One moment they're betting that I will toss in the towel and the next I'm assistant to the store detective. Kathy shakes her head at me, her eyes narrowed.

So much for making friends.

The detective directs Lucille to take us to the fourth floor. Past all the offices, right next to Mr. Selfridge's locked door, is a small separate room with Treasury engraved on a gold plaque. Detective Betts opens the door, revealing wall-to-wall Mosler safes. Not one, but two . . . three . . . four . . . five.

My mouth falls open.

Fuck. Tommy is going to kill me.

"The girls don't know that the jewelry on display is fake," she says proudly. "We're the only store in London that does this, but others will follow. With the rise in theft, I imagine all the stores will lock away their jewelry by the time the holidays arrive next year."

An uncomfortable shudder sweeps through my body. "There are jewels in all of them?" I ask aloud, desperately trying not to let my voice shake while I balance a fine line between excitement and dread. Five safes mean five times the loot, but it also means I'll need to somehow find a way to keep this room free of eyes long enough for Tommy to crack each safe. A distraction, a big one.

She nods curtly. "Mr. Selfridge is a genius with his displays, and he desires to have the customers see the product firsthand . . . but not even he could have predicted the Forty Elephants. If we didn't fight back in our own way, they'd steal us out of business." Observing the safes closely, she continues, "Imagine their horror when they proudly take all their stolen diamonds to fencers . . . only to find out . . ." Her mouth turns upward, and amusement lights up her entire face.

I'm speechless. Even as I try to pull words from my mouth, nothing comes out.

"Those girls think they're so clever." She laughs richly, folding her arms over her chest with a grin. "Little do they know, we can be clever too."

We continue like this for the rest of the day—her beaming with confidence while I study the ins and outs of the building, go over the party plans countless times, and ultimately toy with a handful of different scenarios that will give Tommy enough time. None feels flawless.

Each potential plan has holes—holes that could end with one of us, if not all, wrangled up by Betts in an instant.

No. The distraction is going to need to be bigger.

By the time she sends me home, she is restless, bouncing on the balls of her feet in anticipation of the party while I'm deep in thought, considering how I'm going to destroy that confidence.

I just need the right plan, and the right timing.

Maggie picks me up so we can head over to the 43, saying nothing until we arrive. She pulls out a smoke and lights it, flicking the burnt match against the side of the building. After she takes a long puff, she hands it to me. I try not to let my body betray me, but my eyes automatically drift to Rob's flat.

We haven't spoken since I told his brothers I knew what he was doing, and right now I long for him more than ever.

"How was your day?" Her tone is indifferent like she's just trying to make conversation.

"Detective Betts made me her assistant," I reveal. "I'm supposed to help her spot theft during the party."

A snort escapes from her lips. "How did you manage that?"

"Dumb luck?" That's not the truth though. The only reason she trusts me so wholeheartedly is that I gave her Charlotte. "But I only gained favor with her because I did something horrible. You were right. Not even she would imagine criminals to be so cruel."

She nods slightly. "Would you take it back?"

My throat constricts. I don't want to lie to her. "Would I take back the advantage I have now? No. You told me during my audition that women like us must do things other women won't. You were right, but I'm sorry I didn't tell you about Charlotte sooner."

I see something bordering on understanding in her expression when she says, "Let's put it behind us and focus on today. We need Kate to get into that party."

It takes some convincing to get Kate to agree to speak privately with us, but she finally breaks and leads us inside her office. She immediately moves to her desk and begins sorting through stacks of papers while we stand waiting. There are pictures of her daughters dotting the walls and a few crates of booze, but little else. It's practical and functional—the opposite of Mary's lush, self-important space.

"Make this quick, will you? I've got a busy night ahead of me."

Without even taking a seat, I succinctly tell her the plan, our recent setback with Pearl—although I don't mention her by name—and our current need to gain entrance through someone already on the guest list.

"You're doing this behind Mary Carr's back? Breaking her rules?"

"The rules she designed to keep us from profiting when she's not around? Yes."

She snickers a little. "I called it when she recruited you. I told her you were a leader, not a follower. She ignored my advice though. She was so certain she could control you."

"Your advice?"

"I told her to get rid of you." She pulls back her shoulders. "Given your threat to me recently, what on earth makes you think I'll help you?"

"We can give you a cut," I say grudgingly.

"I don't want a cut," she says.

"Then what do you want?"

She retrieves a bright red invitation identical to Pearl's from her desk and gazes at it with little enthusiasm. "I usually don't go," she says frankly. "Though I'm impressive to Mr. Selfridge, none of the city's elite think a woman owning a nightclub cuts a fine figure. I'm usually just the source of gossip and slander." She takes a long moment to consider it, averting her gaze between us. "One of my daughters will be home for the holidays; she's about your age. You can pose as her friends attending the event with me. However, you must look the part. There can be no question of you belonging there."

"You're going to get us in?" Something about this isn't right. "If you don't want a cut, what do you want, then?"

"A favor."

"What favor?" Maggie asks, narrowing her eyes.

"I don't need one now, but eventually, I might."

Maggie scoffs. "You want us to be in your debt?"

"It's good to have a gang of collectors in your pocket for a rainy day," she quips.

"Fine," I say. "We agree. Right, Mags?"

"Yeah," Maggie concurs. "You've got a deal." We shake hands and walk out, but before I can close the door behind me, Kate says, "What did you do to my bartender?"

I'm alarmed that just the mention of him makes my chest ache. "What do you mean?"

"He quit last night, said he was leaving the city altogether. I assume you broke his heart, and now he wants nothing to do with anything that reminds him of you."

Not exactly what happened, though not entirely off the mark. "I don't know what you're talking about," I lie, and turn again to leave.

"It's worth it, by the way."

I hold the door and glance over my shoulder, "What is?"

"Losing people to get what you want most. We are not supposed to be ambitious, Alice. We are supposed to be meek, humble, and gracious. We are not supposed to have power. Those of us that do will be lonely."

I don't like that she knows so much without knowing anything at all. "So then it was worth it for you? What did you have to sacrifice to become the infamous Kate Meyrick?"

"Everything," she answers simply, but with no sense of regret in her tone. "I gave up everything."

I won't let her see how much her words affect me, and I give her a terse nod before letting the door swing shut. Back inside the club, I take a last look around. Maybe we don't make it out of this score, and I'll never see this place again.

"We need to get ready, keep our minds right," Mags says to me immediately. "Don't let Kate get to you."

"My mind is right," I tell her. "I just need to get some air. I'll meet you back at The Mint. Check on Tommy for me?"

She reaches for my arm. "You're going to see him? I thought we agreed that you'd give him up?"

I take a deep breath, trying to collect myself. "I'm going to see him. You said no more secrets, so I'm not going to lie to you. If he's leaving, I want to say goodbye."

I anticipate a crude remark or a lecture, but instead, her features soften. Her hand falls from my arm to my hand, and she gives it a little squeeze. "Last time?"

I nod. "Last time."

I exit the club and take the stairs to Rob's place. A battered suitcase sits outside the open door. I say his name, but it comes out as a hoarse whisper. I lift my knuckle to give the door a knock but find it's already cracked open. I peer inside.

Rob's gathering his books, sorting through them one by one. He looks up at me, keeping his face blank when he says, "Alice."

I ease inside.

"Kate said you were leaving the city."

He tosses the books in a bag with little delicacy. "Yes, well, apparently, Mary is getting cozy with the commissioner and trading secrets. The juiciest one being that I am, in fact, a liar."

"What happened? Did the commissioner threaten you?"

He hesitates. "I leave tonight. Does it even matter to you? My brothers told me what you did. You used me against them."

I take a short breath, still feeling like I might burst into tears, but I search my mind for the last conversation I had with his brothers and use it as fuel to stay composed. I pull my shoulders back and lift my chin. "Your brothers saw a woman succeeding at something and tried to take it for themselves! I offered to pay off Mary's debt, but they refused. They wanted to keep the girls collecting under their rule to continue adding to what Mary owed. If you think I was going to let them take it away and keep the girls for themselves, then you don't know me at all."

"Yes, yes, Alice . . . the protector of women," he says wryly, running his fingers through his hair. "Would you truly do it? Sell me out?"

"No."

"If it were between The Mint and me?"

"Don't make me answer that."

"Do you want to know what I think about every night?"

"No."

"Do you want to know the first thing on my mind in the morning?" I hold his eyes fiercely. "No."

"Do you want to know who I was willing to become the Demolitions Man again for?"

My mouth dries up in response, and I can't keep control of the pain in my chest.

He plops down on the bed. "You."

"You know this is never going work." I ease down next to him and finally let the tears flow freely. I place a hand on his knee and drop my gaze. "I told you if I found a good man, I'd run as far away as I can. You need to let me run, Rob."

He pulls me close with a shake of his head. "We can leave now—you and me. Take the next train to wherever. I've always wanted to travel. We'd have no commitments, no obligations. I won't ask you to be my wife. Just be the woman I lay next to every night."

He pulls me in to kiss me, and I kiss him back, letting myself melt into the moment. I imagine it. Traveling somewhere far away where I'm not Alice Diamond or Diamond Annie. I'm just a woman with a man. Maybe we'd get a dog and work together at the local pub. No weight on my shoulders, no promises I'd have to keep.

I don't even know if I'd be playing a part or if I'd just discover an entirely new me. I savor the fantasy as I breathe in his musky smell and memorize the pattern of the quilt on his bed. I burn it all into my brain, the same way I did Charlotte's face.

Another casualty of war.

Another sacrifice.

"You're too good for me," I tell him. "You want peace, but you brought the Demolitions Man back because of me. Because of me, you hurt more people."

"No," he protests. "It's not like that. I wanted to help you."

"Because of me, you are becoming the very thing you want to leave behind. Only instead of being controlled by your country or your brothers . . . your feelings for me control you. You are a beautiful man, Rob. You want to be a good man. You can't be one with me."

He throws his hands up in bitter frustration. "You think you are irredeemable, but that's not true! Anyone can be saved."

I shake my head in disagreement, then stand up to look him in the eyes. "What I have done, what I will do, it's bigger than a man and a woman. It's bigger than love. It's bigger than me."

"What does that even mean?"

I look down and close my eyes dreamily. "I will take what Mary started and do something even more extraordinary. Dangerous and lonely . . . but extraordinary. I want it. I want it more than—"

"More than me," he says, finishing off my thought solemnly.

I straighten up, cleaning my face off and buttoning up my coat, eager to leave before he convinces me to reconsider. "Where will you go?"

He presses his lips together. "To protect his reputation, the commissioner wants me to be an informant still, but a real one. I'll be going through proper training to be a genuine officer." He laughs at the irony. "On the other side of the law."

"I don't understand," I admit. "How does he benefit by taking you away from your brothers? He won't have another source of information, will he?"

"This isn't about information. He no longer trusts me because Mary told him I was playing both sides. The press would have a field day if they found out. The entire city would doubt his leadership, say that the gangs control London. To prevent that, I will become an officer. My father would roll over in his grave."

I make a face. "You don't have to do any of this. You could leave."

"I do what he wants, and maybe I return with more power to help my brothers. Maybe I don't return at all."

"Maybe?" I force my shoulders down to soothe the sting of goodbye. He manages a smile. "Maybe."

He takes my hands and tucks a small note into them. "Here's my new address, should you change your mind. I will write to you."

I laugh through the tears and reach for his face, running my fingers down his cheeks. "I will write you back, baby face."

He kisses my hands. "I regret nothing. Not my feelings for you, or what they made me do." He gestures to the door while choking back a cough. "Get out of here, Alice Diamond. Go show London what a girl from The Mint can do."

Chapter Twenty-One

The day before the party, the detective spends much of her time reiterating her plan for the evening and my role in it. Though we're the only two detectives at the party, Mr. Selfridge hired a number of men to guard different posts, secure rooms, and help keep invitations in order. I memorize their stations to relay back to the girls later.

Betts says I'm to look like a guest, dressed up like a lady, casually milling about unnoticed while she stands firm in the corner with her men scouting the crowd from afar. I'm to signal her if I spot anyone, but other than that, make no conversation or other indicators of my assignment.

She wants me invisible.

Such anonymity is a relief. I'll be able to steer her away from the girls while they collect and give her enough false hints to ruin her night. At first, the idea of having the upper hand with the law empowered me, but I've grown fond of her—an inconvenient fact I've chosen to ignore.

Even if we're similar and I sympathize with her desire to be taken seriously, I have to focus on the girls, my family—*our* success. She is the enemy. A clever one, at that, but still.

Before leaving for the day, I catch a quick smoke break with Lucille down in the tunnel. If the girls take the stairs during the party, they'll be able to get down to the basement without any of the lift attendants being any the wiser. The detective won't be anywhere near the stairs, and the bargain basement will be closed for the party.

I'll get Tommy upstairs to the staff wing, and afterward we'll have a straight shot out of the building.

"I said yes to my man," says Lucille, breaking my train of thought. She hands me her cigarette, flashing the ring on her finger in the process. "Plan to do it after Christmas. I thought I might invite you if you'd like to come."

I smile at the thought. "I'm happy for you, Lucille." I don't plan on working here after Christmas, but I don't want to say anything to ruin the joy on her face. "I'd love to be there."

She blushes with pleasure. "So how's it been, working with Detective Betts?"

"Surprisingly enjoyable," I answer. "She's like the rest of us women trying to make it in the world. I thought she'd be intimidating, and at first, she was. But then I realized we're not so different."

"You seem as different to me as black and white," says Lucille. "You don't see me catching a smoke with her, do you?"

I smile at her kindness. "You're a real treasure, Lucille. That man of yours ever decides you don't deserve the best, tell me." I clear my throat, remembering that even with a friend, I have to be careful with my words. "I've got a brother, he'll take care of him."

As we turn to go back into the basement, I take a last glance down the tunnel. It's a bumpy path of untouched construction. I don't know why Mr. Selfridge stopped working on it, or when he plans to start up again, but for now, it's a light in the darkness. Our path to freedom. We can carry everything to the Tube station and use Maggie's car as our getaway. If I were to close my eyes, I could envision it now.

"Any idea when he will finish this project?" I ask.

Lucille shrugs in response. "Maybe never."

Before going home, I stop at the hospital to visit Pearl with a box of Selfridges chocolates, tiptoeing into her room only to find her very much awake, doodling in a small notepad on her bed. Her face is still a bruised mess, but her hair has been washed and styled. It's tousled down her shoulders, wavy and clean.

She spots me and smiles weakly, putting down her pen. "Alice?"

Her quavering voice overwhelms me. I place the chocolates down and reach out to embrace her gently. She sniffles into my shoulder, pulling back after a moment to get a better look at me. "I didn't think I'd ever see you again."

I push a lock of hair behind her ear and sit down beside her on the small bed, taking her hand. "I came before, but Harold was here. He sent me away. I snuck back in today to see you."

A sudden alarm fills her. She releases my hand and looks at the hospital room door. "You should go then. He comes every day around this time."

"I'm not scared of him. Let him come."

I'm not. Not at all.

"No, you need to leave, Alice. Leave and don't come back." Her voice rises higher. "Should he see us speaking to each other, there could be consequences for me. You need to go."

I stand up firmly. "We found another way into the party. Kate Meyrick. We can still pull everything off, and I can still get you the new life you want."

"We were fools to think a simple heist could solve all our problems," she says, choking up. "There's no other life. No other future. This is it."

I shake her roughly by the shoulders, hopeful I might be able to get her back. Retrieve her daring soul stuck inside this frightened body. "Don't you dare say that. You are a survivor, just like me. I'm getting you out of London. I'm getting you away from him!"

She shakes her head, yanking herself out of my grip. "Please, please go. I can't leave London. I can't leave him. I won't survive without him. I won't." She reaches for a small bag on the bedside table. "The keys to my flat are in there. Take them. I won't be going back there."

I pick up the bag but try to make her take it instead.

"I mean it, Alice!" she shrieks, shoving the bag away with a repulsed frown.

In all the time I've known her, she's never been entirely broken. She's always rebelled, clung to the idea of a new life, believing that one day, she'd leave him and get the independence she's so fiercely wanted for years. But I sense no hope in her voice now. Only terror. A broken kind of fear that hurts my soul. She lived through his last attack, but a part of her died.

"I beg you, just leave with me." I take her hand, hold it tight, even as she struggles to pull it free. "I promise you don't have to be afraid anymore. We'll go somewhere he can't find us. You can start over. Be anyone you want to be. Please, just trust me."

"No!" Her shout is frantic and loud and sends me reeling back like I've been slapped. "I *did* trust you, and that was foolish! Putting my faith in a maid that I hardly knew. Pathetic. I should never have done it. I have everything I could ever want in life, more than most. There will be no more talk of running away, and if you show up again, I'll have the nurses alert the police. Now go. Leave now, Alice. Don't come back."

Still, even with how hurtful her words are, I stand my ground until a nurse walks in to see what all the commotion is for. When she takes in the scene in front of her—Pearl sobbing and me with my feet planted defiantly—she drags me into the hallway with the force of an ox. "Don't make this harder on her. There's a time to fight, and there's a time to walk away. You need to walk away."

The sheer urgency in her eyes tells me she knows the truth, and like me, she's unable to fix it. I bite my lower lip and let out a shaky breath. "He will hurt her again. I'm just supposed to accept that?"

She looks around nervously and then back at me. She tilts her head, directing me to the exit. "Mr. King will be here shortly. Get out of here before he sees you. You need to accept what you cannot change and walk away before you get yourself into the kind of trouble you can't get out of."

Maybe I can't do anything now, but something has to be done.

"Someone has to teach him a lesson," I grind out. "Someone has to show him that he can't get away with this."

"That someone isn't you," she says simply. "And he's already gotten away with it." She snaps her fingers and points to the exit. "Go home, girl."

That night, for one last party in case things go horribly wrong, the Hill boys host a dinner. They decorate their section of Chinatown with beautiful red and orange banners. Music fills the air, and paper lamps wind along the streets, illuminated by the candles inside them.

Evelyn, Rita, and Vera celebrate with drinks and dancing, while Maggie reviews tomorrow's schemes with Eli and Patrick in their private gambling den with Tommy listening carefully. I wait outside the den by the door, forcing Rob and Pearl from my thoughts to note the merriment all around me.

Rita and Vera spot me and sashay over with a little tap dance.

"We got you something," squeals Vera.

Rita hands me a medium-sized velvet box with a set of diamond rings. One for each finger. They glisten in the lantern light—bright rainbow flashes. I don't know what to say, so instead of words, I just stare. I've gotten used to having beautiful things while collecting for Mary, but these are beyond anything I've ever seen before.

"We snagged these from the warehouse before the coppers got in. We want you to have them. You didn't have to let us do this with you," says Rita. "You could have turned us down."

Vera gives me a one-sided smile. "And how glorious will it be to watch you strike a man across the face with them on?"

I let out a shaky sigh. "We could still mess this up and all be in jail together come Christmas morning."

Vera shakes her head. "No, we will pull this off."

"We will," agrees Evelyn, emerging to join us with a firm nod. "We're survivors. But most of all, we long for someone to believe in us. You do, in the truest of ways. Thank you, Diamond Annie."

I hold the rings in my hand, marveling. It's funny how these sparkly diamonds can somehow remind me that I have expanded my family. I'm not alone.

"Thank you," I say to them.

They swarm around me for a group embrace, and I'm overwhelmed by the feeling of sisterhood. I needed this reminder of why I'm doing this and why I've made the sacrifices I have. But it also reminds me of my real sister and my mother's plea that I see her before everything goes down, so I go inside to grab Tommy, and the two of us head to the Savoy.

A bellboy directs us to the Savoy Grill, where we wait for Louisa at the bar. I watch the diners, all well-dressed and happy as they relax after the theater, enjoying a meal and cocktails with friends. This place is literal and metaphorical leagues from the slums Louisa is used to, and I can't help but be thankful that she's had this chance to experience something nicer.

I imagine her meeting a man one day and being swept away in one of those dreamy romances that only exist in books. Some handsome, kind businessman who stays at the hotel, falls in love with the beautiful, sweet maid cleaning his room, and whisks her off to his manor on the coast where they live happily ever after.

That makes me think of my brother, doing his best to forge his own fairy-tale ending. "Thank you for coming, Tommy." I lean my head on his shoulder.

He shrugs, glancing around the place judgmentally as if wondering how many of these people deserve their cushy lives. "Beats testing locks in front of Patrick and Eli. Been at it for days with them."

"How are you doing?"

"I unlock nine of ten."

"And the one you don't?"

He grins wickedly. "I mess up on purpose just to see their faces."

I smirk back at him, feeling the dread fill my chest until my heart is hammering wildly. "How's your work going with the safe?"

His jaw drops in offense. "You mean all *five* safes?"

"You don't have to get into all of them, Tommy," I insist, something I've been repeating to him for days. "There won't be enough time for that. Just getting into one will be successful enough."

He runs his hand down his face, then to my surprise, lets out a belly laugh. "If you think I'm not going to attempt all five, you don't know me at all."

I shake my head and reach out for his hand. "Just don't get yourself caught."

Louisa finally arrives, dressed in a lovely but straightforward sweater and pleated skirt. Her hair is cut and styled into a flattering bob, making her look years older than she is. "Alice, Tommy."

Tommy gets up to hug her, but she takes the slightest step back, so he kisses her cheek instead. "I hardly recognize you, Lou. You look beautiful, like a proper lady."

"You do," I agree, and she shoots me a dubious stare, not bothering to come over and let me kiss her, just primly taking a seat.

"Where are you living?" I ask. Mum told me, but I'm trying to make conversation. Normal conversation. Nothing about The Mint, or the score, or how everything between us feels broken.

"There are staff quarters," she says. "I room with a few of the other maids. It's pretty jolly. We go dancing. Sometimes we see a show. It's a nice setup."

Her voice is polite but distant, something I notice right away.

If Tommy picks up on it too, he isn't fazed by it. "Baby is growing good."

Her eyes light up at the subject change. "I still can't believe you're going to be a father."

"Me either," he admits. "I imagine the wife will come to her senses one day and leave me, but for now, I'm doing my best by her."

I finally crack. "You should come home more," I tell her. "If not for me, to see Mum at least."

"I'll try," she says dismissively. "It was good seeing you both, but I should get back. Take care of yourselves." She stands up to leave, and I chase after her, telling Tommy to wait for me out front as I take hold of her arm. "Louisa, please stop. We can't be like this forever."

"I've been doing fine without you," she reasons, looking me up and down. "And you look like you've been doing fine without me."

I feel a painful tightness in my throat and need to swallow to find my voice. "Louisa, Tommy and I are planning something . . . and I just wanted to see you—"

She lifts her hands to stop me. "I don't want to know! Please, don't tell me anything. I just want you to leave and go back to The Mint. You don't owe me anything, Alice."

"Did you love him?" I ask, growing frustrated. "Did you love Jacob so much that you'd spurn me because of what I did to him?"

She jeers. "How blind you are to think this is about him. This is about you!" She points to me bitterly. "You and your vanity. Every day of your life, you've been out to prove something to everyone. You could have let Jacob go that night, but you didn't. You could have killed him in the bedroom, but you didn't. You had to take him out in front of everyone just to show how strong you are."

"Father has done the same thing with other people hundreds of times," I counter defensively. "Why is it a problem when I do it?"

"It's a problem when either of you does it. It's all the same with you and him: the violence, the death, the bloody battle for territory. I don't want power. I don't want the pain and fear that come with it. I just want to have fun with my friends, buy pretty things, and live a perfectly normal life like everyone else. If I need to be as far away from you as possible to have that, then so be it."

She glances around the lobby to see who is watching. "Please don't come back here, asking around for me. My papers say my name is Louisa Finch, and she doesn't have siblings."

I want to say more, so much more, but maybe I owe this to her.

If I'm fighting for the gang and for The Mint to have the freedom to make their own choices, I should let my sister have that same freedom.

Even if she uses it to stay away from me.

On the drive back, I don't know how hurt I am until my fingers shake. I lose my breath entirely and struggle to find it, inhaling frantically to calm myself down. I need to be strong, but I don't want to be right now. I want to mourn the loss of Louisa, Rob, and Pearl. I want to scream until all the regret and shame empty out of me.

I park Maggie's car back in Chinatown, but before I can get out to disappear into some corner to cry, Tommy yanks me toward him and wraps me in a gentle hug. The grief fogs my mind, and I get lost in the moment, not caring if hours or days pass.

I bury my head in his coat, letting out a muffled sob. He makes soothing, shushing noises and pats me on the back. The change is strange, him comforting me, but I welcome it. Perhaps I've needed it more times than I care to admit.

"Attagirl," he says softly. "Let it all go. I won't leave you until you tell me to."

I return home to The Mint for the night, knowing that the wise thing to do is sleep. My body is fully aware of the dangers that will come if I'm not well rested for the coming days, but my mind resists, and I drink. I drink too much, for too long, while Tommy and Mum loom over her table, further studying our exit on a makeshift map. I cannot get Pearl's words out of mind, or my goodbye to Rob. His sweet, dreamy offer of a new life with him far away, where I don't owe the world anything.

The more I drink, the more I consider packing my bags and running to Victoria Station to chase him down even though it's been hours and he's likely long gone.

"Alice!" Maggie rushes through the front door, and I sit up from my slumped position on the sofa.

Maggie's face, shining with fear, startles me nearly sober. "What is it?"

"It's Louisa."

The air grows still, and we all rush out of the house in such a panic that even though I'm stumbling to keep my steps straight, I'm somehow fully aware and ready. Outside, the night air is cool with a stillness that makes me uneasy. On the fog-smoked street, Ralph emerges with Louisa in his arms.

Mum lets out a primal shriek and runs over to check on her. "What happened?"

"A car drove by and tossed her out," he says softly, holding my sister tightly, rocking her as if she were a baby instead of a growing girl. "Two dames, I think. Twins?"

Maggie snarls, red in the face. "Twins? Are you sure?"

The gin still has my head cloudy, but I manage to blink away the haze to walk side by side with Ralph until he enters the shop to lay her down on the sofa.

She's purple and bloody, dressed just like I left her hours ago. How did the twins find her? Were they following me?

"Is she dead?" Maggie's voice cracks. "Please tell me she's not dead."

Mum shakes her head, watching Louisa's chest rise and fall in a slow but steady rhythm. "Not dead, just hurt."

"They left a note pinned to her dress," reveals Ralph, holding it out to me while I stare in horror. But I don't take it; I'm far more concerned with her rising chest, fearing it might just stop.

Tommy takes it from Ralph and reads it aloud. "Given your betrayal, I believe this is fair. But I know what you're planning, Annie, and should you follow through, next time she will not be returned alive. I did warn you. Love, the Queen of the Forty Elephants."

"She knows," Maggie states the obvious. "She knows about the score . . . She knows where Louisa works . . . How does she know all this?"

"Her power is information," I say flatly. "And her information is endless . . . which means her resources are endless. Which means . . ." I pause, closing my eyes to settle my racing thoughts.

"Which means?" Tommy presses me on.

I try not to stiffen or show the fear swelling in my gut. "We have another threat to consider during the score. One that is entirely unpredictable and capable of hurting all of us."

Tommy slaps his sides. "Oh, that's it? Grand! Let's just add it to the list." He lifts his hands in the air to create a mock list. "Arrest, losing everything, lives ruined, and then, of course, the threat of impending death from a crazy bitch somehow pulling strings in jail." He runs his fingers through his hair roughly.

Louisa groans. "Tommy, will you stop talking? My head already hurts."

Mum leans in to caress Louisa's swollen face. "Oh, sweet girl."

"I'm sorry, Louisa." The words come out a whimper, every ounce of strength in me vanishing in an instant. "I won't let this happen to you again."

The eye that isn't swollen shut looks at me. "You can't promise that," she utters breathlessly, tears streaming down her cheek.

My own eyes dare to water. "I should have kept you closer."

"I don't want your promises. I just want you to teach me how to make sure it never happens again. You will teach me, Alice. I don't want your protection. Just teach me how to be strong."

I lean in and cradle her close, the same way my father did me when these streets got the upper hand, threatening to break me. "I'll teach you," I promise her, keeping my voice even. "This will never happen to you again."

Chapter Twenty-Two

The daylight hours on Christmas Eve at Selfridges are solely reserved for the children. Dazzling events are staged throughout the store for them, from puppet shows to gigantic gift towers made of wrapped dolls, toy whistles, and candies. Mechanical toys are on display, and Santa Claus is at the center of it all, wishing children a happy Christmas from his grand velvet chair surrounded by gifts. He hands each child a package as they leave.

The detective treats this as our matinee performance, and I don't disappoint her. I spot several rascals slipping trinkets into their pockets and coats—small wooden soldiers and gilded lockets. It kills me to do it while parroting her boastful attitude, but I still feel like I must prove myself. Keep her on the hook so she won't doubt me later tonight when I draw her away from the girls.

Mr. Selfridge arrives in the afternoon, greeting everyone with a warm smile. He looks older than I expected but still dapper, and dressed to impress. He shakes his employees' hands, and they thank him for their holiday bonuses. He knows their names, every single one of them, and appears to be as down-to-earth as they come—a man of the people, a famous public figure nobody would want to steal from.

"The lovely Alice." He greets me with a firm handshake, and admittedly, I feel a bit starstruck. "Detective Betts has told me so much about you. I know you'll do me proud this evening, and I hope you'll consider staying with us after the holidays."

I nod like a giddy child. "Thank you for this opportunity."

"No, thank you." And then he moves on like the butterfly he is, wandering through the store with his finger high, pointing to things out of place or that need addressing.

The detective dressed me to look like another fine lady in the crowd while she is wearing her usual blazer and homely skirt with her hair pinned up in the same unfashionable plaits. Her blatantly schoolmarm image is one way of warding off potential theft, she explained to me in detail, while another is to have someone like me blending in where she can't.

An observer moving with the masses, exceptional and unnoticed.

The store closes at dusk, giving the staff just enough time to get everything ready for the party. We roll out long red rugs around the store and set up festively decorated tables. We replace the toy displays with eye-catching arrangements of expensive couture and glittering jewelry. One room is being used to showcase a brand-new, gleaming Rolls-Royce, and a large feast is being prepared for the guests to enjoy as they are serenaded by a string quartet. Some shop attendants stroll the party, ready to offer delicious strudels and small cakes alongside champagne.

The detective and I stand on the shop floor near the display counters with other employees while the guests enter. Women stride in lightly, as if they're walking on clouds, dressed in velvet and furs, silk and chiffon. Their necks, ears, and fingers are dripping with emeralds and diamonds that shine like beacons as they emerge from smoggy Oxford Street. They cling to men in Bond Street shirts, felt hats, and custom frock coats. The truly wealthy of London are sporting their most extravagant ensembles.

The guards at the door check invitations off from a long list while the guests marvel at the elaborate displays honoring the Women's Royal Naval Service and Remembrance Day, and a unique congratulatory exhibit for Nancy Astor, the first woman to take her seat in the House of Commons.

I walk around the tastefully dressed mannequins that flaunt the newest Paul Poiret, Coco Chanel, and Jeanne Lanvin fashions, momentarily losing my sense of the world, getting lost in all the colors. Mr. Selfridge is genuinely a master of his craft.

Unfortunately for him, so am I.

I wait for the girls to arrive, bouncing on the balls of my feet anxiously for what feels like hours. The detective peels off to her stationed perch, leaving me to wander alone. I play like I'm scanning the crowd but keep looking toward the doors every few seconds.

"Keep your eyes on the guests already inside," Betts says, suddenly coming up behind me. "You will not spot a thief coming in. Only going out. And try not to look so nervous." She shakes her head with a rueful laugh. "Relax. You don't want anyone to realize you're on the lookout."

"Forgive me," I say with a sigh. "There's so much to be mindful of."

She places her hand on my shoulder. "You'll do fine. Just stay focused on the task at hand."

I nod and shift my body, purposely averting my eyes from the front entrance. After a few moments, when I finally see them sweep into the store, the relief that washes over me brings an immediate lightness to my step, and I nearly rush over to greet them before reminding myself why we're all here in the first place. Rita and Vera are the faces tonight, dressed in attention-grabbing bright blue and gold gowns with daringly low-cut necklines and covered in intricate beading that glints in the light, while Maggie and Evelyn follow behind in gold and yellow silk gowns with pearl embellishments.

No one questions their arrival with Kate Meyrick and her daughter—they have followed Kate's instructions about looking the part to a tee, and one would never guess that they weren't the Meyrick girl's friends.

We all spot each other and tuck our hair behind our right ears, a silent signal to let the collecting begin. I waste no time weaving in and out of the crowd to run interference.

They spread out, and the detective, somehow sensing incoming trouble, starts gravitating toward them. I divert her attention every time, though, by making up random sights and suspicions. The girls confidently slither through the crowd like snakes. Rita and Vera enchant all around them with sparkling conversation while their partners skillfully dip their hands into pockets and behind displays. If I see a particularly choice target, like the fat matron littered with jewelry by the band, I walk toward her and cough twice to signal my partners.

The advantage to a party like this, even given the specific guest count, is that everyone is preoccupied with its exhibitionism. After a year of waiting, the idea that they're here and part of the crème de la crème makes them all act like children. They're too distracted by the ensemble of never-before-seen luxury goods displayed by Mr. Selfridge to pay attention to the people around them. The few conversations being had are short and impersonal. A passing hello and goodbye as they continue to move along the current as the girls mingle among them unnoticed.

It's like a perfectly orchestrated dance, and watching it makes me miss collecting. I haven't so much as swiped a hatpin since I started working here. I've passed up embroidered gloves, a velvet scarf, a delicate gold wristwatch, the most beautiful items, and it pained me to resist the urges.

About an hour into the evening, something calls Detective Betts away to the lifts. The girls speed up during her departure, boldly collecting larger items from countertops and displays before she returns.

Everything is working just like we planned it. No, even better than we'd planned. I feel on top of the world. Then the lift bell dings, and the doors open. I turn to smile at the detective, but she greets me with a dark, animalistic expression. She spots me, and her eyes say it all. *I know who you are.*

In less than a minute, she's in front of me with a scowl that freezes me in place. "May I have a word?"

I swallow. "Now?"

The room spins.

"Yes, now."

I walk with her to the lift, and Maggie watches, giving me a terse nod. Behind her, I spot the twins, Grace and Norma, strolling into the party, dressed in identical tiered velvet dresses and dramatic wraps with large sable cuffs. They each have one arm looped around an older gentleman between them, and they've had no trouble getting in the party either.

As the lift doors close, they both look up at me and grin in unison. All I can think about is strangling their tiny necks. But I hold it together and turn to Detective Betts as we sink below the party. "What's going on? Shouldn't one of us be out there?"

Silence. Nothing but silence.

"I'll do the talking, Diamond Annie."

Chapter Twenty-Three

The lift opens, and she guides me through the bargain basement to a small room at the end of the corridor. Inside is just a desk littered with paperwork and boxes of files.

I pull my shoulders back as I follow, but as the echoes of our shoes bounce off the empty underground walls, a wave of fear hits me. I pull my hands to my sides and fiddle with my dress, fingering the fabric as my forehead grows damp and sweaty. There's nobody down here to protect me and nobody helping the girls navigate the crowds.

"Where are you taking me?" I make sure the only thing coming out of my mouth is spite. Maybe there's still a chance I can talk my way out of this and leave Alice Black's character intact.

But before I realize what's going on, she slaps a set of handcuffs around one of my wrists, locking the other manacle to an exposed steam pipe. I panic and try to wrench out my hand, but she briskly takes the key from the lock and buries it deep into the pocket of her blazer.

"I got an anonymous tip that Alice Black used forged references to get hired here and that she is one of the Forty Elephants, cleverly taking this position at Selfridges to case the store. I knew something was off about you from the very beginning. I knew."

"Anonymous tip?"

She stands against the wall opposite me, looking like a cat with a bowl of cream.

"I haven't the faintest clue what you're talking about."

"You know, I'm not even upset that you've turned out to be a thief or that you're sitting here lying to me. Lying is natural for your kind. I'm upset that you slipped past me. That I didn't follow my gut and push you hard enough because of that little informant scene you pulled." She shakes her head with disappointment. "The woman, Charlotte, was she in on it with you? She certainly seemed genuinely frightened when she was crying her eyes out as the coppers dragged her away."

I hesitate, feeling the tension in my throat making it difficult to swallow. "Charlotte didn't know. I used her to gain your trust."

Her eyes widen at my confession. "You betrayed one of your own to fool me? Have I deeply underestimated you girls?" She looks down, then around, as if she's desperately trying to make sense of my words. "Is Mary Carr somehow planning this from inside her cell? How?"

I give her a tense grin. "Mary Carr has nothing to do with this."

She throws herself into a chair, listening intently. "You mean you planned this all alone? I've never even seen your name in the reports. That means you're a fresh recruit. And how does the new girl get to run her own operation when the boss is in the can?"

"By not following the rules," I reveal with a shrug. Did I plan all this from the start? Absolutely not. Am I angry everything fell into place for me? Absolutely not. "Mary and I didn't see eye to eye."

She laughs cynically and starts breathing hard. "You're lying. You wouldn't cross her. This is her plan, isn't it? Tell me the truth!"

"You have me handcuffed to this desk. Why would I lie?"

"You girls never work alone!" The disbelief shakes her. "This isn't the method. This is all wrong."

I don't know why I'm enjoying her shock so much. She thought she knew everything there was to know about the gang, and maybe when Mary ran it, she did. But I'm not Mary.

"Are there more out there?" She points to the door.

"Yes."

She scrambles a bit, then stands up and straightens her dress. "Turn them in, and I'll forget I got a tip. I'll still get the credit for the capture, and you'll get your freedom." There it is again, her ambition, so raw and on display. She's unashamed of it and how far she'll go to prove herself to the men above her.

I shake my head, then slowly exhale. "I can't do that."

She cocks her eyebrows. "Why not? Don't you have a family? Someone that depends on you?"

"I do," I emphasize strongly. "And if I give the girls up, I can go back to them and forget any of this happened. It's tempting, but I won't do it."

Her jaw tightens, and she gets closer, desperation in her voice when she pleads, "They decided what path in life to take! We all have a choice. I'm giving you one now. One that will unbind you from this."

I force my eyes to look past hers. "Catching a handful of girls won't stop these crimes. You know that, don't you? There are plenty of lost girls in this city looking for a home. Even if Mary and I are both gone, someone else will just rise after us. Your ambition, my ambition—it's not going away. This is just the beginning."

"A handful of girls is a win in my book," she snaps fiercely, her voice loud and callous.

I look down at my feet, making sure my next words are slow and measured. "But do you know what would give you the ultimate win? What would bring her entire enterprise to a grinding halt?"

Through gritted teeth, he barks, "What?"

"You said it yourself: her connections." I think of Mary's large ledgers, all filled with pages upon pages of cramped writing. All the information the commissioner would need to keep her operation buried. "Maybe we can make a deal?"

She places a hand on her chest with a gasp. "No! You don't get to make propositions! I'm giving you a chance, just this once. Identify the girls here at the party, and you can leave out the back. When Miss Waller inquires about you, I'll say you unexpectedly decided to quit. You'll be a ghost to me; one I will gladly leave in the past." She looks down. "Exposing you will only embarrass me."

I rub my temples with my free hand. "I can't do that."

She stands up and bolts for me, taking my chin with impossible strength as if I am a child that needs to be taught a lesson. "Then you're a bloody fool, and you'll suffer like one. You'll be taking all the credit for everything they steal tonight!"

I jerk my head away without breaking her gaze. "Your weakness is that you'll do anything to prove yourself to the men that give your orders. Me? I don't give a damn what men think of me. You follow the rules . . . I make my own rules. Don't you want to start making your own rules?"

She stares long and hard into my eyes, and I wonder if my words are doing something. Changing her mind? Making her think twice? But before she can say anything, a thunderous sound erupts all around—a boom that shakes the entire foundation of the building. I thought I'd be primed for it, but my heart leaps to my throat, and I throw my free hand over my head frantically as if the entire building is about to come down on us.

I hear shouting from upstairs, chaos in the streets above.

"What was that?" She stares at me directly, but my shell-shocked countenance must imply ignorance. She's quick to move to the door and search the hallway for anyone who might have information. Then, strangely, I see her entire form stiffen, and she backs inside awkwardly.

Maggie follows her through the door with a small handgun pointed directly at the detective. She's got a shopping bag full of merchandise, a large fur coat with hidden interior pockets stuffed to the brim, and an air of terrifying indifference that shows she won't hesitate to pull the trigger.

The detective takes a step back, glancing past her. "How did you get down here?"

"I know this building inside and out," she says in a smooth monotone. "All the girls do. We know every entrance and exit."

Even the ones not on the map. In particular, our ace in the hole—the tunnel that will ensure our escape.

She frowns. "The stairs are guarded. All entrances are covered. You and your friend may get out of this room, but you won't get out of this building. I'll alert security."

"I thought you might." Maggie motions to my cuffed hand. "I assume you have the key. Take the cuffs off her now!"

The detective bristles at the command as she removes the handcuff from my wrist. In the exchange, I snatch the key from her without breaking eye contact and quickly switch the cuff from my wrist to hers, snapping it shut and tucking away the key. "I arranged the anonymous tip."

She is stricken with dismay. "You? Why?"

"I needed you down here . . . because you're good, Betts. You're very good. You were right. You knew everything about us, how we work, what we do. The only way to fool you was to give myself away. Because there's nothing you love more than a win."

Her nostrils flare as she tugs her handcuffed hand, rattling the pipe. "You'll pay for this. I swear it! I know your name. I know your face."

"I'll be in touch."

I leave her quickly, and Maggie shuts the door behind us, muffling the detective's yells for help. "We're ready to leave. All the girls are waiting at the exit door."

"Have you heard from Tommy?" I ask, breathlessly following her. "If he's not with them, I'm going back up to get him."

"You can't go back up!"

"Then I'll wait for him! Go, Maggie!"

A sound coming from the nearby stairs sends us leaping to each side of the staircase door just as a security guard storms through. Maggie pivots about with the gun still in her hand, only to find herself smack in front of Tommy, who is dressed in a guard's uniform.

He laughs teasingly and holds up one hand in mock surrender, leaving the other one firmly gripping a large duffel. "Watch where you swing that thing, Reaper!"

I embrace him breathlessly, the sound of his laugh leaving my heart in a flutter. "You did it?"

"No faith in me? I'm offended."

Maggie cackles. "You sneaky sod! No trouble with the safe?"

He grins. "*Safes.* All five. And I never have trouble. Now you two want to get out of here or what? This thing is heavy like a ton of bricks."

The girls are waiting down the corridor with full coats and pockets, bags on each arm filled to overflowing with jewelry and silk scarves. The three of us hurry to meet them. "You're right. We need to leave now."

As we jog, I think about the detective's statement that we'd never get out of the building. "How did you get down here? Did you take the stairs like Tommy?"

"No, we had help."

"Help?"

We reach the lifts, where Lucille stands nervously inside one of them, holding the door open.

"Lucille?" I can hardly believe my eyes. I frown at Maggie. "Lucille, did she threaten you?"

"No," she answers warmly. "They said they were your friends and that you could use some help."

I want to thank her and apologize all at once. I want to explain to her that I'm not just some criminal, that there's a reason for this. "Lucille—"

"I don't want to know," she blurts. "You were kind to me when I needed a friend." She manages a half-smile. "I'm returning the favor, and if the coppers ask, I'll just say you forced me."

Tears fill my eyes. Not just because of Lucille's kindness, but because we're nearly out the door. Against every odd, we've done the impossible.

"Go on now!" Her voice becomes urgent. "You don't have much time before security comes looking for Detective Betts." She closes the lift and leaves us to it.

We rush through the bargain basement and push open the door to the half-constructed tunnel, hurriedly making our way around the debris and climbing a quick flight of stairs at the end to make our way out. Maggie pushes open the door, and we sneak into the station, moving past a group of listless passengers, too tired this late at night to care about anything going on around them. It feels too good to be true.

"I'm parked outside the station," says Maggie, almost running to the nearest station exit. She still looks ill at ease instead of jubilant like the rest of us. She doesn't consider it a win until we fence the goods. Until we get paid.

"I can't believe we did it!" Rita exclaims.

"I've never collected so much in one night," adds Evelyn.

They both look to Tommy. "It's true, what they say about you? That there's no safe you can't break?"

He shakes his head at the compliment. "We haven't won yet, ladies. Let's get out of here."

Vera nods in agreement. "What happened in there with the store detective?"

"A story for the car," says Maggie in agitation, but we all halt when familiar voices emerge at the exit end of the station.

"Now, now, not so fast, girls," taunts Norma, while her sister whips out a gun. Small, like the one Maggie has on her.

The onlookers littering the station scatter at the sight of the gun, fleeing in different directions.

"This is from Mary," says Grace, eyes darkening maliciously as she fires.

No chance to scream or think or move. I stare down the barrel of the smoking gun with a strange kind of acceptance. If this is it, at least I'm going out having made a name for myself and giving my family a fortune they can use to take care of themselves.

At least the girls are set.

I defied the odds. I accepted the challenge and won.

I close my eyes and feel a lightness take over, and I let the chaos of the station fade away until I hear nothing. I wonder if I'll die slowly, bleed to death in front of the girls, or perhaps Grace is an expert shot, and it'll be smooth. Fast.

Surely I'll go to hell with all the blood on my hands.

Evelyn screams, and the sound is so shrill and loud that it leaves my ears ringing. I open my eyes to look down at my dress, but Tommy's in front of me with just enough strength to turn around to face me with a weak smirk before he collapses to the ground.

The bullet didn't get me.

It got him.

Not Tommy. Not fucking Tommy.

I sink to the ground with him, desperate to turn back time, but when I see the blood seeping through his shirt, a stabbing pain grips my stomach, twisting it into a knot until my entire body convulses. "Tommy!" I cry out, clutching his head. "Why did you do that, you bastard!"

Vera, Rita, and Evelyn run at the twins to grapple the gun, but my vision goes blurry. I pull his head into my lap as the grief surges through me, my lips trembling when I mutter, "You will be fine! You hear me? You will make it! You always make it! Not a damn thing in this world can kill you, Tommy."

He reaches for my hand and holds it tightly. "I thought it was about time that I save you."

I shake my head. This can't be happening. It's not happening.

He looks up at me again, wide eyes peering into mine, tearful but somehow unafraid. "Take care of her, will you? Take care of the baby. If it's a boy, name him Tommy."

"And if it's a girl?" I choke out the words.

"Tommy," he says, one end of his mouth turning up before he coughs blood.

He's dying in my arms, and I can't do anything to help him. I push my hand into the wound at his side to apply pressure and stop the bleeding, but there's too much of it.

"I know you will take care of my family, Alice. You always . . . you always do."

He lifts his hand to my chest, his palm flat against my beating heart. But I'm too much in shock to say the words I should to reassure him when he needs it the most. I can't accept this is real.

He's dying, and I mourn the part of me dying with him. The part that believed I could save the people I love. All the warmth abandons my body at once, leaving only pain behind. Everything I didn't treasure about him in life, all the things I told him I did not love about him, are more present than ever, shadowing any memories we shared as children when there was laughter and warmth. I didn't tell him I loved him enough. I didn't enjoy my time with him enough.

How could I, when every year, month, day, and hour felt like a fight to survive? We never stood a chance at something normal.

I'm at a loss for breath as salty tears stream down my face. Try as I might to steady myself, I can do nothing but heave and shake. I need something. I need vengeance. I need to see someone else bleed for Tommy.

I look up at Maggie, still holding the handgun, and snatch it from her.

I focus on Grace among all the girls fighting and struggling for control. "Stop," I shout, and the girls step back, leaving Grace for the taking. Even facing down the barrel, I can't sense any fear in her eyes.

"This is for Louisa." A single shot to the shoulder. "And this is for Tommy." Then another to the chest. Norma cries out as Grace flattens to the ground.

Evelyn, Rita, and Vera back away from the scene in shock.

I move the gun toward Norma, who is sagging over Grace. She looks up at me, and I recognize that the monster in her eyes is the same one in mine. Her chin trembles, and she looks down to her sister, who gives a final shake before going limp.

Maggie reaches for my arm. "Don't, Alice! Send her back to Mary so she knows what happened. There's a point to make here—make it."

I don't know if she means it or if she's simply trying to prevent me from killing Norma, who didn't pull the trigger. Either way, I lower my hand.

She takes the gun away and roughly strips Norma of everything she'd stolen from the party. "Go. Get out of here now!"

"I'm not leaving her!" She gives us both an intense, fevered stare. "I'm not fucking leaving!"

Maggie leans down and in a heavy, low voice says, "You leave now alive, or you leave the way your sister did."

Chapter Twenty-Four

Maggie is talking to me, her voice distant and somehow close all at once. The girls all keep going while I shatter before them into a thousand tiny fragments. Inside I feel still, like time has stopped, and then I slowly realize I can't feel my heart beating in my chest. Maybe she shot both of us?

I want to die.

My brother wanted out, and I brought him back for this score. It's my fault he's dead. It's my fault his child won't know him, and Christina will be alone.

I did this to everyone.

I cry so hard into his body that it takes my breath away, so I silently will him back to life, shaking his shoulders and sobbing wordless apologies into his chest.

"We need to get out of here," utters Maggie in a broken voice. "We need to go. Detective Betts will have alerted security by now. Coppers must have heard the gunshots. We've got to go."

My vision expands outward to take in the entire scene before me. We have everything: all the merchandise, Tommy's vault stash. In every way but one, we won.

Eli and Patrick run up, breathless, with debris from the explosion littering their overcoats. I look up at Eli, blinking rapidly to clear the water from my eyes. He looks down at the mess— the bloody scene of Tommy's and Grace's bodies—and his mouth falls open. His hands shake, and for the first time in as long as I can remember, his eyes gloss over. "What the fuck happened here, Mags?"

"Mary," she reveals hesitantly, "sent Grace to kill me . . . Tommy took the shot."

Patrick lifts his hands to his mouth and turns away.

Eli drops to his knees and reaches out for my hands, soaking his fingers in Tommy's blood to make me let him go. "Where do you want to take him?"

He's asking me where I want to bury him.

I shake my head.

"Alice, you need to answer me. It won't be long before they flood this Tube station with coppers. They're right outside now, trying to find out who set off the bomb. If we stay any longer, we're dead. Do you hear me, girl? We're dead."

"The river," I stutter. "He loved the river. But we need . . . we need to get my mother."

He nods and keeps hold of my hands, squeezing them tightly. "Patrick and I will take Tommy, get your mum, and meet you at our place by the river."

Our place by the river . . . where we spent so much time dreaming together between kissing. A place I remember being so blissfully, foolishly happy.

"I will take care of this, Alice. I'll take care of everything."

And I know he will, but still, the words slip out of my mouth weakly, "I can't leave him."

"I'll keep him safe with me. You know I will. But you need to leave. Maggie will drive you and the girls out of here."

Maggie nods slowly in my direction.

I close my eyes. I have a hundred sides, light and dark and countless shades of gray. I have to suppress the others to cling to the dark numbly—embrace the violence of myself. The woman that doesn't back down—the leader who took The Mint and kept it.

A killer. A collector. A businesswoman.

Alice Diamond.

When I open my eyes, I look at Maggie anew. "Let's go, Mags."

Our path along the Thames is illuminated only by our electric torches as we sullenly approach a graveyard near an old paper mill, where my dad claimed to have buried his parents a long time ago. A mile or so away is the Greenwich Pier, and even during the first light of Christmas morning, men are already bustling up and down the dock.

Tommy loved the river ever since we were kids—it made him come alive. He'd watch the boat race at Putney Bridge and buy tickets to the Henley Royal Regatta every year. He even told me once that he fantasized about running away to sea after reading *Treasure Island*. This is the closest I can get him to his dreams now.

"Are we burying him?" Maggie asks.

"Not here. Let's put him in the water."

We gather rocks to weight his pockets and cement blocks from a nearby factory to place on his chest. This isn't the funeral he deserves. He deserves a mass said in church and a casket filled with flowers. People he loves saying beautiful words about him and sharing their memories.

The least I can do is give him a peaceful resting place. Mary robbed him of his life and now his deserved funeral.

There's one thing left I can give my brother, but only if I move fast enough. Vengeance. Mary must pay for this.

Eli and Patrick arrive, and my mother leaps out of their motorcar like a cat, pouncing and hissing her way to me. Louisa, still weak, follows her but turns away when she sees them pulling Tommy's body from the trunk.

Mum balls her fists, ready to throw a punch. "You did this! You killed him! You killed him!"

Maggie rushes between us to stop her by snatching up her arm. "Tommy wouldn't want this!"

Mum shoves at her. "Like you give a damn what Tommy wants! He's got a baby coming . . . What are we going to tell that babe?"

I keep the sob clogged in my throat with a heavy swallow, then search the motorcar for Christina. "Where is she? Where's Christina?"

"She fainted when she heard about Tommy," she utters. "Left her with Ralph. Don't want to lose another soul today, certainly not to your hands."

Eli and Patrick load Tommy's body with the rocks and cement blocks we collected, then pull my brother's body to the river. I walk to aid them while my mother sinks to her knees, head buried in her hands. She's crying so loudly that the sound grows hoarse, and I fear she'll lose her voice. We throw him in, and I watch his body sink into the murky water while Mum's wailing rings in my ears. The sound of loss, the grief of losing her son, the dismay that her daughter didn't protect him . . . it weighs on me until my knees give out and the earth spins.

Before I can fall, two hands grip my shoulders with bruising strength to keep me from dropping. "No, no," says Eli, supporting me as he turns me around to face him. I put my hand against his chest to push away but end up collapsing into him. "You got two choices. You fall down . . . or you keep standing. God help what happens next if you keep standing, Alice."

I heave into him, his words drifting in and out of my ears slowly. I want to stop sobbing, but I don't know how. He reaches for my face and pulls my head back so he can speak into my ear directly, his hands shaking against my hair. "You got pain . . . you take that pain and use it."

"Alice?" Maggie steps over to us and takes my hand. "What do you want to do now?"

I pull back and suck in a breath, then hold it for a long moment. I think of that day I met Mary at the café—the smugness on her face when she talked about her achievements. The promises she made and how easily I fell for them.

Our last words, when she assured me if I betrayed her, she'd have measures in place to get her vengeance. I open my mouth, and the words slip out of their own accord. "Blood for blood."

Maggie exhales long and slow, and her face hardens before me. She nods in agreement. "Blood for blood. But how? We can't get her when she's locked up."

"We start by making it impossible for her to rebuild."

I stare down at Tommy's watery grave, contemplating my next move. We have the advantage because we have the goods. I can't kill her in jail, but I can ruin her life outside of it. "We need to go see the McDonalds."

"Maybe we should do this tomorrow," Maggie advises. "Take some time to mourn."

"I don't want time," I say more coldly than I intend to. Time to rest will just turn my thoughts against me, make them race to the darkest place imaginable. "I want you with me, but the rest of the girls should go back to Chinatown so everything can be fenced straightaway."

Maggie nods. "Everything?"

"No, wait, not everything. You and I will take half, plus whatever else you have on you. That will more than cover what Mary owes Wal and Wag. Once we pay up with them, then they have no stake in her or her operation anymore. So when I kill her, they have no reason to seek retribution. We'll be tied to nothing and no one."

She doesn't respond right away, and I let the words settle inside me. It's a plan now, embedded in my bones.

"You're sure about this?"

"I am," I say flatly. As much as I search for warmth—a comforting smile to give her, assurance in any form—I can't find it. "Will you do this with me?"

There's no hesitation in her voice when she says, "Yes."

Eli and Patrick take my mother and Louisa to The Mint, while Maggie and I head to the Elephant. I say little on the drive, and Maggie doesn't try to force conversation. I study my hands, using a handkerchief to attempt to clean Tommy's blood off my palm and fingers, but no amount of scrubbing gets the rust-colored stain off my skin.

When we finally arrive, the sun has fully risen, and it's merciless, offensively bright in my eyes. I long for the night, the dark, smoggy street.

Despite the early hour, Wag and Wal are inside. I wonder if they have families waiting for them to celebrate Christmas morning or if this is just another day of the week. Business as usual.

They jump up as soon as they spot us, watching intently as Maggie and I bring in the haul and spread it along the bar, so everything gleams in the morning light.

I expect them to look impressed, but Wag says aloofly, "Mary brings us cash, never the plunder."

"You're big boys," I counter. "And I'm not Mary. You can hawk this yourself." My voice is hoarse and uneven, my thoughts still on Tommy. But I clear my throat and match Wag's matter-of-fact tone in a blink. "This should cover her debt and then some. This ends any business you have with the Forty."

"I suppose this means you pulled off the impossible?"

"That's none of your business." I flash him a cheeky look. "But yes."

It's evident from their identical shocked expressions they never thought I'd be able to do it. Wal clears his throat. "Where do you go from here?"

"The girls and I will be setting up shop in The Mint. We won't need the flats anymore. We don't need your connections either. We don't need *you*."

Wag scowls. "If we don't have some kind of friendship, what's to stop us from naming you as the mastermind responsible for the biggest heist of the year? The commissioner will be hunting you, all of you. Rob's gone. You can't use him against us again."

I signal Mags to take the reins, and she steps forward. "The same thing that will stop us, along with my brothers, from naming you our enemy."

"Same goes for The Mint," I add.

Wag's expression darkens. "You think the Hill boys will follow their little sister's lead?"

Mags smiles proudly. "Yes, because she can guarantee they'll see a profit." She takes a set of beautiful silver hair combs from the bar and inspects them pointedly. "With Alice leading us, no store in London is safe."

Wag stares back at me. "The Elephants, the Hill boys, all of them? You think you can manage it?"

"I know Maggie and I can," I say. "We can handle anything."

Wal shakes his head. "But it's lonely on the streets without friends, Alice."

I cross my arms over my chest. "Friendship is earned."

Wal points at Wag. "We're listening."

I grin. "We can be friends if we can be partners. We help each other without having to give you any of our territories or sacrifice any of our relationships."

"What do we have to gain from that? We can't have The Mint or control of your operation, and you say you don't need our political connections."

Maggie answers. "We'll be teaching the girls how to fight. Fists, guns, knives. The lot. You're waging war against Sabini, and he's building his forces. You need to do the same. We're the allies he'll least expect to be a threat."

Wag chews on his lip as he considers what we've said. "We'll make it known to the streets we're allied, and we can continue to provide security when you need it for bigger scores. But this is all on the condition that if we need to go to war, you'll come when we call."

"And if we need you, you'll do the same," says Mags adamantly. "We paid Mary's debt and then some—you know we keep our word. But how do we know you will?"

I think about Charlotte, wondering if I can use their connections to right a wrong. "One of our girls, Charlotte, got pinched for a theft. Can you see to it that she's freed?" I tilt my head. "You know, show us some of those brilliant connections Mary liked to brag about. Or was that a lie?"

Wag clears his throat. "We'll see what we can do."

I add one more thing—the most important thing of all to me at this very moment. "I have a last condition of our friendship. When Mary gets out, you keep away from her. You don't take meetings with her, and you don't let her get close to any of the girls. She's iced out of everything."

"What happened last night?" Wag takes in my appearance, looking me over dubiously until his eyes land on the dark stain spread across the front of my coat. "Is that blood?"

"Mary had it out for her tonight," answers Mags. "She sent two girls to shoot her after the heist, but Tommy stopped the bullet."

"Tommy is dead?" Sympathy pinches Wag's face. "We're sorry for your loss."

"We won't stop you from seeking your revenge," agrees Wal.

Wag lets out a deep sigh of disappointment. "It's a shame. Your brother was a pain in the arse, but he was a talent. There was nobody like him."

I choke back an emotional outburst and dip my head slowly. "No, there wasn't."

"Consider Mary Carr blackballed . . . and our friendship sealed."

Wag spits into his hand and extends it to me. I know what this means. There's no going back. No chance at the average life Louisa longs for or the whirlwind adventure Rob asked me to take with him.

I won't be a wife or a mother.

Once I do this, I'll be a new player in London's gang wars. A force all my own.

I spit into my palm to shake Wag's hand and then Wal's. Maggie does the same.

"Welcome to the business," they say to us with great finality.

Outside the pub, back at the car, Maggie asks, "You implied we have our own connections in there. What were you talking about?"

"Are Mary's ledgers still at Pearl's old place?"

She nods.

"I've got a plan."

I wait in the rooftop garden at Selfridges for a long while. It's bitterly cold this high up, but thankfully the morning is still and the wind is calm. Again I imagine what it must look like here in the spring, teeming with fresh greenery and colorful blooms. A few days have passed since the score and the bombing, but police still scatter below, trying to piece together what happened.

One of the lifts finally opens, and Detective Betts walks out cautiously, staring at a note I paid to have delivered to her. She looks puzzled as she inspects the terrace.

When she turns my way, I walk out from behind a pillar and take a seat at a nearby bench with one of Mary's ledgers in my hand. The rest are in a valise, tucked away safely back at Mum's shop.

She freezes when she spots me, slowly moving her hand toward the cuff at her belt. I laugh.

"You're a fool for coming back here," she snaps, each step a thundering stomp into the snow until she reaches the bench. "We found a dead body you left on your way out. Guessing it's one of your girls?"

"Have a seat," I say, patting the spot beside me. "I have something I want to give you."

She doesn't look like she intends to oblige until she notices the book in my hand, and curiosity gets the better of her. She sits down at the far end of the bench with her lips pressed tightly together in a disapproving line. I imagine if she had a gun right now, she'd happily use it to force me down the lift and into Commissioner Horwood's arms.

"I meant what I said before about us being similar women who want similar things. In the brief time I worked with you, I grew fond of you. How could I not respect your drive? Your desire for the men around you to recognize that you are just as capable as them. We are on different paths in life, but the choices that surround us are the same. Even if it's difficult for you to believe."

She searches my features. "Where are you going with this? Why did you come back? What is that in your hand?"

I tap the book's leather cover. "This is one of Mary Carr's black books. One of her many ledgers. They're filled with all her contacts—fencers, buyers, store security guards, salesclerks, crooked cops, and dirty politicians. There's even a judge listed in there who might interest the commissioner. You said it yourself: this knowledge is the real win."

Her entire body language changes. "Did you come here to gloat?"

"I came here to give you this ledger. Not all of them, but one at a time, so long as we remain friends."

"Friends?"

"I want to do everything in my power to destroy Mary Carr's operation so it never sees the light of day again. That's where you come in." I open the book. "There are receipts in here too, and notes about various blackmailing opportunities for certain people if they should ever betray her. She was a smart woman, Mary. She knew how to keep and control a business."

Betts stands and takes a step back. "What's your reasoning for doing all this?"

I shrug as nonchalantly as I can. "It's simple. She took something precious from me, so I'm taking everything from her."

"She won't just let all this happen." Her shoulders tense. "She will come after you for this."

"I'm not afraid of Mary Carr."

She leans forward, eyes filled with disbelief. "Who are you? Where the hell did you come from?"

I look down and fiddle with the finger of my glove. "I'm your friend from this point on. I take care of my friends."

"But what does that mean for you? Are you taking her place in the gang?" Her eagerness is obvious.

"Do you really think I'll tell you that?"

She sucks in a breath. "That means yes. You know who I am and what I'm tasked to do."

"This information will make your career."

"I don't make deals with criminals." Her eyes widen as she spins on her heel back toward the lifts. "No matter how tempting the deal may be."

I stand up and call after her. "You can say you found it with the dead girl at the Tube station, or you went back to check the tunnel and found it buried under a bench. There's no reason for anyone to doubt you. You'll be taken seriously. All of London will know your name. I'm giving you a chance you might never get again."

She stops but doesn't turn around to face me. "But at what cost?"

I move so we're face-to-face. "I'm going to take what Mary started and transform it. In exchange for these ledgers, you'll stay out of my business. If you see me on the streets, you ignore me. If I reach out for a favor, you oblige. We're friends, and you'll never see me in Selfridges again. Should you decide to take these books and lie to me, making a promise of friendship you don't plan to keep, there will be consequences."

Something about my voice scares her, but she hurriedly pretends to study the ledger in my hand so I can't see her fear. "What happened to the girl at the Tube station? How did she die?"

"It's better you do not know," I say, dangling my prize in front of her. "Do we have a deal?"

She says nothing in response, just looks longingly down at the book as if envisioning the impact it would make on her life. All the things she could accomplish with it. But I notice resistance too. It's in the way she stands and breathes. She gingerly takes the ledger and flips through it nervously. "There's a page ripped out."

"Someone I plan to protect." A seamstress I plan to use in the future, as well as Kate. It's the least I can do to repay her for the help.

"I can't do this," she says, cradling the ledger in her arms.

"Doing this doesn't make you a criminal. This is just what it is to be a woman in a city run by men. If we want them to take us seriously, we must do things other women won't do. We have to make choices, take risks, and live with them."

She squares her shoulders and exhales, our breath frosty between us. She looks up to meet my eyes again, this time with certainty, then speaks with steely resolve. "We have a deal."

I return to where we threw Tommy in the river and lie down and cry until my mouth is dry and my stomach is rumbling from hunger. I can't remember the last time I ate.

"I still have more to do," I say to him. "But I promise I'll be back soon." I blow a kiss to the water before making my way to the pier, where I find a hackney to take me to Pearl's hideaway.

When I reach the door, Maggie opens it to greet me. "Where have you been?"

Inside, a collection of women waits for me. Not just Rita, Evelyn, Vera, and Maggie, but a dozen more. They barely all fit in the small space, standing shoulder to shoulder.

I shudder off my dirt-smudged coat and look at them, waiting for someone to say something.

Maggie smiles. "We're all in this with you, Alice. We're here for you."

Having five women in the gang is one thing, but having nearly twenty is another entirely. Leading them means agreeing to protect them and being responsible for their successes. They'll look to me for answers, which I'll need to have.

I need to assure them, comfort them, discipline them.

"It will not be like it was," I say aloud. "We will have to change. Become stronger. Learn how to defend ourselves. Take on bigger, riskier scores. The kind that will set us up with an unbreakable empire. It will not be easy."

"We know," says Rita.

"We want to change," adds Evelyn. "All of us."

"Just tell us what to do," agrees Vera.

Despite everything dark and cold inside me, there's so much hope in them I bask in its warmth and feel myself smile. I've lost something inside me, a light I can't get back, but I've found a new one.

A life that's my own.

Chapter Twenty-Five

ONE WEEK LATER

I wait in silence at Victoria Station with my mother, Christina, and Louisa. The headline of the newspaper in my lap reads, "Plunder at Selfridges Is an Attack on All London's Shopkeepers," followed by another article that lists arrests made with the help of Mary's ledger. I fold it up when I hear the train coming and glance at my mother.

She's said but a handful of words to me since we lost Tommy, and I have every reason to believe she'll keep it that way. I took her son away, and there's no changing it.

Christina hasn't spoken to me either, but that's because she bursts into tears every few minutes, followed by a series of measured breaths to calm herself down.

Every time I'm with them, the weight of my shame presses on my chest like a mountain of stones, but I find ways to distract myself from the guilt. At least I'm keeping my promise to protect Tommy's wife and child, the only way I know how—by getting them as far away from London as possible.

As far away from *me* as possible.

"There will be someone to pick you up in Birmingham," I say, handing my mother a small haversack of cash and other essentials. "She'll take you to where you'll be staying. You'll be safe there. I'll send more money every week. But I'm sending enough now to set you up with a new shop, a better one."

She takes the bag with a forced smile. "Is this the last time I'll see you too? Will you be in a grave for our next meeting?"

"Mum, stop," demands Louisa. "This is not what Tommy would want."

"Please come with us, Louisa," Mum begs, reaching out to pull both of Louisa's hands tightly against her chest. "I'd sleep better at night with you beside me."

"I'd sleep better if you left," I agree. We've both been fighting to get her to leave for her own safety, but she stubbornly resists.

She leans in and kisses Mum's cheek. "I'm staying. One Diamond in The Mint is hardly a show of strength, and I still have things I'd like to learn from Alice."

Too much she'd like to learn. Ever since our grand heist and her unfortunate run-in with the twins, she's a changed girl with no desire to run away anymore. It thrills me to have her back, but at the same time, I long for her to be nestled safely in her room at the Savoy. I asked too much of Tommy and lost him.

I can't do the same to her.

The full weight of my sadness crushes me, and I yearn to embrace him and feel his arms around me. My vision blurs, but I rapidly blink away the tears.

"Tell your father where we are when he gets out, and make sure you go see him and tell him what you've done."

"What I've done? I seem to recall you saying Tommy owed me one last job." My words turn venomous, and I immediately regret them— she doesn't deserve to share the blame for his death.

"A job! He owed you a job. Not his life!" Her bottom lip quivers. "You were supposed to take care of everything . . . you always take care of him."

"I know," I utter, more whimper than words.

The train lets out a piercing whistle.

"I'll write to you," I tell her.

"Don't bother. You have a new family now," she says bitterly, giving Louisa one last look of longing, so painful that I feel it too. "You will come to see me?"

Louisa nods.

We wait on the bench long after the train leaves the station until I finally open the paper again. "Police Suspect the Forty Elephants, under New Leadership, for Selfridges Robbery."

Louisa reaches for the paper and gently takes it away from me, tucking it between us. She offers me no comforting words, just reaches for my hand to interlock our fingers. "What will you do now?"

I chuckle softly. "Don't you mean, what will *we* do now?"

Her face beams, just like it did months ago when I told her about my first night at the 43, and I think maybe I can still keep my promise to her.

A new life. The sun. Everything she could ever want.

My family home has changed over the last week. The outside is freshly painted, and a new wooden sign that reads Lady Diamond's hangs outside. Eli and Patrick took over the opium den next door to be their new operations hub, and just across the street, work has started on a set of flats for the girls to live in.

Maggie is on the street waiting to greet me when I drive up. "Things are looking good inside." She flashes a newspaper in front of me. "Hear what they're calling Detective Betts? Lady Sherlock Holmes. Commissioner Horwood has made a dozen arrests." She lets out a secretive chuckle. She's the only person I told about the deal I made with the detective. No more secrets.

"I only scanned some of the headlines," I say. I take the paper and read it over while Louisa rushes inside to see the place. "Despite arrests, London shopkeepers fear the new Queen of Thieves and demand further justice," I read.

Betts is on the front page, standing with Commissioner Horwood. The papers have dubbed her "the best store detective in London."

Maggie arches her brows. "You want to come inside and see the place today?"

I've avoided entering the shop, sleeping in a room at the back of Ralph's pub, too overwhelmed with memories of my mother and Tommy. Moments I want to cherish yet can't muster the strength to face.

"Come on," she urges, pushing me to the doorway. I hesitate to step forward but gradually will myself inside.

The floors and the walls have been cleaned and refinished, and part of the downstairs has been transformed into an office with a window that overlooks the street. Inside, it's decorated with a large Persian rug and a walnut desk. I run my fingers along the edge of the desk before sinking into the plush chair behind it.

From the doorway Maggie is smiling. "Business looks good on us, don't you think?"

Louisa plops down on a new overstuffed chaise and pulls out a book from a bookcase stacked with fresh titles.

Maggie mutters quietly, "I don't think she's got it in her, Alice."

"To be one of us?" I question.

"You're not going to let it happen, are you?"

"Not if I can help it." I drop my voice to a whisper. "She doesn't need to know that though. Let her get lost in her books."

I want to properly thank Mags and her brothers, who have handled all these renovations, but I need to talk business first. "We need a warehouse. Any ideas yet?"

Maggie nods. "I think I found a place, but it could use some work. We must keep things here until it gets fixed up."

"Oy, ladies," Rita calls to us from the door. "You've got a visitor."

I get up from the chair and peer out through the office window. Kate Meyrick is standing outside the shop with her hands buried in her coat pockets, looking like a fish out of water. I walk out to greet her, and Maggie follows. "Are you lost, Nightclub Queen?"

"I thought I'd come to say hello," she says, looking around. "The place looks marvelous. I see you're putting your wealth to good use."

Maggie crosses her arms over her chest. "Why are you here, Kate?"

"You didn't just get a hankering to go slumming," I add. "Get on with it."

She quirks her lip ruefully. "That favor you owe me. I'm here to collect."

"Of course you are," Maggie deadpans.

"What can we do for you?"

"There's a copper I pay handsomely to sweep certain things down at the club under the proverbial rug and to give me fair warning of any raids. His compensation is more than adequate, but last week he decided he wanted more."

"How much more?" I ask.

"Too much more. He threatened to sell me out if I didn't give him what he asked."

Maggie frowns. "What do you want us to do about it?"

"I want you to convince him that our arrangement is fair and to continue to accept the amount I currently give. I also want you to teach him a lesson. I don't like to be threatened."

My lip pulls up. "What kind of lesson?"

She shrugs nonchalantly. "Nothing too hard to learn."

Maggie grins. "Sounds like a fun job for me."

"That's it? Take care of this, and we're even?" I ask.

"We're even."

Maggie and I silently nod at each other in agreement. "Done. Why don't you drink to it with Maggie, give her his information, and we'll take care of it."

Before moving away, Kate rests her hand on my shoulder. "I know what it's like to be where you are, so this is a favor I give freely. When the time comes that you don't know how to continue, my office door will be wide open for you."

I huff. "Don't hold your breath waiting for me to walk through."

She laughs and follows Maggie to a table in the back while I go outside. Evelyn is playing with her daughter, Cora, in front of the flats being built for the girls. Cora is chasing a stray cat down the street, and they both look happy—and at home.

A smile tugs at the corners of my mouth.

Eli walks out of the building next door and approaches me quickly. "Alice! Do you like the shop? We've been working on it day and night."

"It looks great," I say. "Thank you, Eli."

"Thank you," he counters, observing the streets with contentment. "This partnership is beneficial for us both. So, what's to come? Are you planning your next score yet?"

"Only minor jobs for now. We need to lie low for a week or two, let the coppers think they've got the upper hand. Then we strike."

He turns so he's facing away from me and clears his throat. "You know . . . if you need something done, something that maybe you don't want the girls or Louisa knowing about, we'll be happy to oblige."

I blink slowly. "What do you mean?"

"I mean that as a leader, there will be things you have to do in the dark. Things that should stay in the dark. We'll provide security, help transport the goods, give you names when you need them, but we can also be the people you call when you need something unmentionable done."

"You mean if I want someone killed?"

He snorts. "Not that you need any help, but you understand my meaning?"

"I do," I say in a more serious tone. "And there is something I'd like your help with."

His eyes widen, interest piqued. "What do you need?"

"Bring someone to me. I'll give you the name."

"Right now?"

I glance back at the shop and shrug. "The sooner, the better."

The warehouse Maggie has chosen is an abandoned slaughterhouse from the smell of it—a faded mix of rancid offal and blood that turns my stomach. It's a dusty, messy wreck with little to offer aside from its massive space, something I believe we'll need in the coming months. It needs work before I'd want the girls to see it, but it's ours, and that alone is enough to leave a satisfying feeling of warmth inside me. We're starting over from the ground up, but in all the right ways.

Eli and Patrick drag my chosen target inside the building and tie him down to a chair in front of me with thick rope. He's screaming but the sack secured over his head stifles his cries.

I brace for the moment, long-awaited, gathering all the bitterness I've stored away just for him. I nod to Eli, and he removes the sack to reveal a flustered Harold King.

He tugs at his arms tied to the chair and gazes around with a wild expression. I'd be willing to wager that a man of his stature has never experienced this kind of treatment before nor been put in a situation where he has no control or influence.

A man like Harold has never felt powerless.

This is the way I like him.

He stares at Eli and Patrick and finally notices me. That's when genuine fear seems to hit him, draining the color from his face. He must be asking a hundred questions inside his mind right now, the most important being: How does a maid have the ability to have thugs bring a man like him to a place like this? What kind of authority does she possess that allows her to stand over him?

"What is the meaning of this?" he bellows. "Turn me loose at once! I'm friends with Commissioner Horwood! I'll have you locked away for this for a long, long time."

I turn to Patrick, who is slowly putting on a set of brass knuckles. He pulls them tight around his fingers before throwing his fist down into Harold's face to quiet him. Harold lets out a whimper in response.

"I'll be doing the talking today, Mr. King."

I think of Pearl. Her broken, damaged face. How he manipulated her with fear, turned her into the very creature he always wanted—a dog on a leash. I signal Eli this time, whose punch is more vicious. It sends King toppling over in his chair so that his entire body slams to the ground.

I bite my lips to quell the smile tugging at them.

Patrick lifts him back up. Now his mouth is a mess of blood.

He coughs shakily. "Don't kill me. I have money. I have so much money."

I press my finger to his forehead. "This isn't about money."

He gapes at me, nonplussed. "Everything is about money. Name your price." Then he gawks at Eli and Patrick desperately. "What she's paying you, I'll pay more."

I take a step back and signal them.

This time when his chair hits the ground, they don't stop. They land sharp kicks to his stomach and face until one eye is black and swollen and blood pours from his mouth and nose. When he speaks again, it's a cry for mercy.

I think back to what he said to me in the hospital, and I crouch down on the ground next to him. He's a heaving, disfigured, bloody mess. I pull at his hair until his head swings upward, and he meets my eyes dead-on. "I think you'll come to be a happier man when you realize this world no longer belongs to you. You do not have all the power. What I give to you, I can take."

I stand up and let his head thunk to the floor. "Kill him, but make it look like an accident. Nowhere near his home . . . I don't want any of this coming back to Pearl."

I put my coat back on and leave the factory, a satisfied grin on my face to greet the brisk, refreshing air outside. I reach for something inside my coat, Rob's note, scribbled with his new address. I call to Eli in the warehouse, where he's wrangling Harold's body.

"I'll be leaving for a few days."

He pauses, and his eyes narrow. "Where to?"

"Seeing a friend."

I head back to the shop to pack but find Ralph waiting for me outside, more chipper than I've seen him in years. "Alice! I talked with the men. It turns out Alister and Richard were onto something. They do want more. They want to expand."

"All right," I say agreeably. "If that's what they want for The Mint, then that's what we'll do, but I'll need their help."

"I'll bring them," says Ralph.

I grin triumphantly, feeling my heart race with an excitement I can't hide. "Not just the men. Bring me their wives and daughters."

Acknowledgments

To start from the beginning, a huge thanks to the writers, actors, and producers of *Peaky Blinders*. More specifically, the female characters. They left such an impression on me that I couldn't help asking myself, "Why didn't the women just run the gang?"—a question that led to extensive research where I discovered Alice Diamond and Brian McDonald's book highlighting the wild adventures of the Forty Elephants.

My husband, who never gave up on me through all the anxiety and doubt. Fifteen years later, you're still finding ways daily to remind me I can accomplish all my dreams. Thank you for the long nights of writing and brainstorming, our three beautiful children, and the endless dedication.

Pitch Wars and Sajni Patel—you took a risk on a project that needed so much work in very little time. All my Pitch Wars friends, Samantha Rajaram, Mindy Thompson, Jessica Olson, and Jessica Froberg, for providing companionship and advice during tough, sometimes impossible times. Laura Lashley, you incredible source of endless positivity and humor. I don't know how I could have gotten through revisions without you.

Carrie Pestritto, my agent extraordinaire! You are a joy to work with, endlessly patient, and I've gotten so lucky that we share the same vision for most projects. The team at Blackstone, more specifically Addi Black. Thank you for being so passionate about this book.

Lastly, to the obscure, dangerous women of history waiting to be shared more profoundly with the world—my goal is to find you all.